W9-BOM-225

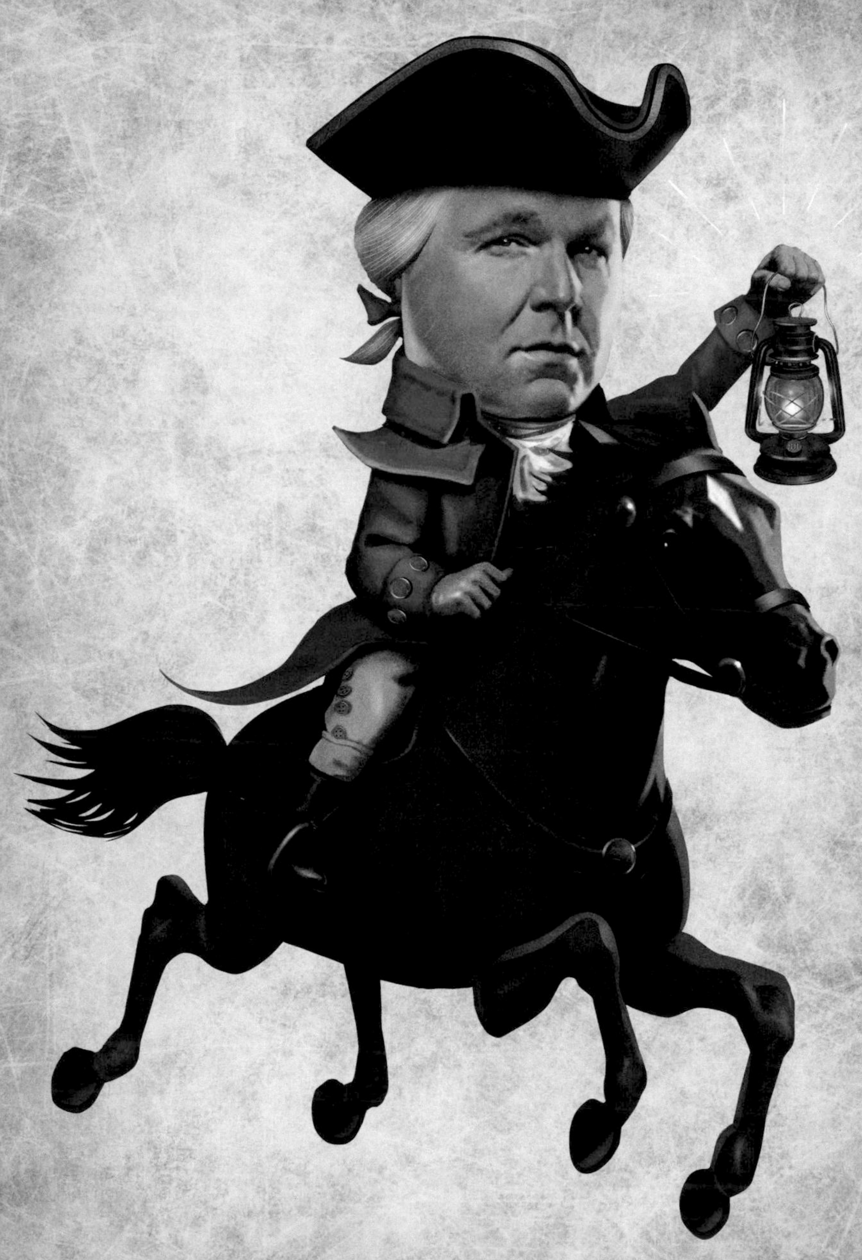

Shining the light on history

Rush Revere

AND THE BRAVE PILGRIMS

and

Rush Revere

AND THE FIRST PATRIOTS

Two Time-Travel Adventures with Exceptional Americans

RUSH LIMBAUGH

THRESHOLD EDITIONS

NEW YORK LONDON TORONTO SYDNEY NEW DELHI

Threshold Editions
An Imprint of Simon & Schuster, Inc.
1230 Avenue of the Americas
New York, NY 10020

This Threshold Editions paperback edition November 2020

For information about special discounts for bulk purchases,
please contact Simon & Schuster Special Sales at
1-866-506-1949 or business@simonandschuster.com.

The Simon & Schuster Speakers Bureau can bring authors to your live event. For more information, or to book an event, contact the Simon & Schuster Speakers Bureau at 1-866-248-3049 or visit our website at www.simonspeakers.com.

Interior design by Ruth Lee-Mui

Manufactured in the United States of America

1 3 5 7 9 10 8 6 4 2

Library of Congress Cataloging-in-Publication Data

ISBN 978-1-9821-5936-8

Rush Revere

AND THE BRAVE PILGRIMS

To Vince Flynn,
this book's Guardian Angel

This cutaway view shows passengers and

the Mayflower for

KEY TO DRAWING:

1. Poop deck
2. Half deck
3. Upper deck
4. Forecastle
5. Main deck where most of the Pilgrims were housed
6. Crew's quarters
7. Large hold
8. Special cabins
9. Helmsman with the whipstaff controlling the tiller
10. Tiller room
11. Captain's cabin
12. Beak
13. Bowsprit
14. Foremast
15. Mainmast
16. Mizzen mast

crew as they would have been packed into the 1620 crossing.

A Note from the Author

We live in the greatest country on earth, the United States of America. But what makes it so great? Why do some call the United States a miracle? How did we become such a tremendous country in such a short period of time? After all, the United States is less than 250 years old!

I want to try to help you understand what "American Exceptionalism" and greatness is all about. It does not mean that we Americans are better than anyone else. It does not mean that there is something uniquely different about us as human beings compared to other people in the world. It does not mean that we as a country have never faced problems of our own.

American Exceptionalism and greatness means that America is special because it is different from all other countries in history. It is a land built on true freedom and individual liberty and it defends both around the world. The role of the United States is to encourage individuals to be the best that they can be, to try to improve their lives, reach their goals, and make their dreams come true. In most parts of the world, dreams never become more than dreams. In the United States, they come true every day. There are so many stories of Americans who started with very little, yet dreamed big, worked very hard, and became extremely successful.

The sad reality is that since the beginning of time, most citizens of the world have not been free. For hundreds and thousands of years, many people in other civilizations and countries were servants to their kings, leaders, and government. It didn't matter how hard these people worked to improve their lives, because their lives were not their own. They often feared for their lives and could not get out from under a ruling class no matter how hard they tried. Many of these people lived and continue to live in extreme poverty, with no clean water, limited food, and none of the luxuries that we often take for granted. Many citizens in the world were punished, sometimes severely, for having their own ideas, beliefs, and hopes for a better future.

The United States of America is unique because it is the exception to all this. Our country is the first country *ever* to be founded on the principle that all human beings are created as *free* people. The Founders of this phenomenal country believed all people were born to be free as individuals. And so, they established a government and leadership that recognized and established this for the first time ever in the world! America is a place where the individual person serves himself and his family, not the king, or ruling class, or government. America is a place where you can think, believe, and express yourself as you want. You can dream as big as you can and nothing is holding you back.

This book on the Pilgrims is part of the great tale of how the United States of America came to be. The Pilgrims came to our shores more than a century and a half before our country was established in 1776, but their reasons for coming to the

"New World" helped to sow the seeds of our nation. The story of the Pilgrims and their arrival in the "New World" has been taught for hundreds of years and in that time the story has been tweaked and changed by people to the point that it is often misunderstood. I want you to know the real story. What really happened, who the Pilgrims really were, and what they did when they arrived.

Let me introduce you to my good buddy Rush Revere! Together, we are going to rush, rush, rush into history and the story of the Pilgrims!

NEWFOUNDLAND
PLIMOTH
CAPE COD
NEW ENGLAND
VIRGINIA
ATLANTIC OCEAN
N
W
E
S

Prologue

The sea was wide, cold, and blustery. The large wooden ship rocked hard against the rolling waves. I'd been on the *Mayflower* for only thirty minutes but already my head was leaning over the side just in case I had to "feed the fish." Water splashed up from the side of the hull and then rained down upon the deck.

"You there!" a voice shouted from nearby.

I turned around to see a sailor staring and pointing in my direction. He was a couple of inches taller than me. His shoulders were broad and his beard was black and scraggly with a thin scar above his cheek.

"That's right. I'm talking to you. Get your landlubber legs over here and below deck!"

Couldn't this sailor see that I was in no position to move, let alone walk across the ship when the deck felt like a washing machine with the spin cycle on extra high?

No, of course not. For starters, washing machines didn't

exist in the year 1620. I turned back toward the sea as another wave of nausea swelled inside me.

Maybe my decision to teleport aboard the *Mayflower* and journey with the Pilgrims hadn't been such a good idea after all. In fact, maybe now would be a good time to time-jump back to modern-day America and get some seasickness pills.

Yes, that's it. I could get the pills, stabilize my motion sickness, and then return before the ship reached the New World.

Suddenly, someone grabbed my arm and spun me around. I nearly jumped into the water when the large sailor shouted directly into my face!

"The whole lot of you makes me sick!" he said. "We should throw all you Saints overboard. What's your name!?"

Saints? This was not my first encounter with someone from the past. Although I was feeling extremely queasy, I tipped my hat and introduced myself while trying not to fall over. "I'm not a Saint or a Separatist. I'm Rush Revere," I said. "I'm a history teacher from the twenty-first century. I've come to—"

"The twenty-first century! Blimey! You're mad! The whole lot of you! You think I care if you make it to New England?" The sailor laughed as he pushed his face into mine and said, "I don't. In fact, I'd rather feed you to the sharks and be done with you."

His breath smelled foul, like rotten fish. I gagged and suddenly I vomited as the boat lurched to the side and sent me facefirst into the unsuspecting sailor. We tumbled to the deck and I rolled up against the railing. I sat up, realizing that I felt a great deal better. Unfortunately, I couldn't say the same thing about Stinky Fish Breath. He was covered from head to toe in my regurgitated lunch.

"Argh! You puked all over me! You piece of scum! I'll throw

you overboard!" He scrambled to his feet and charged at me like a bull targeting a matador.

My horse, Liberty, was aboard the *Mayflower,* somewhere. "*Liberty!*" I yelled, stumbling backward. "I could use a little help over here!"

Now look, I know what you're thinking. What's a horse doing on the deck of the *Mayflower* in the middle of a storm-tossed sea? Good question. The truth is, my Liberty is no ordinary horse.

The ship rocked back and forth as water surged again over its bow and crashed down on the deck as if a large waterfall had been turned on and off. The sailor was only a few feet away and closing fast. I scanned the length of the *Mayflower,* searching high and low. Another rush of water nearly swept me off my feet. I looked down to see a large fish flopping around. The boat rocked again and the fish slid right between the legs of the sailor.

Not a bad idea, I thought. Right before the sailor grabbed me, I dove headfirst through his legs. For a split second, I thought I was through and beyond his grasp. The sailor's beefy hand grabbed my leg, then my coat, then hoisted me up by my collar.

"I hope you can swim!" yelled Fish Breath.

From over his shoulder I finally spotted what I had been searching for.

"And I hope you can fly!" Liberty replied to him.

Oh, yes, Liberty can talk. I told you he wasn't an ordinary horse. Before the man could even turn around to see who had spoken, Liberty kicked his hind legs and sent the sailor sailing high into the air and then he fell into a web of nets.

"Perfect shot!" Liberty said.

"You appeared in the nick of time," I said, starting to feel sick again.

"Leaping to the *Mayflower* in the middle of a storm wasn't my idea!" Liberty said, speaking very fast. "Yes, I can leap to different times in American history, but I'm not a weatherman. And horses don't like boats. There's an awful lot of water surrounding us and this constant rocking back and forth, back and forth—it's making me hungry." Liberty turned his neck from side to side as if searching for the nearest feedbag. "Do you know where we can get some food around here?"

I slipped onto Liberty's saddle and said, "Please, let's not talk about food. Right now I need you to open the time portal."

"Back to the future?" Liberty grinned.

"Yes! Back to modern-day America, please. Just try not to leap us into a tornado!"

Liberty started galloping and yelled, *"Rush, rush, rushing from history!"*

A swirling circle of gold and purple appeared on the deck of the *Mayflower*. As it grew bigger, Liberty bolted for the center and jumped through.

We were back in modern-day America.

Chapter 1

The school bell rang and a few more students rushed into the classroom followed by Principal Sherman. The principal of Manchester Middle School was not a small man. If the door frame were any smaller, the principal would have to duck his head and twist his way into the classroom. I stood outside in the hallway as the door closed but watched and heard what was happening through the door's small window.

"Attention, everyone, please take your seats," said the principal with authority. He stood at the front of the classroom, hands at his sides, while his eyes scanned the desks and chairs. "I have an important announcement."

The room went silent. It was apparent that Principal Sherman did not tolerate disrespect. "I have some unfortunate news," he said. "Your teacher, Ms. Borrington, needed some extra time away from the academy to help care for a sick family member. In the meantime, I feel very fortunate to have found such a qualified replacement. You know that at Manchester Middle School we have the smartest and most educated teachers. It is my pleasure to introduce you to your substitute, Mr. Revere."

As if on cue, I opened the door to the classroom and walked in. As Principal Sherman prattled on about the importance of giving me their whole attention, I walked over to the chalkboard and grabbed a piece of chalk. In the upper left corner I wrote my name.

R-U-S-H R-E-V-E-R-E.

Principal Sherman then turned to me and said, "Mr. Revere, the students of Manchester's honors history class are now in your charge. I kno-o-o-o-ow," he said, turning to the class and then back to me, "they will give you their utmost respect." While he walked past me on his way to the door he lowered his head and whispered, "If the boy in the back row with the red baseball cap gives you any trouble, please send him to my office." Without another word, he opened the door and disappeared.

As I turned to the students, I noticed a hand in the air from a girl with blond hair and two perfectly placed pink bows. Before I had a chance to even call on her she asked, "Your first name is 'Rush'? That's weird. And why are you dressed like . . . that?!" she said.

I could tell that this student was all business. If there were a pecking order in this class, she would probably be at the top of the food chain. I looked at my seating chart and replied, "Thank you, Elizabeth. Do you go by Liz?"

She rolled her eyes and nearly grunted, "No, unlike some people, I have a real name. It's Elizabeth."

"It's a lovely name, if you like four syllables" I said, winking.

"If you must know, my real name is Rusty. But when I was your age, my favorite class was history. In fact, I found myself rushing to history class every day I had it. I would rush from my home, rush down the street, rush through the school until I was sitting at my desk. Eventually, my teacher started calling me 'Rush' and it stuck."

Two girls leaned over and whispered to each other. One pointed at my pants and giggled. Ah, yes, my clothing! Certainly, my colonial shirt with a waistcoat and an outer coat over it, as well as knickers, stockings, and a three-cornered hat, was enough to make me look like I was ready to go trick-or-treating.

"You're probably wondering about my clothing," I said. "Can anyone guess who I'm dressed as?"

A couple of students raised their hands and I pointed to each one.

"George Washington?" said the first.

"Good guess, but no. However, I am dressed as someone who fought in the same revolutionary war as George Washington and they assuredly knew each other."

"Are you Thomas Jefferson?" asked another student.

"No, however, another good guess. Mr. Jefferson lived during the same time, but I don't think he could ride on a horse fast enough as if he was flying from city to city."

Then the boy with the red baseball cap raised his hand. He was smirking at me, the kind of look you give with the intent of hitting the bull's-eye on a dunking machine. Reluctantly, I pointed to him.

"Then you must be Peter Pan," he said.

The students burst out laughing, and now I understood the warning from Principal Sherman.

I quickly glanced at the seating chart and then replied, "Mr. Thomas White, is it?"

"I go by Tommy," he said. "And I think Tinker Bell just flew out the window so you might want to go catch her."

Again, the class laughed. I smiled politely and waited until the room was quiet again. Tommy appeared to be gathering up his history book and backpack.

"Are you planning to go somewhere, Tommy?" I asked.

"Aren't you sending me to the principal's office?" he asked matter-of-factly.

This time I laughed. I could see that the entire class looked confused. Apparently, Mrs. Borrington did not tolerate the silly antics from a class clown. "Absolutely not! If I did, you would miss the most exciting history lesson of your life!"

"Um, for the record, history is not exciting," Tommy said. "Seriously, I have to stay?"

"Well, I hope you choose to stay," I said. "I love your imagination, Tommy. That's exactly the kind of mind I want all of you to have as we discover history together, discover the stories of the exceptional people who made us who we are today. I dress like this to help your imaginations. For as long as I can remember, my boyhood idol has been the famous American patriot Paul Revere. He was a silversmith. He took part in the Boston Tea Party. He developed a system of lanterns to warn the minutemen of a British invasion. And, of course, the event that he's most famous for is his midnight ride in April of 1775."

Tommy eased back into his chair. I could tell he wasn't convinced that history was exciting, yet. But I could see a hint of curiosity on his face.

"Imagine that it's midnight," I said. "It's very dark outside. You hear the hoot of an owl and, perhaps, see bats fly through the air under a full moon. You're on a secret mission to ride as fast as you can to warn the colonists that the British are coming! Raise your hand if you're up for the challenge!"

Several of the students raised their hands, mostly boys, including Tommy. However, I saw one girl in the back of the class who raised her hand, too, but then quickly dropped it. Hmm, I had noticed this girl earlier. She didn't laugh when the rest of the class laughed. She looked very comfortable sitting in the very last row in the corner. Her dark hair had a blue feather clipped in it. She wore jeans with a hole in one knee, but I could tell it wasn't a fashion statement. I looked at the seating chart and noticed the girl's name, Freedom. What an unusual name. Personally, I couldn't help but be a fan!

"Ah, I see we have several brave souls who are ready to ride like Paul Revere. However, in order for you to ride, you're going to need a horse." I paused. Nothing happened. This time, a little louder, I repeated every word slowly: "I said, we're going to need a horse!" I glanced at the door. I paused, again. Still nothing happened.

The students looked at me very confused.

I sighed. "We're supposed to have a special guest join us, but it appears he's running late. Excuse me while I go and see if he's lost." I walked toward the door, opened it, and glanced down the hallway. Nothing. I walked down the hall toward the front doors of the school and passed by the door to the teacher's bathroom. I paused, considering my options. I heard the toilet flush and then I heard what sounded like the clomping of horse hooves. I rolled my eyes and pushed the door open. Sure enough, there stood my horse, Liberty, admiring himself in the mirror.

"Liberty!" I shouted.

Startled, Liberty bumped into one of the bathroom stalls and knocked the door halfway off its hinges.

"You missed your cue and your entrance. I'm trying to teach a history lesson and you're an important part of that," I said.

"You really shouldn't sneak up on large mammals like that," Liberty replied. "See the damage we can cause. Not my fault. I'm the victim here. And I'm pretty sure you're a few minutes early. Besides, it's not like I wear a wristwatch or carry a smartphone," Liberty replied.

"My apologies. It would be my pleasure if you would care to join me," I said sarcastically as I held open the bathroom door for him.

"That's more like it," he said as he walked past me without looking in my direction.

Liberty stuck his head out the door and looked both ways. When he didn't see anyone, we walked toward my classroom.

"Now, remember what we talked about. We don't want to freak out the students the first day by showing them a talking horse," I said.

"Yes, yes, of course. My lips are sealed," said Liberty as he pantomimed zipping his lips with his hoof.

"Good. Now, I'm going back in. Listen for your cue."

I returned to the class and was glad to see that no one had left.

"I apologize for the delay. As I was saying, it was a midnight ride from Charlestown to Lexington when Paul Revere shouted, 'The British are coming, the British are coming!' This would not be complete or even possible without a noble and swift horse! Please welcome our special guest, Liberty!"

Liberty pushed the door open and strutted into the classroom.

The students in the front row leaned back, utterly shocked at what they were seeing.

"No way!" said Tommy. "You actually brought a horse into school? This is so cool!"

Most of the class was standing by now, watching Liberty prance around the front of the room. From the way Liberty was soaking up the attention, you'd think he was standing in the winner's circle at the Kentucky Derby.

Several students still looked flabbergasted. They watched Liberty as if he were a mythical unicorn and crowded closer to him. The girl named Freedom, however, stood five steps back from the rest of the class. Was she afraid? No, not afraid. Unsure? Yes, that's it. She was looking at the other students, unsure of whether she was welcome to join them in their new discovery.

"Don't get too close to us, Freedom," said Elizabeth, who stood at least two inches taller than the other girls in the class. "The horse might smell you and run away."

Freedom stepped back to her desk and sat down.

"Class, I assure you that Liberty is very friendly. There's no need to be alarmed. He doesn't bite and fortunately, he's potty-trained," I said, still irritated that Liberty was late.

Liberty snorted at my last comment, clearly insulted, and flicked his tail into my face. His horse hair tickled my nose and before I could stop it, I sneezed!

It happened so fast that Liberty instinctively said, "Bless you."

I froze, wondering if anyone had heard that. Liberty froze, clearly worried if I had heard that. The students froze, clearly trying to determine if they had heard that. Finally, one of the students broke the silence and slowly said, "Did your horse just say 'Bless you'?"

"My horse? T-t-talk?" I stammered, looking back and forth between the students and Liberty. "Uh, well, yes. I've taught him a couple of words, sort of like a talking parrot. Words like 'bless you.' I mean, what else do you say when someone else sneezes?" I said, trying to laugh it off.

Then, without warning, I sneezed again, "Achoo!"

This time Liberty said, "Gesundheit!"

Again, the students were wide-eyed and speechless. This was not going as planned. The *horse*, as they say, was out of the bag. So I decided to confess, sort of. I sighed, again. "The truth is Liberty is an exceptional learner. He's very bright and, of course, he loves American history. So as long as you can keep this a secret I can keep bringing Liberty to our class. Agreed?" I said, hoping it was enough.

You would have thought I had just asked if each student wanted a million dollars! A flurry of responses came rushing back at me, "Yes! Okay! I'll keep it secret! I'll do it. I'm in!"

"Well, then, it appears we're unanimous," I replied. "Wonderful." I turned to Liberty. "Is there anything you'd like to say?"

Liberty let out a big, horsey "Neighhhhhhhhhhhhhh."

The students looked at each other and then back at me. Tommy was the first to speak and said, "Not very impressive for a talking horse."

I turned to Liberty and mumbled, "Seriously, that's the best you can do?" Then I turned back to the class and laughed. "Liberty has quite the sense of humor," I said. Clearing my throat, I looked at Liberty and spread my arm toward the class and said, "Liberty, the jig is up. Your cover has been blown. Go ahead and tell the class whatever you'd like."

Liberty smiled and I could only imagine what was about to

Mr. Rush Revere
LIBERTY
MANCHESTE
M
MANCHESTE
M
FOOTBALL

come out of his mouth. He inhaled deeply, and then in one long breath he repeated the Preamble of the Constitution!

"*We the People* of the United States in Order to form a more perfect Union establish Justice insure domestic Tranquility provide for the common defence promote the general Welfare and secure the Blessings of Liberty to ourselves and our Posterity do ordain and establish this Constitution for the United States of America," he said, gasping for air.

Spontaneously, Liberty was showered with praises. "Awesome!" "Cool!" "Sweet!" "Unbelievable!" "No way!" "Wicked!" "Whoaaaaaa!" "Dude!"

Liberty took a bow or two.

"Show-off," I said out of the side of my mouth.

Liberty ignored me as the students came to the front of the class and surrounded him, touching and petting his mane and fur. "You're too kind," he said.

Tommy started scratching behind Liberty's neck. "Oh yes," said Liberty. "Right there, a little to the right. Yes, that's it, right behind my left ear. Ahhhhh."

"How did you say that in one breath?" Tommy asked.

"I bet you could do it if you tried," said Liberty.

I rolled my eyes and realized that my class was officially horsing around. "All right, class. Back to your seats," I said. "Show-and-tell is over. Thank you, everyone. Please be seated."

The students returned to their seats and I decided we had spent enough time on the introduction and pleasantries. "Class, I want you to put away your history books. Of course, books are wonderful, but when I'm teaching you won't need them."

"Mr. Revere," Tommy said with his hand in the air. "Not to be rude, but I'd rather hear Liberty talk."

"I knew I would love this class," Liberty said, jumping in. "You know, horses have been an important part of this country."

Oh no, I thought. Here he goes.

Liberty continued breathlessly, "You could say we're the backbone of America! We've lived among the Native Americans, we've fought in the greatest battles, we've carried all the early presidents! One of my favorite riders was George Washington! Now, he could ride. He also knew how to brush down a horse. The trick is using long strokes and starting at the top of—"

"Thank you, Liberty," I butted in. "You've been a wealth of knowledge, but I think we can save the horse-brushing lesson for another day—"

This time, Tommy butted in. "Wait, did he say he carried President George Washington? That was more than two hundred years ago."

Liberty opened his mouth and then shut it.

"I think what Liberty was trying to say is . . . well . . . he's referring to my method of teaching," I said quickly, not ready to introduce the concept of a time-traveling horse.

"That's right," Liberty said, rescuing me. "Having Rush Revere as a teacher is like going to the movies! You all like live-action movies, right?"

No surprise that the students all said yes.

I walked over and pulled down the white projector screen. "History is a mystery until it is discovered. Your job is to use your imaginations as if you're actually there. I'm going to help you. The 'movie' you are about to see will make it appear as if I've gone back in time."

Liberty winked at me.

I continued: "Your job is to try to identify where I'm at, who

I'm talking to, what event is happening, and why it is so important."

As I was speaking, Liberty walked over to the chalkboard, grabbed a piece of chalk with his teeth, and wrote, "Where? What? Who? Why?"

"Together, we're going to discover the truth about history," I said. "Are you ready?"

The students nodded. However, I could tell that Tommy was still not convinced he wanted to be here.

As Liberty walked over to dim the lights, I walked over to the digital film projector and attached a small antenna to receive signals from my smartphone. Then I gave the class one final instruction: "The movie will start in just a minute. I'm going to walk Liberty outside for a breath of fresh air. I'll return shortly."

"What about the popcorn?" Tommy asked.

"An excellent idea, Tommy," I replied. "Tomorrow, you'll have fresh buttered popcorn."

A quick flurry of cheers came from the students.

"And I'll bring the red licorice," Liberty said. "Not long ago I was watching one of my favorite movies, *Seabiscuit*. It was the final race and Seabiscuit was coming around the last bend heading for the finish line, and I, of course, was on the edge of my seat. I couldn't take my eyes off the screen so I blindly grabbed for a piece of licorice, but instead of eating it I accidentally stuffed it up my nose."

My horse, I thought, the comedian. I rolled my eyes as the class laughed. I pointed Liberty to the door at the back of the room and walked over to join him.

"When the movie is over, we'll review what you saw," I said.

Liberty and I slipped out into the hallway, and I jumped onto

Liberty's saddle. I pulled out my smartphone and tapped the camera app and switched it to video mode. As soon as Liberty jumped through the time-portal I would tap RECORD and video our adventure, which would be transmitted to the film projector back in the classroom.

It's a miracle that it works but this way the students could see and hear exactly what Liberty and I were experiencing.

"Do you have your seasickness pills?" Liberty asked.

"Already took one," I replied.

"Good, because the last time we were on the *Mayflower* you looked like green Jell-O," he said with a laugh.

"No time to spare, Liberty. Let's go!"

Liberty bounded down the hall and said, *"Rush, rush, rushing to history!"*

A vertical swirling hole of purple and gold began opening in the middle of the hallway. It grew in size as Liberty approached.

I grabbed tighter to the horn on Liberty's saddle and shouted, "Sixteen twenty, Holland, the Pilgrims!" All I could do now was hope we landed on dry ground.

Right before Liberty jumped through the time portal, I had the feeling we were being watched. I turned my head and the last thing I saw was someone's head dart back inside the classroom, someone with long dark hair and a flash of blue.

Chapter 2

The trip through the time portal was like jumping through a hoop. Instantaneously, we landed in Holland. I quickly surveyed the geography and discovered we were in a field not far from the small Dutch port of Delfshaven. Thankfully, we were alone. Wildflowers with yellow and maroon blossoms buzzed with honeybees. An apple orchard was not too far to our left.

"Oh, look, apples!" Liberty said. "My favorite!" He started trotting toward the nearest tree. "You know that apples are an excellent source of dietary fiber—and vitamin C, too?" he said. "Of course, apples also have plenty of essential minerals like potassium, calcium, magnesium—"

"Liberty, my brilliant friend," I butted in. "Your nutritional understanding of an apple is impressive, but we're here on a historical quest. Let's gather some apples and stick them in your saddlebag, quickly. We need to head over to where that ship is." I pointed to the harbor.

"Oh, all right," Liberty sighed as we began plucking apples.

I opened the saddlebag and we both dropped them in. After about twenty apples, we journeyed over to the port. I could smell the salty sea, watch the water push up and back along the beach, and hear the sound of seagulls as they soared above us. Liberty trotted toward a large gathering of people near the shore. I noticed their colorful and bright clothing.

"Pardon me," I said to a young woman wearing a long green woolen dress and a linen cap that came down over her ears. She was walking toward the shore and carrying a cat that seemed very curious about Liberty. I smiled and continued: "I'm looking for the Pilgrims, I mean, the Puritans. I understand their plan is to sail to the New World." For a split second I worried that I might have missed them. I added, "They're probably wearing dark, drab clothing. I assume the men have tall, black stovepipe hats."

The woman turned in my direction but didn't stop walking. She stared at me as if I were some strange animal at a zoo. She quickly replied, "If you're looking for the Puritans, you've found us."

These? The Puritans? I had always imagined the Pilgrims in clothing that was black, white, and gray. However, these people wore clothing that was dyed every color of the rainbow! A yellow shirt, blue breeches, green stockings, a red dress, a purple knitted stocking cap . . . I was sorely mistaken to think that I knew what the Pilgrims wore every day. It was time to get my class involved.

"Class," I said, "these are the real Pilgrims." I pointed the lens of my smartphone toward the large group that had gathered. "In the year 1620 they were known as Puritans or Saints or Separatists. Many of them separated themselves from the Church

of England and escaped to Holland, where they could practice their religion without being bullied by King James and his bishops." I pointed toward the big ship in the harbor. "I can see that several men, women, and children are boarding smaller boats to take them to that larger ship anchored in the harbor. Let's go find out the truth."

Liberty and I approached the large gathering. I called to the first man we approached and said, "Excuse me, sir, but is the ship out there the *Mayflower?*"

The man turned in my direction. He looked about thirty years old and could have passed as a movie star. He was tall with brown hair and a cleanly trimmed beard. He wore a leather hat that shaded his face from the sun, a long-sleeved light blue shirt, blue breeches, and green woolen stockings. I could see he was comforting a woman in a long woolen red dress. He had his arm around her and I could tell she was crying. I quickly said, "Oh, I'm sorry, I didn't mean to bother you."

The man looked at Liberty and then to me and said, "It's no bother. I'm not familiar with any ship called *Mayflower.* The ship out yonder is the *Speedwell.*"

That's odd, I thought. Where was the *Mayflower?*

"You look bewildered," said the kind stranger. "Can we help you? Are you looking for someone?"

"As a matter of fact, I am," I replied. "I'm looking for one of the leading members of the Puritans, a Mr. William Bradford."

Immediately, the woman stopped crying and the man stepped in front of her. He responded, "I'm William Bradford. Do you come bearing bad news?"

Surprised at my sudden discovery, I jumped off Liberty and reached out to shake his hand. "Mr. Bradford, it is an honor to meet you! I'm a big admirer and I would love to be of assistance to you." When I realized I was still shaking his hand, I let go and just smiled.

William looked back at the woman, who I assumed was his wife, and then back to me. He said, "I'm sorry, but have we met?"

"Technically, no," I replied. "But I was told I could find you here." I fudged the truth a little and continued: "You see, I'm a history teacher—an historian, of sorts, and a Pilgrim, in spirit. Your Puritan faith fascinates me and I would love to follow you to the New World."

"I see," said William. "A fellow Puritan is always welcome to join us. We are boarding the *Speedwell* now. Many of us are saying goodbye to friends and family who are staying in Holland."

"Do you mind my asking why you're leaving? This looks like a beautiful country and a wonderful place to raise a family," I said, looking around and spreading my arms as if to show William everything he was leaving behind. That's when I noticed Liberty following a man pushing a wheelbarrow loaded with large cheese wheels. I hoped the horse was behaving himself.

"Looks can be deceiving," William said. "We lived in Leiden, Holland, for twelve years, but it is not our home. Originally, we came from Scrooby, Nottinghamshire, England. But the government forced us to choose between following our faith and following the law."

"What did you do?" I asked.

"We chose to follow our faith. So we left in search of a land where we could be free to believe and worship without persecution. We found that in Holland. We even created the 'Pilgrim Press' and printed papers to help spread the word about religious freedom. But now we need a community that protects our families from evil influences. Some of our members, including our older youths, are beginning to leave the Puritan faith because of what they see and hear from our Dutch neighbors. It is for this reason we have decided to start fresh in the New World."

I nodded with understanding and said, "It appears your wife will miss this place."

William's wife quickly looked away from me. I could tell she was trying desperately not to cry, so she tearfully excused herself. William reached for her but she was now beyond his grasp.

"My wife, Dorothy, and I have decided to leave behind our three-year-old son, John. The journey is expected to be dangerous. We have wrestled in mighty prayer to know whether or not we should bring him. We believe that God has told us that John would be safer if he stayed. He will be cared for, but, as you can imagine, the decision has been particularly painful for Dorothy."

Again, I nodded, trying to show support. I knew that William and his wife were only trying to do what was best for their toddler. However, I also knew that other Pilgrims had chosen to bring their young children.

William interrupted my thoughts and said, "I apologize. I have yet to ask your name."

Before I could respond, screams turned our attention toward the shops. Women were running toward us while dodging several large cheese wheels as they rolled toward the water. I had a funny feeling I knew who was behind this. When all the cheese wheels came to a stop, I looked for Liberty. I presumed he was hiding.

I turned back to William and said, "Thank you very much for your time. I'm Rush Revere, and I look forward to visiting with you more on the *Mayflo—*" And then I remembered what

William had said. The ship the Pilgrims were boarding was not the *Mayflower*. "Is this the ship you're taking to America?" I pointed to the harbor.

"It's one of them," he said. "We purchased the *Speedwell* here in Holland. However, we need another. We have friends who are looking into hiring a ship in London. Hopefully, it'll be bigger and better than this one. We have many families and much to bring to the New World. Both ships are expected to meet in Southampton, England, before we embark for America."

I couldn't remember the fate of the *Speedwell*. Did it travel with the *Mayflower* all the way to America? Was it shipwrecked? Did it sink? I know that William Bradford sailed on the *Mayflower* to America. So he had to survive the trip back to England, but what about the other men, women, and children? I turned my thoughts again to my new Puritan friend and thoughtfully said, "I think it will be best if I meet you in England."

Confused, he asked, "Are you not traveling with us on the *Speedwell*? Do you have another ship coming for you?"

I stared at him as I searched for what to say. Finally, I replied, "Yes, well, I, um, I'm waiting for someone. And I have some supplies I still need to gather. And I . . ."

"No excuses, my friend," William said, smiling. He firmly put both hands on my shoulders and stared straight into my eyes. With great sincerity he said, "There is no need to fear. Take courage. God will bring us to the New World. Whatever adversity we face will only make us stronger." He shook my hand. "I hope whoever you're waiting for comes soon. And I hope our paths cross again. Safe travels, Rush Revere."

As he left to find his wife and board the ship with the other Pilgrims, I marveled at his courage, determination, and faith.

Before leaving for the New World in 1620, the Pilgrims prayed at the Old Church at Delfshaven, Holland.

William Bradford as a young man.

I was eager to know what happened to the *Speedwell*, curious to reach England and meet the other travelers, and eager to experience life upon the *Mayflower*. First, however, I needed to find Liberty and return to our classroom. I was very curious to know what my students had learned and a little worried to know what Liberty had been up to.

Fortunately, I didn't have to look very far to find Liberty. I heard his high-pitched whistle coming from a bright-colored shop at the corner of the street. That's when I saw his head peeking around the corner. Was he hiding? When I was close enough to speak to him I asked, "Why are you hiding behind this shop?"

"Funny you should ask," Liberty said with a grimace. "First things first: I need you to pay the shopkeeper of this store."

"You broke something," I said.

"No, I did not break something," Liberty replied. "Just because I've broken things before doesn't mean I can't be trusted to try on wooden shoes in a small Dutch shop because I want to prove to that doubtful shoemaker that horses are wonderful cloggers!"

I looked down at Liberty's hooves only to discover four bright yellow wooden shoes with red tulips painted on each of them. "Liberty, you're going to have to remove those shoes and return them immediately," I said.

"An excellent idea, theoretically," Liberty replied. "The problem is . . . I can't. They're stuck. How I got them on I have no idea. But these wooden babies are wedged on pretty tight."

I reached down and tried to pull one off. Sure enough, they stuck like superglue.

Facing page: Pilgrim woman with shawl joined by Pilgrim man with musket circa 1620.

I sighed with frustration and said, "What am I supposed to do, enter you in a horse-clogging competition? Oh, brother. Liberty, I insist that from now on you stay by my side and do exactly what I say. Your freedom to choose as you please is becoming troublesome!"

Liberty calmly replied, "You're sounding an awful lot like King James."

"Excuse me?" I asked, not sure what he meant.

He smiled and said, "Here's the thing. I'm a curious horse. I can't help it. It's just who I am. Discovering new things that interest me is what makes me happy. I love that we can travel together and discover the truth about history. But what interests you may not always be what interests me. Forcing someone else to like the things you like, or to do the things you do, is not what freedom is about, is it?"

"Of course not," I said humbly.

"From what I heard near the cheese cooler, King James didn't want the Puritans to have the freedom to choose what they believed. He just wanted them to stay with the Church of England and do exactly what he said, or else! But the Puritans believed that the Church of England practiced many things that the Bible never taught. So some Puritans called themselves 'Separatists,' because they wanted to separate themselves once and for all from the Church of England. I even heard one of the Puritan women say that the king threw an entire family into prison just because they chose to believe differently than he did."

I had a sick feeling in my stomach. I felt horrible for trying to force Liberty to do what I wanted. "I'm sorry, Liberty," I said. "You're absolutely right. Will you forgive me?"

"Of course I'll forgive you. You're not the only one who makes mistakes," he said as he lifted up a wooden shoe and waved it at me.

"All right," I said, "time for plan B." I walked into the shop, placed four gold coins on the counter, smiled at the shopkeeper, and walked back outside. "And just for the record, I hope you never feel forced to do anything. I'm glad you're a curious horse. And I'm especially glad the Pilgrims had the courage to believe and think for themselves. Otherwise, America might not be a free country." I lifted myself onto Liberty's saddle and said, "I think it's time we head back to the future!"

"Wait, you want me to run in these?" Liberty complained, staring at his shoes.

"Well, you said you could clog in them," I replied.

"Well, yes. But clogging and running are two different things."

"I won't force you," I said, smiling, "but humor me, will you? Back to modern-day America."

"This is so embarrassing," Liberty said pouting.

He willingly trotted back to the same field that we'd arrived in. His trot turned into an awkward half gallop. With a little more speed he said, *"Rush, rush, rushing from history!"*

With one jump we soared through the swirling time portal and landed back in the hallway at Manchester Middle. I knew the time portal created a sixty-second delay of any footage from my smartphone to the digital projector. We had just enough time to slip into the back of the classroom without being noticed. We watched the students as they watched Liberty and me race back through the field and jump into nothingness. The movie ended, and Liberty flipped on the classroom lights.

Tommy raised his hand and said, "Just for the record, I'm not a big fan of King James. He sounds like a real party pooper. He probably got too many wedgies when he was a kid."

"As you can imagine, these Pilgrims weren't big fans of the king, either," I replied.

"They should've just done what the king told them to do," Elizabeth blurted out.

Surprised, I turned to Elizabeth and asked, "Do you do everything someone tells you to do?"

Elizabeth rolled her eyes and looked at the girl next to her. That girl, who I assume was one of Elizabeth's groupies, raised her hand and said, "What Elizabeth is trying to say is that no one tells her what to do."

"Ahh," I said. "Well, then it sounds like you would've made a great King James."

"You mean Queen James," Elizabeth said, suddenly realizing she had just called herself by a boy's name.

Several students tried to cover up their laughs but Tommy couldn't resist and said, "Hey, James. What's up?" He put his hand in the air as if to give Elizabeth a high five.

She ignored him.

"In all seriousness," Tommy said, "I liked that William Bradford dude. He was cool. Too bad he and his wife didn't bring their little guy with them."

"Let me ask everyone the same question. If you were William Bradford, would you have taken your three-year-old son on a death-defying voyage across a tempestuous sea?"

I heard several halfhearted responses. "Probably." "Maybe." "I think so." "I guess."

I had almost forgotten about Freedom until she raised her

hand like the tallest mast on the *Mayflower.* "Freedom, you have an opinion?"

Freedom's dark eyes reminded me of that same determined stare that William Bradford gave me right before he boarded the *Speedwell.* Freedom spoke from somewhere deep within and said, "I could tell they loved their son, more than anything. They only wanted what was best for him. It took courage for the Pilgrims to leave their homes and travel into the unknown. But it takes more courage to travel into the unknown and leave someone you love behind."

"Well said, Freedom," I replied. "And who knows, maybe they thought they could come back for him someday. Or maybe someone else had planned to bring him to America when he was older. I don't know. What we do know is that more than anything, the Pilgrims like William and Dorothy Bradford were real people ready to give their lives for their freedom, no matter the cost, no matter the pain, no matter the sacrifice."

Suddenly, something yellow shot from the back of the room and would have struck me in the head if I hadn't dodged it at the last second before impact. It hit the chalkboard behind me and splintered into several pieces.

From the back of the classroom, Liberty's eyes were as wide as cannonballs. With a surprised smile he said, "By golly, those wooden shoes do come off! I was beginning to wonder. I think a larger size would've fit better. Of course, now it's going to be rather difficult to clog in only three shoes. Anyway, the trick to getting them off is to leverage this hoof like this and wedge the other by pushing down like that and . . ." Again, the second shoe shot off like a rock from a slingshot, but this time it whizzed to the left and crashed through an outside window.

"Oops," Liberty said.

I rolled my eyes, but before I could say anything else the door to the classroom opened. Principal Sherman walked in, looking alarmed, and asked, "Did I just hear the sound of breaking glass?" His eyes locked on the broken window. "How did this happen?" He turned to the class and then to me and asked, "Is anyone hurt? How did the window break?"

Curious, the entire class turned around to look at Liberty, and I wondered why Principal Sherman wasn't equally alarmed at the fact that there was an actual horse standing at the back of the classroom. However, upon further inspection, Liberty was gone.

"Well, is anyone going to answer me?" Principal Sherman asked again. "Mr. Revere, do you have an explanation?"

"An explanation?" I stalled. "Well, yes, of course." I realized that Principal Sherman would eventually find a yellow wooden shoe outside the classroom window so I began: "We were discussing the Pilgrims and how they left England to escape religious persecution and settled in Holland along their journey to the New World. I brought a wooden Dutch shoe from my trip to the Netherlands as a bit of show-and-tell and—"

Principal Sherman interrupted me and said pointing, "You mean like the one that's broken and splintered on the floor here?"

I had forgotten about that one. "Yes, and apparently, wooden shoes are not very sturdy."

Principal Sherman walked over to the window and saw the second wooden shoe lying on the grass near a big oak tree. "And yet that one looks just fine," he said.

I joined him by the window and said, "Um, wood is stronger than glass?"

He was not amused. He continued his classroom interrogation: "I've still not heard a reasonable explanation for why the window is broken."

"Yes, I was getting to that," I said, wondering if this would be my last day teaching at Manchester Middle School. "Let me start by saying this has been an excellent class and—"

Before I could finish whatever it was I was going to say, Tommy jumped up from his seat and shouted, "I did it!"

I was not expecting that.

Principal Sherman took a deep breath and didn't look a bit surprised.

I could not let Tommy take the fall for Liberty's antics. "I can assure you that it was somewhat of a bizarre accident," I said.

"Yes, I'm very well acquainted with Tommy's 'accidents.' But not everyone loves a class clown. Tommy, you'll report to my office as soon as class is over," said Principal Sherman, who nearly growled when he finished.

"If you'll permit me, Principal, I have an appropriate consequence for Tommy's outburst," I said.

"Continue," the principal said while straightening his tie.

"We both know how much Tommy lo-o-o-oves history," I said. "I think the appropriate punishment is to keep him after for detention in my class. I'm happy to give him an extra history lesson that he's bound to never forget."

I could see that Principal Sherman was pondering the idea and examining Tommy's reaction. Tommy didn't disappoint. His face showed pure misery. The principal smiled and said, "I like that! In addition, Tommy will write on the chalkboard, 'I will not throw wooden shoes through glass windows' one hundred times."

"I like your style, Principal Sherman," I said.

"And I like yours, Mr. Revere, especially that tricornered hat. I need to get one of those," he said. "I'll have the custodian clean up and repair the window immediately." With that he turned his huge shoulders and exited the classroom.

Relieved, I let out a long breath.

"What happened to Liberty? How did he get out of the room so fast?" Tommy asked. I could hear several other students ask similar questions.

Thankfully, I was saved by the bell before I had to answer their questions. Class was over. As the students grabbed their backpacks, I said, "Tomorrow, we'll continue the journey with the Pilgrims. Thank you, everyone. Class dismissed."

As the students began filing out of the room, I noticed that Tommy stayed behind for his detention and extra history lesson.

I noticed that Freedom stayed as well. I was pretty sure that it was her head I saw dart back into the classroom just as Liberty and I had jumped through the time portal.

If I didn't know any better I'd think Freedom was on to me.

Chapter 3

Freedom crossed her arms and leaned back in her chair. Tommy looked back at Freedom and then back to me, shrugging his shoulders. Freedom stared at me like I might disappear if she looked anywhere else. I finally asked, "Freedom, is there something I can do for you?"

She was twisting her hair between her fingers. I could tell she was pondering whether she wanted to say something or not. She looked across the room at Tommy and then back at me. She was a pretty girl with very tan skin. She flipped back the blue feather in her hair and then pushed the rest of her long black hair behind her shoulders. Finally, she spoke and said, "He never left."

"Excuse me?" I asked. "I'm not sure I understand what you're referring to." Actually, I knew exactly what she was referring to, but I decided to play dumb.

"Liberty, he's still in the room," she calmly said. "I can

smell him. Horses have a strong scent. And if you look closely, you can see his image outlined against the back wall." Still sitting at her chair, she turned around and traced Liberty's outline with her finger.

"I don't see anything," Tommy said as he strained to see what Freedom was pointing at.

It was apparent that Freedom had a gift. She acted as sure as if she were pointing at the sun. Questions raced through my head. Could I trust these students about the time-travel abilities that Liberty and I enjoyed? Would they be able to keep the secrets about our historical missions? I decided to take a chance and said, "As I mentioned earlier, Liberty is an extraordinary horse. In addition to his language skills, he has the ability to disappear."

"Not disappear," said Freedom. "He's blending into his surroundings like a chameleon."

Suddenly, Liberty reappeared right where Freedom had pointed, gasping for air. "I couldn't . . . hold my breath . . . a second longer," said Liberty, still trying to catch his breath.

"What the . . . !" Tommy exclaimed. He looked at Freedom, then to me, then back at Liberty. "Did he just appear out of thin air? That's awesome! I mean, that's the coolest trick ever! How do you do that?"

Explaining the impossible is never easy, but I tried my best and said, "Soon after Liberty and I met we discovered that when Liberty holds his breath he can turn invisible. Well, he's invisible to most people," I said, glancing at Freedom. "It's sort of like when you hold your breath and your face begins to turn red or even purple. When you let out the air, the color in your face returns to normal. It's the same principle with Liberty."

"Except he turns invisible," Tommy said. "Coolest. Thing. Ever."

"Frankly, I'm surprised that Freedom can see through the disguise," I said. "I've seen Liberty vanish at least a hundred times and I'm still not always sure if he's in the same room."

Freedom smiled and replied, "I've had lots of practice tracking animals with my grandfather."

Tommy walked over and touched Liberty on the back just to make sure he was real. "That is so cool how you can change like that," Tommy said.

Liberty smiled and said, "I think we need a name, you know, since we all know the secret. We could be the Four Musketeers! Or the Fantastic Four! Or the Four Amigos! Or—"

Tommy started laughing and said, "Your horse cracks me up!"

"Don't encourage him," I pleaded.

"I like him, too," said Freedom. "But he is more than a horse. He must be a spirit animal. There is an Indian legend about animals that can talk to humans."

I pondered the idea and replied, "I don't know Liberty's whole story. Even Liberty doesn't know what happened exactly. Liberty, tell them what you remember the day you traveled to modern-day America."

Liberty cleared his throat and slowly began: "It was a dark and stormy night. . . ."

"Liberty!'

"Seriously, it was! I don't remember the year but I do remember that in the evening we used only candles and lanterns. Oh, and I remember George Washington. Oh, and Paul Revere. His story is one of my favorites because who doesn't love the fact that he was racing a horse to warn the Minutemen that the British were coming. I mean, if you ask me, the horse is the real hero."

I jumped in and said, "I've concluded that Liberty is originally from the revolutionary time period and lived during the Revolutionary War. His memory is spotty, but he has several strong memories during the 1770s. The Boston Tea Party, the ride of Paul Revere, the Battle of Bunker Hill, the public reading of the Declaration of Independence . . ."

"And I specifically remember hearing that in 1775 Alexander Cummings invented the flushing toilet!" exclaimed Liberty.

"I've never heard you mention that," I said, surprised.

"It just popped into my head," Liberty replied.

"But that doesn't explain how Liberty ended up in modern-day America," said Tommy.

"Or the fact that he can talk and turn practically invisible," Freedom added.

"Yes, well, let me try to explain," I said. "Liberty remembers a lightning storm—"

Liberty butted in: "I'm not a big fan of lightning. Just the thought of it gives me the willies."

I continued: "It appears that lightning may have struck Liberty and created a supernatural phenomenon or a time portal that thrust him forward in time to our day. The electrical properties that charged through his body and the vortex that sent him to the future changed him physically and mentally. He can not only talk and disappear, but he's also . . ." I paused, trying to formulate the right words.

Freedom finished my sentence and said, "A time machine."

"What?" Tommy said, confused. "Did I miss something? Did you just say 'time machine'?"

"He's more like a time portal," I said, to clarify. "He has the ability to momentarily open a time door to anywhere in history. Well, more specifically, anything that touches American history."

Tommy started laughing. "Okay, this is a joke. I'm onto you. This is some reality TV show called 'The Biggest Bozo Who Believes Anything,' right? Where are the cameras?" Tommy started looking around the room. He then looked at Freedom and back at me; both of us were dead serious.

"You believe this guy?" Tommy asked Freedom, sticking his thumb out at me.

Freedom replied, "You've just seen and heard a talking horse who turned invisible, but you won't believe he can travel through time?"

"Hey, I might be crazy, but I'm not that crazy, okay?" Tommy said. He got up from his desk and started pacing the floor. He took off his baseball cap and combed his fingers through his blond hair. He sighed, "I have to think about this for a minute."

"We probably shouldn't show them the other thing I can do, should we? I mean, he seems a little freaked out right now," Liberty said.

"No," I said, firmly. I took a deep breath. "I need to finish our story. I believe the lightning created the time portal that brought Liberty to the modern day."

Tommy put his baseball cap back on and said, "Okay, okay. Maybe it is possible. I mean, I don't think the lightning hit him directly. Technically, a direct hit would have killed him. But I guess there's a possibility that several bolts could have simultaneously hit the ground around him, creating an electrostatic prism, and maybe the positive and negative charge carriers combined with the acoustic shock waves created some kind of time hole that sent Liberty to the future."

Freedom and I were stunned by Tommy's explanation.

"Aren't you a football player?" Freedom said. "You're never this smart in our other classes."

"Yeah, well, I really wouldn't fit in with the other guys on the team if I admitted that I'm a science geek," Tommy replied.

I patted Tommy on the shoulder and said, "Exceptional thinking, Tommy. Now then, where was I, oh yes, when Liberty arrived in our time he appeared at the intersection of Washington Boulevard and Lincoln Avenue in front of that iced-tea factory. It was late at night and I was leaving the factory dressed as Paul Revere."

"Wait, you were dressed like Paul Revere? Like you are now?" asked Tommy.

"Yes, that's right," I said. "I'd been hired as part of a promotional campaign. My Paul Revere self was printed on banners, billboards, buses, even on the side of bottles. It was rather embarrassing but it paid good money. Anyway, as I was saying, I was leaving the factory dressed as Paul Revere when I had the strangest feeling I was being followed."

Liberty was nearly trotting in place and excitedly said, "Oh, oh, oh, can I tell this part? I was so happy to see someone I recognized. Well, I mean, I'd never met Rush Revere before but I recognized his clothing. It was the only thing that felt like home. I first saw him on a billboard and then on the side of a bus. And when I saw him walking out of the iced-tea factory I was like, 'Ahhhhhhhh! That's him!' But there were all these traffic lights and cars and horns and they sort of freaked me out because I'd never seen or heard any of these things before, so I was like, 'Ahhhhhhhh!' I ran across the street, weaved my way through traffic, and nearly stopped when I smelled the heavenly scent coming from the peanut vendor, and I was like, 'Ahhhhhhhh!' It smelled so good! But I couldn't stop because I didn't want to lose sight of Rush Revere. I knew he could help me so I started following him."

"That's right," I said. "And after weaving my way through town for a couple of miles I realized that the strange horse, no offense, was not giving up. Of course, I was very curious why a horse without a rider would be following me. I decided to simply stop walking and wait for him to catch up."

"I'm glad you did, but if I were you there's no way I would've stopped. I mean you might be a mugger or a zombie or even worse, a vacuum cleaner salesman!" Liberty said.

I continued: "Anyway, I had to pinch myself several times when Liberty starting talking. And when we discovered he had the ability to open a time portal I was reluctant to jump through. Nevertheless, I did and it was the beginning of our adventures through history."

Tommy turned to Freedom and said, "You realize we can't tell anyone about this. Seriously, Mr. Revere would get fired and, even worse, I'd probably get invited to join the Chess Club."

"What's so bad about the Chess Club?" Freedom asked defensively.

"Sorry I brought it up. It's just that at a different school I was in a chess club. One word, *boring*! No competition. I pretty much wasted everybody. And then all these chess nerds followed me around like I was their king. No thank you."

"There's no reason why anyone else needs to know about our secret of time travel," I said. I turned to Freedom and asked, "I'm fairly certain you saw Liberty and me jump through the time portal earlier today, correct?"

Two if by Tea®

Freedom nodded and said, "Yes, I did. At first I wasn't sure what I saw. As I said, I thought Liberty must have been a spirit animal. Maybe you were a great shaman. I did not know. But I'm glad to know the truth."

"So, wait a minute," Tommy said, "are you saying that when we saw you in the movie, you were actually time-traveling, literally?"

"I know it's hard to believe," I said. "But as the saying goes, 'seeing is believing.' Liberty, I think it's time for another history lesson. Tommy, are you ready to experience firsthand some American history?"

Tommy looked at Freedom, then to Liberty, who nodded wildly, and then back to me. He finally said, "You mean, now? We can do that? I mean, of course I want to go. My football coach won't be happy that I skipped practice, but," Tommy said laughing, "I'll just blame it on the new substitute history teacher. Oh, and I need to be home for dinner or my mom won't be happy, either."

"No problem," I said, "and, Freedom, how about you?"

Freedom glanced at the clock on the wall and looked disappointed. "My grandfather will be here to pick me up any minute," she said. "Can I go another time?"

"Absolutely," I said.

"Thanks," Freedom replied. "I better go. I'm sure my grandfather is waiting." She grabbed her backpack and started for the door. She looked over her shoulder and said, "Bye, Mr. Revere; bye, Tommy; bye, Liberty."

Freedom stared intently at Liberty one last time. She winked and exited the classroom.

"Did you just hear that?" Liberty asked.

"Hear what?" Tommy questioned.

"I heard Freedom's voice echo in my head. She said, *Don't have too much fun without me,* right before she left the classroom," said Liberty.

Fascinating, I thought.

"Maybe you just imagined it," said Tommy.

"Help me rearrange these desks so Liberty has some running room," I said.

We quickly pushed the desks to the sides of the room. I climbed up onto Liberty's saddle and invited Tommy to join me.

"Where are we going?" Tommy asked, sounding a bit unsure.

"The *Mayflower,* of course," I said.

"Uh, I've never been on a ship before," Tommy said sheepishly.

"Good to know," I said. "If you feel yourself getting nauseous I have medicine for motion sickness. But I don't want to give it to you unless you really need it."

Tommy said, "Let's hope I don't need it."

"Before I have you get on Liberty, I want you to watch what's going to happen. Liberty will open a literal time portal right here in this classroom. He and I will jump through first. We'll find you some seventeenth-century clothing and then return for you."

"What? You don't think people in 1620 are wearing blue jeans, sneakers, and a T-shirt that says 'Manchester Football'?" Tommy winked.

I smiled back and said, "I happen to know that American football wasn't started until 1879, so the answer would be no."

"We'll be back in a flash!" Liberty said.

Tommy looked doubtful. "So, I should just sit down and watch this? What exactly is going to happen? Is lightning involved? I mean, that's how it happened the first time, right?"

"It's a bit hard to explain," I said. "That's why I want you to sit this one out and just watch."

"Can we get you anything while we're gone? Something to snack on. A beverage, perhaps?" Liberty asked.

Tommy plopped down at a random desk along the side of the room, grabbed his backpack, and pulled out a Snickers bar. "I'm good. I'll just sit here and play WordSlammaJamma on my phone. Just before class I got my highest score, 126 points with the word *quillback*."

"What's a quillback? Some kind of porcupine?" Liberty asked.

"No, it's a fish. A carpsucker, actually. Pretty common in lakes on the east coast. They're easy to spot because one ray of their dorsal fin is longer than . . . oh, sorry, sometimes my inner nerd comes out," Tommy said, apologetically. He took a bite of his candy bar. "So, how long is this trip of yours going to take?"

"You'd be surprised what can happen with a time-traveling horse," I said, winking. "Let's go, Liberty."

As Liberty started galloping he said, *"Rush, rush, rushing to history!"*

The time portal started to open. Tommy watched as a circular pattern of gold and purple swirled in the center of the classroom and quickly expanded until it was the size of a large satellite dish. Liberty jumped through the center and disappeared. A second later the portal closed. Tommy was still chewing his first bite of Snickers when the time portal reopened and Liberty jumped back into the classroom.

"Cool!" Tommy said as he jumped out of his seat. "That was whacked-out! The portal thingy! I saw it! There were these swirling colors and then you jumped through and vanished. That was crazy! Seriously, I saw it but I still don't believe it. Wait, why are you back so soon? Did you forget something?" Tommy asked, confused.

"We're finished. We have your clothes," I said, pulling my traveling bag over my shoulder and tossing it on the floor near the desk Tommy was sitting at.

"And we brought you back a freshly baked carp pie," said Liberty.

"You got me a what?" Tommy asked.

"A carp pie," Liberty clarified. "You know, like a meat pie, but with fish. You seemed so excited about the word *quillback* that I thought you would enjoy eating it. It looks delicious, I mean, if you're into that sort of thing. Personally, I'm a vegetarian, but the cook seasoned it with pepper and salt and nutmeg and then baked it with raisins, lemon juice, and slices of orange peels with just a sprinkle of vinegar, and voilà!"

I opened the lid of the serving tray to show Tommy the seventeenth-century dish. He swallowed his bite of candy bar and looked at the fish like it was an alien artifact from Mars.

"How is this possible? You weren't gone for more than five seconds," Tommy managed to say.

"Well, it actually took us closer to an hour," I said. "We had to visit two different clothiers to find all the items I was looking for. I hope it all fits. And then Liberty was absolutely set on getting you this carp pie. I must admit, it was very thoughtful of him."

I covered the fish with the lid and Tommy took the tray, not really knowing what to do with it.

I said, "When it was time to come back to the modern day, Liberty returned to the present at the same time we'd left, give or take a few seconds."

"I told you we'd be back in a flash," Liberty said, smiling.

"You can do that?" Tommy asked. "I mean, I guess you can because you did. Sorry, still trying to wrap my head around the fact that time travel is even possible."

"Don't think about it too much," I said. "Why don't you take the bag, slip down to the bathroom, and change. When you get back, we'll all jump through the time portal and begin our voyage on the *Mayflower*."

"Um, okay, sure. Sounds good to me," Tommy said. "Oh, and thanks for the fish. Not much time to eat it now. Maybe I can just leave it in the classroom and then when we return back to the present in a 'few seconds' it should still be warm, right?"

"You catch on fast," I said.

Tommy set the tray on the teacher's desk, grabbed the bag of clothes, and left the room. He returned a few minutes later looking like a seventeenth-century Pilgrim boy. He wore a short-sleeved, off-white linen shirt with a collar. Over that he wore a blue doublet that buttoned down in the front. In addition, he wore green baggy breeches, yellow stockings, leather shoes, and instead of his red baseball cap he wore a brown wide-brimmed hat. Tommy handed me the bag with his modern-day clothes, pointed to what he was now wearing, and said, "I assume you intended me to wear these clothes, right? There was a dress in the bag, too, but it really wasn't my style."

I chuckled. "I forgot about that. Yes, I purchased a dress for Freedom. I thought she might need it the next time we time-jump." I slipped the bag into a bottom drawer in the teacher's desk.

Tommy lifted his heel out of his shoe and put it back again. "For the record, these shoes need some padded insoles. And these pants, what are they called again?"

"Breeches," I said.

"Yeah, these breeches are really itchy."

"Well, you look great!" I said from on top of Liberty's saddle. "Now jump up behind me."

Tommy seemed unsure of what to do and said, "I've never been on a horse before."

"No worries," I said, "we'll make this easy. Liberty, walk over to the teacher's desk so Tommy can climb on from there."

When Tommy was sitting behind me I said, "Hold on to the saddle. Liberty is a smooth jumper and he's getting better at where he lands, but just in case. . . ."

"For the record," Liberty defended, "I've been one hundred percent accurate since we accidentally landed in Boston Harbor."

"Let's not forget the Civil War battlefield," I reminded him.

"Well, it's hard to forget when you keep bringing it up. Back then I was a novice, but I think I've come a long way, not to mention that I did save you from that cannonball."

"What cannonball?" Tommy asked, curiously.

"A story for another time," I said. "Liberty, we need to land undetected on the *Mayflower*."

"Got it!" said Liberty as he galloped forward. *"Rush, rush, rushing to history!"*

The time portal opened just as it did moments earlier. As clearly as possible, I pronounced each word, "September sixth, 1620, Plymouth, England, the launching of the *Mayflower*." I had found that giving the exact date, location, and name of the historical event helped Liberty get us to where we needed to be.

The sensation of jumping through time was always the same. A rush of air sent goose bumps all over my body, the hair on my arms stood on end, and for a split second it felt like it does when

you're swinging backward on a swing set. Yes, backward, probably because we were heading backward in time. The sensation happened only when we were airborne and passing through the portal. Once we landed, the feeling was gone.

Two seconds later, we landed on what looked like a cobblestone street behind some large crates and barrels. As we peered out from behind the cargo we immediately saw a large sailing vessel about a hundred feet in length and twenty-five feet wide that was moored alongside a stone wharf. Three tall masts with square-rigged sails stood like the queen's guards at Buckingham Palace as men, women, and children carrying few possessions walked down a dozen or so stone steps and then crossed over a wooden gangplank to board the ship.

"That's it!" I exclaimed. "That's the legendary *Mayflower* with the original Pilgrims as they board to sail to the New World! This is truly an exceptional moment for America. This little ship with a hundred and two passengers is going to cross the wide Atlantic Ocean, more than three thousand miles, with no guarantee that they're going to make it. Imagine how nervous or scared you might feel."

"Thank you, Captain Positive, for the pep talk," said Liberty.

"Let's try and board with the Pilgrims," I said. "Liberty, I doubt they'll let a horse on the ship so you'll need to follow closely behind and stay under cover."

"Ten-four. Going into stealth mode in three, two, one," Liberty said as he took a giant breath and disappeared.

"How will we get on if they have a passenger list?" asked Tommy as we walked toward the ship. "What if they don't have any more room for two more passengers?"

"I happen to know that many of the Pilgrims had second thoughts about traveling to the New World and decided to stay in England," I said.

"You mean they were nervous or scared about going?" Tommy asked.

I nodded, then continued. "Yes, and I imagine others were persuaded not to go by family or friends. Or perhaps the trip from Holland to England made them realize that a longer voyage to the New World would be more than they could handle. Right up before the *Mayflower* left for the New World there were many passengers who changed their minds and 'jumped ship,' as they say."

"Well, then, they might be happy to see us," Tommy said.

As we reached the gangplank William Bradford recognized me and said, "Rush Revere! It does my heart good to see you again. And is this the person you were waiting for in Holland?" He smiled affectionately while straightening Tommy's brown leather hat.

"Yes, this is Tommy," I said as I put my arm around Tommy's shoulder. "His parents are gone so I'll be caring for him on this voyage."

"It's a pleasure to meet you, Tommy," Bradford said as he reached out his hand to Tommy, who shook it. William turned back to me and said, "Let's talk some more after the ship sets sail. The captain is very eager to leave. He says the winds are perfect. We're just waiting for one more family and . . . oh, here they come. Wonderful. We should be leaving in a minute or two."

"We'll wait for you on deck. It'll be an honor to talk some more with you," I said with great enthusiasm.

Robert W. Weir's rendering of Pilgrims embarking from Delfshaven, Holland, on July 22, 1620. William Brewster (holding the Bible), William Bradford, Myles Standish, and their families. This painting is on display in the U.S. Capitol Building Rotunda.

Pilgrims and "Strangers" boarding small boats heading toward the *Mayflower* in Plymouth, England, 1620.

Boatloads of people waving farewell to the *Mayflower* as she leaves Plymouth for America, September 6, 1620. Original Artwork: after Gustave Alaux.

We continued past William and crossed the gangplank to board the *Mayflower.* As I stepped onto the upper deck a chill went through my body. The kind of sensation you get when you walk into the front gates of Disneyland. Or the feeling you have when you wake up knowing that it's Christmas morning!

"Unbelievable," said Tommy. "I just checked my phone and it says I have service. Not sure how that's possible but I think I'll send Freedom a text from the *Mayflower.* Let's walk over closer to the bow where we can take a picture without anyone watching. Plus if Liberty is behind us he'll want a place to get another breath of air."

"Good idea," I said.

Seagulls flew overhead, their calls competing with about a hundred or so passengers who were crowded near the aft and starboard quarter of the ship. I assumed they were calling to family and friends who were standing near the steps of the wharf. The sailors were calling back and forth to each other as large sails plumed from the square rigging. It was time to sail. The gangplank had disappeared and the ship was no longer anchored to the wharf. We were drifting out to sea!

As the ship rocked leeward for the first time, Tommy stumbled to the ship's railing as if he had just entered an ice-skating rink without ever having ice-skated.

"I'm good," he said. "I guess I don't have my sea legs yet. I'll get the hang of it." He let go of the railing and balanced himself with his hands out to his sides as if he were surfing. "This is so awesome."

I smiled at Tommy as he continued to "surf" but I was also curious to know where Liberty was. I called, "Liberty?" There was no sight of him and no answer. I looked over the ship's railing to see if I could spot him somewhere on the wharf. I didn't see him. Tommy saw the concern in my eyes. Oh boy, I thought. It's one thing to lose a cat or dog. But I wasn't sure how to start searching for a lost magical horse!

Chapter 7

The captain don't like passengers snoopin' around his ship!" someone yelled behind us.

We spun around and saw a sailor who wore an off-white long-sleeved shirt, a dingy orange vest, and a dark blue knit cap. He had a black scraggly beard and a thin scar along the side of his cheek. He climbed down off the forecastle and landed sure-footed on the upper deck of the *Mayflower*.

"We're just, um, exploring the ship. Is there a problem?" I asked in my most convincing British accent.

The sailor looked at us as if he was still digesting what he saw. In a gruff voice he said, "Yeah, you're the problem. You're another Puritan, aren't you."

It didn't sound like a question, nor did it sound friendly, but I responded anyway. "We're traveling with the Puritans as they travel to the New World, if that's what you're asking."

As the sailor walked closer I had a déjà vu moment. He

looked very familiar. Had we met before? Perhaps he looked like someone from the future. I couldn't put my finger on it.

"I'm sick and tired of all you Puritans," the sailor said. "I'm sick of your praying and your holier-than-thou attitude. You should've all stayed in Plymouth with the others. Better yet, I wish the *Speedwell* would've sunk and taken the lot of you with her. It was bad enough having some of you on the *Mayflower*. Now I'm stuck with all of you."

I must admit I was surprised by this sailor's hatefulness against the Puritans.

The sailor gave a wicked smile and said, "I guess there's one good reason to have you on board."

"That's the spirit," I said.

Tommy nudged me and whispered, "I don't think this is going to be a compliment."

The sailor continued: "We'll have plenty of food for the sharks!" He laughed.

Suddenly, I remembered where I'd seen him. Of course—he was the sailor that I encountered the first time I had time-traveled to the *Mayflower*. How could I forget the person who almost threw me overboard? Obviously, he wouldn't remember that first meeting, because for him that part of history hadn't happened yet.

Just then Liberty appeared directly in front of the sailor, deliberately snorted, took another deep breath, and then disappeared.

I think I was just as surprised as the sailor. On second thought, maybe not. The sailor had slimy horse snot oozing down his face.

"What the . . . where did . . . that was a . . . ," the sailor muttered as he tried to wipe away the snot.

"Rush Revere!" a voice called from the front of the ship.

The sailor quickly went about his business as if he had not been talking with us. I turned around to see who had called my name. I was thrilled to see my Pilgrim hero William Bradford walking toward me with his wife, Dorothy.

"Rush, you joined us in the nick of time," said William.

"Yes, well, better late than never," I said, laughing.

We all had to catch our balance as the bow of the ship plowed over a wave. A light spray of water splashed over the ship's railing. The large sails of the *Mayflower* no longer rippled like they did closer to the coast. Out in the open ocean they billowed like parachutes, pushing the boat westward.

William said, "You get used to that after a while. Have you had time to tour the ship?"

"No, not really," I said. "I was just talking with Tommy. He's a bit lonely without his horse. But there really isn't any room for a horse on the *Mayflower,* is there?" I asked, hoping I'd get the answer I was looking for.

"Unfortunately, no," said William. "The only place I can think of where a horse might fit and stay protected from the wind and waves is the capstan room."

Bingo.

"What's a capstan?" asked Tommy.

"And where's the capstan room?" I asked, hoping Liberty was paying attention.

"The room is located on this deck but it's at the aft of the ship. The capstan is kind of a pulley," said William. "It's used to move heavy cargo between decks."

"Thank you," I said. "Very interesting. Well, I'm hopeful we can find and train another horse when we get to the New World."

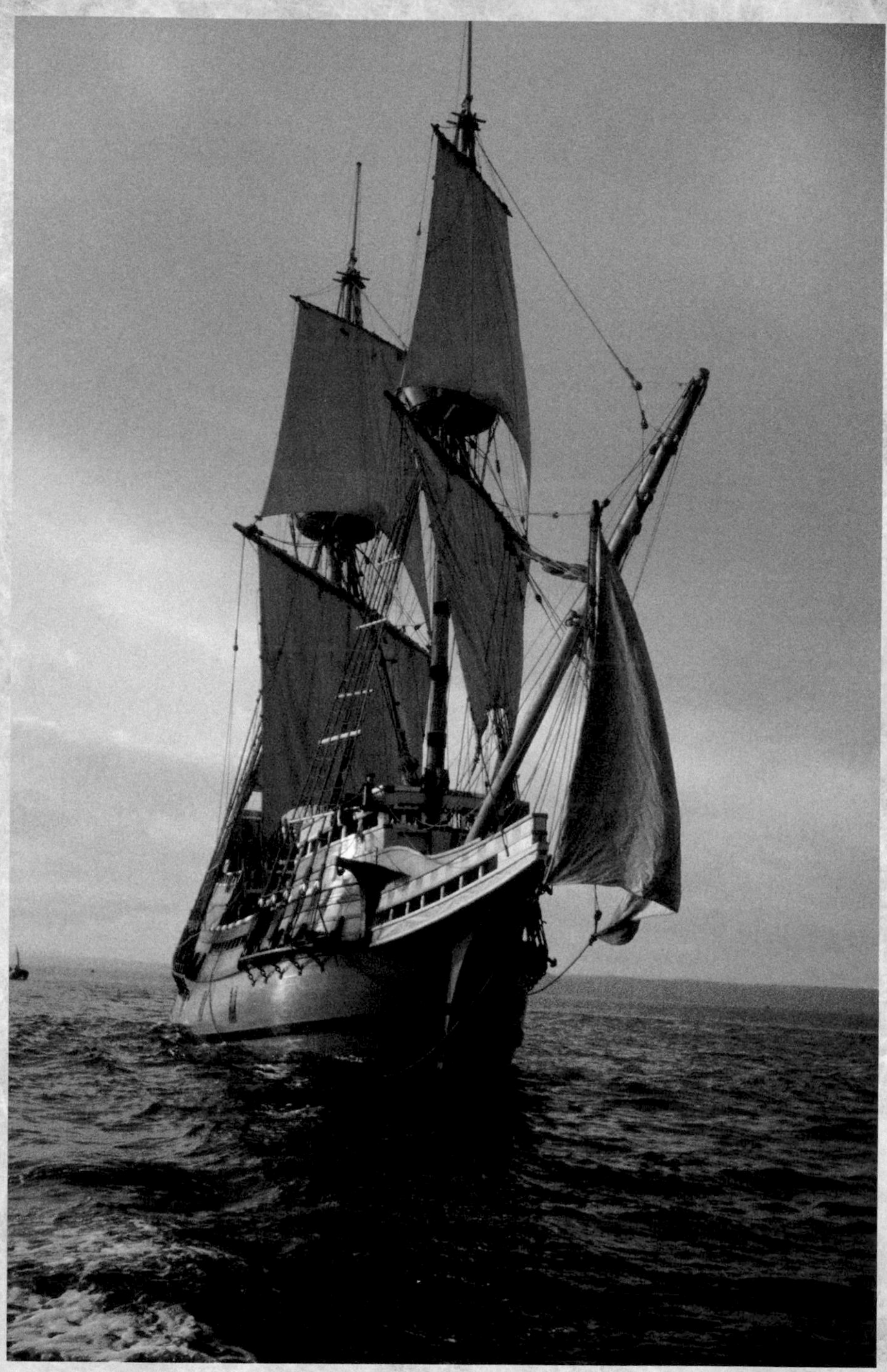

Mayflower II in calm seas.

"How many decks are there on the *Mayflower?*" asked Tommy. "I mean, where do people sleep?"

"Good question," said William. He pointed toward the top aft end of the ship, "That up there is the quarterdeck. That's where you'll find the captain's cabin. The deck we're standing on is the upper deck. The galley or ship's kitchen is to the bow."

I knew Liberty wasn't around or he would have asked for a personal tour of the kitchen and then he would have volunteered to be the *Mayflower*'s official taste tester!

"Below this deck is the tween deck. That's where most of the passengers are living and sleeping. We also have a small pen for our smaller livestock, including chickens. And below the tween deck is the cargo hold where we store our flour, barrels of water, and other general supplies."

"William," I asked, "tell me, how are things for you? How can I help with your voyage?"

"Our numbers are dwindling. There used to be nearly one hundred and fifty Puritans traveling to the New World. But the trip has been hard on many of our people. After several attempts of trying to sail two ships to America we decided that the *Speedwell* was not seaworthy. It leaked like a sieve. Three times the crew tried to patch her up, without success. The first attempt was at Southampton after a very wet and worrisome journey from Holland. But a leaky ship will not keep us from the freedom we desperately want. We will make it to our new home!"

That's when William gave me the most reassuring smile. It's no wonder the Pilgrims were ready to follow him to the New World. He was inspiring to listen to. I was ready to follow him, too.

"You said that there used to be nearly one hundred and fifty Puritans," I said. "How many are there now?"

"The passengers of the *Mayflower* include about fifty Puritans. The crew refers to us as Saints. The other half are Adventurers, also known as Strangers."

Tommy whispered in my ear, "Sounds like two football teams playing on *Monday Night Football,* the Saints versus the Strangers."

I smiled as William continued: "We had to include others if we stand a chance of starting a new settlement in the New World. It's not ideal but it's a step closer in getting us to our new home."

"I really like your ship," said Tommy. "And I happen to know you'll make it to the New World."

"Really?" William said, smiling. "You say that without a shadow of a doubt in your voice. I wish more of our members had your same positive attitude and conviction."

A gust of wind came up and William quickly grabbed for his hat. He looked up at the sails and said, "I believe that heaven is helping us. We should give thanks for such a prosperous wind. Come, let us find Elder Brewster."

As we followed William, the boat rose and fell with greater force. The winds were getting stronger and the swells were getting bigger. We were far out to sea now. Dark clouds pushed across the Atlantic Ocean. More frequently, water splashed up and over the ship's railing. Imagine what it would be like in the evening when it was pitch black outside. Waves crashing, winds howling, thunder cracking, and the ship rocking fiercely against the waves. I imagined a monstrous wave that rocked the ship so hard that it capsized. The thought was terrifying and I quickly pushed it from my mind. It was easy for me to do because

I knew that the *Mayflower* made it to the New World. But none of the Pilgrims knew that. And yet, William Bradford spoke as if he did know. His faith allowed him to stay optimistic despite the raging storm.

We arrived at the hatch door that led down to the between decks. Other passengers were lined up and climbing down the ladder. When we were close enough to climb down, the smell caught my attention immediately. Tommy whispered, "Whoa, this is ten times worse than our locker room at school. It smells like a boatload of stinky socks down there."

As quietly as possible I responded, "There should be about a hundred people down there, with no windows and not a lot of room."

"That's like the time we had our family reunion at my house and like a hundred of my relatives crammed into my living room for a few hours. It was so crowded and most of my cousins are really annoying."

"That was just for a few hours," I said. "Now try it for a few weeks or months and instead of your relatives you have to hang with a bunch of people from your church and the other half is a bunch of people you've never met."

Tommy's eyes were wide with concern. "Seriously? All in the same room? Oh, that would get old really fast. I mean, I think an hour would be too long with some people. And the smell down there must be a lot stronger. I don't know how they did it."

Tommy followed William and I followed Tommy.

When I stepped from the bottom rung of the ladder to the tween deck I had to bend my knees and lean forward to enter the room. Tommy was standing up straight but it looked like his head touched the wood ceiling. Hunched over, we tried to follow William through a maze of people. The only light that came into the room was from the open hatch. It was dim but there was enough light to see that every family had a small living space. Some families had built wooden dividers that served as walls and provided them with a little privacy. We heard voices all around us; many of them were children saying things like:

"How long do we have to stay down here?"

"The sea is making me sick again."

"I have to go potty."

"Can I go find the puppy?"

I thought that last comment was odd, but with all the voices it was hard to be sure what I heard. Occasionally, water dripped through the upper deck and onto my head and neck. Tommy tapped me on the shoulder and whispered, "This place is creepy. And I think someone or something is following me."

"Not to worry," I whispered back. "We won't stay long."

Suddenly, a little boy, probably five or six years old, jumped out of the darkness and into our path. He looked up at Tommy and said, "Pardon me, but have you seen the puppy?"

Tommy crouched down until he was eye to eye with the little boy and said, "Sorry, little dude, I haven't seen a puppy."

Suddenly, the little boy jumped up and down, shouting and pointing to something behind Tommy: "Puppy, puppy, I see the puppy!"

Still crouching, Tommy turned around and stared up into the eyes of a giant-sized dog only inches from his face. The dog's huge tongue licked and slobbered excitedly as Tommy fell backward until he was on his back and the dog was now standing over him. The little boy laughed and laughed.

"That's the puppy?" Tommy asked still lying on the damp floor and trying to cover his face with his arms.

William smiled and said, "That's what they call him. He's actually a giant mastiff. And there's another dog, a spaniel. Two dogs and a hundred and two passengers."

Other children joined the first little boy and they all started petting the dog. It was large enough that the smallest of the children could probably ride it like a horse.

I leaned over to help Tommy to his feet. He grabbed my hand and while hoisting him up I forgot about the low ceiling. "Ouch," I said.

"It takes some getting used to," said William. "Are you all right?"

"I'll be fine. No worries." I could already feel the raised bump on the top of my head.

"The *Mayflower* was not built to be a passenger ship. It's a cargo ship. However, as you can see we've converted this crawlspace into our living quarters," said William.

I looked around and could vaguely see that many passengers were lying down on rugs or sitting on chairs, chests of clothing, or leaning up against casks that were probably filled with water or beer. Many looked seasick, with chamber pots close by in case they had to vomit.

Tommy turned to one of the children who were petting the dog and asked, "Do you have to stay down here all the time?"

"Not all of the time," said a girl who was about eight years old. "Only when the wind is really pushy and the waves are really big."

"The waves don't feel really big from down here," Tommy said.

Overhearing the conversation, William crouched down to his knees and spoke to all of the children, including Tommy. "It's true that this deck can be very deceiving about what's happening outside. But the *Mayflower* is a special kind of ship. Have you ever seen a duck float on top of the waves? It just sits there, perfectly balanced while easily floating up and over and around the water. Well, the *Mayflower* is like a duck." William reached out and while gently pressing against a little boy's nose he made the noise "quack, quack." The children laughed.

A young teenage boy who was standing nearby raised his hand and said, "I haven't seen a duck, but I have seen a seagull. Or at least I think it was a seagull. I'm not sure because I didn't see it float very long before a giant shark three times the size of the *Mayflower* jumped out of the water and ate the whole thing in one gulp."

"It's true," said a second boy, about the same age as the first. They looked like brothers. "I saw the same shark. In fact, I saw it following the *Mayflower* just a few minutes ago."

The young children stood there looking horrified, their eyes nearly as big as their opened mouths.

"D-d-did you really see such a shark?" a little girl finally asked.

"No, he did not!" said a man coming from behind the two teenage boys. Although it was dark, I could tell that he was shorter than William but probably close to the same age, maybe a little older. He looked like a strong man with broad shoulders. His red beard and mustache were neatly trimmed and he wore fine clothing, with a sword hanging from his side. I could see Tommy's eyes fixed on the sword.

He grabbed the ears of both of the teenage boys and forced them to their knees. He spoke with authority and while twisting their ears he said, "I warned you Billington boys. I told you I wouldn't put up with your nonsense. You will now tell these children the truth."

Painfully, the boys spoke as fast as they could. "We didn't see a shark." "Ouch, or a seagull." "We're sorry for scaring you." "Ow, it was just a fib." "We were just teasing you." "That really hurts, it won't happen again. . . ."

"Thank you, Captain Standish, that will be enough," said William Bradford.

Like two fish being released in a shallow pool, the boys darted for the other side of the darkened ship.

"Let me introduce you to Captain Myles Standish," said William. "Captain Standish was with us in Holland. He will be handling our colony's military matters in America."

Tommy leaned close to me and whispered, "I'm glad he's not our substitute teacher. He doesn't mess around. My friend's dad was in the military, and let's just say no one wanted to get on his bad side. Captain Standish seems stricter than Principal Sherman."

We exchanged introductions and Tommy immediately asked, "Will you teach me how to fight with a sword?"

"I'd be delighted," said Myles, "but ear-twisting can also be very effective." He winked and smiled while messing up Tommy's hair. "When the weather gets better I can teach you the art of swordfighting on the upper deck."

William asked Myles, "Have you seen Elder Brewster?"

"I believe he's returned to the captain's cabin to—"

Before Myles could finish his sentence a loud bell started to ring. "Ding, ding. Ding, ding. Ding, ding." Through the open hatch we heard someone shout, "Man overboard!"

As we hurried to follow William and Myles back to the hatch and up the ladder, I noticed several families calling out for sons and daughters, husbands and wives. Like a hen rushing to gather her chicks, fathers and mothers were frantically searching for their own children, hoping whoever went overboard wasn't one of their own.

We rushed up the ladder, through the hatch, and onto the upper deck. It was like we landed on a different planet. Although it was much brighter and the air much fresher, the wind was howling through the ropes and rigging, and giant waves looked like they could smother the *Mayflower* at any moment. We were drenched from the water spraying in every direction. We scrambled toward several sailors shouting and pointing at something in the water.

"He fell over the ship's railing right there!" a sailor shouted.

An older man was barking orders to the crew and I assumed he must be the captain of the *Mayflower*. He was wearing a long coat with a stocking cap similar to what the sailors were wearing.

William called to the older man, "Captain Jones, look over there!" He pointed to a rope attached to the upper sail. "It looks like it's dragging something."

The captain looked doubtful but in a split second yelled at the crew, "Get that topsail halyard out of the water!"

I studied the end of the rope that was lost in the waves behind us. For a few seconds, I saw something that looked like a body lift up out of the water and then become consumed again by another wave.

"A man!" I shouted. "He's hanging on to the end of that rope." I wasn't 100 percent sure but I believed William Bradford's suspicion was correct.

"He's caught in the rope. He's already dead!" shouted a sailor. "Leave him for the sharks."

"I give the orders around here, sailor!" shouted Captain Jones. "Get that halyard out of the water! And that man still better be on the end of it or I wouldn't want to be you!"

Captain Jones's voice was so loud and so threatening that the crew looked more afraid of the captain than they did of the storm. Within seconds they had the rope and began pulling with all their might. "Heave, heave, heave!" they shouted in unison.

It felt like buckets of water were being thrown on us from every direction. The ship rocked again and again. It was almost impossible to stand up without holding on to something. I tried to keep my eye on the end of the rope that the sailors were hauling in, and hoped to spot the dangling body, but I slipped and slid across the width of the twenty-five-foot deck. It might have been fun if I were at a water park. As I looked back to where I was standing, I saw that William had joined the sailors and was pulling the rope as well. Tommy was on his hands and knees nearly twenty feet away. He was dangerously close to the railing and as he attempted to stand the boat suddenly lurched leeward. Helplessly, I saw Tommy slip and tip over the ship's railing headfirst. I scrambled toward Tommy but realized I just wasn't close enough to help him. Fortunately, Myles Standish was. He reached over and grabbed Tommy's right leg in the nick of time. Just as Myles was slipping, I reached out and grabbed his arm as he continued to pull Tommy back onto the ship.

"I'm taking the boy to the captain's cabin! You should come, too!" shouted Myles.

"Thank you, Captain Standish!" I yelled, not fully realizing

An artist's rendering of William Brewster.

An artist's rendering of Myles Standish.

the gravity of what had just happened. "I'll follow you in just a minute!" I wanted to witness the rescue of the man in the water.

I yelled to Tommy, "Go with Captain Standish! I'll be right behind you!"

The sailors continued to heave and pull the rope in rhythm. The end of the rope was nearing the rudder. It reached the aft of the ship and then the hull. Without question, there was a man hanging on to the end of that rope with fierce desperation.

"Grab a boat hook!" shouted Captain Jones. "Haul him up and snag him with the hook!"

After several more minutes, the man was hauled back into the boat. He rolled to his side and coughed up seawater.

"Take him to my cabin!" the captain ordered.

Two sailors pulled the man to his feet. They helped him up the ladder to the quarterdeck and into the captain's cabin.

"He's lucky to be alive," I said as I patted William on the back.

"Not luck," William said. "It's a miracle. Surely, this is a divine sign. We will ask Elder Brewster. Whenever there is doubt or fear among the passengers we can always turn to him for guidance and strength. He has great wisdom and spiritual strength." As William opened the door to the captain's cabin he turned back and said, "Elder Brewster always provides a sense of calm in troubled times. I'm eager for you to meet him."

"Did I hear my name? Am I needed?" asked a man dressed in a long blue robe. His high collar and stately appearance reminded me of someone of religious authority. He had kind eyes and his peppered hair was thin and receding. He was sitting across from Myles Standish and Tommy. They all stood and rushed over to us when they saw the sailors help the stumbling man to a bed.

"Elder Brewster," said William. "John Howland fell overboard but was saved."

"If he had followed the rules and stayed below deck during a storm he wouldn't look like a drowned rat," said Myles.

"You say he fell overboard?" asked Elder Brewster, sounding greatly concerned. "And yet he is back on the ship? Tell me what happened."

William explained all that had happened.

"Extraordinary," said Elder Brewster.

John started coughing again. He breathed deeply as his eyes scanned the room. "I can't believe . . . I'm alive. . . . Thank you for saving me."

"John, my dear boy, what were you doing on the upper deck during a tempest?" asked Elder Brewster.

Breathlessly, John replied, "I'm sorry. Truly, I am. I was sitting in my space down below in the tween deck. The passengers next to me were seasick and both threw up in their chamber pots. The stench was more than I could handle. I just needed some fresh air. I felt the walls of the ship's hull closing in all around me, and down below it didn't feel like the weather was a raging tempest. So I climbed the ladder as fast as I could, opened the hatch, and jumped out only to find that I had entered a terrible fury."

"Do not condemn yourself, John," said Elder Brewster. "Your salvation from certain death is a miraculous sign. Everything happens for a reason. God has chosen to save you, which I believe means we are certain to make it to America."

William looked at me and nodded in agreement.

The wind blew in as Captain Jones entered his cabin and removed his heavy coat. I guessed he was fifty years old. His hair and beard were gray. He wore a blue stocking cap like the other sailors but his clothing was cleaner and more distinguished. He said, "I'm sorry for my delay. How is the passenger?"

"He's alive," said William.

"He's welcome to stay here until he fully recovers," said Captain Jones.

William approached the captain and said, "I want to personally thank you for acting quickly and ordering your men to do the same. It's apparent your crew respects you."

Captain Jones laughed, "Ha, they respect me or fear me. Either way, it got the job done. But I warn you, there are sailors on this ship that would rather see all of the Puritans fed to the sharks."

"We are used to being bullied and threatened, Captain Jones," William said.

"Rest assured," said Elder Brewster, "we will not retaliate. God will smite those who afflict the righteous, just as he saves those who are good and true."

I thought about the sailor who already threatened me, twice. I believed the warning from Captain Jones. But I wondered if the captain believed the words of Elder Brewster.

As the captain talked to the other Pilgrim leaders, Tommy walked over to John's bed and said, "Dude, I can't believe you hung on to that rope. That was amazing! You're like the seventeenth-century version of Chuck Norris."

John looked at Tommy, confused. "My name is John Howland. I know not anyone named Dude, but apparently you mistake me for some stranger by that name. And I know not of any Chuck Norris. But it sounded like a compliment, so thank you."

William introduced me to both Captain Christopher Jones and Elder William Brewster, the current religious leader of the

Puritans. They invited Tommy and me to stay in the captain's cabin until the storm blew over. While we waited, Captain Jones offered us some salted beef.

"This is pretty good," Tommy said, chewing. "It's just like beef jerky."

"Jerky?" Myles questioned. "I'm not familiar with that word."

Still chewing, I butted in and said, "Oh, it's an old family recipe."

As we finished our sticks of salted beef, I walked over to William and said, "I just wanted to say that I think you make a fine leader."

William said, "Thank you, Rush Revere. I'm not sure about being a fine leader. I just do what needs to be done."

"Even if it means risking your own life?" I asked.

"I would risk my life to do the right thing every time. When I was a young boy I became very ill. I had to stay at home. I had time to read many books, especially the Bible. I promised God that I would try my best to make the right choice every time. I am far from being perfect. My wife will tell you that," William said with a smile. "But I will do everything I can to help make our colony, our New World, our land of America a place where religious freedom comes first. If we can become a nation under God and put our trust in Him, I believe we shall prosper."

I pondered those words and realized how important they would be to our Founding Fathers.

The ocean settled sooner than I expected. It was still drizzling outside but I realized it would be a good time to find Liberty, before the upper deck got too crowded. We thanked our guests and excused ourselves.

"I hope Liberty is okay," Tommy said.

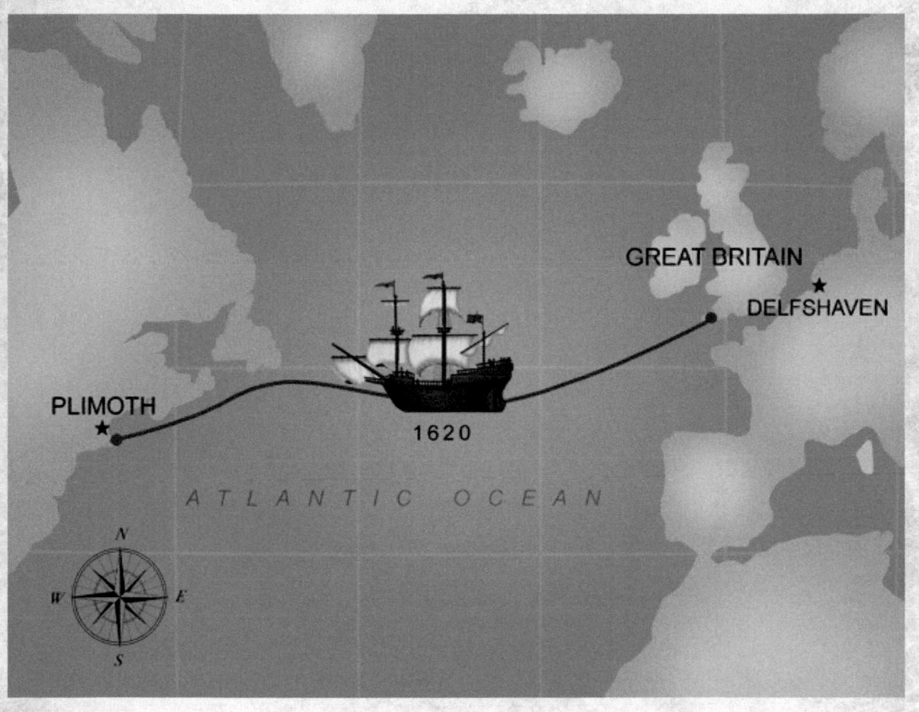

Route of the *Mayflower,* 1620.

We walked across the quarterdeck, down the ladder, and to the door of the capstan room. We opened it and found Liberty wedged between a side wall and the wooden levers of the capstan, sleeping peacefully.

"Liberty," Tommy said.

Nothing.

"Liberty!" Tommy shouted.

Still nothing.

"Here, let me try," I said. I opened Liberty's saddlebag and pulled out an apple that we had picked in Holland. I waved it in front of Liberty's nose.

With his eyes still closed, Liberty wrapped his lips around the apple and chewed heartily. I grabbed several more apples and fed them to him one by one. He kept his eyes closed while he chewed and said, "I must have taken a nap. Ships always do that to me. The more the rocking the more tired I become. Did I miss anything?"

"Nothing too important," I said, still feeding him the apples. "But it's time to jump forward to the end of the *Mayflower* voyage. There's a new land to discover! There are Indians to befriend and a new colony to build. And a celebration to be had called Thanksgiving!"

Liberty's eyes popped open and said, "Thanksgiving! Pumpkin pie. Cranberries. Squash and green beans and carrots and corn and peas and those miniature pumpkins! Now you're speaking my language! What are we waiting for?" With a burst of energy he walked out onto the open deck and vanished into thin air.

"What we need now is a distraction so Liberty can create the time portal and we can jump through it," I said. "Anyone have an idea?"

"Whoa, is that a real whale?" Tommy said while pointing starboard, off the bow of the ship.

"Very convincing, Tommy," I said. "You're a very good actor. Now we just have to convince everyone else on deck."

"I'm not kidding, look!" Tommy said.

I turned around and, sure enough, a giant sperm whale nearly sixty feet long surfaced the water. And not just one, but several whales. An entire pod of sperm whales was just two hundred yards off the starboard bow. Sailors called to each other and pointed in the direction of the whales.

"Quickly, now's our chance. To the opposite side of the ship!" I whispered.

The diversion worked. Liberty reappeared and we slipped onto his back. Liberty said, *"Rush, rush, rushing to history!"*

I echoed his words with "November ninth, 1620, the *Mayflower.*" Nobody noticed as we jumped through the time portal.

Chapter 5

Darkness concealed our return to the *Mayflower*'s upper deck. However, the sun was close to rising and would soon stretch its rays across the eastern horizon. A light breeze drifted across our faces, reminding us that winter was just around the corner. We appeared to have landed on the ship we left from, except instead of September it was now November. It was still too dark to see much, but I was worried about the condition of the passengers and crew. I knew they lacked food and water. I knew they lacked good nutrition, particularly vitamin C, in their diet. Certainly, this would cause many to suffer from scurvy—a disease known to cause swollen and bleeding gums and ultimately, death. And, most important, I knew they lacked hope. For days and weeks the Pilgrims hoped that they would find land. They hoped for an end to the miserable conditions they had to endure. Now, after suffering for two months, there was still no sign of dry ground. Even I could feel the grip of hopelessness trying to strangle me. I quickly turned to Liberty and Tommy in an effort to break the despair I was feeling.

"Nice jumping, Liberty," I said, scratching him behind the ear.

"Aw, shucks! I bet you say that to all the magical horses who leap you across the Atlantic Ocean," Liberty said, grinning.

Tommy jumped off Liberty's saddle and said, "Hey, if there are other horses like you, I want one!"

Curious, I asked, "If you had a horse like Liberty, what exceptional event in American history would you visit first?"

"Hmm," Tommy thought, "that's a tough one. Probably 1969, when Apollo 11 launched into space and Neil Armstrong became the first man to set foot on the moon. That would be awesome!"

"Oh, I remember watching that on television," said Liberty. "When he landed on the moon he said, 'That's one small step for man, one giant leap for mankind.' Although, personally, I think a giant leap through time is more impressive."

"Wait, you mean that if you wanted to you could time-jump to the moon?" Tommy asked.

"Well, if a cow can jump over the moon, certainly a horse can!" Liberty huffed.

"All right, kids," I intervened. "Let's get back to business. It's almost light enough now to see what's happening on the ship. In fact, I think that's Captain Jones and William Bradford up on the poop deck."

Tommy burst out laughing and asked, "Did you just say 'poop' deck?"

Then Liberty started laughing. "It's funny when you say it like that! Poop deck. Poop deck."

I rolled my eyes and waited until the two of them stopped laughing. "Are you finished? Honestly, you're acting like a couple of five-year-olds."

"Um, actually," Liberty tried to say, "I *am* five."

Then they both started laughing again. In fact, watching them laugh made me start to laugh.

"For the record," I said, smiling, "the 'poop' deck is the deck above the captain's cabin, built in the rear or stern of the ship. I believe the name originates from the French word for stern, *la poupe*."

More laughter. Tommy and Liberty were leaning on each other now, laughing hysterically, and saying in their best French accent, "La poupe, la poupe."

"Liberty," I said, "I think you better disappear and hide yourself in the capstan room. I think someone is approaching." Instantly, Liberty vanished as we heard a familiar voice say, "I'm glad to see someone can laugh under the circumstances. Who goes there and why all the frivolity?"

As the voice got closer we saw Myles Standish, his sword still hanging from his side. His clothes were haggard and he smelled like he hadn't bathed in days or weeks or even a couple of months. However, despite his appearance he was smiling.

"Hi, Captain Standish," said Tommy, standing up straight.

"Oh, hello, Tommy. Hello, Rush. I was thinking about you just the other day. I'd meant to come find you but with all my duties I'm afraid I've not been very attentive. I must say it's good to see you in such fine spirits. Hearing you laugh put a smile on my face. I can't remember the last time I smiled. Thank you for that," said Myles.

"It appears our laughter may be contagious," I said.

"Let's hope it spreads quickly. Our people are beginning to doubt. Elder Brewster is encouraging as many as he can. He reminds us to pray day and night. But so many are sick. We are nearly out of water, and we have little food. We've had much contention and despair among the passengers and crew. Thankfully, the cruelest of them is no longer with us."

"Did someone die?" asked Tommy.

"Yes, lad. We've kept it quiet because we didn't want to worry the rest of you below deck. Many days ago one of the sailors, a vile, profane, and arrogant man, was stricken with disease and died in a wretched way."

A thought occurred to me and I asked, "I remember one sailor with a scar above his cheek. He was heartless about our seasickness and threatened to feed all the Puritans to the sharks. Was it him?"

Myles nodded. "The very one," he said. "That sailor mocked our suffering and cursed our people endlessly. He swore and hoped to cast half of us overboard before we came to our journey's end. Yet he himself was the first to be thrown overboard. The word has spread that it was the just hand of God who did it."

Tommy raised his hand as if he were in the classroom and asked, "Captain Standish, what happens when people get sick on the *Mayflower*? Is there a doctor's office on the boat?"

"No, Tommy, not really," said Myles. "We have people who care for the sick but there isn't much that can be done when the illness is severe."

"Do you ever feel like you want to give up and go back to Holland?" asked Tommy.

"No, son," Myles said, firmly. "Abandoning this voyage is out of the question, at least for me. We must go on despite the hardships. If we give up now, we will never know what land is ahead. If we turn this vessel around, we will be back to a place where we cannot really be free."

"Do you think the king would put all of you in jail?"

"Perhaps," said Myles, "even if we made it back to Holland without anyone knowing, we couldn't go to our own church. The Church of England would tell us how we must act and how we must think."

Tommy's brow was furrowed as he thought about what Myles had said. "Yeah, I don't like when people try to control me. My mom always tells me to think for myself and not just follow the crowd. She says I should stand up for what I believe even if it's not popular."

"It sounds like you have a very smart mother," said Myles.

"Yeah, and she's also really strict about me doing my chores around the house. You'd probably really like her."

Myles laughed and said, "You are an incredibly bright boy, Tommy. I'm glad you are here. You fit in perfectly with our mission.

"Come, Rush Revere and Tommy," he said. "Let me take you to Captain Jones and William. He's navigating the ship from the poop deck."

I gave Tommy "the look."

Both of Tommy's hands went into the air. "Hey, the joke's over for me. That was so 1620," he said, winking.

As we walked to visit with Captain Jones and William, Tommy said, "Captain Standish, I never really got a chance to thank you for, you know, the way you caught me. I mean, you

Mayflower in rough seas, 1620.

were lightning fast. And then how you lifted me up by my leg. You were like the Hulk. Anyway, thanks for saving my life."

Myles stopped and looked at Tommy. He finally said, "Tommy, I don't know if I'm any stronger or faster than any other man. But if I've learned anything while living among the Puritans it's that everything happens for a reason. Simply, you weren't supposed to fall off this ship. It wasn't your time."

Boy, is that the truth, I thought.

Myles continued: "I'm glad I was standing next to you when you fell overboard. I'm glad I could save you. But my part in helping you is over and yours has just begun. Think of it as a second chance. What will you do with your life now that you couldn't have done if I hadn't caught you?"

"Wow, that's deep. But I get it," said Tommy.

"Good," said Myles. "Go do something great with your life, Tommy. We'll talk more soon. And your first sword lesson begins when we get to dry ground! A man is always better off when he knows how to protect himself and his family!" Myles turned to leave, but then stopped with a quizzical look and asked, "Did you say I was like the Hulk? Who or what is the Hulk?"

Tommy paused for just a second and replied, "Oh, well, he's just this guy back home. Sort of a hero. He's really strong and pretty much invincible."

"Thank you for the compliment. I think I would like to meet this Hulk someday," Myles said, smiling. He then turned on his heel and headed for the ladder.

When Captain Jones and William Bradford saw us, William said, "Rush Revere! Please forgive my neglect. It's good to see you. I assume you've been surviving with the others below deck? I know I shouldn't assume but with so many passengers suffering from seasickness, including my wife, I've found myself unable to visit everyone I'd like."

"No worries," I said. "Tommy and I are definitely surviving and feeling very optimistic today!"

I noticed Captain Jones held a three-foot-long stick on which was attached a sliding crosspiece. I assumed it was sort of a compass. That's when Tommy asked, "What's that in your hand?"

"It's a cross-staff," said Captain Jones. "It helps me know where to steer the ship. I place it up to my eye and measure the distance between a star, the moon, or the sun and the horizon. It helps me calculate the ship's position. But with all the bad weather it's been difficult to know for sure how far we are from land."

Curious, I asked, "And where are we supposed to be by now?"

"By now I expected us to be at the Jamestown Settlement on the Hudson River." At that point in history, the Jamestown settlement extended all the way up the mid-Atlantic coast to what is now New York. "But with all the storms it looks like we have traveled much farther north than I expected," said the Captain.

Tommy whispered to me, "Too bad they didn't have a GPS."

William added, "By Captain Jones's calculations we should spot land in a day or so."

"Look," said Tommy, pointing up into the morning sky. "Isn't that a seagull? And there's another! I'm pretty sure those seagulls are coastal birds."

In the moment Tommy finished speaking we heard a sailor shout from above, "Land, ho!"

Passengers started streaming out from the hatches that led to the tween deck. Many were lifted and helped up the ladder, too sick or weary to walk on their own. Their expressions were mixed between hope and doubt as if they couldn't believe their ears. The bow of the ship pointed westward as all eyes raced to see what they hadn't seen for more than two months. Land! Sure enough, a distant strip of land could be seen on the horizon. As soon as the Pilgrims on the upper deck saw the outline of dry ground, they fell to their knees and began to weep. Others shouted for joy and almost everyone found someone to hug. Elder Brewster called the Saints together, and even some of the Strangers came, and together they offered a word a prayer. They knelt to give thanks to God for persevering and protecting them. After they prayed, they sang a hymn. Some were too emotional to sing as they watched the approaching land and simply cried tears of relief. Even the sick and weary looked to have renewed health and strength.

I noticed William had a giant smile on his face and what looked to be a tear in his eye. He said, "We left Plymouth, England, on September sixth and today is . . ."

"November ninth," Tommy finished. "You've been sailing straight for sixty-five days!"

"Very good, Tommy," said Captain Jones. "And many of the passengers have been seasick for all sixty-five days."

William breathed deeply and nearly laughed when he said, "They are not feeling sick now. They are exceedingly happy and grateful that God has preserved us over this vast and furious ocean."

"And it looks like a beautiful day," I said. "Soon we'll be on dry ground."

"Yes," the Captain agreed, "but remember, we are far north of our original destination. We were supposed to land at the Hudson River. Instead, it appears we are headed toward New England—Cape Cod, to be exact."

"It is needful that we find our way to the coast as fast as

possible," said William. "Our provisions are low and many passengers are sick and even diseased."

"We sail by the wind," said Captain Jones. "Right now, the wind is coming from the north. We'll sail to the coast and follow the coastline swiftly to the Hudson River."

They all agreed and soon a colony of seagulls flew overhead, welcoming the *Mayflower* as it drifted out of deep blue waters and into emerald green. Passengers crowded the starboard side of the ship and watched with keen interest at the thick forest of trees and bushes with orange and yellow leaves that grew beyond the empty beaches.

I watched these remarkable passengers, amazed at how genuinely tough they were. The kind of hardship they experienced on the *Mayflower* is something that modern-day people will seldom, if ever, experience. And yet these Pilgrims did it with gusto! They hadn't been spoiled by wall-to-wall carpets, central heating, and microwave ovens. They lived and endured hard things because that is just how it was. And so they passed the first test. The next would be the building of a new colony. I knew it wouldn't be easy, but I was sure that these rugged individuals would, again, find a way to overcome any trial.

Myles Standish walked up to us and asked, "What catches your eye out there, Tommy?" Tommy gripped the railing as he stared at the passing wilderness. "Oh, well, I was just wondering what might be in those woods," he said, sounding a little bit nervous.

Myles answered, "All the things that will sustain us. Wood, berries, animals, water, and soil."

"And Indians?" asked Tommy.

"Yes, probably Indians," Myles said. "We will do what we must to protect ourselves. We have swords and muskets and cannons if need be."

"That's good to know," said Tommy.

"Hopefully, we won't have to use them," said William.

As I looked ahead along the coast I wondered if Captain Jones had ever sailed these waters. Surely, every coastline is different and there's always a chance of hidden dangers.

Suddenly, a sailor yelled from above, "Shoals ahead! Turn port side!"

"Aren't shoals like a sandbank or sandbar out in the open water?" Tommy asked.

"Yes," I said to Tommy softly. "And if I'm not mistaken this place is called Pollock Rip—it's a ship's graveyard. If the captain doesn't avoid the shoals the *Mayflower* could get pinned or even shipwrecked. A direct hit could smash the ship's hull."

Waves crashed against the shoals as water swirled up and over the threatening sandbars. The wind died down to almost nothing but the *Mayflower* drifted dangerously closer to the roaring breakers.

"We are in great danger!" said Captain Jones with urgency. His eyes were fixed on the shoals ahead. "A southern wind would be especially helpful right now!"

Calmly, William said, "We've not come this far to shipwreck now. What must we do?"

"Watch for shoals," said Captain Jones. "And keep your people away from my sailors so they can do their jobs."

"With God all things are possible," said Elder Brewster from behind me.

I turned and asked, "Do you have any counsel, any advice?"

"Pray," he said, smiling. "God will make up the difference. He created the heavens and the earth. Surely, He can steer a ship to safety."

Remarkably, the wind began to blow, a southern wind! The sails shifted and the *Mayflower* turned just in time, missing the shoals by only a few feet.

"I'm afraid we won't be landing at the Hudson River. This coastline is too dangerous," said Captain Jones. "Now that the wind has changed directions our best chance is to sail north, back around Cape Cod to New England."

William gave a worried look at Myles, who said, "The Strangers will not like it."

William looked deep in thought and said, "Yes, the Strangers will insist we land at the Hudson."

"Then they can jump off my ship and swim if they want to," said Captain Jones. "I will go and explain to them the situation. I will not have a mutiny on my ship."

"Captain Standish and I will go with you," said William. "Rush and Tommy, you're welcome to come but please don't feel like you have to."

I eagerly replied, "We're right behind you. If there's anything you need, just ask."

"Thank you, Rush Revere, for all the support you've given."

We climbed down from the poop deck to the quarterdeck and then climbed down again to the upper deck. Several passengers climbed up from the tween deck. Liberty was waiting for us on the upper deck.

As Myles predicted, the Strangers were in an uproar when they heard the news. Shouts could be heard from above and below deck. It sounded like a mob. Children were crying and even the giant mastiff was barking at everyone and everything.

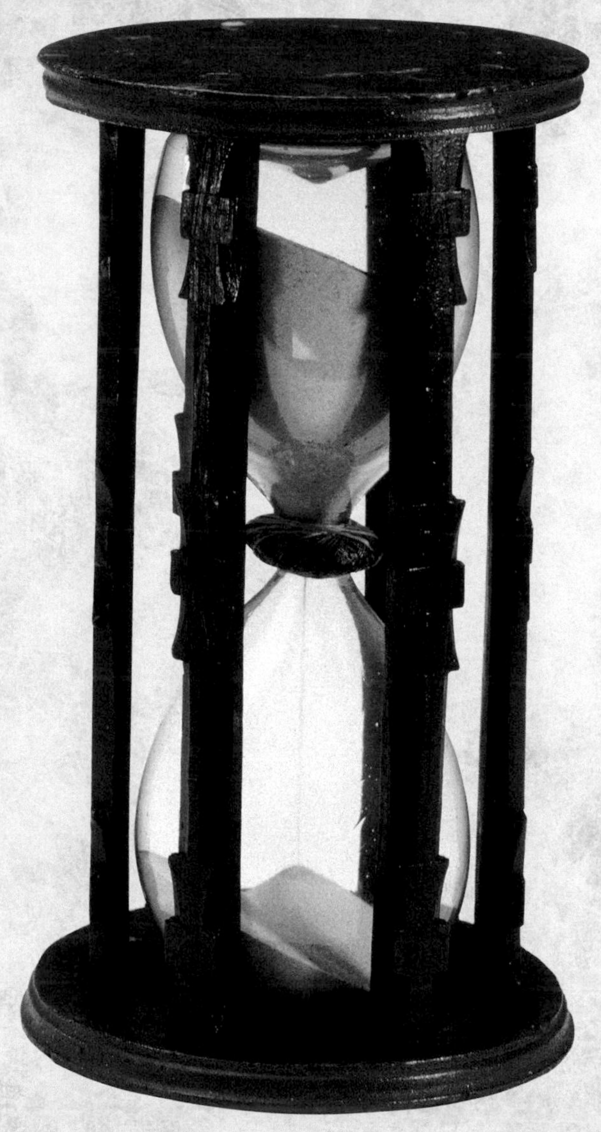

Hourglass used to tell time on the voyage.

Compass dial with lid used to navigate during the day.

Compass and sundial made of silver, ivory, brass, and glass used to tell time during the day.

A nocturnal, an instrument that uses the stars to tell the time at night.

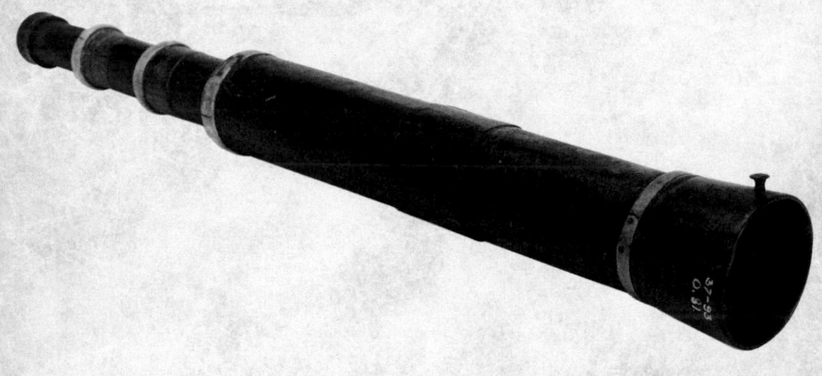

Portable telescope used to view at a distance.

A jack screw similar to this raised houses in Plymouth and saved the *Mayflower* from sinking.

"Please," pleaded William, trying to calm both Stranger and Saint. "I'm sure we can work this out. We've shared the same boat for sixty-five days. We've had our differences but we've come to know each other. We've both suffered and survived together. We've shared our provisions and our stories and our dreams knowing that we, all of us, would be a new colony."

Captain Jones added, "I've seen firsthand how Saint and Stranger have worked together for the good of all. When we were mid-ocean and that monstrous wave cracked one of the ship's core beams, I witnessed how you rallied to find a solution. In desperation, you collectively used a screw jack to help my carpenter repair the fractured beam."

One of the Strangers stepped forward and raised his hands to speak.

"Who is that?" Tommy asked. "Is he a Stranger or a Saint?"

Myles leaned over to us and whispered, "That's Stephen Hopkins, a Stranger. His wife gave birth to a baby boy during our voyage. They named him Oceanus."

Tommy raised his eyebrows and whispered back, "Oceanus?"

Myles shrugged his shoulders and smirked.

"It's an odd name, for sure," I said, "But when the other kids ask him about it he can always say, 'It's because I was born aboard the *Mayflower*.'"

"Yeah," Tommy agreed, "not many people can say that."

Stephen Hopkins spoke boldly: "We agreed to help and use the screw jack because we all had a common goal. We all agreed to settle at the Hudson River. And now we're headed in the opposite direction." He pointed at William Bradford, Myles Standish, Elder Brewster, and the other Puritan members and shouted, "Land where you want, but when we come ashore we'll use our own liberty, for none have the power to command us!"

"Did he just say they'll use their own horse named Liberty?" whispered Liberty. "What are the odds that there are two horses with the same name on the same ship?"

"They weren't referring to a different horse, they said—"

Liberty interrupted: "Well, if they think they're going to use me they better think again. I'm not another man's property. I mean, I used to be but that was in the eighteenth century and just because we're in the seventeenth century doesn't mean I'm going to give up my twenty-first-century freedoms."

Liberty's mouth was so close to my face that his whiskers tickled my ear. I whispered back, "Nobody is going to use you. They might as well try to tame a thousand wild horses with nothing but a whistle."

"Shh," Liberty hushed. "I'm trying to listen to what's happening."

I resisted the urge to strangle my horse and continued listening.

William said, "I understand your frustration. I do. We all have advantages by settling at the Hudson River. However, right now that's not an option. The truth is the only way for this new colony to succeed financially is if we all stay together and work together."

Stephen Hopkins turned to discuss the matter with his fellow Strangers. Before long, they reluctantly agreed that a union with the Saints or Puritans was important for the colony to survive and thrive.

William turned to Captain Jones and said, "Captain, I request that we set anchor at Cape Cod so that we might compose an agreement, something that would bind us all together." He turned to the large crowd of passengers on the upper deck and continued: "We need a document that will help create just and equal laws in our new colony. We'll need a government and a governor, but more important, we must choose this by common consent where majority rules. Once this agreement is composed, I propose that we sign it as a promise to obey and support the rules and laws which we agree to."

I whispered to Tommy, "This is a key moment of American history. The agreement that William Bradford is proposing is the Mayflower Compact. It is said to be just as important to American history as the Declaration of Independence."

The passengers agreed to creating the agreement and Captain Jones offered William Bradford his personal cabin and desk to compose the agreement.

I approached William and said, "That was a difficult situation but you handled it well."

"Thank you," said William. "It was the mutinous speeches that made me determined to find a solution."

"And what are you thinking this agreement will do?" I asked.

"It's a good question. By signing this agreement everyone on this ship is agreeing, when we land, to live and work together so that we can survive. It will be a brief outline of self-government. We'll still profess our allegiance to King James but we also need just and equal laws suited to our new settlement and new way of life. We are far from England and so we must do what is convenient for the general good of the colony."

"That is really ingenious," I said.

Signing of the Mayflower Compact on board the *Mayflower* in 1620.

IN the Name of God, Amen. We whoſe Names are under-written, the Loyal Subjects of our dread Soveraign Lord King *James*, by the grace of God of *Great Britain*, *France* and *Ireland*, King, *Defendor of the Faith*, *&c.* Having undertaken for the glory of God, and advancement of the Chriſtian Faith, and the Honour of our King and Countrey, a Voyage to plant the firſt Colony in the Northern parts of *Virginia*; Do by theſe Preſents ſolemnly and mutually, in the preſence of God and one another, Covenant and Combine our ſelves together into a Civil Body Politick, for our better ordering and preſervation, and furtherance of the ends aforeſaid: and by virtue hereof do enact, conſtitute and frame ſuch juſt and equal Laws, Ordinances, Acts, Conſtitutions and Officers, from time to time, as ſhall be thought moſt meet and convenient for the general good of the Colony; unto which we promiſe all due ſubmiſſion and obedience. In witneſs whereof we have hereunto ſubſcribed our Names at *Cape Cod*, the eleventh of *November*, in the Reign of our Soveraign Lord King *James*, of *England*, *France* and *Ireland* the eighteenth, and of *Scotland* the fifty fourth, *Anno Dom.* 1620.

John Carver.
William Bradford.
Edward Winſlow.
William Brewſter.
Iſaac Allerton.
Miles Standiſh.
John Alden.

Samuel Fuller.
Chriſtopher Martin.
William Mullins.
William White.
Richard Warren.
John Howland.
Steven Hopkins.

Edward Tilly.
John Tilly.
Francis Cook.
Thomas Rogers.
Thomas Tinker.
John Ridgdale.
Edward Fuller.

John

Mayflower Compact, establishing the rule of fairness under law in Plymouth Colony, signed by almost all men on board the *Mayflower*.

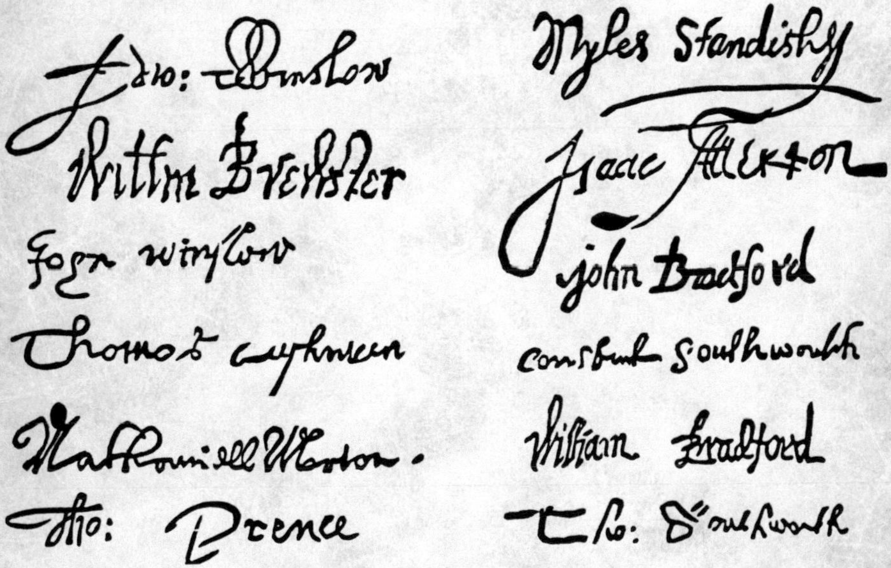

Signatures of several Mayflower Compact signers, including William Brewster, Myles Standish, and William Bradford.

"If we can get everyone to agree it will be," William said with a chuckle.

I patted him on the back and said, "I predict that this very agreement you're proposing will be referred to by many English colonists who will settle in America in the years to come. In fact, it might very well be the beginning of a greater constitution for all Americans."

"You are always thinking of the future, Rush Revere," said William, smiling. "I like that about you. If you'll excuse me, I have some writing to do."

William and several other passengers climbed the stairs to the captain's cabin.

"I love happy endings," whispered Liberty.

"Ending?" I said. "Liberty, this is just the start. In a way, this is like Neil Armstrong landing on the moon."

"It is?" Tommy questioned.

"Absolutely! The Pilgrims may not be the first to discover the New World but their footprint in New England will eventually lead to the making of the United States of America."

"Wow," Tommy said. "I never thought of it like that."

"It's hard for me to think about anything with an empty stomach," said Liberty.

I grabbed a few more apples out of Liberty's saddlebag and fed them to him. Tommy and I ate an apple as well.

When we finished Tommy asked, "Hey, do you think we could climb up and watch them sign the Mayflower Compact?"

"You took the words right out of my mouth," I said.

"Don't worry about me," Liberty sighed, obviously trying to make us feel guilty for leaving him. "You're off to watch one of the most important events in American history while the rest of us get stuck out in the cold. It reminds me of that one Christmas reindeer. . . ."

"Rudolph?" Tommy said.

"Yes! Rudolph, the red-nosed reindeer. He wanted to join in the reindeer games, but the other reindeer wouldn't let him."

"How thoughtless of me," I said. "You're absolutely right. We should be filming this so I can use it as a teaching moment back in class."

"Um, well, that's not exactly what I . . . ," Liberty tried to say.

I added, "And I'll find you the biggest and juiciest carrots when we get home. Deal?" I asked.

"All right," Liberty sighed. "I suppose nothing says I love you and I forgive you and I'll make sure I include you the next time like a big, juicy carrot. Or a fresh head of cabbage. Or large, crisp turnips. And I'm especially fond of cauliflower. . . ."

While Liberty continued daydreaming I whispered to Tommy, "Let's go."

When we reached the quarterdeck to the captain's cabin, we turned to wave at Liberty, who looked deep in thought.

We shuffled into the crowded room as many Saints and Strangers surrounded the captain's desk, where William Bradford was sitting and composing the agreement. Most men were standing but Myles Standish sat close by William. Myles wore his breastplate and helmet and looked as if he was ready to pounce upon anyone who objected to William's composition. Overall, the room had a peaceful mood. Finally, William dipped the quill into the inkwell and signed his name at the bottom. He dipped the quill again and handed it to Myles Standish, who signed his name. One by one, the men in the room began signing their names. As men exited the cabin, other men entered to sign their names.

As the signing continued, Tommy whispered, "Try taking my picture with your smartphone. I'll squeeze my way in so you can get me by the Mayflower Compact, okay?"

"I'll do my best," I said.

Tommy squirmed his way to the table and then stood on his tiptoes, smiling a big cheesy grin. I stood at the back of the room, removed my phone from my pocket, and as discreetly as possible took a picture of Tommy's first event in American history.

When Tommy made it back to me he said, "We should go and get Freedom. I feel bad that she hasn't been here to see all of this. I don't want her to miss the Pilgrims' landing."

"Good idea," I said. "We'll slip away before anyone notices."

We exited the captain's cabin and climbed down the ladder to the upper deck, but when we looked inside the capstan room for Liberty he wasn't there. That's odd, I thought.

"There he is," Tommy said, pointing to the far side of the ship. For an instant, Liberty appeared and then disappeared. What was he doing? I wondered.

We quickly walked over to where we had last seen him and whispered, "Liberty! What are you doing?"

Liberty reappeared right next to us. Pointing at the hatch that led to the tween deck he said, "Something fishy is going on down there, and I'm not talking about fish. I watched two teenage boys who looked very mischievous climb down this ladder and say something about shooting off a musket. I have a bad feeling about this."

"I'll go check it out," said Tommy. "I'll let you know what I see."

I paused to think about whether or not that was such a good idea. Finally, I said, "All right, but just take a look and then come right back up and tell us what you see."

Quick as a cat, Tommy sprang down the ladder. After a couple of minutes his head popped up and he said, "It's the Billington boys. You know, those teenagers that Myles scolded for scaring those little kids with that shark story. They're playing with their dad's musket. I think they're going to try to shoot it."

"That doesn't sound good," I said.

"Yeah, and it gets worse. I noticed they're sitting near a barrel of gunpowder. If the gun ignites the gunpowder . . . ," Tommy said, assuming we knew how his sentence would end.

"Ka-boom," said Liberty. "Neil Armstrong won't be the first man on the moon. The Billington boys will be."

"Tommy, run and get Myles," I said. "I'll climb down and try to stop them."

Before either Tommy or I moved, we heard a loud musket blast from the deck below. Immediately, Liberty took a deep breath and disappeared. We waited two more seconds and were relieved when the rest of the ship didn't blow up. Instantly, the captain's door swung open and several men streamed out of the cabin, including Captain Jones.

"Who fired that musket?!" the captain yelled.

Tommy and I pointed to the hatch that led to the tween deck.

I whispered to Tommy and Liberty, "This would be a good time to time-jump. Let's head away from the commotion."

As men and women crowded around the hatch and climbed

down to the tween deck, we mounted the now-visible Liberty and I said, "Back to modern day."

The last thing I heard before we jumped through the time portal was the captain yelling, "Francis Billington, if I ever see you with a musket on my ship again I'll strap you to the topmast and let the crows peck out your eyes!"

Chapter 6

Upon returning to the classroom we dismounted from Liberty. Tommy walked straight to the teacher's desk and grabbed his modern-day clothes. I asked, "So, Tommy, did you enjoy your adventure with the Pilgrims on the *Mayflower*?"

"Best. Detention. Ever!" he said. "I can't wait to go again."

"What do you think you'll remember the most?" I asked him.

"That's easy. I'll never forget the looks on the Pilgrims' faces when they saw land again. I mean they were so happy, they were crying. Even the men were crying. I know they were tough and put on brave faces, but when they finally saw the end of their journey it was like that rough exterior melted away."

"Real gratitude can do that to a person," I said. "Giving thanks with all our hearts is an emotional experience.

When we're truly grateful for something, we sometimes show it through tears of joy."

"I have a sister named Joy," said Liberty. "And she cried a lot, too, but not from gratitude. It's a long story but basically she was madly in love with this stallion and she thought he loved her, too, but then he left her for another mare and boy did the waterworks flow after that."

"I'm running to change my clothes," Tommy said. "I'll be right back." He ran to the door and slipped out.

I went to the teacher's desk, grabbed a piece of paper and a pencil, and wrote down some items that might be useful before we time-jumped back to the Pilgrims.

"I hope you're writing down a grocery list," said Liberty. "I believe I was promised a smorgasbord of fresh fruits and vegetables."

"Perhaps we should hang a feed sack to your neck so you have something to snack on twenty-four/seven," I said with sarcasm.

"Now you're talking," Liberty said with delight. "Oh, I almost forgot." Liberty walked over to the chalkboard, picked up a piece of chalk with his teeth, and then wrote on the chalkboard, "I will not throw wooden shoes through glass windows 100 times."

Tommy returned looking like a twenty-first-century boy again. He tossed me the traveling bag and I slipped it over my shoulder.

"Nice job, Liberty," Tommy laughed. "That looks like something I would do."

"Just trying to help out a . . ." Liberty gagged and then swallowed. "I think I just swallowed that piece of chalk."

"Well, I'm going to run over to the football field. I can probably catch the last half of practice," Tommy said. "Hey, I can bring this carp pie to my football coach. Maybe he'll forgive me for being late."

"Football, now *that* sounds interesting," Liberty said.

"Do you mind if we watch?" I said.

"Sure! We have a big game on Saturday. We're playing against our archrivals. But I also don't want to miss swordfighting with Captain Standish. That guy is cool. Do you think we'll be back in time for me to play in the game? It's so weird that I want to go to history class instead of football!"

"No worries, we'll be back. That is, if Liberty doesn't get lost wandering through a carrot patch searching for the perfect carrot," I said teasingly.

"No kidding," said Tommy. "Or he might wander into an Olive Garden for an all-you-can-eat special! I'm pretty sure the restaurant would lose money in that deal."

Liberty butted in and said, "Hello, I'm standing right here. And since when have I put my stomach before time-jumping?"

"Every time!" we said together.

As we slipped out the classroom door, Liberty held his breath and vanished. We walked down the hallway on our way to the outside door. Unexpectedly, Principal Sherman bounded around the corner and nearly tackled us.

"Mr. Revere," the principal said. "I hope Tommy behaved himself during detention." The principal raised his eyebrows as he looked at Tommy.

I couldn't tell if Liberty was close by or not. I looked at Tommy and then back at the principal and said, "I'm confident that Tommy learned a valuable lesson today."

"Oh, really?" questioned Principal Sherman. "Forgive my suspicion, but I've had other experiences with Tommy that have created a different belief. In fact, I'll even place a wager, a whole quarter for each item of history learned." He towered over Tommy like a monstrous wave threatening the *Mayflower*. "Anything, Tommy? Any tiny piece of information that might have slipped through to that brain of yours?"

"Hmm," Tommy replied. He glanced at me and I recognized that look. It was almost imperceptible, but I could see it. It's the same look that someone gives when playing chess just before saying "Checkmate."

"All I can say is Mr. Revere really knows his history," said Tommy. "You wouldn't believe all the stuff he had me do, I mean, learn. We started clear back in 1620 when the Pilgrims sailed from England to America. Did you know their voyage on the *Mayflower* took sixty-five days and more than three thousand miles? Almost everyone was seasick except for the sailors, who bullied the Pilgrims and teased them by calling them Puritans or Saints, but they were actually only half of the passengers. The other half were called Strangers, who were furious about not landing at the Hudson River and there was almost a mutiny but William Bradford saved the day with the Mayflower Compact that everyone signed which basically meant that they would stick together no matter what. Would you like me to go on?"

Principal Sherman's eyes were bulging. He was about to say something when the outside door at the end of the hallway opened; then a couple of seconds later it closed.

"Well, that's odd," I said, relieved that Liberty had gone undetected.

Tommy held out his hand to the principal and said, "That will be two dollars and seventy-five cents. Cash only, please."

The principal gave Tommy a half grin as he reached for his

wallet. "Impressive," the principal said, handing Tommy the money. "But I'm not falling for it. I don't know what kind of game you're playing, Tommy, but I'm on to you. Mr. Revere, if I were you I'd put eyes in the back of my head." And with that, the principal turned and lumbered down the hallway toward his office.

I smiled at Tommy. "Well said. Now, let's get you to your football practice."

We walked outside and saw Liberty waiting for us in the parking lot. We hurried over to him and climbed on. "Lead the way," I said. As Tommy guided Liberty to the football stadium I said, "Try and meet me and Liberty tomorrow before school. Come a half hour early and call or text Freedom to come as well. If you're up to it, we'll continue our journey with the Pilgrims."

"You bet! I haven't been this excited since Christmas morning," Tommy exclaimed.

Liberty laughed and said, "Except instead of opening Christmas presents, you'll be opening history!"

"You're right," Tommy said. "Who knew history could be so exciting!"

The next morning, Tommy and Freedom were waiting at the school by the time I showed up. "Good morning," I said cheerfully, dismounting from Liberty.

"Hi, Mr. Revere," said Tommy and Freedom.

"Tommy just told me about your journey yesterday. Well, most of it," said Freedom. She was wearing a faded yellow T-shirt and faded jeans. It was hard not to look at her black hair. It was silky smooth, as if she brushed it a thousand times. This morning there was a yellow feather clipped in it. "I'm excited to go with you today. I assume we'll be back before school starts."

"That's correct," I said. "After we're finished in the past we can time-jump back to the future, which, of course, is actually the present. In fact, we can only return within seconds of when we left. And we're unable to time-jump into the future."

Freedom pondered for a second and said, "So, Liberty can jump to America's past and return to our present but not its future."

"Correct," I said. "We've tried to jump to the future but the portal won't open unless we say the right words. *Rush, rush, rushing to history* has proven to be the most effective phrase."

Tommy said, "I told Freedom that today we're going to join the Pilgrims in America."

"First things first," I said. I pulled off my traveling bag from my shoulder and handed it to Tommy. "Your pilgrim clothes are inside. There's a dress for you, too, Freedom."

"It's a lot bulkier than yesterday," Tommy said.

"That's because you'll need some heavier clothing to help keep you warm. Liberty and I had to time-jump to the seventeenth century this morning to collect these."

"Is it supposed to be really cold? I'm a wimp when it comes to the snow," said Freedom.

"Yes, we'll probably experience freezing temperatures. We're heading back to the Pilgrims' first winter. Keep in mind that the Pilgrims landed in the New World and started building their first colony, Plymouth Plantation, in November."

"Anything else we should know before we go?" Tommy asked.

"If you get hungry I brought some additional snacks," I said. "This morning, Liberty ate enough for two horses."

Liberty snorted and said, "It's a well-known fact that breakfast is the most important meal of the day." Liberty paused for just a second and added, "Thank you, Freedom."

"Why are you thanking her? She didn't say anything," said Tommy.

"Yes, she did. She said that she supports my hearty appetite," Liberty replied.

"No, she didn't. I've been standing right here," Tommy argued.

I intervened. "It's apparent that Freedom has a gift. How long have you been able to communicate with animals?"

"Since I was about eight, I think," said Freedom. "My grandfather says that animals can feel what we feel, especially fear. Our emotions are powerful. He trained me to use emotions to speak to the mind of an animal."

"So, you're like a horse whisperer," Tommy said, smiling at her. "I'm good with that."

"Very well," I said, "run inside the school and change your clothes. Liberty and I will wait here."

Tommy and Freedom rushed inside the school and within a few minutes they were back outside dressed like Pilgrims.

"How do I look?" asked Freedom, spinning once in her green woolen dress. She also wore a white linen cap that came down over her ears, and a white apron. Finally, she wore a purple woolen shawl that covered her shoulders and hung down to her waist.

"Marvelous," Liberty said.

"I believe we're ready to go," I said.

"Will we join the Pilgrims right before they set foot on Cape Cod? Is that where Plymouth Rock is?" Tommy asked.

"Actually, no," I replied. "Plymouth Rock wasn't the first place the Pilgrims found. First, *Mayflower* anchored off the coast of Cape Cod at what is now Provincetown Harbor on November 11. It was so cold that a small search party left the *Mayflower*. They needed to first find a good place to build their town before everyone left the ship."

"Ugh, you keep mentioning the cold," Freedom sighed.

"I bet Myles Standish was part of the search party," said Tommy.

"Yes, he was. And so was William Bradford. In fact, William's journal said there were sixteen men who wore light armor and all carried swords and muskets. Can you imagine landing in a place you have never been to with nothing around that you recognize in the cold, cold months of winter?"

"Again, do you have to keep mentioning the cold?" Freedom said. She looked around nervously. "Anyway, I think we should leave sooner than later. The other students will start arriving soon and I'd rather not call attention to myself."

"Good point," Tommy said, scratching Liberty behind the ear. "Let's go. Are we going to land with the search party?"

"No," I said. "It took the search party several trips and many days of hiking in freezing temperatures. They searched all over Cape Cod and were even attacked by Indians."

"Seriously? You had to say *freezing temperatures*. Why don't we suck on ice cubes before we go," Freedom said. "We really don't have time for this conversation." Freedom searched left and right while fidgeting with her apron. "The school bus may have already arrived at the front of the school."

"Wait," Tommy said wide-eyed. "Did you say they were attacked by Indians? I thought the Indians were their friends. How many Pilgrims died?"

Elder William Brewster, Myles Standish, and other Pilgrims pray upon arrival.

"Remarkably, none," I said. "The friendly Indians came later."

"I hope they had friendly horses, too," said Liberty.

"Not to make you suffer," I said to Freedom, "but I only mention the cold, freezing temperature because it may have been the biggest test for the Pilgrims. Think about it. How do you feel when you're freezing? And how would you survive with little food, few clothes, and really no idea where to go? These people were incredible! They had such a will to survive and thrive. Have you ever wanted something so badly you would work and fight and crawl to get it, even if you had to go through things that weren't very fun?"

"Oh, you mean like a house of mirrors?" Liberty asked.

We looked at Liberty in complete confusion.

"You know," he clarified, "the mirrors in the fun house at the carnival. Some people think it's fun to stand in front of them and see their bodies all warped and freakish, but I think it's terrifying. Except I had to do it! I had to go past those mirrors. It was the only way to get to the caramel apples!"

I sighed.

"That was very brave of you, Liberty," said Freedom, patting his side. "Now can we go?"

I finished by saying, "Finally, on December twentieth the Pilgrims settled on the location of their future home, which became Plymouth Plantation."

"Whoa," Tommy said, quickly doing the math in his head. "That means they searched for thirty-four days from the time they landed on Cape Cod to the time they started Plymouth Plantation. They must have been exhausted!"

"And *very* cold," I said.

"And *very* hungry," said Liberty.

"And I'm *very* ready to go," said Freedom.

"And I'm *very* embarrassed for all of you," said a voice from behind Freedom.

We all turned to face Elizabeth, who was already waiting with her smartphone. "Click."

Freedom looked mortified.

Elizabeth smiled and laughed. She was wearing a preppy blue and yellow checkered skirt and vest with a bright yellow bow in her hair. In one hand she was carrying a plate of pink frosted cupcakes. "I'm so glad I got to school a little early today," she said. "I'm bringing my favorite teachers a special treat."

"Thank you, Elizabeth," I said. "That's very kind of you."

Elizabeth gave me a fake frown, "Oh, I'm sorry, I said my *favorite* teachers. Not substitute teachers. My grade doesn't depend on you."

"Don't dis Mr. Revere," Tommy said. "He's an awesome teacher. And I better not see that picture on Facebook. I know where your locker is."

"No worries, Tommy," said Elizabeth. "I wasn't aiming for you. But I did get a great close-up of our poor little Pilgrim girl. And I really like your locker idea. We could post the picture on every locker! You know, in celebration of the Pilgrims."

Freedom sprang forward and tried to grab the phone. "Give me that," she said, as Elizabeth tried to back away.

Elizabeth pushed and Freedom pulled. Elizabeth may have been taller but she had a difficult time struggling with her phone in one hand and a plate of pink pastries in the other. As the two girls twisted and turned, I tried to step in to break things up. But before I could reach either of them Elizabeth's phone flipped up and away from her. As Freedom swung her arm up to catch the phone, she knocked the plate of cupcakes into Elizabeth's face.

"You imbecile!" screamed Elizabeth, wiping pink frosting off her forehead and cheeks. "Look what you've done!"

"I-I didn't mean to," Freedom stuttered.

Elizabeth frantically searched the ground. She squinted through the frosting until she spotted what she was looking for lying in the grass under Liberty. "My phone! Your freakish donkey better not step on it or—"

Crunch.

"Oops," said Liberty. He lifted his hoof but the phone was definitely crushed.

"You are in big trouble," Elizabeth huffed. "I'm telling Daddy." She spun around and stormed back the way she came.

"Now can we go?" asked Freedom. "Before her daddy comes looking for us. Her name is Sherman," Freedom said. "Elizabeth Sherman."

"Elizabeth Sherman?" I inquired. "As in Principal Sherman's daughter?"

"Yep, the very same," said Freedom.

Tommy walked over and picked up a cupcake from the ground. "This one doesn't look like it's been touched," he said, examining the edges. He peeled back the paper and took a big bite. "Izz weely ood," he said.

"Did he just say, *This wheel is hood?* Is that code for something?"

"Yes," Freedom said, "it means let's get out of here. I hear the bus!"

"Freedom, can you ride a horse?" I asked.

Instead of responding, Freedom sprinted and sprang up the side of Liberty and into his saddle.

"Tommy, you next," I said.

"I can't do that," Tommy complained.

"Aren't you the star quarterback?" Freedom teased.

"Yeah, but I'm not a ninja horse whisperer," he said.

Tommy walked over and I boosted him up.

"I'll jump through the time portal behind you, Liberty, let's go," I said.

"*Rush, rush, rushing to history!*" Liberty said.

As the portal opened and Liberty started to gallop I said, "December thirty-first, 1620, Plymouth Plantation, America." I watched Freedom and Tommy bounce on the back of Liberty as he jumped to our next history lesson. As I followed and jumped through the portal I instantly felt the freezing temperature on my face. Thermal underwear never felt so good!

We were at the edge of a forest. The trees were naked. Thin patches of snow rested on a thick layer of brown leaves like random quilt patches covering a blanket. I could hear voices and the distant sound of waves crashing on the beach. The sun was overhead but the weather prompted me to button my coat.

"Where are we?" asked Freedom.

"If we were in the modern day we would technically be in the state of Massachusetts," I said.

"Hey, when you guys talk I can see your breath," said Tommy.

Both Liberty and Tommy exhaled and watched their breath as it crystallized in the air.

"Look," said Freedom, pointing. "Are those the Pilgrims?"

Through the trees we could see a clearing. "Yes, those are definitely the Pilgrims," I said. "And I see a warm fire. Let's go over and see what we can learn."

"Okay, but first can Freedom and I take Liberty and ride to the top of that other hill?" Tommy pointed to a larger hill about fifty yards away. "I bet we could see Cape Cod from there," said Tommy.

"I'm fine with that. But you must stay with Liberty, no exceptions," I said, firmly. "Liberty, I trust you'll keep them safe."

"No worries, boss," said Liberty. "They don't call me 'Liberty the Dragon Slayer' for nothing."

As the three of them trotted away, I started my own course toward the Pilgrims. It was a cold but clear day. The small settlement was located on a flat hill. I saw several men carrying timber and others framing the side of a house. A few men were resting or chatting by a fire. I noticed William Bradford and Myles Standish speaking to each other as they pointed at different parts of the landscape. As I walked toward them I could see the *Mayflower* anchored in the harbor about one or two miles from us.

"We should be able to finish the Common House in about two weeks," said William as I approached from behind.

Myles turned and saw me first, "Rush Revere," he said. "We thought you were dead. Where have you been? Where's Tommy?"

"Indeed," said William as he rushed over and embraced me. "What a delightful surprise. I knew you were still alive. I wouldn't believe anything else. One passenger thought you had fallen overboard. But when we couldn't find Tommy I assumed that when we landed at Plymouth Rock and all the passengers disembarked from the ship, the two of you went exploring."

"That's exactly what we did," I said, relieved that William had assumed my alibi. "Yes, we, um, found a trail of sorts and decided to follow it. It was a foolish thing to do but I was strongly prompted to explore this New World."

"A prompting we have all felt, I'm sure," said William.

"Yes," agreed Myles, "but there is safety in numbers."

"All is well, Myles," said William. "And it appears that Rush Revere is capable of taking care of himself. But where is Tommy?"

"He and a new friend are exploring the top of that largest hill with my horse," I said, referencing the nearby hill.

"Did you say horse?" asked Myles.

"Oh, yes," I said, forgetting that neither William or Myles had ever met Liberty or Freedom. I had been thinking of a reasonable explanation and said, "As Tommy and I were exploring we became disoriented but were fortunate to come across a young Native American girl riding a horse. Strange, I know. But the girl took a liking to us and helped us find our way back to you!"

"No matter," said William. "The important thing is that you're here now."

"So this is your new home?" I asked, changing the subject. "How did you know where to start building?"

"It wasn't easy," said Myles.

"We have struggled, for sure," agreed William. "We searched all over Cape Cod. Some of us explored by foot and others explored using the shallop. Myles and his men survived an Indian attack."

"We have all survived hard things," said Myles. "William has had to survive the passing of his wife, Dorothy."

"Yes," said William softly. He sighed and said, "She died just before we found our new home. Her loss has been the hardest thing. But I also ache for many of our people who suffer because of the cold and lack of food. Many have the chills and cough and no place to get warm. But after thirty-four days since the *Mayflower* arrived at Cape Cod, we have found our home. This is Plymouth Plantation. Or it will be. For now, our people must stay on the *Mayflower*."

"It will make for a fine town," William went on. "When we arrived we found barren cornfields with the land strangely cleared for our homes. There is even a running brook with fresh water."

"Did someone once live here?" I asked.

"Perhaps," William said. "But we can see this place has been deserted for years."

"I heard you mention a 'common house.' What is that?" I asked.

William pointed to the frame on the ground and said, "This will be the Common House. It is one of the first buildings. It belongs to everyone. We've agreed to set aside our want of personal property or personal gain and instead create a community where the houses and buildings and profits belong to everyone. We are trying to create a fair and equal society."

I thought of the Pilgrims on the *Mayflower*. These were tough, strong, and independent people. I thought of them as self-reliant and ambitious. People who came to America to start a new life, build their own homes, work for themselves, and be free people. But what William Bradford was explaining to me seemed like the opposite. Certainly, it would be tempting to live in a society where everything is shared and all your choices are made for you. But is that freedom?

With some courage I asked William, "You say you're trying to create a fair and equal society. Do you think your people will find joy and happiness with this kind of common control?"

William sighed and said, "It will be a test, for sure. At first, the Common House seemed very attractive. This kind of control should guarantee our prosperity and success. But recently I'm beginning to doubt whether everyone will work their hardest on something that is not their own," William said.

"All these men are working on the same project," said Myles. "All week they've used axes and saws to fell trees and transport them to this site. The trunks will be woven together with branches and twigs and then cemented with clay and so forth. Some men do little and some men do a lot. When this house is finished, who deserves the benefit and blessing of having this roof over their head?"

I pondered the question. Was there a right answer? Certainly, no one should be left out in the cold. But at the same time, it didn't seem fair for everyone to be rewarded equally when people who were able to work chose not to. I finally said, "You're right. I think this will be a test. But I know you are both wise enough to figure it out."

"A fine answer, Rush Revere," said William, smiling. "Are you sure you don't want to be governor?"

"Not me. You'll make a fine governor," I said to William.

"If you'll excuse me," I said, "I'm going to track down Tommy and his friend and make sure they're okay."

"I think I can see your horse at the top of Fort Hill," said William as he squinted and looked over my shoulder. "We are building a platform at the top of the hill so we can mount our cannons."

"And soon we will build a fort," said Myles. "I'm sure Tommy will enjoy that."

"Ah, yes, there's nothing like building a fort," I said with pleasure. "I remember building forts in my living room with blankets and chairs. My brother used to always want to be the lookout. He would scream, 'Incoming!' and I would run around making sure all sides of our fort were secure."

"And did you have muskets and cannons?" Myles asked, smiling.

"Not exactly," I winked. "We had Nerf guns! They're very specialized weapons and highly effective in keeping out annoying little sisters."

Myles smiled, "Ah, these Nerf guns are good for little sisters but probably not so effective for savage Indians."

"Not so much," I said, smiling back at him.

Just then one of the Pilgrims working on the Common House called for William.

"Excuse me," said William as he stepped away from us.

"I promised Tommy I would teach him how to fight with a sword," Myles said. "However, it may need to wait until the spring, when it's warmer."

"No worries. I'll tell him and I'm sure he'll understand." I excused myself, again, and headed in the direction of Fort Hill. As I started climbing I heard the clomping of hooves and saw Liberty coming in my direction with Freedom and Tommy on his back.

"We saw Indians!" said Tommy.

"What? Where? How many?" I asked.

"There were only two scouts," Freedom responded. "They were

A re-creation of Plymouth Colony.

The Old Fort and First Meeting House, 1621, Plymouth Colony.

Pilgrims on way to church in mid-winter.

on a neighboring hill, watching us. They wore heavy pelts and furs. They were only curious."

"I'm glad you came straight back here. Good job, Liberty," I said.

"Did you find William Bradford?" Liberty asked.

"Yes, and I'm worried about their conditions, their health. They have little food and this weather is making life miserable for them."

"Let's give them our food," Tommy said. "Didn't you say you brought food or snacks? We don't need them."

"We don't?" asked Liberty, surprised. "I mean, what if we kept an apple and a couple of carrots and a—"

"Liberty!" said Tommy and Freedom in unison.

Liberty sighed, "All right. Sorry, sometimes my stomach takes me hostage."

I sighed and said, "I'm sure your parents would be very proud of you, but unfortunately there are laws to time-traveling and if we give these children a bag of fruits and vegetables it might very well save their lives."

"Is that a bad thing?" Tommy asked.

"No and yes. Your instinct of wanting to help someone is a good thing, of course. But we need to remember that we shouldn't change history. We should learn from it. Unfortunately, tragedy is a part of life. It's a part of history."

"But we could help one person, couldn't we? How could that really change the course of history?" asked Freedom.

"Look at it this way," I said. "Let's say we did help one or both of those girls. Let's say the food and clothing and medicine they receive could and probably would save their lives. Now let's say that one of those girls grows up and marries a cute boy in her town. The same boy who should've married another girl but because of our rescue effort, he never does. She never marries. The children she was supposed to have never happen. Friendships and families and futures are all gone because we helped one person to live when she was supposed to die."

"Does anyone have a tissue?" Liberty sniffled. "I don't know what's come over me. It must be my allergies."

"Okay, I see your point," said Freedom. "But I'm still sad to see them suffer."

"As well you should be," I said. "If we feel and learn nothing from the tragedies of the past, then we'll never know how to truly help avoid those same tragedies in the future. Certainly, we can't avoid all pain and suffering, but we can and should learn from it."

"I think I'm ready to go, Mr. Revere," said Freedom.

"Yeah, me too," said Tommy. "Can we travel to a time in history with less pain and suffering?"

I patted Liberty on the neck and said, "Liberty, it's time to spring forward to March sixteenth, 1621."

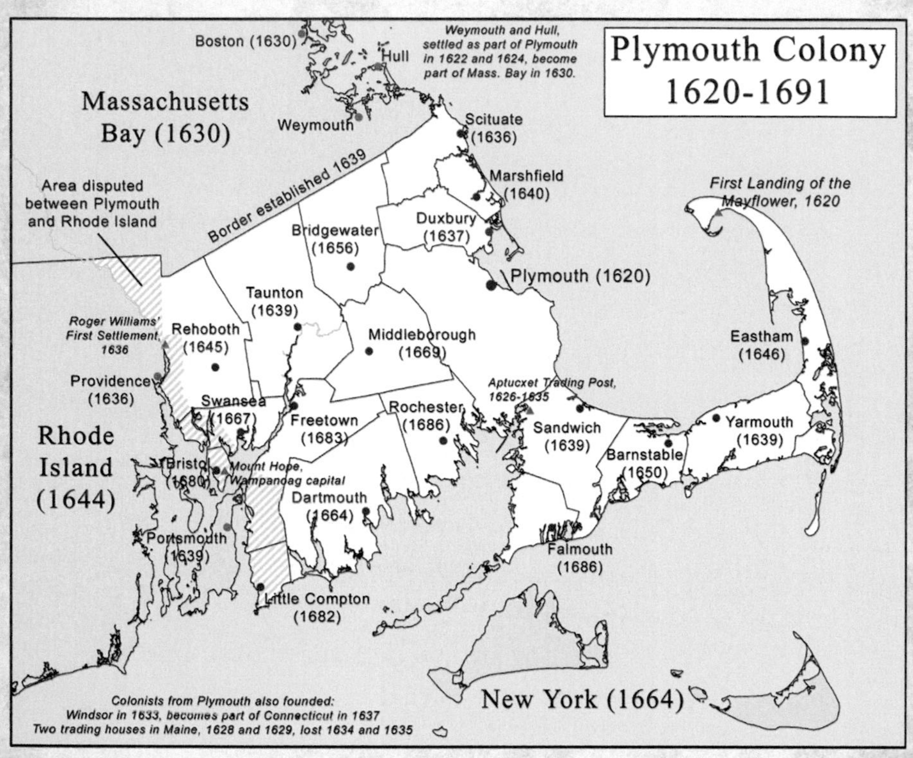

Eventually, the original Plymouth settlement grew into a thriving Plymouth Colony with thousands of Pilgrims.

Chapter 7

Birds *chirped and* flew among the branches of the many oaks, maples, chesnuts, hickories, and pines. The snow had melted and the temperature was at least thirty degrees warmer. About twenty yards away from us stood a deer, her short white tail twitching as she watched us between the trees.

"Can you talk to it?" Tommy asked Freedom.

"I don't think she understands English," Freedom joked. "But, yes, I can communicate with most animals."

"Hellooooooo," called Liberty. "We come as friends. Take us to your leader."

The deer just stood there, watching us curiously.

"Nope," Liberty said. "Nothing. I hope that deer isn't a member of the hospitality committee, because if she is I'm sending a complaint."

I watched Freedom as she stared intently at the deer. Its tail stopped twitching and it began to walk toward us.

Soon the deer was only a couple feet away, and Freedom walked over and stroked the side of its neck.

"You're more than a horse whisperer," Tommy said.

"No kidding," Liberty said. "You're like that girl who calls all her animal friends to help clean the dwarves' cottage. I hope we don't run into a witch with a poison apple. That would be bad."

"Check out all these tree stumps," Tommy said.

"What do you think they did with all these trees?" asked Freedom.

"I'm guessing they built houses," said Tommy. "I mean, I'm pretty sure after they landed in the New World they didn't check in at a Holiday Inn. There wasn't anything here! I mean, they basically were camping for months!"

"Good point," said Freedom. "When I hunt or track animals with my grandfather we camp for a couple of days but then we get to go home."

Tommy continued: "I used to go camping with my friend's dad all the time. He'd make us go really far and deep into the woods, and then we'd pitch our tent. My friend's mom hated it! She used to complain about not being able to plug in her hair dryer or take a shower. That was after one day! I can't imagine what she'd be like after landing in the New World with the Pilgrims. Ha!"

Liberty looked all around and said, "Come to think of it, it doesn't look like there's a drive-through for miles around."

"Nope," I said. "No McDonald's, no Taco Bell, no Kentucky Fried Chicken. Nothing. When the Pilgrims first landed they had to figure out everything from scratch. So what they did was basically try to re-create the town where they lived in Holland."

"That's really cool," said Tommy. "If I was building my own town from scratch I think I'd start with a football field."

"Seriously?" asked Freedom, rolling her eyes. "Before building a house?"

"Okay, well, maybe after my house," Tommy said. "But that would be kind of cool for everyone to be able to hang out at the same place and have some entertainment! Of course, I would be the starting quarterback. Oh, and I would totally invite you, Freedom."

"Thanks," Freedom said. "But I'd for sure have built a house first, a warm house, with a big fireplace so I don't have to camp during the winter! After that, I'd want to build a stable for Liberty."

"Ah, thanks, Freedom, for thinking of me!" said Liberty. "And maybe one of those Jacuzzi tubs with the rotating jets to massage my back."

I ignored Liberty and said, "The Pilgrims kind of built a football field. Well, a large place for everyone to hang out or gather and meet, called a 'Common House.' It was the first thing they built."

"I can see several houses or buildings over there," said Freedom as she peered and pointed through the trees. "Is that the Common House?"

I tried to look where Freedom was pointing and said, "I honestly can't really tell from here."

"What are we waiting for?" said Tommy. "I have a swordfighting lesson to get to."

As we got closer, I could see a dirt street with a row of seven houses with thatched roofs. There were also four larger buildings. One of those must be the Common House. Seven houses didn't seem like nearly enough to house the 102 Pilgrims who arrived on the *Mayflower*. I wonder if some chose to build a

town somewhere else. That seemed unlikely since the Pilgrims signed the Mayflower Compact, so they all sort of decided to stick together! Actually, the Mayflower Compact was supposed to provide just and equal laws for everyone at Plymouth Plantation, the very place we were standing. I'd have to ask William Bradford when I saw him.

I noticed the *Mayflower* was still anchored in Plymouth Harbor. Many Pilgrims, mostly men, were doing various chores: chopping wood, mending roofs, tilling a field for a future garden. A teenage girl was dipping a bucket into a nearby brook. Another girl was reading a book to a small group of younger boys and girls under a big oak tree.

"Let's go see if anyone is home," I said. "I'm especially curious why there are only seven houses."

We approached the first house and found a teenage boy carving a piece of wood with a long knife. He was sitting on a chair that looked too fancy to have been made in America. He saw us approaching and stopped carving.

"Hello there, young man," I said. "I'm Rush Revere. Do you live here?"

"Nah, I sleep across the way," he said. "I just like sitting in Governor Bradford's chair. He brought it from England. We don't have many chairs." He eyed Liberty. "Can I ride the horse?"

I looked at Liberty as he eyed the boy suspiciously. I turned back to the boy and asked, "What's your name?"

"Francis Billington," he said.

"Aren't you the kid who shot the musket on the *Mayflower* and nearly blew up the ship?" Tommy accused.

"You can't prove it," Francis said, standing up and putting the knife inside a sheath.

"Well, maybe it was your brother," Tommy replied.

"You can't prove that, either!" Francis exclaimed.

"Well, Francis, do you know how to ride a horse?" I asked.

"Any dimwit can ride a horse," he said. "I've ridden thousands of horses."

"Thousands?" I said, a bit surprised. "Well, then this one shouldn't be a problem for you."

Liberty shook his head and stomped his hoof.

"It looks like he's twitching to give someone a ride," I said, smiling.

"Good! I hope he's fast. I like going fast. Do you have a stick so I can make him go faster?"

Liberty backed up and huffed.

"You shouldn't hit a horse with a stick," Freedom said, stepping forward and petting Liberty on his face.

"You're just a girl. What do you know," said Francis.

Tommy started forward and I held him back.

"Very well, Francis," I said. "Let's see what you can do."

Liberty rolled his eyes and looked rather annoyed. I wasn't sure how this would play out but I thought the ride could serve a purpose.

I held Liberty's halter as Francis searched for a way to pull himself up into the saddle. He was a tall and wiry boy with curly brown hair. After a couple of unsuccessful attempts he finally managed to swing his leg over the saddle. He looked as comfortable as someone trying to water-ski for the first time.

He grabbed Liberty's reins and pulled left. Liberty didn't budge. He tried pulling to the right, but Liberty was immovable. I had never used a bit with Liberty and therefore he felt no pain every time Francis jerked the reins to the left or right.

"Stupid horse," Francis said. "Why won't he move? I've ridden mules that are smarter." It was the last thing he said on the back of Liberty because the very next second, the horse kicked up his hind legs and bucked Francis high into the air.

Francis yelled loud enough for all of New England to hear. He landed on the thatched roof of the house across from William Bradford's home, but only for a second, before the roof caved in and Francis fell with a thud.

"Francis Billington!" yelled a woman's voice. "How many times do I have to tell you to stop climbing where you don't belong?"

"You have to admit he had it coming," said Liberty.

"Look, there's William Bradford," said Tommy, pointing. "He's coming out of that larger building."

"Good eye, Tommy," I said. "Let's go say hi."

We walked along the row of houses toward the Common House. As we approached William I noticed how tired he looked. I didn't want to say anything, because that would be a little rude, but he really looked a lot older than when we last saw him, just a few months earlier. I couldn't really blame him. After all, he traveled across the entire ocean in a small boat under the hardest conditions, landed in a new place that was completely barren, and needed to build a town for all of the people who relied on his leadership. That makes me tired just thinking about it. Nevertheless, when William saw us he smiled and turned to meet us.

"Hello, Rush and Tommy! I've missed you! I assume you've been exploring, again?"

"Yes, we have," I said. "This New World is a bounteous land."

"It's a lot bigger than England," said Tommy. "I mean, it sure feels a lot bigger but that's probably because of the endless forests and unsettled land."

William agreed. "I only wish I could join you. But for now my duty is here at Plymouth Plantation. And this must be your new friend with the horse!"

"This is Freedom," I said. "We've spent the last couple of months teaching Freedom the English language. She's an exceptional learner." I hoped Freedom would play along.

"Freedom," said William, reverently. "I have to say I love that name. In fact, if I have a daughter someday I think Freedom would be a wonderful name."

"Thank you," said Freedom slowly. "Please excuse my grammar as I have only just learned to speak your language. I was born on the fourth of July, so my mother felt like it was the perfect name for a special day."

"Your English is marvelous. Does the fourth of July have a special meaning for your family?" asked William.

Freedom paused, realizing that the Pilgrims hadn't celebrated the Fourth of July yet. The Revolutionary War hadn't happened and the Declaration of Independence wouldn't be signed for another 156 years. It was only 1620 where we were, not 1776! She looked to me for an answer. As my mind raced for a way to help Freedom, we heard the sound of a loud bell.

"Either we're late for school or it's time for dinner," Tommy said.

"I hope dinner," Liberty whispered.

"Neither; that bell means Indians," said William, as he began searching the surrounding hills.

Pilgrims from every direction were heading for the Common

House. Women and children left their homes and men returned from the field and forest.

William pointed to a neighboring hill and shouted, "There! A single Indian on Watson Hill."

Sure enough, a lone Indian walked with long strides toward a brook that bordered the hill where the Pilgrim settlement was.

William spoke loudly so all within earshot could hear him. "Do not fire your muskets! The Indian walks boldly but he does not look hostile. He is only one and we are many. There is no need to fear. God is with us."

I was amazed watching this group of Pilgrims listen to William so closely. He was clearly the leader that they turned to for direction. Just like on the boat! They all put their muskets down and quietly watched.

Nobody else spoke as the Indian crossed the brook and began climbing the pathway up Cole's Hill. We were now close enough to see that he was a tall man. His hair was black and long but his face had no hair, unlike most of the Pilgrim men. However, the biggest difference was the fact that the Indian was practically naked. A piece of leather covered his waist but his legs and chest were bare.

"Hold your ground," William said firmly to his line of defense.

The women and children had gathered together farther behind us. I looked back and saw several holding Bibles. One mother covered her daughter's eyes and others had turned away from the approaching intruder.

Finally, when the Indian was only five yards from us he stopped, his path clearly blocked by the barricade of Pilgrims. His eyes were the color of tree bark. He had a large bow slung over one shoulder and a quiver of arrows over the other. Then he did something completely unexpected. He smiled and saluted us with much delight and said, "Welcome, Englishmen!"

"Wait, did he just speak English?" Tommy whispered. "How is that even possible? And he doesn't even look scared. He just walked up to us like it happens every day!"

"Shh, let's listen," I whispered back.

A gust of wind caught the back of the Indian's long black hair and it swayed up and over his shoulder. As he scanned the crowd of Pilgrims his eyes caught the movement of Freedom's silky black hair, which also waved in the wind. The Indian stared at her for just a moment, then turned to William Bradford and said, "Me, Somoset, friend to Englishmen."

William responded, "Welcome, Somoset. I am William Bradford, a leader of this colony we call Plymouth Plantation. How did you learn to speak English?"

"Me learn English from fishing men who come for cod." Somoset stretched out his arms and said, "This place, this . . ." He paused, pointing at the harbor.

"Are we playing charades?" whispered Liberty so no one else could hear. "Because if we are my guess is *harbor*."

I offered the suggestion to Somoset and said, "Harbor?"

"Yes," Somoset smiled, "this harbor called Patuxet."

Liberty whispered, "Am I good? Or am I good?"

Somoset continued: "Death come to this harbor. Great sickness. Much plague. Many Pokanokets die. No more to live here."

"You're saying that the Indians who lived in this area died of the plague?" asked William.

"Yes," said Somoset. "Many, many die. Much sadness. And you. Your people. Much die from cold and sickness. Massasoit knows. Waiting. Watching."

Visit of Samoset to Plymouth Colony, where he stated, "Welcome, Englishmen!"

William turned to Myles, then back to Somoset and said, "We come in peace. We only want freedom to live in peace. Who is Massasoit?"

"Massasoit great and powerful leader of this land. He watching you. He knows your people dying. He lives south and west in place called Pokanoket. Two-day journey."

"You must be hungry," William said. He saw Tommy and Freedom standing nearby and said, "Tommy, Freedom, run back to where the women are gathered and ask them for a plate of food and drink for our new friend."

"You got it," Tommy said as he and Freedom raced off to where the women and children were gathered.

William turned back to Somoset. "Please tell Massasoit that we come as friends. We are his friends. Yes, many of our people have died but we are strong."

Myles Standish clearly wasn't as quick to believe Somoset meant no harm. Since he was the main military man of the town, I can understand why! He probably felt he needed to defend and protect his people. Standish was wearing his helmet and breastplate. He firmly held his musket in both hands as if to say, Look here, don't make any false moves! His trademark sword was, as always, hanging at his waist.

Myles said, "Tell Massasoit that we have guns, bullets, armor, and powerful cannons. We are here to stay and we hope we can be friends."

"Together," said Somoset. "Massasoit and William Bradford, together."

"Yes," said William. "Together in peace."

Somoset smiled like he did when he first saluted us. "Me tell Massasoit. Bring Squanto. He speak better English. He help . . ."

Again, Somoset began gesturing with his hands, clearly trying to communicate the right word.

"Translate," whispered Liberty.

"Translate?" I repeated loudly to Somoset.

"Yes," said Somoset pointing at me.

William, Myles, Elder Brewster, and the rest of the Pilgrims looked impressed by my guesses. I turned back to Liberty and whispered, "You're making me look really good."

"I usually do," Liberty softly replied.

Standish, still not quite as welcoming as Bradford, said forcefully, "Who is Squanto?"

Somoset continued, "Squanto translate for Massasoit. Squanto speak like English man. Help Massasoit and William Bradford together in peace."

"We look forward to meeting Massasoit and Squanto," said William. "Will you bring them?"

"Yes, bring them. Return in five moons. But first, stay with William Bradford tonight. Need rest, food. Tomorrow, go to Pokanoket and Massasoit."

Tommy and Freedom returned with a plate of food and a flask and handed them to Samoset.

"Please, eat," said William.

Liberty whispered into my ear, "I can't believe he isn't scared! I'm scared just watching. It reminds me of a late-night movie I saw once. Well, I didn't see the whole movie because I was too scared. I mean if I were Somoset I think I'd wonder if my plate of food was poisoned. Or if I were the Pilgrims I'd wonder if Somoset wasn't secretly plotting to have all his friends sneak into the town in the middle of the night and—"

"You watch too many movies," I whispered back. "I'm guessing

William had a gut feeling. He relied so much on God's grace to protect them traveling across the rough waters for so many months, he just had to trust that this would be okay, too! It's really pretty amazing."

"Either that or Myles has a backup plan!" Liberty softly replied. "He doesn't seem to be joking around with that musket."

"Thank you," said Somoset. Before he took the plate from Freedom he reached out to touch the yellow feather in her hair.

Freedom handed him the plate of food and then reached up and unclipped the feather. She said, "A gift from us to you." Somoset leaned over and Freedom clipped the feather in his hair.

"A fine gift," said Somoset. Then he smelled the food with a curious look on his face.

William pointed to each food item, "This is a biscuit, butter, cheese, pudding, and roasted duck."

As Somoset used his hands to sample each item, William turned to us and whispered, "He seems like an honest fellow and eager to befriend us."

"Yes, but can we trust him to stay with us overnight?" asked Myles, suspiciously.

"Rush Revere, what do you think?" said William.

I cleared my throat and said, "Assuming he was sent to us by Massasoit, if we turn him away we may offend him, which may offend Massasoit. We can't afford to do that."

William turned to Elder Brewster, who said, "I agree. Our kindness may be our best ally."

"Yes, I agree," said William. "I propose we let him stay the night."

Liberty again whispered to me, "William really put you on the spot with that question. I couldn't have dug you out of that one.

Nice job answering him! Maybe you should get your own radio talk show. You know, callers call in with questions and you give them advice and stuff. I'd totally call you!"

We turned back to Somoset, who had finished the entire plate of food and was now drinking from the flask.

"Me like much," said Somoset.

"Come, Somoset. I would like to learn more about this harbor and anything else you can tell us about living here," William said.

This time Tommy leaned over and whispered, "Do you think Somoset really gives him the real scoop? Or do you think he'll hold back and wait for his next move like a game of chess? I mean he sure trusts William a lot without even knowing him! So, maybe he really does tell him everything he knows about this land."

I softly replied, "According to everything I've read, Somoset and especially Squanto became friends with William. I think they realized right away that they could help each other."

As the Pilgrim leaders led Somoset into the Common House, I decided this was a perfect opportunity to time-jump to our next destination.

"Guys, I don't know when or if we'll be eating with the Pilgrims," I said. "They seem pretty busy in there, so I suggest we time-travel to get a quick bite to eat, and then time-jump back in 'five moons' or five days when Somoset returns with Massasoit and Squanto. Liberty, did you catch that?"

"Uh, all I heard was blah, blah, blah, get a quick bite to eat, blah, blah, blah," said Liberty. "Was there anything else important?"

"I'm in," said Tommy. "All I had for breakfast was a stick of gum."

Homes and farmland surrounding Plymouth Colony.

"Is that what they call a breakfast of champions?" Freedom teased.

"What did you eat for breakfast?" Tommy asked Freedom.

"Are you kidding? I was too excited to eat," Freedom said.

"Then let's rush back to the present. Liberty? I imagine you're ready?" I asked.

"I was ready to eat when we got here," Liberty said.

Within minutes we found a secluded place just within the forest. When we jumped through the time portal we were standing in a parking lot behind a Dumpster with a sign that read PROPERTY OF FOSTERS' FAMILY DINER, FAST AND FRIENDLY SERVICE ON WHEELS. As we came out from behind the Dumpster we saw several old-fashioned cars parked in front of the diner. Waitresses with pink blouses, poodle skirts, and roller skates were taking orders and rolling back and forth between the diner and the cars. Liberty wasted no time and trotted up to an empty parking space. Freedom and Tommy were riding on Liberty as I followed from behind.

"You seem like you've been here before," said Freedom.

"Oh, I love a good fifties diner. And this place is especially good," said Liberty in a hushed voice.

I added, "No surprise we ended up here. This is Liberty's favorite place to eat."

Tommy asked, "So you can go and eat anywhere? Any time in history?"

"Any time in American history. However, I've tried to avoid bumping into myself. That could be problematic."

"So what do you recommend on the menu?" asked Tommy.

"Oh, I'm sure everything is good," said Liberty. "The menu has the usual hamburgers, hot dogs, fries, and shakes. But I always get the Veggie Supreme! With extra lettuce, pickles, tomatoes, cucumbers, spinach, sprouts, and guacamole on a sesame seed bun!"

"Guacamole?" asked Freedom. "Seriously?"

"Of course," smiled Liberty. "Everything tastes better with guacamole."

"I think everything tastes better with bacon," said Tommy.

"Well, sure, if you're a carnivore!" Liberty grunted. "I tried bacon once. I thought it tasted like dirty socks soaked in lard."

"You've actually tried dirty socks soaked in lard?" Freedom asked, skeptically.

"Blech! Gross! Who in their right mind would taste a dirty sock soaked in lard! That's disgusting," said Liberty.

Freedom complained, "But you just said—"

Freedom was cut off by the roller-skating waitress who asked for our orders. Freedom, Tommy, and I each ordered the cheeseburger, fries, and shake combo. And I ordered Liberty's usual, three Veggie Supremes, extra everything.

"Don't you think it's strange that she didn't ask why we're dressed like this?" Tommy asked.

"Not really. As I said, this isn't our first time here," I said with a wink.

As we ate our food Freedom said, "It's just really sad that the Pilgrims never had this kind of luxury. They never got to go to a diner and have food prepared for them in minutes. They had to shoot a duck or kill a pig or—"

"Or grow a garden," Liberty added between mouthfuls.

"What I'm saying is we have it easy," Freedom finished.

"True," Tommy said. "I'm pretty sure I would've starved."

I sighed. "Sadly, many of them did starve. In fact, that first winter was called the 'Starving Time.' When we met Somoset I counted the number of Pilgrims who were gathered outside. It was about half the number who arrived on the *Mayflower.*"

"Oh, that's what Somoset meant when he said that Massasoit knew that many of the Pilgrims had died, right?" asked Freedom.

"Correct," I said. "It was probably a combination of lack of food, the severe cold, and disease."

As the waitress rolled away after offering us each a free peppermint candy I said, "Why don't we all take a potty break before we head back."

"Good idea!" Tommy said. "The other luxury the Pilgrims didn't have is flushing toilets!"

Chapter 8

It was officially spring when we returned to Plymouth Plantation in the year 1621. To be exact, we arrived on March 22, five days after Somoset's initial visit to the Pilgrims. We landed near the top of Fort Hill, concealed by a number of trees and bushes.

As we were about to head downhill toward the settlement, I heard the sound of twigs snapping. I looked back to see what it was. Apparently, Freedom had heard the same thing.

"Did you hear that?" she asked.

"Yes," I said. "It sounded like it was coming from farther uphill."

"We're nearly at the top," Tommy said.

"Not farther uphill. It came from somewhere up in that tree," Freedom said, pointing to the large pine tree that rose more than one hundred feet in the air.

"I love those trees," said Tommy. "I'm ninety-nine

percent sure it's a white pine. Did you know that white pines can reach up to two hundred fifty feet in height and as much as five feet in diameter?" Tommy said.

"Who needs the Nature Channel when Tommy's around," said Liberty.

Tommy and Freedom dismounted from Liberty and we all walked closer to the trunk of the large pine. Just as we looked up, a pinecone fell from the interior branches and bonked Liberty on the nose.

"Ouch," said Liberty. "This forest is downright rude. First I get snubbed by a deer and then I get hit by a pinecone. I suggest we leave before we get tarred and feathered!"

Again we peered up into the branches. Sure enough, about thirty feet up was a man. No, a boy of about thirteen or fourteen. He looked tall and wiry and appeared to be climbing down the tree. Suddenly I recognized who it was and yelled, "Francis Billington!"

My call startled Francis and he lost his balance, slipping from the branch. In a split second I realized he was falling backward and away from us. My mind raced at the future implications. If Francis died because of the fall, it would be my fault. Francis was seconds from his death and I would be responsible for changing the course of history. I looked at Liberty, who saw my fear and despair, and suddenly everything on the hill that belonged to this moment in time had literally stopped. A bird had frozen in mid-flight just a few feet from Tommy's head. A squirrel was frozen in mid-scurry as it climbed a tree trunk. Even the twigs from a nearby birch tree were frozen in mid-bend from a recent gust of wind.

"Help Francis . . . quickly," Liberty struggled to say. His voice sounded strained, like he was holding back a locomotive with his mind.

"What's happening?" Freedom asked, a twinge of fear in her voice.

"This is freaky," said Tommy. "Mr. Revere, Francis is . . . he's frozen in time!"

True to his word, Francis hung in the air completely motionless, no strings attached. He was about fifteen feet above the ground that would very likely kill him upon impact.

Suddenly I had an idea. I ran to Liberty's saddlebag and opened it.

"Trying . . . not to . . . blink," Liberty said.

"Just a little more," I said. "Try and hold off time for another twenty seconds." I dug deeper into the corner of the saddlebag, "Found it!" I pulled out a mesh hammock that I had purchased when I thought I might be sleeping on the *Mayflower.* I ran toward the tree and called Freedom and Tommy to join me. "Quickly, you two hold the other end. We need to position ourselves directly under Francis and pull the hammock as tightly as possible."

"Eyes burning . . . bulging . . . twitching!" Liberty was panicked.

"Just a little more," I said.

Just as we finished stretching out the mesh beneath Francis, the air, the forest, the world suddenly came back to life, and Francis fell and landed dead center in the hammock. Thankfully, he wasn't dead. The hammock broke his fall as he slid off to the side and landed on his stomach.

I quickly gathered up the hammock as Tommy and Freedom helped Francis to his feet.

"I'm not dead," Francis said, brushing himself off. "That was a lucky fall. You know, if you hadn't scared me like that I wouldn't have fallen at all!"

"Are you sure you're okay?" I asked.

"I'm fine," Francis said. "You got to do a lot more than that to take out a Billington. That's what my dad always says. Out of twenty-two families who sailed on the *Mayflower,* he said we're one of the few who have all survived since landing in the New World."

You're still alive thanks to Liberty, I thought. *Liberty!* I turned and ran back to him. "You did it!" I said, rubbing his nose.

Liberty half smiled and weakly replied, "Yes, it worked. I actually stopped time for a few seconds. Although I'm still not sure how I did it. It was different than opening the time portal to the past or back to the present. That seems easy compared to this. This was different. It was like flipping a switch in my brain, although it wasn't really in my brain. It was more like a space between time. It was a place between the here and now. I'm sure that sounds completely ridiculous, but it's the best I can come up with right now."

"What else do you remember?" I asked. "Were you scared? Angry? Hungry? What were you feeling? And were you holding your breath or swishing your tail or crossing your eyes? I'm just trying to figure out if there's a pattern and if we could duplicate it."

"I don't think I want to do it again," Liberty replied. "It was exhausting. But I don't remember feeling scared or angry or hungry. Well, I'm always hungry, but you know what I mean. Mainly, I remember sensing danger and having the sudden resolve to do anything I could to help you."

"Courage," I said. "You were feeling courageous. Good. What else?"

"Hmm," Liberty pondered, "I remember keeping my eyes wide open like I was in the finals at the World Championship Staring Competition."

"I don't think there is such a competition," I said.

"Well, there should be, because I think I'd be really good at it!" Liberty sighed, "Anyway, when I finally blinked, everything went back to normal."

Francis finished brushing himself off and said, "I have to get back home. I need to tell the others!"

"Perhaps you shouldn't tell them about the fall," I said. "The important thing is that you're not hurt."

"Who cares about the fall," Francis said. "I'm talking about my discovery. I saw a giant lake of fresh water from the top of that tree!"

As Francis bolted down the hill, I stored the hammock back in Liberty's bag.

"No one's going to believe him," Tommy said. "I should know. There's no way Principal Sherman would believe me if I had some important news to share. I mean I know I goof off in class sometimes, but I'm an angel compared to that dude. And I can promise you that I will never shoot off a musket near a barrel of gunpowder."

"Good to know," I said, smiling. "But from what I know Francis Billington really did find a giant freshwater lake about two miles inland. Just like you said, William Bradford doesn't believe him at first. But, finally, Francis convinces the Pilgrims to scout it out and sure enough, they find it. And the fish and fowl that the lake provides becomes a huge blessing for the colony."

"Like I always say," Liberty yawned, "never believe a trouble-maker unless he's telling the truth."

We slowly headed down the hill toward the Pilgrims' settlement.

"I think I'm going to rest near that large oak tree," said Liberty. "I'm exhausted."

"I'm going to check out the brook," said Tommy. "Want to come, Freedom? Maybe you can talk some fish into letting me catch them."

"I'll come," said Freedom. "But I've never had any luck communicating with fish."

"If you hear the bell, make sure you come straight back," I said.

As we separated, I headed over to the houses. As I approached the first one, I noticed the door was open. Inside, William Bradford sat in his chair with his elbows resting on a crude table. He had a quill pen in one hand and he looked to be writing in a small notebook. He also looked to be in deep thought. For a minute I thought maybe I should leave, but I said to myself how often can you pop in and have a chat with one of your all-time heroes? I mean it's one thing to read about the Pilgrims and the leader of the first colony, and it's another to actually walk through his door and be able to ask him in person any intelligent question you could think of.

I softly knocked on the door.

William turned and said, "Rush Revere, you're always the last person I expect to see but it's always good to see you. Come in. Please, have a seat. I hope your travels have been kind to you?" He pointed to the oak chest sitting near his desk.

"Thank you," I said. "Yes, traveling and exploring have been good to me. I've learned much and hope to be able to share it someday with my history class." I looked around his modest home and noticed a fireplace took up one side of the room, a bed against another wall, and a Bible and silver drinking cup rested on his desk. His musket hung from pegs on the wall. I cleared my throat and said, "It's great to see the settlement growing."

"Yes, it's growing," said William, "but not as fast as it could."

"Why is that?" I asked. "Do you not have enough trees or supplies to build houses?"

"Well, no, not exactly. I can't remember if I told you while we were on the boat or not, but we have a contract with our sponsors in England, the ones who helped us pay for this voyage. The contract says that everything we produce or harvest, like food, furs, furniture, etc., must go into a common store and each member of the community is entitled to one common share. Eventually, we hope to make enough to pay back our sponsors in England. But I'm finding it difficult to get our people to work."

I pondered his comment and said, "So you're saying that everything that is produced, all the profits, go into, let's say, a box. And then everyone gets one equal share of what's in the box regardless of how much work they do or how much they produce."

"Correct," said William, "and some people figure that it doesn't matter how much they work because they're still going to get an equal share of what's in the box. I can't really blame them. I mean what is the incentive to work hard if you know the other person will get the same reward doing little to no work?"

"That doesn't seem very fair," I said. I thought about Tommy's football coach and the question he asked all the boys after practice. He said, "What would you think if two teams playing against each other get the same amount of points regardless of how many touchdowns they make?" The boys booed the coach, and Tommy asked, "What's the purpose of playing if nobody can win?" The coach replied, "Exactly! So get out there this Saturday and play hard! Play to win! There are a few of you who think you don't have to play hard to win a championship. Some of you think you deserve part of the trophy even though you're not giving your best effort. I'm here to tell you that if I see slackers out there, I'm cutting you from the team. And if you don't think that's fair, then you don't understand what it means be a champion!" Then the coach led them in the chant, "Play to win! Play to win! Play to win!" I then thought of the Pilgrims. They initially tried to make everyone winners but soon realized the attempt was failing because not everyone wanted to work hard enough to be champions. The truth is, when we try to make everyone a winner, no one's a winner.

William continued. "We thought people would be happy with a commonwealth, where no one owns property but rather shares what everyone else has. Instead, the idea is bringing much confusion and discontent."

To be clear, I asked, "If no one owns property, then you don't own your house or your garden or your business."

"Correct," William said. "I live here, but the house, the garden, or a business belongs to the community. And it has caused many of our people to do less instead of do more. We thought everyone working for each other would help the community flourish and prosper. But that hasn't been the case because men who work harder and smarter are beginning to wonder why they are putting all of their profits into a common box, as you say, so that other men who choose not to work receive an equal share of the profits. For the first time since the boat, I can see real tension developing! Anytime that I am in the Common House, at least three people come up to me to tell me they don't want to be doing all the work while their neighbor is sleeping! I'm beginning to wonder if the solution to our problems is for everybody to keep what they produce."

A knock came at the open door. "Sorry to interrupt," said Tommy. "Freedom and some other girls started braiding each other's hair and that's not really my thing. So I came to find you."

"Come in, Tommy," said William.

"I happened to overhear your conversation about how some people work harder and smarter but how others get all the perks. I'm not sure why but it reminded me of the county fair."

Tommy surprised me. I thought for sure he'd tell William about what his football coach said.

"I am familiar with fairs, since they have existed as far back as the Romans. But what is this 'county fair' you speak of, exactly?" asked William.

"Oh, well, it's sort of this competition," said Tommy. "People from all over come and see who has the biggest pumpkin or best pies or the largest pig. And the winner gets a cash prize like profits and a cool blue ribbon. People love it. They work really hard to try to have the best garden. They grow amazing vegetables like squash and cucumbers and tomatoes. My mom makes the best salsa and she enters it into the county fair every year and she's won three times!"

"Your mother makes salsa? I'm not familiar with this. Is that something that Somoset showed you?" asked William.

"Oh, no, but it's awesome. It's this great dip for chips! She chops up tomatoes and onions and chili pepper and a little bit of an herb called cilantro! My mouth is watering just thinking about it."

"I like this 'county fair' idea," said William. "Do you think we could have a county fair here in Plymouth?"

"Well, I'm not sure if you would call it a county fair, but you could use the idea if you like," said Tommy.

I looked at Tommy and smiled. I wanted him to know how very proud I was that Tommy was the one teaching!

"We could start by giving people their own plot of land to till, grow, and harvest their own crops on," William said. "Perhaps this could motivate people to work harder and be more creative with their skills, knowing that anything they produce would be theirs to keep. Perhaps a little competition could be healthy!"

I agreed. "Yes, it's quite brilliant! Those who work harder will likely produce more and then be rewarded more. Those who don't will not."

"Yes, I like it. I will consider this some more," said William. "Thank you, Rush. Thank you, Tommy. Our conversation has been very helpful. And next time we should try the 'salsa' you speak of."

The sound of footsteps made us turn toward the door as Freedom rushed in breathing hard. "Indians! Coming down the hill. About four or five."

A second later the bell starting to ring as we jumped up and ran outside.

This time, five Indians approached the settlement from Watson's Hill. As they drew near, I recognized that Somoset was leading them. I couldn't help but feel relieved. I imagine William Bradford and the other Pilgrims felt the same way. The Indians looked tall and strong. Each carried a bow and a quiver full of arrows and two carried several bundles of fur. Some were bare-chested and a couple had furs draped over their shoulders. The Indians stopped at the same place that Somoset had stopped during his first visit.

"Somoset return with Squanto," said Somoset, the yellow feather still clipped in his hair.

An Indian with knowing eyes stepped forward. He held a small bundle of animal skins and furs under one arm. He wore a necklace made of small seashells and his smile was bigger and brighter than Somoset's.

"I am Squanto," he said. "I used to live here in Patuxet Harbor. That was many years ago. I've been sent by Massasoit, the sachem and leader of this land. He permits me to come and speak with you. He will come soon. He is eager to meet you."

"Your English is extraordinary," said William. "How did you learn to speak the English tongue so well?"

"You must be William Bradford. May I call you William?"

"Yes, of course," William said.

The ease in which Squanto spoke English was unnerving. It didn't seem natural. And yet he was a perfect gentleman as he stood there in his leather loincloth and bare chest.

Squanto spoke again. "We have brought some furs to trade as well as some fresh herring to share with you. A small token of our friendship."

Myles Standish, who had also come out to meet the Indians, stood with his armor and musket and said, "When will Massasoit be here?"

"Before the sun sets," said Squanto. "He comes when he is ready. He could be watching us now. Every great sachem has eyes in all the forest. He watches. He waits. You are fortunate that he wishes to befriend you."

"We thank you for the herring," said William. "I'm sure they are delicious."

"They are not for eating," Squanto said. "They are for planting. If you're going to plant corn and grow a successful crop at Patuxet, you will need to fertilize the soil with these." Squanto held up the herring.

"Squanto know much. Smart. Listen to Squanto and live long," said Somoset. "Me leave now. Long journey home."

"Somoset is leaving with his men and returning to his people," said Squanto. "He is a sachem in the land northward."

Somoset nodded.

"But I will stay," said Squanto. "I will help you and do what I can to help Massasoit see that you are his friend and ally."

Somoset smiled and found Freedom among the Pilgrims. He walked up to her and held out his hand. Inside was a leather strap with what looked like a bear claw attached to it. "A gift for you," said Somoset.

Freedom accepted it and said, "A fine gift. Thank you."

Somoset gave one final look at the Pilgrims and then turned northward and left with his men.

Freedom turned to Squanto and asked, "You said you used to live here at Patuxet Harbor many years ago. Why did you and your people leave?"

"I have heard about the girl they call Freedom," said Squanto. "The girl with midnight hair who speaks perfect English."

"Thank you," blushed Freedom.

"Seven years ago, I was kidnapped and taken from Patuxet Harbor, never to see my family or loved ones again. I was put on

a ship and sailed across the ocean to a new world called Spain. Eventually, I sailed to England and learned to speak like you do. Finally, I had the chance to travel back to my homeland. I was eager to see my family, my parents and brother and sisters. But when I returned, there was nothing. Everyone was gone. I soon learned that the plague, a great sickness, had swept over Patuxet Harbor and killed my people. Hundreds and hundreds and hundreds . . ." Squanto stopped talking as he stared off into the harbor. He looked sad and distant.

"I'm sorry, Squanto," said Freedom.

"Yes," said William, "we are all sorry for your loss."

Squanto blinked and a tear rolled down his cheek. "You are kind. And you, too, have suffered great loss. Many of your people have died from sickness. This place has seen great sorrow for both Indian and Englishman. But I will try to change that. Together, we can learn from each other. Come, I will show you how to plant corn that will grow big and delicious."

Tommy nudged William and said, "Sounds like he could give you some nice tips on how to win a blue ribbon for best corn at the county fair!"

William smiled and said, "I like the way you think, Tommy."

As the Pilgrims followed Squanto, I called for Freedom and Tommy. "I think it's time we find Liberty and return to school."

"This has been a great field trip," said Freedom.

"No kidding. Do we get extra credit for this?" Tommy asked.

"Where did everyone go?" asked Liberty. "I had a nice nap over by that oak tree. Do you want to hear about the dream I had?"

"Sure," I said. "You can tell us all about it as we walk to someplace a little more private so we can time-jump back to school."

Tommy and Freedom climbed on the back of Liberty. And as

we walked into the forest to open the time portal, Liberty ended the day the only way a magical horse could.

Liberty said, "I dreamed that I was racing from town to town while carrying your revolutionary hero Paul Revere! Suddenly, a giant bolt of lightning struck the ground in front of me. I dodged it just as another hit the ground and then another. Each time, I barely avoided the bolts. It was like Zeus himself was determined to stop our midnight ride. Just before we reached the final town a lone food cart selling Veggie Supreme sandwiches rolled in front of us and I had to make a split-second decision on what to do. Should I stop and indulge myself with mouthwatering goodness or jump the cart and win the day?"

"What did you do?" Freedom asked with great curiosity. Tommy looked like he was equally interested.

"I don't know; that's when I woke up. I think an acorn hit me on the head. I'm telling you, this forest is out to get me!"

"I think you stopped for a midnight snack!" said Tommy.

"I think you jumped the food cart and saved the day!" said Freedom.

I pondered both answers and said, "You are a time-traveling horse that can stop time! So I think you did both!"

Facing page: Illustration depicting Native American Indian Squanto. He served as guide and interpreter for Pilgrim colonists at Plymouth Colony.

Chapter 9

The morning air was crisp but not cold as we dropped through the time portal and landed on the grass near the back door to Manchester Middle School. Tommy and Freedom didn't waste any time as they slid off the side of Liberty, grabbed their modern-day clothes, and rushed into the school to change.

Birds were chirping in the gnarled oak tree that shaded the back door. The sound of a large engine idling, like that of a garbage truck or a bus, was coming from in front of the school. It must be the school bus that Freedom heard right before we had time-jumped. As we peeked around the side of the school, I nearly stepped in a mess of pink frosting. Ah, yes, the incident with Elizabeth and her pink cupcakes. In a way, Elizabeth was like Massasoit. She was the leader or sachem of this school. Students either feared or revered her. She watched and waited for any sign of weakness in her classmates or any opportunity to send the message that she was in control. I wondered when our next meeting would be. And I wondered what happened in the meeting between the Pilgrims and Massasoit. I doubt Massasoit had brought pink cupcakes. But, hopefully, the two groups had better success at getting along.

Liberty watched the students exit the bus. "I've always wanted to ride inside a bus," he said, "but they simply don't make the seats big enough for extra-large mammals like me. I've seen horses ride in those fancy trailers and get pulled wherever they want to go. They probably get their hooves manicured, their manes permed, and their nose hairs plucked! No thank you!"

Tommy ran outside with the bulging travel bag and handed it to me. "Here are the Pilgrim clothes, mine and Freedom's. Oh, I almost forgot. Here's a letter from William Bradford."

I paused, not sure I heard Tommy correctly. "What is it? Who is it from?"

Slowly, Tommy repeated, "William Bradford, remember him?" He reached out his arm in my direction.

"Earth to Rush Revere, come in, Rush Revere," teased Liberty.

"Yes, yes, of course," I stammered, still trying to figure out how Tommy got a letter from William Bradford. "I'm here, I'm listening. You say it's a letter?"

"Well, actually, it's a sealed parchment, which I've always thought was cool because of the wax seal. Of course, the most common substance used to seal a letter was beeswax or resin. Did you know the pope would seal his documents with lead?"

Native American Indian sachem Massasoit visits the Pilgrims at Plymouth Colony around 1621.

"You're doing it again," said Liberty.

"Too much info?" Tommy asked.

"Oh, I don't mind," said Liberty. "I love the way your brain works."

"Yeah, but I probably sound like I should be wearing really thick glasses and a pocket protector full of pens. Anyway, here," Tommy said as he waved the sealed parchment in front of me.

I took it and examined both sides. Still a little confused I asked, "Exactly how did you get it?"

"After Squanto finished speaking and led the Pilgrims to the cornfield, William slipped this letter inside my coat pocket and asked me to give it to you. He said it was really important, but I forgot about it until I changed my clothes."

"Oh, well, that makes sense. For a second, I thought that William Bradford had figured out a way to teleport mail through a time-travel pony express service."

"Don't get any ideas," Liberty said, eyes narrowed.

"Well, I need to run and get my backpack out of my locker. Freedom already went to her English class. We'll see you in last period for Honors History!" Tommy waved and slipped back into the school.

"Well, what are you waiting for—open it up!" Liberty said, excitedly. "He said it was important! Maybe it's a treasure map! Or maybe it's the first clue to a scavenger hunt! Or maybe it's an invitation to his birthday party!"

I ignored Liberty as I pondered what William Bradford would send to me in a sealed parchment. I slipped my finger between the edge of the yellowed paper and the red seal until the seal broke. I opened the letter and read:

"Do you realize what this is?" I asked, excitedly. "This is an invitation to the very first Thanksgiving! What an honor!"

"I was hoping for a treasure map," said Liberty. "But the part that says 'lots of food' makes up for it. Let's hope they have a great harvest with lots of fresh vegetables! The invitation didn't say anything about what to wear, did it? I mean, I'd hate to come overdressed. I hope it's not formal. Tuxedos can be such a bother."

"Have you worn a tuxedo before?" I asked.

"Maybe I have and maybe I haven't. What's it to you?" Liberty said suspiciously.

I looked at the invitation again and said, "Lucky for you it doesn't mention what to wear, so that means you can come as you are."

Liberty smiled and let out a long, relaxed breath.

That's when I thought I would have a little fun with him. "Oh no," I said as I pretended to study the invitation.

"What is it?" Liberty asked.

"Well, I just noticed that your name isn't on the invitation."

"What!" Liberty snapped. "Let me see that!" I moved the parchment up to his eyes as he scanned the letter word for word.

I continued, trying not to smile. "That's too bad. I'm sure we could bring you back something. A carrot, perhaps."

Liberty's head jerked from the letter to my face. He gave me a penetrating stare as if trying to shoot laser beams from his eyes. His head jerked back to the letter. He stared some more. An idea must have popped into his head because he slowly turned to me with a big, wide, satisfied grin. He asked, "And just how do you think you're going to get to the Pilgrim Party, Professor? Hey,

I like that alliteration. *Pilgrim Party Professor.*" He refocused his attention and gave special emphasis each time he used the letter *p*. "The *point* I *prefer* to *punctuate* is that I'm your ride! You can't get there without me." Liberty smiled and blinked rapidly several times.

I couldn't help but smile and said, "*Perfectly played*. You're right. I'm sure it was just an oversight on William's part. We'd love for you to join us."

"Or perhaps the better way to say that is *I* would love for you to join *me*," Liberty said.

"Touché!" I laughed. As we walked away from the school I said, "Let's go gather some items for our history class as well as for the festival. Then we'll go have some lunch and return before class starts."

"Sounds like a plan!"

"But let's not eat too much. Remember, William said we should come hungry."

Liberty looked at me like he was embarrassed to know me and said, "You did not just say that. For the record, there are three subjects that have always put me at the top of the class: breakfast, lunch, and dinner."

We returned just seconds before the Honors History class started. Liberty, of course, held his breath and walked into the classroom unnoticed. I carried two large grocery sacks and set them down near the teacher's desk. As the bell rang and the students took their seats I reached up to feel the once-sealed letter from William Bradford resting in my pocket. I couldn't help but smile that we were invited to attend the first Thanksgiving.

I quickly welcomed the students and asked for everyone's

Dear Rush Revere,

The experience over the last several months is not something I want to repeat. I cringe at the thought of the many hardships I've endured: escaping from England, leaving my son in Holland, losing the Speedwell, sailing on the Mayflower, enduring miserable conditions overseas, feeling persecuted by Sailor and Stranger, suffering bitter cold and wretched hunger, and especially, losing my wife, Dorothy. The latter is something that nearly crushed me. However, I survived thanks to the friendship and the support of my friends in the New World. I consider you one of them. You always seem to show up at just the right time and at just the right place. I have struggled to know how to best repay you for your kindnesses. Although I know you expect nothing in return, I've decided to have a celebration of sorts. I feel the winds of change and good fortune are upon us. There is much to look forward to. Please accept this letter of invitation. The details are below. I hope to see you there.

Your true friend,

William Bradford

An Invitation

The First Annual Plimoth Plantation Harvest Festival

When: Late September or early October, 1621

Where: Cole's Hill (Plimoth Plantation)

Who: Rush Revere, Tommy, and Freedom

What: A celebration with games and lots of food

Come hungry!

Seal of the city of Plymouth, Massachusetts.

attention. As all heads turned in my direction, Liberty exhaled and appeared at the back of the classroom. Freedom noticed him but no one else did.

I noticed that all the desks were filled but one.

"Has anyone seen Elizabeth?" I asked.

Before anyone could respond, the door to the classroom jerked open and Elizabeth rushed in. She was so fast that Liberty didn't have time to disappear.

"Ah-ha! Caught you!" Elizabeth yelled, pointing. "See, I told you he had a horse in the classroom."

Principal Sherman was still inching his way through the door. Elizabeth quickly turned and impatiently pulled him into the classroom. In the two and a half seconds it took to look back and pull the principal through the door, Liberty vanished.

"What just . . . How did . . . Where did he go?" Elizabeth asked, confused.

Principal Sherman surveyed the scene.

"He was right there!" Elizabeth pointed as she marched to the back of the room. "Right here!" She spread out her arms as if showing off a masterpiece. She whipped around to the principal, who looked somewhat bothered.

Principal Sherman sighed and said, "I apologize for the intrusion. I always hate to interrupt a teacher's precious time nurturing the fine minds of Manchester Middle School. But Elizabeth was so passionate about it and assured me that you had a horse in your classroom. And not just any horse."

"That's right!" shouted Elizabeth. One of the yellow bows in her hair looked off-kilter. "*Daddy!* It's a talking horse who loves American history. He recited the Preamble to the Constitution.

He took Mr. Revere to visit the Pilgrims. You all saw it! And his horse really does talk! *Tell* him!"

Elizabeth stared at the students, urging them to back her up, but they all avoided her glare.

The principal walked to the back of the classroom and patted Elizabeth on the shoulder. "There, there, my dear. It's all right."

The students were all watching, eyes glued to the scene at the back of the classroom. In that exact moment, Liberty reappeared at the front of the classroom.

"There he is again!" Elizabeth pointed frantically to the front of the classroom. But, again, in the one and a half seconds it took the students to look where Elizabeth was pointing, Liberty had already gasped for air and had vanished again. I stood all alone at the front of the class and waved at all the searching eyes.

Freedom got up out of her chair and opened the back door. She said, "Is anyone else warm? This room feels really stuffy. I'll just leave the door open for a minute."

Smart girl, I thought. I hoped Liberty took the hint and was leaving the room.

"I think I'm partly to blame for Elizabeth's behavior," I said. "There was an accident this morning. . . . Oh, I almost forgot." I pulled out a new phone that I had purchased after lunch. "Here you go. And I do sincerely apologize about this morning."

"Accidents happen," said Principal Sherman. "Let's go to the nurse so you can lie down while I call your mother."

Elizabeth took the phone and started to squawk, "But *Daddy*!" Principal Sherman put his hands on her shoulders and started to leave. Elizabeth looked around the classroom one last time and then quietly exited with her father.

The whole class burst out laughing.

"All right, all right," I turned to the class and said, "enough of that. You all had an opportunity to turn me in, but you didn't. Why?"

"We like you!" said Tommy.

"Yeah, yesterday was awesome," said another boy in the front of the class.

"We hope Liberty comes back," said a girl sitting near the empty desk.

"We don't want to lose our talking horse!" said another boy.

"If that is how you truly feel, I can assure you, Liberty and I will be back. But we wasted enough time and we have an important history lesson today." I went to the chalkboard, grabbed a piece of chalk, and began writing some letters. K-I-S . . .

"Kissing?" guessed Tommy. The class laughed. "I thought this was history class." Then Tommy's face turned serious. "Wait, we're not going to talk about the history of kissing, are we?"

The boys all groaned, and the girls seemed very curious about where I was going with this.

"No," I said, "I'm not finished putting letters on the board." I continued writing,

K-I-S-T-I-N-G . . .

Tommy interrupted again, "Mr. Revere? It looks like you're trying to spell *kissing* and I'm no kissing expert, but I'm pretty sure you're spelling it wrong."

Again, laughter bounced off the classroom walls.

"Thank you, Tommy. But if you'll let me finish, I'll explain." I finished writing each letter. K-I-S-T-I-N-G-V-A-G-H-N. "There! Does anyone know what this says or means?"

All I got were blank stares. Timidly, a couple of students raised their arms.

"Is it some place in Europe?" said a boy.

"Is it somebody's last name?" asked a girl.

Tommy tried one last time and said, "I'm pretty sure it has something to do with a girl kissing a guy named Vaughn."

This time, I found myself laughing. "Imaginative, but no," I said. "Sometimes, what we see is not what is truly there. Most people see Liberty as an average horse. But you know differently. Likewise, most people don't see history for what it truly is. To know the truth about history, it needs to be experienced to be understood. When we begin to know the real people who were a part of real events in history, we begin to see those events differently. Today we are going to visit one of those events. Remember, oftentimes what we see is not what is truly there."

Using the same letters, I rearranged them and spelled T-H-A-N-K-S-G-I-V-I-N-G. "By simply unscrambling the letters, we see what is truly there. Tell me what you think about when you hear the word *Thanksgiving*."

"We get out of school!" said a boy in the back row.

"My family goes to my grandma's house and all our cousins come and it's like a big party," said a girl near the windows.

"I love watching football," said Tommy. "And my mom cooks a big turkey with stuffing. One year my dad tried cooking the turkey, but it didn't turn out so well and the fire department showed up, so, well, now he makes the mashed potatoes and gravy. And, of course, there's always pumpkin pie. I'm getting really hungry just talking about it."

The rest of the class agreed and starting talking about their favorite Thanksgiving foods.

I thanked everyone for their comments and said, "Today we're going to visit the first Thanksgiving. Of course, the Pilgrims didn't call it Thanksgiving. Their celebration was more of a harvest festival. Rather than try to explain it to you, I'd rather you experience it with your own eyes. History is a mystery until it is discovered. Are you ready?"

"Are you going to show us another movie? Do we get popcorn this time?" asked Tommy.

"Yes and yes!" I reached for the large grocery sacks and pulled out two large bags of popcorn, including some paper bowls. I also pulled out several packages of red licorice. The class cheered and several boys gave each other high fives.

"This movie is a documentary on the Pilgrims' first Thanksgiving. Pay attention to what's different and what's the same when you think about your own Thanksgiving." I walked to the back of the class and connected the wireless adapter to the projector. "I'm going to step out of the class to check on Liberty, but I expect you'll be on your best behavior. Enjoy the show." I dimmed the lights and discreetly nodded at Tommy and Freedom. As students were crawling over chairs and desks to get to the popcorn and licorice, nobody noticed the three of us slip out the back door. We hurried down the hall and through the doors to outside, where Liberty was waiting for us behind the gnarled oak tree.

"I have your Pilgrim clothes but you'll have to change when we get there. Liberty, try and get us just inside the forest."

Tommy and Freedom climbed up onto the saddle and Liberty wasted no time. "*Rush, rush, rushing to history,*" Liberty said.

"The fall of 1621, Plymouth Plantation, the first Thanksgiving," I said as I ran behind Liberty and jumped through the swirling time portal.

Chapter 10

I *immediately saw a* drastic change in the surrounding forest. Instead of the mostly green leaves of springtime, now the leaves were various shades of vibrant yellow, red, orange, and purple. It was definitely autumn and it felt like the perfect scenery for celebrating the first Thanksgiving.

Freedom and Tommy were experts at jumping off Liberty. They quickly slipped off their shoes and put their Pilgrim clothing on over their modern-day clothes.

"It feels like we were just here," said Freedom.

"We were," said Tommy. "Technically, we came here this morning. But about seven months have passed at Plymouth Plantation."

I pulled out my smartphone, tapped the camera app, and switched it to video mode. I turned the phone toward Liberty and said, "You're on. The students back in class will be able to see and hear you."

Liberty cleared his throat and said, "Hello, class. It's me, Liberty. I can't wait to get back and visit with all of you. Right now, we're approaching the place where the Pilgrims first settled in America. It's called Liberty's Landing."

"Liberty!" I whispered loudly.

"What?" Liberty whispered back.

"It's not called Liberty's Landing," I said. "You know that."

"I was just making sure you were paying attention. Although I do think 'Liberty's Landing' has a nice ring to it, don't you?"

I rolled my eyes and firmly said, "Get on with it."

"Okay, okay. We're approaching Plymouth Plantation. The Pilgrims have been living here for about ten months. And now a word from our sponsor."

"We don't have a sponsor," I said.

"We don't? Well, we should. The iced-tea factory that you work for should be sponsoring us. Seriously! Or what about Butterball turkeys! Or Stove Top stuffing! Or—"

"Liberty, I think I can take it from here," I said, exasperated.

"For the record, just because I'm a horse doesn't mean I don't have good ideas. Oh, I do. In fact, I have a dream. I have a dream that one day, I won't be judged by the color of my skin but by the content of my character! Wait a minute. That was brilliant! I could build upon that."

"It's brilliant because the Reverend Martin Luther King, Jr. said it first," I said.

"Oh," Liberty said. "It just goes to show how great minds think alike."

I turned the camera toward the Pilgrim settlement. "Class, this is Mr. Revere speaking. You can't see me because, as I mentioned before, the camera I'm using is attached to my coat disguised as a button. We are approaching the festival now!"

"Look at all the Indians," said Freedom.

Sure enough, I counted about a hundred Indians, double the number of English Pilgrims. I looked for William Bradford or Myles Standish or Elder Brewster but none of them could be found.

"Mr. Revere," Tommy said, softly. "I see a bunch of kids playing games over by the brook. We're going to check it out, okay?"

"Have fun," I said.

Tommy and Freedom ran off toward the brook and I started weaving my way through the guests. Finally, I saw a familiar face. Squanto was walking in my direction and waved as I approached. "You must be Rush Revere!" he said. "Welcome!"

"Thank you," I said as we shook hands.

"It is an honor to meet you," Squanto said. "William hoped you would come and bring Tommy and Freedom."

"We just arrived," I said as Liberty wandered toward the tables of food. "Tommy and Freedom ran off to see what games are being played by the brook."

"Smart children," Squanto said. "William recognized your horse and asked that I come find you. Come, he is with Massasoit. I will introduce you to the leader of the Pokanokets. As you can see, he has brought many of his people to the Harvest Festival."

I nodded and said, "It looks like he brought his entire village."

"Before I was captured and taken to Spain. I remember Massasoit had a great army. His people numbered almost twelve thousand, with three thousand warriors."

"That's remarkable," I said.

"Yes, but after years of disease, Massasoit was left with fewer than three hundred warriors."

I remembered Squanto talking about how many of his people died. I didn't realize how great a number that really was. I said, "I assume that Massasoit's visit with William Bradford and the others went well."

"Yes," Squanto nodded. "Very well. Massasoit and the people of the *Mayflower* worked out an agreement of peace. They promised to help and protect each other."

I liked the idea of a peace agreement. I was very glad to see the friendships that had been forged between the Pilgrims and the Pokanokets.

As I followed Squanto through the maze of people, I have to admit, I felt a little nervous and overwhelmed. I'm not usually starstruck, but walking around meeting exceptional people like Squanto, who left such a mark on American history, was just incredible! Not to mention, I was about to meet the man who could command his warriors to capture or kill the Pilgrims like the Indians did with the French sailors who had arrived in previous years. Instead, he chose to befriend them. And from the sound of it, the Pilgrims had helped the Indians as well.

As we approached several outdoor fires, I saw William Bradford standing next to a strong and muscular Native American. His chest was bare but he wore a thick necklace made of white shells. His long black hair was cut short on one side and his face was painted dark red. He had several warriors standing with him. Their faces were also painted, some red, some white, some yellow, and some black. William presented Massasoit with a pair of knives and some copper chains. In return, Massasoit presented William with some furs and a quiver full of arrows. The two men smiled upon trading the items.

Squanto turned to me and said, "Massasoit does not speak English, but I will translate for you." As Squanto approached the sachem, Massasoit turned and acknowledged him. The two spoke briefly and Squanto pointed in my direction. Both Massasoit and William turned and upon seeing me, William rushed over to greet me.

"Rush Revere, as always your timing is perfect. I see that Squanto has found you," William said. He took my arm and led me to Massasoit. "It is my pleasure to introduce you to the Indian king, Massasoit."

In his native tongue, Squanto translated for William and then introduced me to the king.

I reached out my hand toward Massasoit and he shook it with a strong grip. He looked to be about thirty-five years old and as lean and fit as any professional athlete. He smiled and spoke a language that was complete gibberish. I smiled back and nodded my head.

Squanto said, "He says that you have a strong name, like a rushing river."

Massasoit spoke again and Squanto said, "He asks if you have brought anything to trade."

I felt bad that I had nothing to trade with the Indian leader. Or did I? I slipped my hand into my pocket and pulled out the peppermint candy that was still there from our trip to Fosters' Family Diner. I said, "I have nothing to trade but I do have a small gift." I handed a piece of candy to Massasoit, who accepted it in his palm. He looked at it closely.

"Peppermint candy," I said. "You'll need to take off the wrapper, then place it on your tongue and suck it. It's sweet like honey."

Squanto translated my words and Massasoit placed the hard candy on his tongue. His eyebrows raised and he nodded at the warriors next to him. He smiled and spoke briefly as he continued to suck.

Squanto said, "He says your gift is good. He likes it very much."

Then Massasoit spit the candy into his palm and offered it to the warrior on his right, who took it and placed it on his tongue. One by one, the Indians surrounding Massasoit each took a turn sucking the candy and tasting the peppermint until it made its way back to the Pokanoket leader. Obviously, no one in the seventeenth century was familiar with germs or bacteria and how they can be passed along by the food we eat, the surfaces we touch, and even by the air we breathe. But they knew good candy when they tasted it!

William spoke. "Squanto, please tell Massasoit that our home is his home. And thank him, again, for the five deer that he brought to our celebration."

As Squanto translated, I turned to see the many deer, ducks, and wild turkeys that turned on wooden spits, roasting over the outdoor fires. Meats and vegetables were thrown into large metal pots similar to Dutch ovens and were simmering over hot coals.

"It smells delicious," I said.

"Squanto, Massasoit, if you'll excuse me. I'd like to show Rush Revere our settlement," said William.

Squanto translated and Massasoit nodded.

As William and I walked away, Squanto stepped alongside me and said, "I have a gift for Freedom. If it is acceptable to you, I would give it to her before she leaves."

"I think that would be wonderful," I said.

"Very good," Squanto nodded. "I will get it to her. Thank you, Rush Revere. You have been a good friend to William."

"And Squanto has been a good friend to me and our settlement," said William. "He taught us where to hunt and fish, how to plant and grow the best crops, what herbs to use for medicines, and how to trade for supplies with other tribes. We believe he's been sent from God as an instrument to help us grow and prosper."

"You are too kind, William," said Squanto. "God, as you say, rescued me from slavery in Spain. The Catholic friars, holy men, helped me escape. They risked their lives to free me so that I could return to my native land. I have much to be grateful for. And I choose to show my gratitude by serving my new friend and holy man, William Bradford."

I could see how Squanto would consider William to be holy. The Puritans prayed many times a day and they never worked on the Sabbath. They tried to show compassion to all men and women and looked for solutions to their problems without violence.

With great admiration I turned to William and said, "Mr. Bradford, I must thank you so much for inviting me. I am beyond honored."

William replied, "Tommy is a good lad. I wasn't sure if I

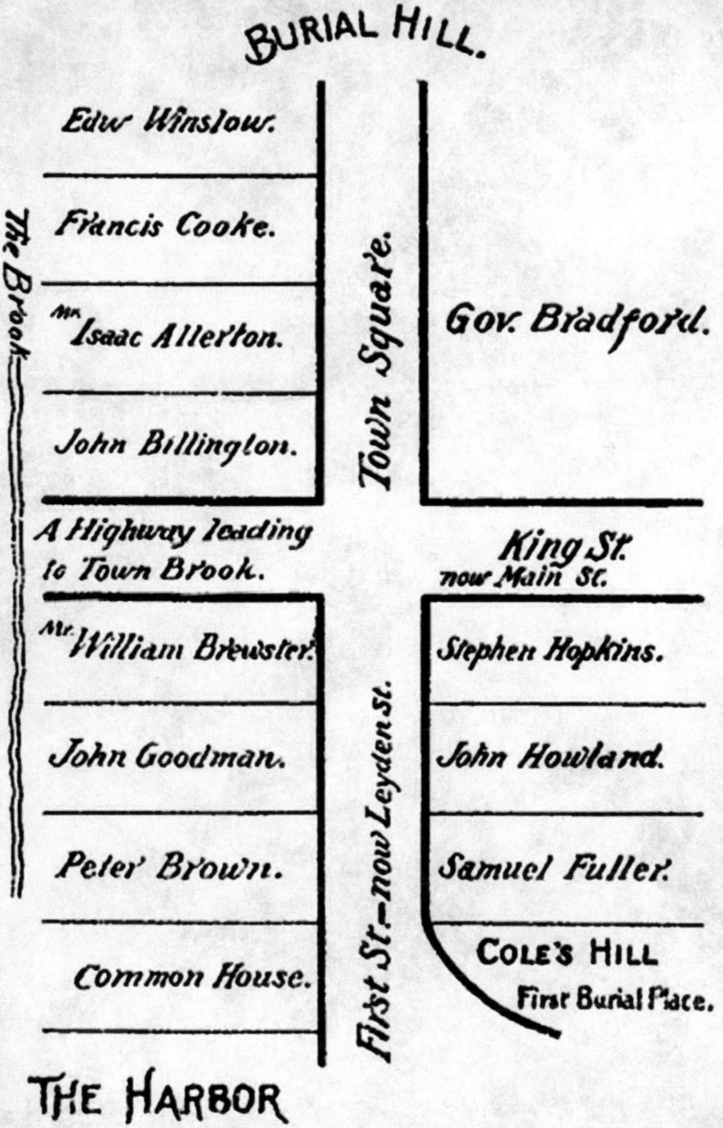

BURIAL HILL.

Edw Winslow.

Francis Cooke.

Mr. Isaac Allerton.

John Billington.

The Brook

Town Square.

Gov. Bradford.

A Highway leading to Town Brook.

King St. now Main St.

Mr. William Brewster.

John Goodman.

Peter Brown.

Common House.

First St.—now Leyden St.

Stephen Hopkins.

John Howland.

Samuel Fuller.

COLE'S HILL

First Burial Place.

THE HARBOR

Map of private land in Plymouth Colony, including the home of William Bradford.

would see you at the Common House, but I knew he would find a way to get my letter to you. I wanted you to be here to celebrate with us. We all have so much to be grateful for on this day."

"Yes," I agreed, "everyone seems so joyous, far different than a short while ago."

"It's true," said William. "But the real difference came when every family was assigned its own plot of land to work. That was the turning point! They were permitted to market their own crops and products. This had very good success. Men and women worked harder and much more corn was planted than otherwise would have been."

"The turnaround to success is truly extraordinary," I said. "And you say that it all happened soon after you stopped sharing the profits that gave every man a common share or equal amount?"

"Yes, at first we really had great expectations and high hopes that all the people would embrace the idea of a commonwealth. But it didn't work. In fact, it almost ruined us. We learned that it wasn't actually fair at all."

"But William is a smart man," said Squanto. "He gave people their own land. He made people free. No more slaves to a common house. They set up trading posts and exchanged goods with Indians."

William nodded and said, "In no time we found that we had more food than we could eat ourselves. We realized that our profits would soon allow us to pay back the people that sponsored our voyage to America. In fact, we expect more Puritans to arrive and surely more Europeans will come to trade with us."

I smiled at what William was saying. This, of course, is something that America has long since learned, but I marveled at how quickly the Pilgrims figured it out. When people have individual freedom to work, build, create, market, and make a profit for themselves, the community prospers faster than it would when these freedoms aren't available to men and women. It was obvious that this first Thanksgiving wouldn't be possible if William Bradford hadn't boldly changed the way the Pilgrims worked and lived.

"If you'll excuse me," said Squanto. "I must check on Massasoit. And then I will find Freedom and give her my gift."

"Again, it's a great honor to meet you," I said.

We said goodbye and Squanto slipped back into the crowd at the exact same time as Myles Standish walked up to us. He said, "He'll make a fine military man."

"Excuse me?" I asked, confused.

"Your boy, Tommy," said Myles. "I found him by the brook. He's quick as a snake and light on his feet. I was very impressed. He's a natural. I hope you don't mind that I gave him a gift."

"A gift? I'm sure he was thrilled to get a gift from you," I said.

"Indeed he was! He said his mother might be worried and I told him, 'Nonsense!' He should wear it proudly, day and night."

"Thank you, Myles," I said. "And, um, exactly what was it that you gave . . ."

My words were drowned out by the sudden sound of pounding drums and the loud shrieks coming from near the outside fires. I turned to see Indians dancing around a fire ring, their faces streaked with paint. Both Indians and Pilgrims smiled as they watched the performing Pokanokets twirl and bend and wave their arms as they sang and chanted to the drums. After several minutes the mesmerizing dancers finally stopped and several Indians whooped and hollered for more.

I turned toward William, who handed me a plate of food. "I'm sure you haven't had time to eat yet," he said. "Myles won't be joining us. As you may know, he, too, lost his wife last winter and is eager to find someone to marry. He fancies a young lady and has gone to court her. Please, sit, join me."

I thanked him and took my plate, which was loaded with food, including sliced turkey, a stew of meat and vegetables, and bread pudding. We ate until my belt felt like it was two sizes too small.

"Come," said William. "We will walk off this fine meal. I have something I want to show you."

We walked along the row of houses toward the harbor. When we reached the shore at Plymouth Bay we walked south along the sandy beach and then followed a trail that led slightly uphill toward a giant granite boulder the size of a large elephant. We climbed until the ground was level with the boulder, which stuck out of the side of the hill and into the ocean. My natural instinct was to step onto the rock and look out over the shoreline. The breeze was cool to my face. The waves were soothing as they rocked back and forth along the beach. Sandpipers pecked for sand crabs just before running from the approaching waves.

"You are standing on Plymouth Rock," said William. "We used this rock to guide the *Mayflower* back to this place after we found it on one of our discovery expeditions."

I had heard of Plymouth Rock since I was a little boy. I imagined a shallop or small boat could have used this rock at half tide as a dock for the Pilgrims to step onto dry ground rather than wading through frigid waters.

"I have tried to be like this granite boulder, steadfast and immovable," said William. "It has not been easy. But God has made the impossible possible. The Bible says we should build our house upon the rock. I have thought about this since we arrived. I have thought about this through each of our trials in the New World. Though the winds may blow and the storms may rage, the rock does not cower in fear. Do you know why?"

I waited for William's response, eager to know the answer.

He continued, "It is fearless because it knows where it belongs."

I paused before I said, "And you know that the Pilgrims belong here at Plymouth Bay."

"Yes," William said, nodding. "And each of us can be fearless and strong like this rock when we know, without a doubt, where we belong and what we should do. God helps us to know these things. I knew we would make it to the New World. I knew we would find a home like Plymouth Plantation. I knew, eventually, that I would need to give each family their own piece of land and allow them the freedoms to enjoy the profits of their labor. And I know, today, that this land will prosper and become a great nation. And it will remain a great nation as long as we are one nation under God."

"Thank you, William," I said. "I have treasured our time together and I will do my best as a history teacher to make sure that people across America never forget you or the Pilgrims."

Before we turned back toward the festival, I slipped out my phone and discreetly took a picture while William was distracted by several seals playing in the harbor below.

When we arrived back at the first Thanksgiving I said, "Thank you, again, William. I wish you the very best in everything you do."

"The same to you," said William.

He clasped my shoulder and we embraced. We said goodbye and I decided to head over to the brook to find Tommy and Freedom.

Several children were playing a variety of games like keepaway and leapfrog and hide-and-seek. Some Pilgrim children were playing tic-tac-toe in the dirt. Another pair was playing checkers with an old, water-damaged checkerboard and two different-colored stones. Finally, I saw two children sitting on tree stumps and in between them on a third stump was a very pristine but old-looking chessboard with elaborately carved chess pieces. Oddly, one was a Pilgrim boy with a sword hanging from his belt and the other was an Indian girl with a deerskin dress trimmed with fur and matching moccasins. She also wore a necklace of shimmering shells and two hawklike feathers in her hair. An odd pair of chess opponents, I thought. Both had their heads down intently studying the chessboard.

The next second the girl moved her queen to its final resting place and said, "Checkmate."

The boy was motionless, apparently stunned.

As the girl raised her head I quickly stopped the video on my smartphone and asked, surprised, "Freedom, is that you?"

"Hi, Mr. Revere," said Freedom. "Is it time to go?"

"Where did you learn to play like that," said Tommy.

"Playing chess is a lot like tracking animals," said Freedom. "I hunted you. And you stepped right into my traps."

"Huh?" asked Tommy, completely bewildered. "Let's play again," he said, determined.

"Not now," I said. "We need to head back to the modern day. Has anyone seen Liberty? Oh, and by the way, where did you get the Indian dress?"

"It was a gift from Squanto," said Freedom. "We talked for a little while. He said I should be proud of who I am and that I shouldn't care what people think of me. He knows a lot."

I thought, I'm sure he does.

"Yeah, and Myles Standish gave me this awesome sword!" Tommy unsheathed it and sliced it through the air. "We practiced for like an hour. It was so fun!"

"I bet it was. But let's not do that when we get back to the classroom, okay?" I asked politely.

I jumped when whiskers tickled my ear and I heard, "I sure wish they had a livery here."

"What's a liberty?" Tommy asked.

"Not a liberty," said Liberty. "I said a livery. It's like a spa for horses."

"Oh, yeah, I thought you said liberty, not livery. Hey, that's sort of a tongue-twister," said Tommy. "Try and say 'livery liberty' ten times really fast!"

"Oh, that's easy," said Liberty. "Livery liberty, liverty libery, libery livery, oh, hogwash."

As we walked to the place in the forest where we first arrived, I told Tommy, Freedom, and Liberty about my conversation with William Bradford.

"That's awesome that you got to stand on Plymouth Rock!" Tommy said.

I looked back at Plymouth Plantation and marveled at what the Pilgrims had accomplished. These people accomplished the impossible. They survived the unthinkable. And they started a new way of living that would influence the making of the greatest country in the world. The Pilgrims taught us that religious freedom comes with a price. They paid it with their lives while others lost the people they loved the most. But their sacrifices would not be in vain. I would miss my time with William Bradford. He was an exceptional American and someone who truly made a difference in the making of the United States of America. Of course, he would never fully see how the Mayflower Compact influenced the future lawmakers who ultimately created the Constitution. But I was excited to return to class and review what we had learned with the other students.

"So where are we going to go on our next time-travel adventure, Mr. Revere?" asked Freedom.

"Eager to go already?" I asked.

"Absolutely!" said Tommy.

"I've decided to visit Liberty's hometown and home time," I said.

"Really?" asked Liberty, excitedly.

"It's time to experience the history of the events leading up to the signing of the Declaration of Independence."

"There's no place like home!" Liberty said. "Unless your home is in a country ruled by a ruthless king or sitting under a lightning storm or on top of an active volcano or in the path of stampeding elephants or on top of a termite farm or in the path of a falling comet or . . ."

Tommy, Freedom, and I simply smiled at each other as we listened to Liberty's endless list. My life has never been the same with a time-traveling horse, I thought. And I wouldn't have it any other way!

Where do we go next?

A Final Note from the Author

Can you imagine being on the *Mayflower*, crossing a wide-open ocean with crashing waves shaking the boat? What about landing in a place you have never been and needing to build everything in your town from scratch? The Pilgrims truly were an amazing group of people who risked everything in order to be free and live as they thought best.

William Bradford, Myles Standish, William Brewster, Squanto, and Samoset were all brave and courageous figures! These were ordinary people who accomplished extraordinary things. Our country's history is filled with just these kinds of people. Their stories are both unbelievable and fascinating! I am really looking forward to sharing more of that with you in future books.

My buddy, Rush Revere, and his horse, Liberty, can go anywhere in American history anytime they want. How cool is that? I really hope you join us all for the next great adventure!

Quick, who taught Tommy how to swordfight?

Acknowledgments

For years, people were telling me I should write another book. I would shrug them off, giving one excuse after the other. I just wasn't inspired to write more political commentary.

Then, in early 2013, my wife, Kathryn, suggested an entirely different idea. She reminded me how often I talked about the importance of young people learning the truth about American history. She knew my frustration with what many kids are learning today and suggested that I tell the amazing stories of our country's founding in an easy-to-understand way. This concept did excite me and changed my entire attitude about writing another book! Suffice it to say, Kathryn was indefatigable in shepherding the entire thing, creating, coordinating, and assembling all elements. Thank you, Kathryn, for being an exceptionally bright, talented, loyal, and wonderful person to share my life with.

After hearing about the idea, my good friend the late Vince Flynn put me in touch with Louise Burke at Simon & Schuster, who helped to bring this all to life. Thank you to Vince, Louise, and everyone at Simon & Schuster, especially Mitchell Ivers.

Thank you sincerely to Jonathan Adams Rogers for being an instrumental part from the very beginning. He spent long dedicated hours helping to develop this concept from infancy.

My sincere appreciation goes out to Christopher Schoebinger for providing considerable assistance with writing, editing, and reaching a younger demographic. Spero Mehallis worked closely with Chris Hiers to create tremendously impressive illustrations, allowing history to be told in a creative way.

My brother, David Limbaugh, is an unwavering source of support. He is there for me at all times in all endeavors, and I am extremely grateful.

Photo Credits

PAGE

ii Chris Hiers
viii De Agostini Picture Library/Getty Images
xiv Chris Hiers
13 Chris Hiers
18 Chris Hiers
21 Chris Hiers
26 © Jon Hicks/Corbis
27 Project Gutenberg
28 Getty Images
44 Chris Hiers
51 Chris Hiers
54 Architect of the Capitol
55 © Woolaroc Museum, Bartlesville, Oklahoma
56 Getty Images
62 National Geographic/Getty Images
68 © Richard Schecht/DEA Picture Library/Getty Images
74 Project Gutenberg
75 Photography Collection, Miriam and Ira D. Wallach Division of Art, Prints and Photographs, The New York Public Library, Astor, Lenox and Tilden Foundations
77 Chris Hiers
81 Chris Hiers

PAGE

89 © Pilgrim Hall Museum
96 © National Maritime Museum, Greenwich, London
97 © National Maritime Museum, Greenwich, London
98 © National Maritime Museum, Greenwich, London
99 © National Maritime Museum, Greenwich, London
100 © National Maritime Museum, Greenwich, London
101 Wikimedia
105 The Library of Congress
106 Archive.org, The Library of Congress Collection
107 Getty Images
121 © Corbis
126 Chris Hiers
132 © Amy Riley/Getty Images
133 Photography Collection, Miriam and Ira D. Wallach Division of Art, Prints and Photographs, The New York Public Library, Astor, Lenox and Tilden Foundations
133 Getty Images
136 Hoodinski/Wikimedia
140 Chris Hiers
147 Picture Collection, The New York Public Library, Astor, Lenox and Tilden Foundations
152 The Library of Congress
168 Chris Hiers
170 Getty Images
174 © Corbis
177 Chris Hiers
179 Chris Hiers
180 Wikimedia
193 Wikimedia
199 Chris Hiers
202 Chris Hiers
209 McMaster, John Bach. *A School History of the United States.* New York: American Book Company, 1897
210 Penelope Adams Rogers

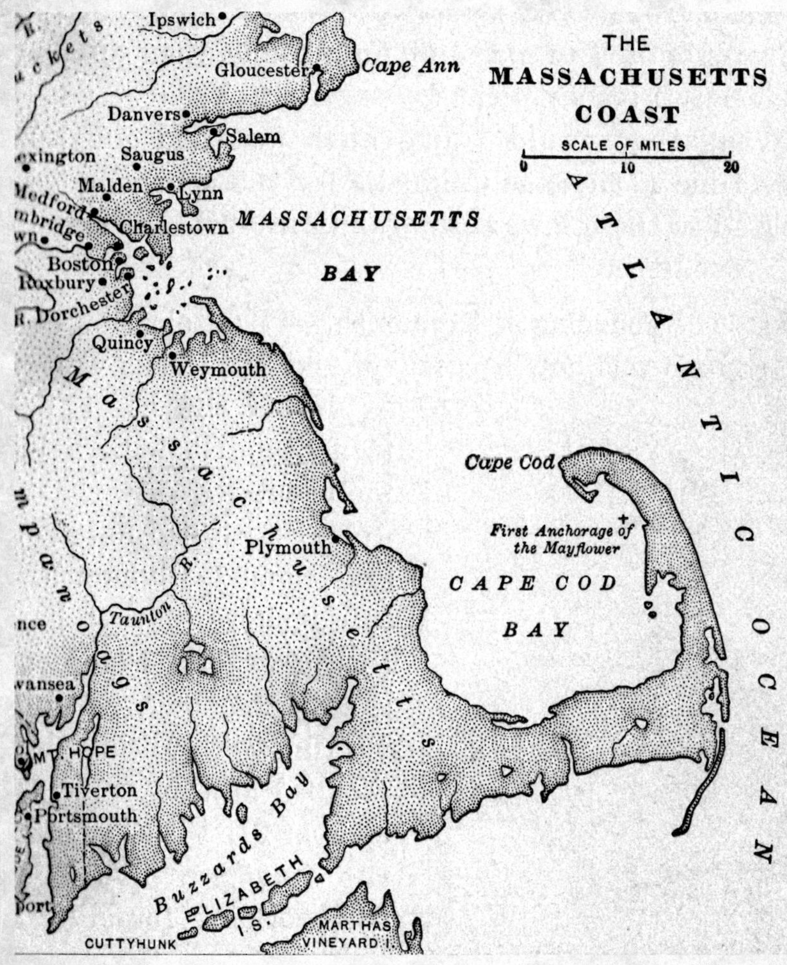
THE
MASSACHUSETTS
COAST
SCALE OF MILES
0
10
20
Ipswich
Gloucester
Cape Ann
Danvers
Salem
Saugus
Malden
Lynn
Charlestown
Boston
Roxbury
Dorchester
Quincy
Weymouth
MASSACHUSETTS
BAY
ATLANTIC OCEAN
Cape Cod
First Anchorage of
the Mayflower
Plymouth
CAPE COD
BAY
Taunton
Massachusetts
MT. HOPE
Tiverton
Portsmouth
Buzzards Bay
ELIZABETH
IS.
CUTTYHUNK
MARTHAS
VINEYARD I.

PLYMOUTH ROCK
LANDING PLACE OF THE
PILGRIMS
1620
COMMONWEALTH OF MASSACHUSETTS

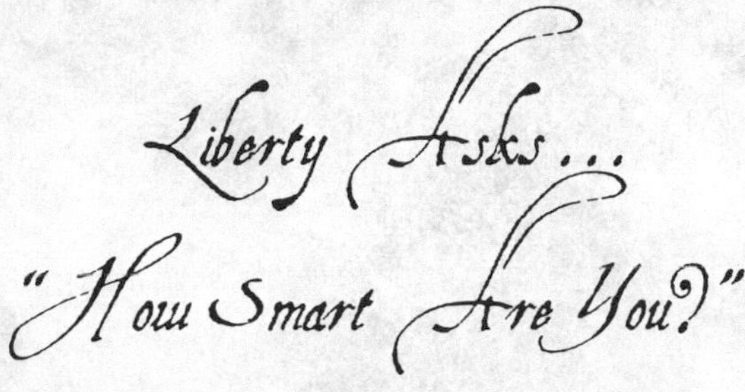

Liberty Asks . . . "How Smart Are You?"

(Beware—He Thinks He Can Stump You!)

1. What was the name of the boat the Pilgrims used to cross over the wide Atlantic Ocean?
2. Where did the Pilgrims start their journey?
3. Where did Rush Revere, Tommy, and your favorite horse time-travel to first?
4. Who was the main leader on the boat?
5. Where did the Pilgrims land?
6. What color were my shoes in Holland?
7. What did we all say before we traveled back in time?
8. Who showed Tommy how to sword fight?
9. What did Squanto teach Freedom to do?
10. Who invited Rush Revere to the "First Thanksgiving"?
11. What was the name of the house where the town gathered?
12. Why did the Pilgrims brave the crashing waves to reach a new land? What were they searching for?
13. Were there any children on the boat? If so, who?

14. Were there any pets on the boat? Not including horses!
15. Who fell overboard? Not including Tommy!
16. In what state is modern Plymouth?
17. Who was the governor of the Plymouth colony when Rush Revere left?
18. What is the most misunderstood part of the "First Thanksgiving"?

Looking for answers?

Visit www.twoifbytea.com under Tea The People!

Rush Revere

AND THE FIRST PATRIOTS

To my audience, the genuine people who make this country work.

In honor of our friend Vince Flynn, "Keep The Faith!"

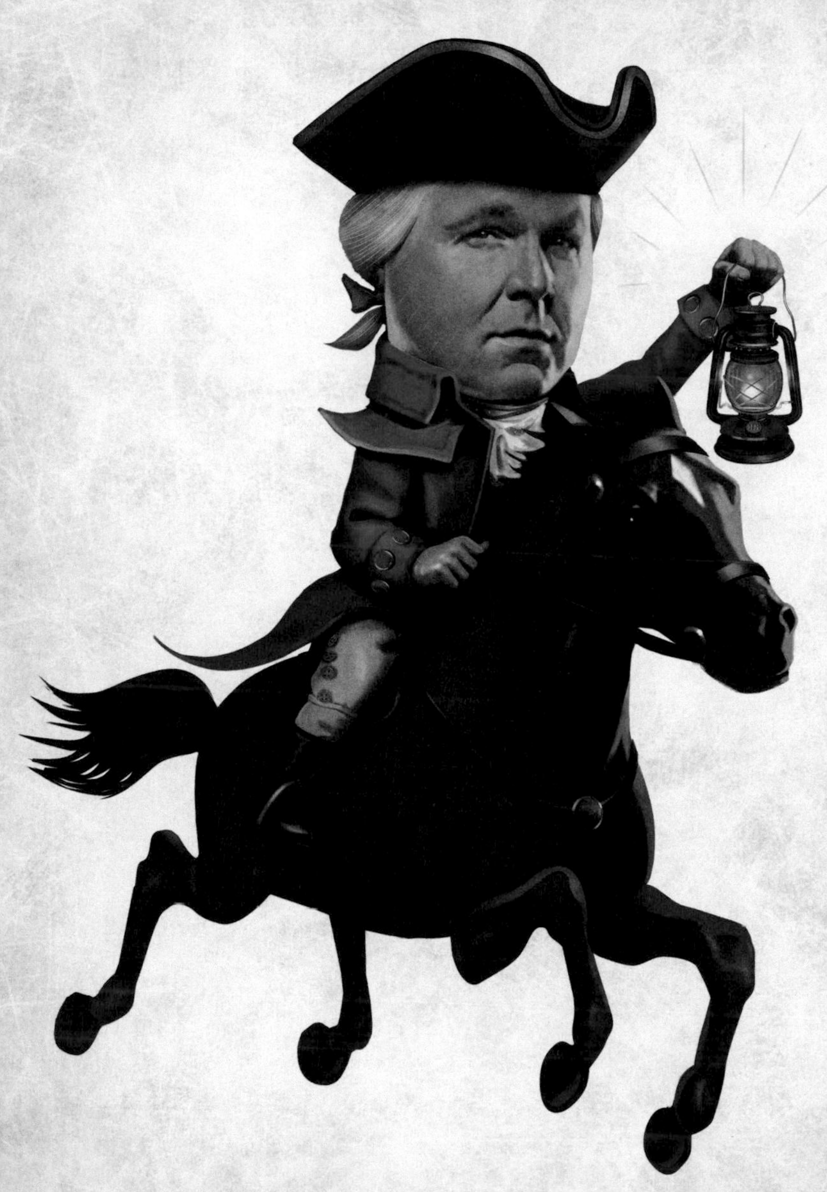

Foreword

I have dedicated this book to some people I often talk about, people for whom I have the greatest respect and admiration. These are the everyday, anonymous people we don't know by name, who are out there working hard, trying their best to play by the rules and do what is right. They are not trying to become famous, because they don't have time. They are focused on things they consider far more important than fame and notoriety. These people define the uniquely American spirit. They are the people who, I like to say, "make America work."

These people truly define and exemplify what is great about this country. Their toil and productivity created an abundance of goods, services, and compassion the likes of which the world had never before seen. Because of them, the Unites States of America became a beacon of hope and inspiration for people all over the world. Americans are some of the most generous, dedicated, courageous, and sincere people in the world. More often than not, the moment a tragedy or natural disaster happens in a small hometown or anywhere in the world, Americans sprint to help "thy neighbor" not only because they can but because they choose to.

The Pilgrims planted the seeds of all of this. After they arrived in what became Plymouth Colony on the *Mayflower* in 1620, under the leadership of William Bradford, they not only survived in the very tough conditions, they thrived. The Pilgrims and Native Americans shared tips of survival. The colonies grew rapidly in size and population. Small towns developed with streets, stores, hospitals, and libraries.

The Pilgrims paved the way for future Patriots to bond together and stand up for their beliefs. Many everyday people, people who were not famous at the time, took grave risks to voice their opinion, especially when counter to mainstream thought. From the early days of the Pilgrims onward, the people of the original colonies wanted to be free: free to believe in God and practice their religion, free to provide and care for their own families and futures, free to own their own property, and free to speak out against those who wanted to control their lives. We are all the descendants of the people who held these first American ideals.

If it hadn't been for these everyday people, people who faced difficult circumstances and overcame what seemed like overwhelming odds, transforming themselves into the leaders of their time, our country would not be the wonderful place it is today. We should never lose sight of this. These leaders took chances—great risks—and thought far beyond their own lives for the greater good of others.

This is the American spirit that we share with our ancestors.

Children across the country have been writing in to me, talking about reading *Rush Revere and the Brave Pilgrims*. Parents, grandparents, stepparents, and siblings from Honolulu to Bangor are sharing the message about true American history:

a message that recognizes our failures and challenges, yes, but also one that does not focus on these failures and challenges alone! One that celebrates freedom and the American spirit!

I love America, and I want you—and everyone!—to also love America. It is my fervent hope that in learning the history of our country you will be inspired to learn about the people, traditions, and institutions that make this a great country so that you will someday make your own contributions to these ideals. And someday maybe you will become a leader yourself. I really want you to be among the millions of ordinary people who accomplish extraordinary things and make America work.

So now it is time to delve into a new adventure and learn about some other people who stood up and got involved in order to further their dreams. My good buddy Rush Revere and his hilarious pal Liberty are going to take you back in time to the mid-eighteenth century, where you will meet some of the first Patriots!

So hold on tight and here we go . . . let's *rush, rush, rush into history*!

Prologue

Smoke billowed from the center of the large rioting mob. The year was 1765 and I was walking along a busy street in Boston, Massachusetts. Large colonial buildings surrounded me on either side; most were two-story rusty-red brick buildings but some were taller, three or four stories. Many shops and businesses lined the street—a silversmith, a candle maker, a clock maker, a bakery, a furniture store. The shops seemed endless. The last time I was near this location was 1621, soon after the Pilgrims landed on the *Mayflower*. It had grown tremendously! I wish my good buddy William Bradford could be with me! When I last saw him at the first Thanksgiving, he told me he knew Plymouth Colony would develop into an incredible country we call America! He was right, of course!

As I thought back to my conversations with William, I completely lost track of where I was going! All of sudden I found myself approaching hundreds of men dressed in colonial clothing looking eager to pick a fight. They were yelling things that I couldn't really understand, but it didn't sound like they were very happy. I noticed the smoke I had seen earlier was still coming from the center of the crowd!

Liberty, my horse, spoke loudly enough to be heard over the shouts of the mob and said, "If that's a fire up there I don't think they're roasting marshmallows. It's too bad because I do love a good marshmallow, but only if it's slightly browned on the outside and gooey in the middle. I mean I know some people like to set their marshmallow on fire and then quickly blow out the flame, but then all you get is that charred and blackened outside crust that tastes like charcoal. Not that I've ever eaten charcoal but I . . ."

"Liberty!" I said. "I appreciate knowing how you like your marshmallow cooked, but we're on a top-secret historical mission, remember?"

"Oh, yes, got it, Captain," Liberty said as he started humming the theme song to *Mission: Impossible*.

"Liberty!" I said. "Shhh."

"I was just trying to set the mood," he replied.

"Let's see if we can squeeze our way through the crowd and find out what's burning," I said.

"Call me crazy but normally I don't like to walk toward fires! I mean, can't we just assume they aren't making s'mores and hightail it out of here?"

"What happened to 'Got it, Captain'?" I asked with a grin.

"Right, okay. I'm in. Luckily, I'm wearing my fireproof saddle. Not! But seriously, you won't hear a peep out of me unless I catch on fire!"

"That'll never happen," I said with a wink. "You're too *cool* to ever catch on fire!"

"Well, that's true." Liberty smiled.

As we made our way toward the smoke I heard a number of comments that were very revealing about the mob's mood and motivation.

"This should send a message to that bloody King George III," said a man who wore his hair in a ponytail.

"Yeah, he thinks he can tax us and take our money to pay for his debts and support his military in America. We didn't vote for that!" said another man who wore a white wig.

"That's right," said a third man. "No taxation without representation!"

I was leading Liberty by his halter as someone bumped into me from the side. He might have knocked me down if I hadn't been holding on to Liberty.

The man slurred his words when he asked me, "Are you in support of the King or against him?"

I was caught by surprise. I'd intended to only observe what was happening. I quickly came up with something on the fly and replied, "Oh, well, I'm against anyone or anything that tries to control the people and withhold their freedoms."

"How do I know you're not just saying that? Maybe you're in support of the King and his Stamp Act and you're just saying you're not so we don't beat you to a pulp!"

I quickly realized that maybe Liberty was right! Maybe we shouldn't have walked toward the smoke, but my inquisitive mind just had to know!

"Who can vouch for ya?! Maybe you're really a spy!" shouted another man.

I felt several pairs of eyes glaring at me and realized I had no witnesses, no one who could vouch for my loyalty to the colonies and to this new America. The men stepped closer. It was obvious they weren't playing around. My palms started sweating and my heart was racing. I felt a nudge from my side. Liberty was trying to get my attention but I was frozen. He nudged me again with his nose, prodding me to hurry up with an answer. Hmm, think, Revere, think. Aha! Got it! Sure hope this works, I thought.

I finally said, "I do have someone who can vouch for me: my horse!"

The men surrounding me burst out laughing at the thought of it.

"Did you just say your horse can vouch for you!" said the man with the white wig.

It was clear that none of them believed me.

"Yes," I said with as much confidence as I could. "You see, I'm so passionate about America's freedoms that I've trained my horse, Liberty, to support the cause of freedom as well."

"You're going to have to do better than that," said the man with the ponytail, who got right in my face and grabbed my collar with both hands as if he was about to throw me.

"I will prove it," I said.

The man holding my collar released his grip and said, "You had better."

I straightened the collar on my coat and turned to look at Liberty. I asked, "Are we in support of King George?"

Liberty shook his head from side to side with big, sweeping strokes. When he finished he stuck out his tongue as if he were disgusted about something. My accusers thought this was very amusing as they all laughed out loud. Whew! I thought, wiping my sweaty palms on the sides of my pants.

I steadied my voice and said, "Are we against King George and the unfair taxes that he burdens us with?"

This time Liberty nodded and let out a high-pitched squeal that sounded like "heeeeeeeeee!"

I looked each of the men in the eye and said, "Do you know how long it takes to teach a horse verbal commands like that?" I wanted to say about ten seconds if he's a magical, time-traveling horse that can talk. Instead, I said, "It takes weeks and months, especially if the horse is stubborn and pigheaded!"

Liberty turned in my direction and gave me *the look*. The kind of look you give to someone when you think you might have just been insulted.

"Thankfully, I have a brilliant horse who can smell tyranny a mile away and who fights for freedom. In fact, this horse should be the mascot for the thirteen colonies! After all, his name is Liberty!" I said, proudly.

The performance seemed to work, as the three men slapped me on the back! "Good on ya! We'll see you later at the tavern. Only Patriots allowed."

"Sounds like a plan," I said, still nervous inside but trying to sound confident.

"Holy smokes!" I said, letting out a breath as they left.

"Go on, admit it, I came through for you, right?" Liberty teased. "I'm going to answer that for you. Liberty saves the day! Oh, and by the way, you didn't look nervous at all," he said with a heavy dose of sarcasm, "especially when that guy with a ponytail was about to put you in a headlock!" He laughed like it was the funniest thing he'd heard all week.

"Go ahead and laugh it up. The truth is, I was scared that they were going to use me as a punching bag!"

"I would never let that happen," Liberty said with a determined look. "You should always know that I've got your back, Rush Revere. Always! After all, we are best friends!"

I sighed with relief and smiled. "Thanks, Liberty," I said. "I owe you one, possibly even two."

"But you still want to know what's up with all the smoke? You know, we could just leave," Liberty prodded.

"Aren't you curious to know what's making all that smoke?" I asked.

"Not really," he said, sounding almost bored. "My nose only smells smoke, not food. Why start a fire if you're not going to cook something?"

Food was never far from Liberty's thoughts.

"Come on, let's continue our mission," I said.

We got close enough to see a bonfire blazing right in the middle of the street. We could hear the men shouting things like "Repeal the Stamp Act!" and "No more stamps!" Several members of the mob were throwing what looked like newspapers, books, and documents of all kinds. Even playing cards were being tossed in and consumed by the flames. And each item had a stamp on it.

"I know what this is," I said to Liberty. "The colonists are protesting the Stamp Act by throwing stamped documents onto the bonfire."

"I don't get it. What does the stamp have to do with anything?" asked Liberty.

"King George passed the Stamp Act without consulting the colonists. He basically decided that everyone in America who purchases anything made from paper should have to pay an extra charge for it—it's called a tax."

"No wonder they're ticked off. Didn't the colonists come to America to get away from the King's rule and be free from this kind of thing? It doesn't sound like the King really wants to let them go!" said Liberty.

Just then a voice shouted, "Redcoats! About two dozen with guns and bayonets are coming!"

I could see the glint of the bayonets. I could hear their boots against the pavement getting closer and closer. "Come on, Liberty! We better get out of here!"

I didn't have time to jump onto Liberty's saddle so I just sprinted as fast as I could. Liberty galloped ahead of me, looking back now and again to see if I was close behind.

"Now you want to run!? You could've listened to me when I said it was a bad idea to walk toward the fire, but nooooo," Liberty said.

Most of the mob dispersed from the scene as the fire was left unattended and burning in the street. We kept running until we were a safe distance away from the commotion. Finally, we slowed down to catch our breath.

As much as I wanted to stay to see what happened next, I knew it was time to hit the road, and fast! I said to Liberty, "Remind me to tell you more about the Stamp Act later."

"It's funny because whenever you say Stamp Act I think you're saying Stomp Act. You know, like stomping or clogging. Maybe I should put together a stomp act about the Stamp Act!"

"If you did I'm sure it would be something unforgettable! But first, let's get out of here before we run into British troops. Let's head over to that side street. I saw an alley earlier that should conceal us when we jump through the time portal."

I lifted myself up onto Liberty and we trotted over to the alley.

"Let's go!" I said as I gripped the horn on Liberty's saddle.

"Rush, rush, rushing from history," Liberty said as he started galloping toward the brick wall at the end of the alley. A swirling gold and purple hole started to open in front of the wall. Two more seconds and we jumped through the cosmic hole—our time portal to the twenty-first century. I was excited to get back to modern-day because tomorrow I had a very important appointment with the principal of Manchester Middle School!

Chapter 1

Hundreds of students wearing gold and black sweatshirts, hoodies, and jerseys swarmed the football stadium like honeybees in a hive. I guessed that the mascot of Manchester Middle School was a yellow jacket or hornet, but my suspicions were soon put to rest when I saw the actual mascot enter the field with a fluffy golden mane around a large catlike head. Obviously, Tommy, my favorite history student, played for the Manchester Lions. Whoever was inside the mascot costume was very acrobatic as the lion jumped up and did a perfect backflip. He or she stuck the landing and then pumped a large paw into the overcast sky as hundreds of students and families cheered with excitement.

I was glad to be back at Manchester Middle School and curious to know why the principal had asked to see me in his office after the game. You see, my horse and I had recently taught the Honors History class while the full-time teacher, Ms. Borrington, was on a leave of absence. I know what you're thinking. Did I just say I was teaching with a horse? Yes. Yes, I did. My horse, Liberty, is not just any horse. He's, well, special. He's sort of like the Lone Ranger's horse, Silver.

In fact, after I took Liberty to watch the Lone Ranger movie he said, "I should've tried out for the part of the Lone Ranger's horse, Silver. The part where Silver races across the top of those western buildings and then leaps onto that moving train was impressive. But that was clearly a stunt horse. Besides, if they had picked me I could've carried on an actual conversation with Tonto! Not to mention my superior good looks."

I didn't say he was humble, I said he was "special." Yes, Liberty can talk. Oh, and he can time-travel, too. What better way to teach history than actually going there. Jumping back in time is very cool!

I followed several students into the school stadium and started searching for Tommy. He had bright blond hair that was usually easy to spot. I was pretty sure he'd be at the game since he's the starting quarterback—a gifted athlete but a closet genius.

As I walked parallel to the sideline, looking up at the bleachers I heard a voice yell, "Mr. Revere, heads up!" I turned toward the green field and saw a distant player throw a football that was now spiraling directly toward me. The ball soared directly over a Lion who tried to intercept the ball but missed by just a few inches. Instinctively, my hands reached out and, surprisingly, I caught it. The Lion turned around and crouched in a defensive pose as if daring me to try to get past him. Then it motioned for me to come forward with its large mascot paws. I looked beyond the Lion at the player who threw the football. He waved and

I could see that he was smiling. Actually, he was laughing really hard! Wait a minute, that's Tommy!

Right then, I felt a hand pat me on the back. I turned and saw a familiar sweet face. "Freedom!" I said. She was another favorite student with some special gifts of her own. Her long, silky black hair had a purple feather clipped in it that complemented her tan skin and dark eyes. But it was her smile that was the most welcoming.

"Hi, Mr. Revere, it's great to see you again!" she said. "Looks like Tommy picked you!"

"What do you mean *picked me*?" I questioned.

"He picked you to challenge the Lion," she said, her smile even bigger than before. "It's a school tradition. Before every game the quarterback throws the football into the crowd. Typically, he picks someone who's walking along the sidelines. Whoever catches it gets to take on the Lion."

"And exactly what does *take on the Lion* mean?" I asked. By now it sounded like every person sitting in the bleachers was chanting *Run! Run! Run! Run!* Over and over, louder and louder, the crowd was clearly eager to see me in action, whatever that was. The Lion kept jumping up and down waving his large paws back and forth, encouraging the crowd to chant louder.

Freedom continued, "Oh, that means you have to try to get the ball past the Lion. If you do, then it's sort of considered a touchdown! It means good luck for our team if you score, and bad luck if the Lion sacks you."

"Sacks me?" I squeaked. "Here I thought I was only coming to the game to cheer on Tommy. Not be in the game."

"Oh, you can do it, Mr. Revere!" Freedom said, still smiling.

"Good luck!" She patted my shoulder and disappeared into the crowd.

"Come on! Run! Run! Run!" the crowd endlessly chanted.

Well, I decided it was time to show Manchester Middle School just what Rush Revere was made of. My Pilgrim hero William Bradford didn't doubt his goal of reaching the New World. He led the *Mayflower* ship from Europe to America, across the huge waves, water crashing on the deck of the boat. The Pilgrims learned to overcome their fear. They took every challenge head-on. They used their skills and their ingenuity to prosper and find success. If the Pilgrims could do that, I could figure out how to win this challenge and not be completely humiliated in front of the entire school!

I gripped the ball tighter against my side and started running. The crowd erupted with cheers as they saw me fearlessly take on the football feline. I moved a little to the left; the Lion moved with me. I moved a little to the right; the Lion adjusted again. When I was only five yards from my opponent I put the football behind my back and concealed it with both hands. It felt awkward running with a football behind my back, but it was all part of the plan. I slowed at four yards, a little slower at three yards. The Lion tilted his head, obviously confused as to why the ball was behind my back and why I was slowing. In that split second of confusion and with only two yards between us I bent forward ever so slightly and flipped the ball up and over my head. Before the Lion could react, the football soared above its shaggy head. I sprinted past the bewildered beast and turned to catch the ball as it drifted down. Pedaling backward, I reached out, caught the ball, and then landed on my backside. Immediately the crowd burst into cheers. Apparently, I had scored! I looked up and saw the Lion with his paws in front of its mascot face, shaking his head. Tommy ran up to me wearing his gold football helmet and said, "You did it! That was amazing! Nice job, Mr. Revere!"

"Whew!" I said as I stood up. "Thank you! A little positive thinking and hope for the best goes a long way!"

As Tommy and I walked to the sideline he said, "I'm really glad to see you! I kept hoping you'd come back to Manchester. Does this mean you're back to teach?"

"I'm not sure yet. Principal Sherman asked if I'd stop by after the game for a chat. He didn't say what it was about, but I knew I shouldn't miss it! I'm really glad he called or I wouldn't have known about the game. I was hoping you were playing today."

"I'm going to tell Principal Sherman that you have to come back!" Tommy said. "You're awesome! I mean you're the first substitute teacher that makes history remotely interesting or at all memorable!"

"I appreciate the compliment," I said, "but that might not be a good idea. If I remember correctly, Principal Sherman thinks you're always up to something. The troublemaker!" I smiled.

"That's a good point!" Tommy said with a laugh.

As we got to the sideline Tommy looked around and asked, "Hey, where's Liberty? I don't see him! Or smell him, for that matter!"

"No, Liberty has the day off," I said. "He's at a horse spa! A livery, remember?"

Tommy laughed. "That horse is so spoiled! A horse spa? As in massages and pedicures?"

"Ha, yes! That's what he calls it. He's actually just getting a bath but don't tell him that."

Freedom joined us from the bleachers. "Hi, Tommy," she said, seeming happy to see him. "Good job, Mr. Revere! I knew you would do it! You told us on the *Mayflower* not to doubt you and you were right!"

"Ha, I'm pretty sure I was talking about why the signing of the Mayflower Compact was a really important part of history, not about taking on the school mascot in front of a roaring crowd!" I said with a grin while brushing a grass stain off my knee.

Tommy chuckled and asked, "Hey, are you going to stay and watch the game?"

"Of course!" I said. "I sacrificed my body to get past your Lion and bring you good luck!" I winked at Freedom. "Speaking of good luck, that reminds me! Almost forgot!" I reached into my pocket and pulled out two musket balls given to me by Myles Standish, the military leader for the Pilgrims. "Do you remember when we all traveled back in time with Liberty to Plymouth Plantation in the year 1621?"

"How could we forget? That wasn't your average day at Manchester!" Freedom said.

"Quick pop quiz! Who was Myles Standish?" I asked.

Tommy laughed. "That's easy! He was the cool Pilgrim guy that taught me how to swordfight! He reminded me a lot of my friend's dad who was in the military and really strict. But Myles was still really nice. And he knew everything about fort building, which rocked!"

"Correct, Tommy, spot on! He was the military leader for the Pilgrims! Well, I brought something with me from Myles. I forgot I had them until Liberty and I got home." I held out my hand to show Tommy and Freedom the musket balls. They were as small as marbles but made of lead. They were round, smooth, and very shiny. "Myles told me that when the Indian Squanto stayed with the Pilgrims he taught them many things, like where to find the best striped bass, bluefish, and cod or how to catch eels or where to hunt for ducks and geese and deer."

"Wait! Did you say eels?" asked Tommy with his eyes wide.

"I did," I said, nodding. "Slimy, snakelike eels!"

"Awesome! I wish Squanto would've taught me how to hunt for eels!" said Tommy.

"You were probably busy swordfighting," Freedom teased. "Squanto taught me how to plant corn just like the Indians did back in the early, early, early colony days. And he gave me a special necklace."

I continued, "Let me finish my story. After coming back from fishing, Myles was gutting a big fish and inside he found these two musket balls."

"Really? The fish ate the lead balls? Wow, that fish must've been really hungry! I don't even think Liberty would eat lead balls!" said Tommy.

"Sure he would," I said, laughing, "if they were dipped in honey! Anyway, when Squanto heard the story he said that it was a sign of good fortune, a sign of good luck. He promised Myles that if he rubbed the musket balls between his fingers while making a wish, the good fortune from the balls would rub off and help him succeed in his next task!"

"And? Did it work?" Tommy asked with excitement.

I smiled and replied, "Myles rubbed the musket balls together each time he went hunting or fishing, and every time he had great success!"

"But that doesn't necessarily mean it was caused by—"

Freedom tried to say before I discreetly elbowed her in the shoulder as Tommy reached for the musket balls.

"I'm going to try it," Tommy said. He rubbed the balls between his fingers and said, "I want to have my best game today. No interceptions!" He handed me back the musket balls.

"Good luck, Tommy," I said.

"Yeah, good luck," said Freedom, smiling.

"Thanks, guys! Gotta go!" Tommy ran off toward his team.

Freedom and I headed back to the bleachers and found a place to sit. When the game ended, Tommy had completed four touchdown passes, a rushing touchdown, and zero interceptions! The Manchester Lions beat the Benedict Bulldogs 35–14. Call it luck or coincidence or whatever you like, but the fact is, Tommy had a super game! It's amazing what a positive mental attitude can do. Of course, a little bit of luck never hurts!

Soon thereafter, Freedom left with another friend and I decided to head over to the principal's office. As I was leaving the stadium I saw Tommy run over with his helmet off. His curly blond hair was matted to his head but his blue eyes were as lively as ever.

Tommy said, "Thanks for coming, Mr. Revere. It was great to see you. I think those musket balls must've worked! Tell Myles 'thanks' the next time you see him. By the way, have you gone back to see Plymouth Rock or visited your friend, William Bradford?"

"No, I haven't recently," I said. "I've really wanted to see how everything is progressing in the colonies, but I just haven't had the time."

"Are you working at the iced-tea company?" Tommy asked.

"Yes, and I've been helping a friend start a small business. I tell you, starting a business isn't easy! It takes a lot of long hours and hard work!" I said.

"Well, if you ever do time-jump to visit the first Pilgrims again, I want to go!" said Tommy. "I'd love to check in with all those guys, including Squanto! In fact, I made the coolest fort in my backyard with my new buddy, Cam. He just moved here from Colorado. I told him that I learned fort building from Myles Standish."

"And what did Cam say?" I asked curiously.

"He thought I was totally full of it! He said, 'Yeah right, and I bet you learned how to skateboard from Tony Hawk!'" Tommy said, imitating Cam.

"Do you blame him?" I asked, smiling. "Does Cam go to school here?"

"He just started. I'm trying to get him to try out for the football team. Hey, maybe you can get him into our Honors History class!" Tommy said.

I looked at my watch and realized I needed to hurry or I'd be late for my appointment with the principal.

"Well, it's great to see you, Tommy! You were a star out there today! I better get going and see what Principal Sherman wants."

"C'mon, Tommy!" yelled one of Tommy's teammates. Tommy waved goodbye to me and ran off while I headed into the school.

Although it was late in the day, there were still several students in the hallways. I saw Principal Sherman speaking to a couple of students near his office. I'd forgotten how he towered over everyone else. I'll admit that he made me a little intimidated. As I approached, the principal excused the students he was talking to and said, "Hello, Mr. Revere, thank you for taking the time to meet with me."

88

Principal Sherman was all business and got right to the point. He said, "Mrs. Borrington is going on vacation to the Caribbean to celebrate her wedding anniversary. Therefore, Manchester Middle School would like to invite you back to teach her class in the interim. We are low on substitute teachers and most of the kids seem to like your style."

"Thank you," I said. "History is my specialty and I think the students are wonderful."

"I say 'most of the kids' because there is one student that doesn't like you much."

"Oh, that's too bad," I said. Even though I was sure the disgruntled student was the principal's diva daughter, I asked, "What's the student's name?"

"Well, it's actually my daughter, Elizabeth. She strongly encouraged me to not have you return. However, I interviewed several other students who are enrolled in Honors History and they vouched for you as a competent teacher."

"I'm encouraged that the students feel this way and I'm happy to return to teach Honors History," I said. "And I do apologize that Elizabeth did not have the same experience that the other students shared. She's more than welcome to attend my class, if she would like to try it again." I decided it probably wasn't the best time to tell him that his daughter can be a bit of a brat!

"I'll see you tomorrow then, bright and early," said Principal Sherman as he excused himself.

I was excited about the chance to teach again. My first lesson covered the journey of the *Mayflower* from Europe to the New World! Personally, this had always been a favorite part of American history for me. It always amazed me that a group of 101 people would decide to set sail across the wide, scary ocean without really knowing where they were headed! It's not like they had an airline ticket and knew which airport they were landing at with a welcoming committee! They set out to find a new land of true freedom, where they could be themselves and improve their lives. I'm sure they couldn't have done it without strong leaders, like William Bradford, who rallied them together just when the journey was looking to be a lost cause! My mother used to do that on long car rides. Every time my brother and I thought we were going to go crazy waiting to stop for McDonald's, she would say, "Rusty, remember, it's mind over matter! Just think how much better that Happy Meal is going to taste knowing you went through long hours of pain and suffering to get it!" I always knew she was exaggerating! We weren't really suffering in the back of the car. The Pilgrims, however—they really struggled. They spent sixty-five brutal days with little food, cramped into a very tight space, in terribly hard conditions, with waves crashing all around them in the dark of night. I get a little seasick just thinking about it. Just like my mom, William Bradford encouraged the Pilgrims to keep their faith and trust that God would help them survive and prosper. When they finally landed in the New World, sadly many of the Pilgrims died that first winter due to the freezing temperatures, starvation, and disease. But William Bradford held their heads high, reminding them that they had set out on the journey to build a better life in a new place and that is exactly what they did!

William knew that the best way for each of the Pilgrim families to prosper in their new way of life was for each family to have a plot of land where they could build a home and work for themselves. Instead of putting all of their goods into a communal chest, William Bradford encouraged the Pilgrims to be on the same team, yet work hard to take care of their own families. He knew they would try their hardest if they knew they could keep the rewards of their hard work and labor. It's a lesson I've always tried to teach my own students. What if they all studied really hard for a test but no matter how hard they worked they would all get the same B grade as everyone else? Why would they ever try for an A?

Under William Bradford's leadership the Pilgrims quickly prospered. They befriended and traded with the Native Americans. Soon after, other ships like the *Mayflower* came to America after hearing the success that the Pilgrims were having. In only twenty years, that first colony, known as Plymouth Plantation, grew from fifty people to two thousand people, with new colonies being built throughout New England. Of course, this was just the beginning—the beginning of America's independence from England.

As I walked down the hall, my mind raced thinking about what the next lesson should be! It can't be boring, I thought. Why not just pick up where I left off? Absorbed in my own thinking about exceptional Americans like Benjamin Franklin and Patrick Henry, I was surprised to hear someone say, "Mr. Revere?"

I didn't recognize the voice at first until I looked down the hall and saw the principal's daughter, Elizabeth, in a purple pleated skirt and a pristine white blouse with her hands on her hips. Her long blond hair had been expertly curled and there was a purple headband perfectly placed on the top of her head. She looked surprised to see me and said, "I thought my dad said you weren't coming back? Ugh. I guess this means you're teaching Honors History again."

"Oh, hello, Elizabeth, great to see you," I said in the most positive way I could.

"Don't you have some horse stalls to clean or something? I mean, really!" she said in a feisty tone.

I ignored her insult and while smiling I said, "As a matter of fact, I'm all done cleaning today and was just thinking about my next history lesson. And I do hope you'll choose to be in my class!" Win them over with kindness, I always say! I was determined that this little diva was not going to get the best of me.

Elizabeth huffed and said, "I see you still have your outfit on. You do know it's not Halloween, right? That's not until October, the month *after* September."

I forced a smile on my face and nearly had to bite my tongue so I wouldn't say something I would regret.

She continued her insults and said, "Seriously, the 1700s called and they want their clothes back! In fact, why just send the clothes? You should seriously consider getting a one-way ticket."

Ever so charming, I thought. I took a deep breath and said. "Yes, Paul Revere is still my hero and I must say I like this colonial jacket a lot. I know you don't like me much, but I'd like to propose a peace treaty. Similar to what the Pilgrims proposed with Massasoit and the Pokanoket Indians when they first arrived in the colonies of the New World. What do you say?" I asked.

"I say you are ultra-weird, but whatever floats your boat. I'll be in your class but on my own terms. And don't think for a second that you've fooled me. You may have stumped my father, but I know you're up to something. I'll find out what it is," she said as firmly as ever.

Populations in towns in the American colonies were growing extremely quickly, as in Lexington, seen here.

"Well, great, that's a start!" I said. I wanted to roll my eyes and tell her she was extremely irritating, but I knew that wouldn't be the best approach. Patience, Revere, patience, I thought.

After saying goodbye to the little darling, I walked down the hall and back toward the football field. That's when I felt my phone buzz. It was a text from Tommy. It said, "So? R u coming back?"

I texted, "Yes, teaching tomorrow!!!! Get ready to meet Ben Franklin!"

Tommy texted, "No way! Sounds amazing! TTWL!"

I texted, "TTWL? You mean, TTYL? Talk to you later?" thinking I was very hip.

Tommy responded, "Nope, I mean TTWL. Time travel with Liberty!!!!!"

I smiled. Yes, I thought. We would definitely need Liberty. It was time to pick him up from the livery. I had better go get him some apples, I thought. The best way to win Liberty over is always through his stomach.

Chapter 2

The sky darkened above Manchester Middle School as gusts of wind sent oak leaves cartwheeling over the grass. From inside the classroom I peered through the windows at thick, ominous clouds that seemed to be waiting for just the right moment to douse the school with buckets of water. The Honors History class was the last period of the day and I wondered if Liberty and I would have to travel home in a torrential downpour.

Liberty watched the swirling clouds and said, "Those look like thunderstorm clouds—cumulonimbus to be exact!"

"I'm impressed you know the meteorologist term for this kind of cloud," I said.

Liberty still watched the skies and replied, "After my incident with the lightning I make it a point to know as much as I can about the weather. In particular, how to avoid lightning strikes."

"Maybe it's your electrifying personality that attracts the lightning," I said, smiling.

Liberty turned to me and said with a smirk, "Well, there's not much I can do about that. Some of us are born with an extra dose of charm and charisma."

The school bell rang, which meant that the students would begin arriving in the next few minutes.

"Do you think Elizabeth will return?" Liberty asked.

"I think so. Something tells me she likes keeping me on my toes! She's a handful that one," I said as I double-checked the projector and made sure it was ready to transmit any video footage from my smartphone.

"That's a nice way of putting it. You do remember she tried to fire you as a substitute teacher by catching you with a horse in your classroom? A talking horse!" Liberty winked.

"Yes, but I know the kind of game she's playing," I said. "Elizabeth considers this her school, her territory. My intent wasn't to challenge her authority or remove her from power. Yet she feels threatened by my presence. I imagine it's similar to how the Native Americans felt when the Pilgrims started arriving in the New World. William Bradford befriended the Indians and created peace. It worked for him so I'm going to try to do the same."

I could see that Liberty was thinking about what I had just said and then he replied, "I think some people don't want peace. Instead, they want control. They want people to obey without question. They want to rule with an iron fist. You of all people know that history is full of leaders who were intolerant of others when they tried to stand up for freedom."

"Indeed," I said. "But I consider myself a peacemaker. I'm going to reach out to Elizabeth with peace in mind. The kind of peace that can only come when people or, in this case, students are treated with respect and fairness."

"Well, good luck with that, Mr. Positive!" Liberty said with a grin.

"Wait, that's exactly what we should go over in today's history lesson," I beamed. "By the way, you better disappear for now. After class starts we're going to meet outside for a little scavenger hunt."

"Ooooh, like hunting for Easter eggs?" Liberty said. "I love finding the plastic eggs filled with jelly beans. They are yummy-licious."

"Yes, just like that except we're not hunting for chocolate or eggs. I hid some other cool things outside of the classroom earlier this morning. Kind of a show-and-tell game!" I said.

"Alrighty, I'll meet you outside. But I warn you, the first sound of thunder or the first sight of lightning and I'll be inside faster than you can spell *cumulonimbus*."

"Spell it? I can't even say it!" I said.

"I can," said Tommy, who was the first student to slip into the classroom. He continued, "Cumulonimbus, spelled c-u-m-u-l-o-n-i-m-b-u-s."

"Liberty," I said, "quickly, dematerialize!"

"Oh, that's a good one! D-e-m-a-t- . . ."

"No!" I interrupted, "this isn't a spelling bee. You need to vanish, disappear, dematerialize now! Principal Sherman could come into the classroom at any second!"

"Oh, got it, Captain! See you outside!" Liberty inhaled deeply and disappeared. As long as he held his breath he was invisible.

Tommy laughed and said, "It's hilarious that he calls you *captain*!"

"Yeah, he thinks he's quite amusing," I said.

Tommy walked over to his desk as I walked to the front of the class. Although I had only taught this Honors History class for two days a few weeks ago, I felt completely at home as if I had been there for years. Freedom walked in and went right to her desk at the back of the class. Just before the bell rang, Principal Sherman entered the room followed by a tall and thin African-American boy with a backpack over his shoulder.

"Hey, Cam!" I heard Tommy say as he waved his hand and smiled.

Cam gave Tommy a simple nod and grinned. They seemed to have that best-friend kind of connection where they know what the other is saying with one look. Cam wore a black button-down long sleeve shirt. He wore a dark leather wristband that almost blended in against his dark skin. He appeared at first glance to be a happy kid and he had this look in his eyes, like he knew more than he was telling.

Principal Sherman spoke: "Allow me to make a quick introduction. This is Cameron. His family just moved here."

"My mom calls me Cameron, but I like to go by Cam," he said.

"I like to call students by their formal names," said Principal Sherman. "Cameron, this is Mr. Revere. He's teaching temporarily until Mrs. Borrington returns. Cameron tells me that history is one of his favorite subjects so I'm sure the two of you will get along splendidly. Now, if you'll excuse me I must get back to my office for another appointment." True to his word, the principal lumbered toward the door and exited.

I noticed all eyes in the classroom were on Cam. I turned to him and said, "Welcome, Cam. Before you take your seat, perhaps you could tell us something about yourself." He looked at me as if to say my clothing was a bit outdated. I noticed he paid particular attention to my boots. Ah, yes, my boots. Very comfortable, I must say.

"Um, okay, sure," Cam said, turning his attention toward the class. He had the kind of smile that felt contagious and lit up the entire room. "Like the principal said, my family just moved here from Colorado. I like to play sports, video games, and build forts with my new neighbor, Tommy." He gave Tommy a nod. He clearly wasn't shy!

"Thank you, Cam," I said. "Welcome to the class. Does anyone have any questions for Cam?"

A girl with curly brown hair asked, "Do you play football for the Lions?"

"No," said Cam, "but I went to the game yesterday and saw Mr. Revere juke out our mascot!"

The class applauded with whooping and hollering.

I raised my hands to quiet the class and said, "Thank you, but I was lucky. If there are no other questions then we'll—"

Suddenly, Tommy raised his hand as if reaching for the ceiling. He looked frantic like he had to go to the bathroom. I responded, "This looks urgent, Tommy. You have a question for Cam or are you going to tell us you have ants in your pants?"

The class laughed and Tommy said, "Touché, Mr. Revere. Nice one. But I wondered if Cam was going to tell us about his fake eye?"

"Tommy," I chastened, "this is hardly the place. Cam, I apologize for—"

"Oh, it's okay," said Cam. "It's no big deal. I pop it out and show people all the time."

Cam brought his cupped hand up to his eye as he dropped his

chin to his chest. He covered his right eye and gently squeezed his eye socket. When he pulled back his hand, his right eye was closed and sure enough, an eyeball sat in the palm of his hand. The only sound came from the wind outside as the students stared in silence.

"Putting it back in is the hard part," he said as he gathered the eyeball between his fingers. "Sometimes it gets slippery and . . . oops!" The eyeball slipped from his fingers and landed on the desk closest to him. As it bounced and rolled across the desk-top, the girl sitting at the desk screamed like someone had just dropped a hundred snakes on her lap. In fact, the entire class sounded like they were screaming and gasping and grossing out as the eyeball rolled off the desk, bounced off the floor, and started rolling across the room as feet quickly jumped up and out of the way.

That's when I noticed Cam grinning and Tommy laughing hysterically. In fact, Cam had both eyes open with eyeballs in both sockets. I folded my arms and gave Tommy *the look*. However, it was difficult to keep a serious face. When Tommy saw me he quickly jumped out of his seat, ran toward the eyeball, and scooped it up. More gasps and more "ewwwwwws" as he casually put the eyeball in his pocket and returned to his seat.

When the class finally calmed down, Cam said, "I'm sorry, Mr. Revere. Tommy said you liked practical jokes and promised me you'd be okay with it."

I couldn't help but smile and said, "I think this deserves a round of applause." I started to clap and the students joined me.

"Bravo, Tommy and Cam, for a very convincing performance."

Tommy was still giggling, which made Cam start to laugh

again. Then Cam said, "It's a classic prank, the ol' *introduce the new guy with the fake eye*."

Trying desperately not to laugh, Tommy said, "The look . . . on your faces . . . was priceless."

"You know what they say, Tommy. What goes around comes around," I said.

"Yeah, especially a rubber eyeball from the dollar store," Tommy said as he covered his mouth and burst out laughing again.

I'll admit that the laughter and innocent prank put me in a good mood. "All right," I said, still smiling. "Cam, why don't you take that seat in the middle." I pointed to Elizabeth's empty desk. "We may need to shuffle the seating chart later but for now I think we're good."

Cam walked over and settled into his new seat.

"Today we're going to go on a little history scavenger hunt," I said. "I know that it's a little windy outside but it hasn't started raining yet so let's quickly see if we can do this. Let's all walk outside near the back of the school."

After a minute or two we were all outside. It was barely windy and I wondered if this was the calm before the storm.

As I asked for everyone's attention, I saw Liberty suddenly appear behind the students. I continued, "Of course, our class wouldn't be the same without Liberty!" I reached out my hand in Liberty's direction. The class turned around and immediately smothered Liberty with praise and affection. Dozens of hands petted his sides, nose, and mane as they commented how much they missed him. Liberty just stood there like he was taking a long, hot shower.

"That's Mr. Revere's horse," I heard Tommy tell Cam.

Rush Revere's Honors History Class
DEMATERIALIZE
M
MANCHESTER
MIDDLE SCHOOL

"Sometimes Mr. Revere will sneak him into the classroom. It's a secret so don't tell anyone."

I looked up at the sky and said, "We probably don't have much time. I've hidden six different objects around the schoolyard. Each has a bright yellow ribbon tied to it. I'll give you five minutes to search for them and bring them back to me. Ready, set, go!"

"I see one," said a boy from somewhere in the back.

Instantly, all twenty-five students took off running in different directions. The wind had picked up a little but nothing out of the ordinary. Within minutes the students returned.

"Wonderful," I said. "All of the objects have someone in common. Let's see what you've found. Tommy, I believe you returned first. Show us what you have."

Tommy awkwardly stepped forward while wearing a pair of black swimming fins. He waddled like a large penguin.

"Can you tell the class who invented flippers?" I asked.

"Uhhhh, Aquaman?" he said.

The class laughed.

"Strike one," I said.

"Captain Nemo?" he tried again.

More laughter.

"Strike two," I grinned.

Tommy's eyebrows went up and his eyes went wide as he said, "Ohhhhh, I remember now. It's SpongeBob SquarePants!"

Tommy high-fived several of the students near him, including Cam, as the rest of the class laughed.

"You're in fine form today, Tommy," I said with a smile. "However, three strikes and you're out. Who has the next object?"

Freedom stepped forward as Tommy waddled back to the

other students. She said, "I found this old book." She held it up so the other students could see. She sounded a little confused and read the cover, "It says *Gulliver's Travels* by Jonathan Swift."

"Thank you, Freedom," I said. "The book you're holding is a classic. The person who invented the flippers also loved to read and was very smart. Most assuredly, he read *Gulliver's Travels*. In fact, when this book was first published in 1726 the person I'm thinking of was only twenty years old."

"Seventeen twenty-six? Whoa, that's a long time ago!" one boy said.

"So this mystery person was born in 1706?" said Tommy. "That's like eighty-six years from the time the *Mayflower* arrived and the Pilgrims landed at Plymouth Rock."

"Correct," I said.

Several students turned to Tommy and looked surprised by his quick calculation.

"What?" Tommy asked innocently. "It was a lucky guess."

"What else did you find?" I asked.

Cam stepped forward and said, "I found this newspaper. The crazy thing about it is that it's the *Pennsylvania Gazette*, printed in 1732. How did you find a newspaper this old, Mr. Revere?"

"Oh, I have a friend that has a way of getting old things," I said, winking at Liberty. "The person I'm thinking of was also a printer. In fact, his newspaper, the *Pennsylvania Gazette*, was the most successful newspaper in the colonies. Does anyone want to guess the man I'm thinking of?"

Nobody raised their hand.

"Very well, there are three more items. Let's see them all."

Three students came forward, with a piece of wood, a kite, and reading glasses. I briefly described each one. "I'm sure you're wondering what a piece of wood has to do with the history mystery man. Well, in 1742 this man invented a new kind of stove. It was a metal-lined fireplace that stood in the middle of a room. It provided more heat and less smoke than an open fireplace and used less wood. This stove was made from cast iron and would radiate heat from the middle of the room in all directions. This stove was a very popular way to warm your home if you lived in colonial America. In fact, it's still used today."

"What about these crazy-lookin' glasses?" asked a boy who was wearing them and trying to see through the upper and lower lenses.

"Those reading glasses are called bifocals. The man I'm thinking of created them in 1784. The upper half of the glass lens was for distance and the lower half of the lens was for reading."

"My grandma has a pair of those," said Tommy.

"Yeah, right," said Cam, sarcastically. "You know you have a pair, don't lie."

Cam and Tommy joked around as they playfully slugged each other in the arms.

I continued, "Yes, they're still popular even today," I said.

"Did this guy also invent the kite?" asked a girl who held up the red and white diamond-shaped kite with a long blue tail.

"No," I said. "But this person in history used the kite to experiment with electricity. That's a pretty big clue of who I'm thinking of."

"Benjamin Franklin!" said Tommy.

"Bingo!" I said.

"Isn't his face on the one-dollar bill?" asked a redheaded girl.

"Actually, he's on the one-hundred-dollar bill," I corrected.

Benjamin Franklin

"Did you hide one of those somewhere in the schoolyard, too?" asked Tommy.

"I'm a teacher, not a banker," I said with a laugh. "But Tommy is right about Benjamin Franklin. He is the mystery man of history that invented the swimming fins, owned a printing press, and created the Franklin stove. He loved reading so much he established a library. And in 1753 his experiments with electricity enabled him to create a device that could protect homes and buildings from the destructive force of lightning bolts."

"The lightning rod!" shouted Liberty.

He'd been so quiet, I'd almost forgotten that Liberty was with us.

"A very useful device," Liberty explained. "A lightning rod is an iron rod attached to the top of a house or building and connected to a wire that is attached to another rod that's in the ground. Since lightning is typically attracted to the highest point of a building, the electric charge from a lightning bolt will strike the rod and the charge is conducted harmlessly into the ground. I remember now that our large barn back home had one at either end of the roof."

That's when I noticed Cam staring at Liberty with his jaw open.

"Am I seeing things or did that horse just talk?" he mumbled.

Tommy, who was standing beside Cam, said, "Oh, that's right. I should've warned you about that. He's a talking horse."

Cam slugged Tommy in the arm again and laughed, "Whatever! Where I come from the horses don't talk! Nice practical joke!"

Cam was smiling and Tommy looked at me and shrugged like he wasn't sure what to say next.

One of Ben Franklin's most famous inventions—bifocal glasses.

Benjamin Franklin on the front of the U.S. $100 bill.

As a boy in Boston, Benjamin Franklin made a pair of swim fins. In comparison to modern-day swim fins, his version was shaped more like an artist's palette.

"Seriously," Cam continued, "that looked like he was actually talking. That's got to be the best prank ever."

Just then the sky lit up and within a few seconds the sound of thunder made all of us jump. Liberty stepped back and yelled, "I'm out of here!" He bolted away from us and out of sight as he rounded the corner of the school.

"Everyone, please head inside. We don't have much time before the bell rings and class is over. So let's meet back at the classroom and finish up today's lesson."

As we headed back inside, random raindrops started to fall from the sky and by the time we were back inside the classroom the drops had turned to a heavy shower.

The six Franklin objects were placed on the teacher's desk and once everyone had settled in their seats again I said, "We only talked about some of the inventions and discoveries that came from Benjamin Franklin. There were many others. But it's clear that he was devoted to improving life. He was a successful businessman, inventor, scientist, and politician. Why do you think he was so successful?"

"Because he tried new things?" said a boy in the front row.

"True, I'm sure that had something to do with it. Anyone else?" I asked.

"Because he had a wild imagination," said a girl with short hair and freckles.

"Yes, it would certainly take a big imagination to do some of the things he did."

I noticed Freedom raised her hand and I eagerly called on her. She said, "It sounds like he was a hard worker and kept really busy. He wasn't afraid to try new things. And I bet he didn't spend all of his free time playing video games."

I replied, "True! Video games, movies, iPads, smartphones, or any of the electronic things that we spend time with today didn't exist when Benjamin Franklin was alive. Think about how much time kids today spend playing video games or watching TV. Now, these aren't bad things to do but if you used that same amount of time instead to think like Benjamin Franklin, what might you be able to do? What could you create or invent? Your ideas might very well change the world!"

"What's up with Freedom knockin' our video games!" Cam whispered to Tommy. Tommy and Cam fist-bumped and then Cam raised his hand and asked, "That's cool how he invented all that stuff, but wasn't Benjamin Franklin one of the Founding Fathers of America? Didn't he spend a lot of time defending the rights of the colonies?"

"You're absolutely right, Cam," I said. I had forgotten that Cam's favorite subject was history. "In fact, right after Benjamin Franklin invented the lightning rod you could say he was *struck* with an idea to unite the colonies.

"You mean, he had a brain-*storm*?" Tommy said, smiling and reaching out to Cam for another fist bump.

A flash of lightning followed immediately by a loud crack of thunder overhead made everyone jump in their seats. I could hear the heavy rain on the roof of the school.

I brought my attention back to the students and said, "Yes, Tommy, Franklin had a brainstorm. Like I said earlier, Franklin was a smart man. He was a genius. He was passionate about freedom and ready to defend America with his wit and wisdom! And it was the Stamp Act of 1765 that convinced him that it was time to tell England what he really thought."

"What's the Stamp Act?" asked a girl in the front row.

"I'm glad you asked," I said. "Tomorrow, Liberty is going to introduce us to the Stamp Act with a special musical presentation, something you will not want to miss!"

"You mean, Liberty, your horse?" asked Cam.

"Yes. Liberty's a very talented horse. I don't want to give anything away. Just be sure to come tomorrow and you'll be in for a special treat."

Just then, the school bell rang and the students started gathering their backpacks and exiting the room. Freedom, however, came to the front of the classroom. She looked rather panicked and whispered, "Mr. Revere, we have a situation."

"Oh?" I asked. "What seems to be the problem?"

"It's Liberty," she said. "Right after that loud thunderclap I reached out to him with my mind. I sensed he was scared. That lightning and thunder felt like it was right on top of us. Anyway, he's in the teachers' lounge waiting for us."

"That's quite the gift you have, Freedom," I said. "Very convenient. And I wasn't aware that your telepathic ability to speak to animals could reach beyond just a few yards."

"Well, usually, it can't," she said. "But I've grown a strong connection with Liberty so it's easier. In fact, he's learning to speak to my mind as well."

"Well, thank you for telling me," I said sincerely.

Freedom still looked extremely worried as she glanced over her shoulder waiting for the final students to exit the classroom.

"Is there something else you needed to tell me?" I asked, almost afraid to hear what she had to say.

Freedom opened her mouth like she was about to say something but didn't know how to say it.

Benjamin Franklin in his printing shop.

"Just spit it out, Freedom," I said, encouraging her. "It's about Liberty, isn't it?"

She silently nodded. "He's not alone in the teachers' lounge. He's with, um, he's with Benjamin Franklin."

"Excuse me?" I asked, clearly not hearing her correctly.

"Liberty's not sure how it happened," Freedom exclaimed. "One minute he was hiding in the teacher's lounge, hoping there wouldn't be any more lightning. He said that all he could think about was Benjamin Franklin and his invention of the lightning rod. He concentrated really hard and thought that if Ben Franklin were here we'd all be safe. And that's when the lightning flashed right over the school and the next second, BOOM! Benjamin Franklin appeared out of nowhere!"

I stood there staring at Freedom like she was a ghost.

"Mr. Revere," Freedom asked softly. "Did you hear what I said?"

I snapped out of my trance and took a deep breath. I exhaled and asked, "Liberty told you all of this?"

"Yeah, I mean telepathically he did," she said. "And he's really scared that you're going to be mad at him."

"Tell him I'm not mad," I said. Was I stunned? Of course. Worried? Yes. Feeling like the course of world history may have just been altered? Absolutely. "And tell him we're coming to help." I took out my phone and texted Tommy: "Need your help. TTWL. Meet in teachers' lounge ASAP."

May 9, 1754. NUMB. 1324.

The PENNSYLVANIA  GAZETTE.

Containing the Freshest Advices, Foreign and Domestick.

A copy of Franklin's *Pennsylvania Gazette*, May 9, 1754. His newspaper was the most successful in the colonies.

Chapter 3

Freedom and I raced down the hallway to the teachers' lounge. I could still hear the rain coming down outside but thankfully the lightning and thunder had ceased.

When we stopped in front of the door Freedom said, "I better wait out here and keep guard."

"Good idea," I replied. I quickly slipped inside the teachers' lounge. Sure enough, Liberty was standing over a man dressed in colonial clothing who was awkwardly lying on a long orange couch.

"Are you sure you're not angry?" Liberty asked timidly.

"I assure you I'm not mad," I said, forcing a smile. I walked closer to get a better look. The middle-aged man appeared to be unconscious but his face looked surprisingly peaceful. "Whoever this is, he's a dead ringer for Benjamin Franklin," I said.

"You mean he's dead?" Liberty shouted, sounding panicked.

"Who's dead?" Tommy said as he walked into the room. "What the . . . who's that?"

The door opened again and Freedom peeked inside. "You should try and keep it down . . . Wow! So it really is Benjamin Franklin!" She slipped in all the way and put her back to the door.

"Benjamin Franklin!" Tommy exclaimed. "You killed Benjamin Franklin?"

"He's dead?" Freedom panicked.

"Yes! I mean no. I mean I don't know, it all happened so fast!" Liberty whimpered. "I'm going to prison for killing Franklin, aren't I!"

I kneeled down to feel the man's pulse. "He's not dead. But how did he get like this?"

"Like—I told—Freedom," Liberty tried to explain through gasps of anguish and despair. "The lightning flashed, the thunder boomed, and then Mr. Franklin appeared out of nowhere. I think I wished him here."

"Sort of like how you can stop time when you concentrate hard enough," Freedom explained.

"The shock of traveling through time must've been too much for him and he passed out," Tommy said.

"I was close enough to push him onto the couch. He almost collapsed onto the floor. That must count for something, right?" Liberty said pleadingly.

For the first time I looked closely at the face of the supposed Benjamin Franklin. He had wrinkles in his broad forehead and under his eyes. He had a large head and the little hair he had was blond but graying. His leather shoes, cream stockings, and sea-green breeches and coat were clean but somewhat plain. For the first time the realization that I was kneeling above the legendary Benjamin Franklin hit me like a ton of bricks.

"What's in his hand?" Tommy asked.

In his left hand were several pieces of parchment with cursive writing on them. I quickly browsed the pages and after reading several sentences a sense of panic overcame me. "Oh my," I gasped.

"What's wrong?" Freedom asked.

"This appears to be notes for a speech. If I'm correct, we may have just snatched away Benjamin Franklin before he could persuade the English government to repeal the Stamp Act."

"And that's a bad thing, right?" Liberty worried.

"I don't know yet," I said. "What I do know is that we have to get him back to the past immediately. Lucky for us it doesn't appear that he's completely aware of what's happened. Let's try to get Mr. Franklin onto Liberty's saddle. Liberty, move over here so it's easier for us to hoist him up."

As Liberty moved his large equine body, someone tried to enter the teacher's lounge. The door pushed open only a few inches and Freedom pushed back to close it. "Hey! Open the door," Elizabeth yelled. "I saw Freedom go in there and I've been listening to your conversation. Let me in!"

Liberty backed up to the door and helped Freedom keep it shut.

"What do we do?" Freedom whispered.

"We stick with our plan," I softly said. "Tommy, Freedom, on the count of three we lift Mr. Franklin onto the saddle. Liberty, keep that door shut."

"That I can do!" Liberty said firmly.

"Hey! I said open the door! I can wait out here all day if I have to," Elizabeth threatened. "I know I heard Mr. Revere and his circus horse. And I'm pretty sure I heard Tommy's voice, too. And from the sound of it some dead guy named Franklin. So I'm going to give you thirty seconds to open the door. After that, I'm bringing my dad and you know how big he is. He'll have this door open in no time!"

As Elizabeth finished speaking we adjusted Franklin's body onto the saddle and I slipped on behind him.

"I'll try and be back in a flash," I said.

"We can't let Elizabeth catch us in here," Tommy said.

"Um, she already has," Freedom whispered matter-of-factly.

"No, she hasn't," Tommy replied. "Technically, she only saw you come in."

"She said she heard our voices," Freedom said.

"Well, when she only finds you in here she'll think again," Tommy said, smiling.

"So you're leaving me here?" Freedom whispered with wide eyes.

"It'll be worse if Elizabeth finds all of us together," Tommy pointed out. "If she just finds you, well, just tell her you were sleepwalking and ended up in the teachers' lounge."

"Sleepwalking?" Freedom shook her head. "That's a lame excuse."

"You'll think of something," Tommy said.

Freedom sighed, "Fine, just go. I'll figure it out."

"Do we have enough room to time-jump in this small room?" Tommy asked.

I hesitated and said, "Well, we've never tried it with this much space but—"

"I can do it," Liberty interrupted. "I'll do anything to get us out of this mess."

I turned to Tommy and said, "You'll need to jump right behind us. We're headed to England, 1765!"

Tommy raised his eyebrows and said with a smile, "Cool."

"Let's go, Liberty," I said.

In his loudest whisper, Liberty said, *"Rush, rush, rushing to history!"*

Like before, the circular portal of swirling purple and gold instantly began to open. I held tightly to Liberty's saddle and Benjamin Franklin and said, "London, England, 1765, let's return Benjamin Franklin to the Palace of Westminster." With a hop, skip, and a jump Liberty bolted up and through our door to the past.

As we landed the jolt caused Benjamin Franklin to stir. Groggily, he began to come to.

"Quickly," I said, "help me get him to the ground."

With Tommy's help we lowered him to a freshly cut lawn. Immediately, I noticed a heavy fog that surrounded us. I couldn't see much but I could hear the distant sound of horses. Yes, in fact I could see a faint outline of two horses pulling a carriage. Large trees bordered a nearby dirt road that disappeared into a fog bank.

"Who are you?" Benjamin asked as he looked up at me from the grass.

"Let me help you up, Mr. Franklin," I said with eagerness. I grabbed Ben's hand and pulled him to his feet.

He stood, brushed himself off, and said, "I'm afraid I'm a bit disoriented. I was riding in a carriage and on my way to give a

speech to Parliament and then . . ." He paused. "Let me think, oh yes, there was a brilliant white light and for a second I remember staring at . . . at a horse." He turned his head and stared at Liberty. He pointed, "That horse!"

I tried to divert his attention and loudly exclaimed, "Benjamin Franklin! You really are Benjamin Franklin! It's a great honor, sir. You're a legend. An American hero. And we're standing here! With you! Right now! Talking. With you." He was a very big deal back then. It's sort of like running into the president! Not exactly, but a big deal.

"I don't think we've met, sir," said Benjamin. "You seem to know my name and though I'm flattered by your compliments I'm afraid I've much more to accomplish in my life to ever be called any of the things you've mentioned. So, tell me, what is your name? And who is this fine young man with you?"

I was giddy at the sight of one of the Founding Fathers of the United States of America. He was shorter than I was, probably about five feet nine or ten inches, but he was larger than life! Standing right in front of me! He put me at ease as he smiled and waited for my response.

When I continued staring, Tommy grabbed my arm and shook it a little, "Mr. Revere? This is the part where you introduce yourself."

I snapped out of my momentary dream and then realized it wasn't a dream. Benjamin Franklin was actually speaking to me. I took a deep breath and said, "Yes, of course, I'm Rush Revere, history teacher and fellow American."

"Ah, yes," said Benjamin. "I thought you might be from the thirteen colonies as your accent sounds a little non-British."

Franklin as chief of the Union Fire Company of Philadelphia—
the first volunteer fire department in Philadelphia.

"Oh, yes," I said, laughing, still feeling a little lightheaded. "I'm from the United States of America."

"Pardon me, the united what?" asked Benjamin.

Tommy whispered, "Mr. Revere, the United States hasn't been invented yet, remember?"

"What an interesting thought," Benjamin said. "I'll have to try and remember that."

I composed myself and said, "It truly is a great honor to meet you. I apologize for sounding like a bumbling idiot." I turned to Tommy and said, "This is one of my students, Tommy."

Liberty cleared his throat for attention and sidestepped close.

"Oh, and, of course, this is Liberty," I said with a little bit of apprehension. I was worried that Liberty's enthusiasm to meet any historical figure, especially one from his own century, might cause him to forget our secret that he was a talking horse. And just like I suspected, he forgot.

"It's a great honor, Mr. Franklin, I'm just glad you're not dead," said Liberty with great enthusiasm.

"Fascinating," said Benjamin as he began to closely examine Liberty like he was an exhibit at the Museum of Natural History. "Absolutely fascinating!"

"Oh, yes," Liberty continued. "You can't begin to know the relief I felt when I found out you were still alive! Whew! Seriously, seeing you standing here brings me a lot of joy! Yes, sir. Joy with a capital *J*."

Benjamin looked into Liberty's mouth and then into his ears and nose. He finally said, "I'm thoroughly impressed. It appears you have the ability to reason and can fluently speak the English language." He turned to me and asked, "Is this an invention of your doing?"

The Library Company of Philadelphia was founded by Benjamin Franklin in 1731.

The First American political cartoon, published in 1754 by Benjamin Franklin in his *Pennsylvania Gazette* to rally the former colonies against British rule.

I gave the best explanation I could. "Yes, well, it was a crazy experiment with lightning," I replied nervously. "Sort of an accident. Impossible to duplicate. But I've nurtured Liberty and helped him adjust to his new abilities and intellect."

"Well, I must commend you for the scientific success that you have achieved," said Benjamin. "Truly, I feel very fortunate to have witnessed your accomplishment. But you would be wise to keep Liberty's gift a secret. I am all for sharing the inventions I have discovered, but your discovery is a . . . a . . . a natural phenomenon! Yes, definitely a wonder to behold!"

Liberty blushed and said, "Ahh, shucks. Thanks, Frankaben, I mean, Benjafrank, I mean, Franklin Benjamin. Doh, I mean, Benjamin Franklin, sir." Liberty blushed, again.

Benjamin stroked Liberty's neck and said, "Yes, Liberty, you are definitely one of a kind. Indeed, most people would pass out in shock at the discovery of a talking horse!"

"Thank you for your counsel," I said. "And Liberty is usually very careful about letting others know about his gift. Aren't you, Liberty?"

"Oh, uh, yes," said Liberty. "But I knew you'd understand, Mr. Franklin. I had a good feeling about you."

"We're just glad we found you when we did! Aren't we, Mr. Revere," Tommy said.

"Definitely! And I'm sure we've taken too much of your time. Certainly, you're here in England for a special reason," I hinted.

"I almost forgot," Benjamin said as he quickly looked at his pocket watch. "What a relief," he sighed. "It appears that time is on my side today."

Time is always on our side with Liberty, I thought.

"As fellow colonists you should join me," said Benjamin. "As a colonial representative of Pennsylvania I've been invited to testify to Parliament about what is happening in the colonies, particularly about the opposition to the Stamp Act. I believe if we cut across this lawn we can hail a carriage."

As we followed Benjamin I found myself smiling at the mere fact that we were about to experience an important moment in American history. It appeared that the fog was thinning and in the distance loomed a massive building that looked like a castle fortress.

"Mr. Franklin," Tommy said. "Are you in trouble? Why do you have to testify? Was there a crime? And what's Parliament? Sorry to ask so many questions."

Benjamin laughed and said, "Asking questions is the first step to discovery! Let me answer your questions in reverse. Parliament is the word we use in England for the English government. King George III regularly meets with Parliament—the House of Lords and the House of Commons—to make rules and laws to govern his people."

Tommy asked, "Do the King and Parliament make the rules for the thirteen colonies, too?"

"Yes," said Benjamin, "and that's beginning to be a problem. In fact, many colonists think it's a crime for the King to tax the colonies. In particular, I have come to testify to members of Parliament why the colonies dislike the Stamp Act so much."

"I remember Mr. Revere mentioned the Stamp Act in our history class," said Tommy.

Liberty cleared his throat and said, "You'd know what the Stamp Act is if you'd seen and heard my Stomp Act!" Liberty said. "I'd perform it for you now but it's just not the same without the music."

"I am still not accustomed to a talking horse," Benjamin said with a chuckle. "Please excuse my laughter. It is simply an expression of surprise and admiration. Are you suggesting that you can also sing?"

"Oh boy, let's not encourage him," I cringed.

"I'm not prepared to sing my Stamp Act song just yet but the national anthem is one of my favorites." At once, Liberty began singing, *"O! say does that star-spangled banner yet wave, o'er the land of the free! And the home of the brave!"*

Benjamin Franklin applauded and said, "I am amazed. And please be assured that your secret is safe with me. However, I am not familiar with this national anthem."

I quickly replied, "Oh, yes, well, it hasn't caught on just yet."

"I think it has potential," Benjamin said. "I especially like the part about the *land of the free and home of the brave.* In fact, it describes America perfectly. Our forefathers who first settled in America from England are some of the bravest people I have ever read about. Men like William Bradford, for example."

"Our class learned all about William Bradford and Myles Standish, who sailed on the *Mayflower* and settled Plymouth Plantation!" Tommy exclaimed.

Benjamin nodded and said, "We owe everything to the brave colonists who first came to America to start a land of the free. And now it is my turn to be brave by fighting for the rights of the thirteen colonies. We can talk more inside the carriage."

Several carriages waited in a row like taxis ready to take people to various destinations in London. Neatly trimmed hedges bordered either side of the road. The grass, the shrubs, the trees were perfectly landscaped. It was a sign that England was an established land with centuries of tradition and order. We waited for a carriage to pass before crossing the road.

Benjamin called to the coachman of the lead carriage with two white horses and said, "Westminster Palace, the House of Commons, please."

The footman opened the small door and Benjamin paid him before we stepped up and inside the enclosed interior. Two purple velvet benches faced each other. Benjamin Franklin sat on one side and Tommy and I sat on the other. I saw Liberty roll his eyes. He was always bothered by the fact that he couldn't fit inside cars or buses and now, carriages.

As the carriage rumbled down the dirt road, I looked out the side window to see Liberty prancing alongside the horses pulling the carriage. From the looks of it he had forgotten about riding inside the carriage and was now flirting like he was a stallion.

Tommy announced, "Wow, this is really bumpy! This carriage could use a pair of shock absorbers."

"I am not familiar with shock absorbers as you say," said Benjamin.

"Oh, it's a device to help smooth out the ride so it's not so bumpy."

"Are you an inventor, Tommy?" Benjamin asked.

"I do like to build things. Do you have any advice for me?" Tommy asked.

"Never let uncertainty or fear stop you. If you work hard and think big you can accomplish anything, especially in a free land like America. There are people that will tell you otherwise. They will say you are not good enough. You are not old enough. You are not smart enough. Balderdash! Do not listen to them. If you have a dream, follow it!"

A view some years later, Hanover Square in London, 1787.

"Thanks!" Tommy said. "I'll remember that. By the way, you said you were fighting for the rights of the colonies. Exactly what rights are you fighting for?"

"I'm fighting against this horrible idea called the Stamp Act. Horrible it is, horrible! Last year, the British prime minister, George Grenville, passed the Stamp Act, the first direct tax on the American colonies."

"I know all about taxes," said Tommy matter-of-factly. "Last year I saved my money to buy this awesome Lego set and—"

"I'm sorry to interrupt," said Benjamin, "but what is a Lego set? I've been gone from the colonies for a couple of years. Is this some kind of new toy?"

"Um, yeah," Tommy said reluctantly. "They're sort of like building blocks but they have pieces that connect together and you can build all kinds of things. I have this Lego set with instructions to build the Death Star, you know, from *Star Wars* and—"

"Tommy has quite the imagination," I said, cutting in laughing as I nudged Tommy.

"Instructions to build a star of death? For children? Interesting," mused Benjamin.

"Anyway," Tommy continued, "I knew the exact price of this Lego set because I wrote it down and looked at it every week. I did lots of chores and worked hard and saved my money. When I had earned enough my mom took me to the store to purchase it. I put the exact change on the counter but the salesperson said it wasn't enough. I'm really good at numbers so I knew I wasn't wrong. That's when my mom told me that I'd forgotten about the tax. I thought, the what? The sales tax, she said. And that's when I learned that we pay a little extra on everything we buy and that little extra money, the sales tax, goes back to the government."

"And tell me, Tommy, how did this tax make you feel?" Benjamin Franklin asked.

"Well, at first I didn't think it was fair, but then she said if we all pay a sales tax then that money goes to help run the city. She said this way everyone can enjoy things like public schools, libraries, highways, and police and fire protection. Once I realized all the places and services I get to enjoy because of all the taxes that are collected, I really didn't mind paying a little bit every time I buy something."

"You are a very smart boy, Tommy," said Benjamin. "But what if the money from those taxes wasn't used to build up your city or bless its citizens? What if your tax money was being used for something you didn't agree with? What if there was no real benefit to anyone at all?"

Tommy thought for a second and said, "Well, um, wouldn't that be stealing? That doesn't seem fair."

"And that's why the colonists are angry," I said.

"Yes," said Benjamin. "The Stamp Act is making the colonists pay extra money on something they didn't vote for. It is a tax that gives nothing back to the community. And we believe it is something that Parliament is doing to undercut our businesses and the success we are having."

"But why do they call it the Stamp Act? I don't get it?" asked Tommy.

"It is called the Stamp Act because a stamp is placed on all paper products reminding the colonists that England is still in charge," said Benjamin.

"You mean I have to pay a tax on anything I buy made from paper?" Tommy asked again.

Benjamin replied, "Anything and everything! Newspapers,

almanacs, pamphlets, legal documents of all kinds, ships' papers, licenses, and even playing cards. The act was to be enforced by stamp agents with severe penalties for any who would not pay. However, the colonists are putting a stop to it. Many resist paying the stamp tax. I would not be surprised if someday they rebel against the Empire."

Tommy laughed and said, "That sounds a lot like *Star Wars*."

"Well, I'm not familiar with a *star* war," said Benjamin, "but if the thirteen colonies continue to rebel and resist, it is just a matter of time before the empire strikes back!"

"That's exactly what happens in *Star Wars*!" Tommy shouted. "And then the rebels are forced to retreat until the return of the Jedi!"

I forced a nervous laugh and said, "Ha! Jedi! That's Tommy's special word for hero! Isn't it, Tommy?"

"Oh, um, yeah," Tommy said. "That's right. I made it up. Jedi heroes like William Bradford and Myles Standish! All they wanted was freedom! We can't let them down."

"No worries, Tommy," I said. "I saw colonists in Boston burning anything that had a tax stamp on it. And I've read about how the colonists are threatening the stamp agents. I even heard that one agent was tarred and feathered for trying to enforce the Stamp Act."

Tommy's eyes went wide and asked, "When you say 'tarred and feathered' do you mean . . ."

"I am afraid so," said Benjamin. "It is a barbaric and cruel act to slop hot tar on someone's body and then pour goose feathers on top of them."

"Oh, wow," Tommy said. "This is really getting serious."

As the carriage slowed Benjamin looked out the window and

said, "We have arrived at the Palace of Westminster. And it appears that the fog has lifted."

In 1765, England was said to be the most powerful country in the world and as I peered out the window I saw that the Palace of Westminster was certainly reflective of that power. The massive stone building, originally built in the Middle Ages, had several tall, castle-like structures that overlooked the River Thames. A beautiful courtyard landscaped with well-trimmed shrubs and trees welcomed us. The overall site was breathtaking.

The carriage stopped and as the door opened Benjamin said, "Follow me, gentlemen. I am honored to have you as my guests."

As we exited the carriage I turned to Tommy and whispered, "This building is where the British lords and lawmakers come to govern. In the United States, the Capitol building in Washington, D.C., is the equivalent."

In the courtyard that surrounded the steps leading to two ornately carved doors were dozens of men. I assumed these were the lords and lawmakers of England. They were dressed in the finest waistcoats, vests, and breeches. Most wore white wigs or their hair was pulled back and tied off with a ribbon.

The sound of a large bell rung through the plaza and the men responded by filing into the palace doors.

"Now, let's see if I can get these British gents to repeal the Stamp Act!" said Benjamin as we followed him into the Palace.

We were the last ones to enter the building, so Liberty took a deep breath and slipped in behind us like he was wearing an invisibility cloak.

Chapter 9

Benjamin sat in a wooden chair behind a well-crafted wooden desk in the middle of a large room. On the walls, masterful oil paintings of former British monarchs hung in grandiose golden frames. Exquisitely carved half columns stood against the walls and reached up to a high ceiling. Three hundred seventy members of Parliament sat in theater seating on either side listening to Franklin's testimony about the colonies' reaction to the Stamp Act. Without question, Benjamin Franklin looked exhausted after answering more than 170 questions. He took another sip of water and waited for another member of Parliament to ask yet another question. Secretively, I continued to record the proceedings with my smartphone.

"He's not being questioned, he's being interrogated," Tommy whispered from the back of the room. "I feel really bad for him. He's got to be really tired."

The House of Commons in session in 1710.

"Remember that he is fighting for freedom. Some people fight for it on the battlefield and some fight for it in a court of law," I said.

"Well, it just goes to show how smart he is. These guys in Parliament keep trying to mess with his mind. It's like they keep asking the same questions to see if he'll give different answers," Tommy said.

"Yes, some lawyers and politicians can be very crafty. I don't think they realize who they are dealing with," I said, softly.

"No kidding. I'd totally pick him to be on my debate team," said Tommy with a big grin.

"What did I miss?" asked Liberty, who suddenly appeared behind a large curtain in the back of the stuffy room. Liberty was present for the first thirty minutes of questioning but then disappeared to find a snack.

"They just passed a law that gives donkeys special privileges over horses," Tommy whispered to Liberty.

"What!" shouted Liberty. The word reverberated off the walls and ceiling. Thankfully, it was difficult to know where the sound was coming from.

"Order!" said the prime minister, who acted as the judge and pounded his gavel. "We will have order during the questioning. Next question."

Another member of Parliament raised his hand and asked, "If the Stamp Act is not repealed, what do you think will be the consequences? How will the people of America respond?"

Benjamin sighed but calmly replied, "A total loss of respect and affection for Great Britain."

Another question came from the other side of the room. "Do you think the people of America would submit to pay the stamp tax if it were moderated?"

Again, Benjamin replied, "No, never, unless compelled by force of arms."

Still another question: "Do they realize the British Empire owes a lot of money to those who helped us fight the French and Indian War—a war that was fought on American soil? Do you think it right that America should be protected by this country and pay no part of the expense?"

Without flinching Benjamin replied, "The colonies raised, clothed, and paid nearly twenty-five thousand men and spent millions during the French and Indian war. Candidly, they believe they have paid their part in full."

"One final question for Mr. Franklin," called the prime minister. "We have heard that the Americans claim 'No taxation without representation.' The fact is Parliament has the right to tax the colonies with or without their consent. Can anything less than a military force carry the Stamp Act into execution?"

Benjamin Franklin smiled the most convincing smile he could give and said with boldness, "I do not see how a military force can be applied to that purpose."

Murmurs spread across the great room and echoed off the walls.

"Why may it not?" asked the prime minister.

"Suppose a military force is sent into America. They will find nobody in arms. What are they to do? They cannot force a man to take stamps who chooses to do without them. They will not find a rebellion. They may, indeed, make one."

More murmuring rippled through the large hall and Benjamin Franklin took a deep breath and exhaled. The prime minister stood from his seat, pounding his gavel, and the meeting was adjourned.

"Let's sneak out to the courtyard and wait for Mr. Franklin," I said.

As we walked outside and down the stone walkway I was reminded again how beautiful London was. The courtyard was circular and symmetrical, with a round pond in the middle. A variety of perfectly pruned shrubs and bushes lined a variety of pathways. We walked to the center of the courtyard and Tommy said, "No wonder the Revolutionary War happened. There's no way England and America are going to agree. They both think they're right. And both sides are getting angrier and angrier. This is not going to end well."

"You're right," I said. "The Stamp Act may very well have been the spark that led to America's independence from England. The King and Parliament won't back down. The thirteen colonies are standing firm for freedom. And tempers will eventually reach a boiling point!"

"Speaking of boiling point," Liberty said, "I think most people overcook their food. There's nothing worse than overcooked potatoes or carrots or especially asparagus! Seriously, limp and soggy asparagus is almost as bad as a limp and soggy handshake."

Confused, I questioned, "a soggy handshake?"

Liberty clarified: "You don't want one, trust me. It begins by soaking in the bathtub or playing in a pool for too long and then your hand looks old and wrinkly! Shaking a soggy hand feels like you're holding a slimy, shriveled piece of seaweed. And you're not going to impress anyone with seaweed. Why are we even talking about this?"

I said defensively, "Because when I said boiling point you starting talking about—"

Liberty interrupted. "What we should be talking about is how to help the colonists defend their freedoms!"

I rolled my eyes and said, "I agree. Tommy, do you have any questions about what you heard in there?"

"Yeah, I do," Tommy said. "I'm not sure I understood what *No taxation without representation* means."

"It's the main reason why the colonists are mad," I said. "It's important to understand that the thirteen colonies are still a part of England. They still consider King George to be their king, and they are subject to the rules and laws of the British Empire. So, of course, if they have to live by these laws then they want to help make the laws. Instead, the King and Parliament are making decisions without them."

"You mean like the Stamp Act," said Tommy.

"Exactly! The colonies petitioned Parliament to repeal the stamp tax several times but were ignored each time. Finally, the colonies said, 'no more.' No taxation without representation."

Tommy nodded and said, "It sort of reminds me of this kid named Billy who lived in our neighborhood and had this really cool fort. But he only let the kids on his street play in his fort. I heard it was really cool. It had a pinball machine, and this balloon launcher, and this awesome rope swing! Plus, it had jars full of candy and snacks. Anyway, the kids on my street decided we should make our own cool fort but Billy didn't like that idea. He had a top-secret meeting with the kids on his street and they decided that we could use Billy's fort if we paid to get in. We told him no way, Jose!"

"I thought you said his name was Billy," said Liberty.

"It is," I said. "Jose is just a nickname that rhymes with way."

"Oh," Liberty replied. "You mean like, go take a hike, Mike. Or take a chill pill, Phil. Or go ride a ferret, Garrett!"

"Exactly," Tommy said, laughing. "Anyway, we told Billy that we were going to have our own meeting. We decided we didn't need his lousy fort and we built our own."

"You did just what the colonies did," I said. "They had their own meeting in October 1765. The colonies formed the Stamp Act Congress to figure out what to do and say to England about the Stamp Act."

"I know what I would do," said Liberty. "I would get a big piece of tape and make a line down the center and say this side of the barn is mine and that side of the barn is yours, and if you step on my side of the line then I'm telling Mom! Seriously, I had this brother that was soooo bossy and he thought he owned every inch of our barn and he was—"

I stroked Liberty's neck and said, "It's all right, Liberty. That was in the past. But you bring up a very good point. King George felt like he was the boss of the colonists. He felt like he owned their land and did not want to give it up! That's why he started taxing the people and tried forcing them to buy British products. He was trying to control what they did. He wanted them to think of the British Empire first."

"That's hard to do when you live three thousand miles away," said Tommy.

"The King believed there was lots of money to be made in the colonies," I said. "America was rich in resources like wood, minerals, furs, and especially land. Plus, he sent a lot of British citizens to colonize the New World. You can understand why he was selfish and wanted to maintain his power and make the people feel dependent on England."

"But the colonists are becoming so successful that they really don't need the King or the British Empire, right?" Tommy asked.

"Correct," I said. "America is like a child who is big enough to ride a bike without training wheels. But the King doesn't want to take the training wheels off!"

"Hey, there's Benjamin Franklin," Tommy said pointing.

Sure enough, Benjamin slowly walked out of the Palace of Westminster. He looked like he could use a long nap. We joined him at the center of the courtyard.

"You were amazing in there," said Tommy. "It was like the battle of the minds. Just like when Professor Xavier from the X-Men uses his mind power to fight off the bad guys. Seriously, you're like an eighteenth-century X-Man!"

"Your imagination astounds even me," said Benjamin. "What exactly is an X-Man?"

"Only the coolest group of superheroes to ever exist. Their whole purpose is to fight for and protect our freedoms. Yep, Benjamin Franklin is definitely an X-Man!"

"I have been called a lot of things, but never an X-Man," Benjamin said, laughing.

"I believe you persuaded Parliament to repeal the Stamp Act," I said.

"You must be an optimist," said Benjamin with a wide grin. "Only time will tell. But I want to thank you for your support and for the service you rendered me."

"Thanks, Mr. Franklin, for all your advice. I'll never forget you," Tommy said.

Benjamin put both hands on Tommy's shoulders and said, "Tommy, you are the future of America. I'm an old man and today I feel even older. But when I hear your questions and see the light in your eyes I realize your mind is not much different than mine. Creating new inventions or fulfilling your dreams is

Benjamin Franklin presenting the concerns of the American colonists to the Lord's Council, Whitehall Chapel, London.

simply connecting the dots in your mind. Some ideas have lots of dots and others just a few. But it is all the same process. Dot by dot by dot. The key is to keep going until you reach the final dot. When you do, you will have accomplished something. And with a mind like yours, I know it will be something great!"

Finally, he turned to Liberty and said, "And how could I forget you!"

Liberty smiled and just stood there beaming!

Benjamin placed his hand under Liberty's muzzle and said, "There is no such thing as coincidence, Liberty. God knows where every lightning bolt strikes, if you know what I mean." He winked. "Something tells me you are exactly who you were meant to be. Don't ever forget that."

Liberty's lip quivered just a bit and if he could have I know he would've given Benjamin Franklin a great big horse hug.

"Thank you, again, my friends," said Benjamin. "And when you're back in the colonies if you ever have a chance to meet Patrick Henry I would highly recommend it. I think he's an exceptional American and one of your X-Men," he said, winking at Tommy. "I hope our paths cross again someday." And with that he tipped his hat and we parted ways.

"This was way better than I expected," said Tommy.

"No kidding," said Liberty. "He called you Mr. Future of America! Wow, you're pretty important. I think you should get a T-shirt with 'Mr. Future of America' printed on it."

"Thanks, Liberty, for being my number-one fan," said Tommy. "But I think we should keep this a secret between you and me."

"No problem," Liberty said, grinning. "Now we both have secrets. It's like we're secret members of a secret club of secrets!"

"I hate to break up your secret meeting, but it's time to

time-jump back to Manchester Middle School." I scanned the courtyard and said, "Let's walk over to that tall hedge. It should conceal our departure. Oh, and Liberty, we can't return to the teachers' lounge because we don't know if Elizabeth is still there."

"I hope Freedom is okay," Tommy said.

"I'm more worried about Elizabeth," I said. "I've seen her taunt and tease and insult Freedom over and over again. That kind of thing can be very taxing on a person. One of these days Freedom is going to reach her boiling point just like the colonies. I would not want to be Elizabeth when that happens."

"I say we jump back to the classroom. It should still be empty since school just ended," Liberty said.

"Just ended? It feels like that was days ago," Tommy sighed.

"Good idea, Liberty. The classroom it is," I said.

We traveled to the nearby hedge, and after making sure we were alone, Liberty opened the time portal and we jumped back to the classroom.

"Now I know how Liberty feels. I'm starving," said Tommy as he dismounted from Liberty.

"You see," said Liberty, "I'm not the only one with a big appetite."

"Thanks, again, Mr. Revere," said Tommy. "I better get home." He took off his layer of colonial clothes and put them in his backpack. "I like keeping my modern-day clothes underneath. It's so much easier to change! See ya!" He smiled and quickly left the classroom.

Liberty smiled and said, "So what's the plan, Stan? Should we get something to eat, Pete?"

I tried not to laugh and said, "Good idea."

"Really?" asked Liberty.

"Absolutely," I said. "We need to keep your energy up. We have more time traveling to do!"

When the school bell rang the next day, the students were still busy talking about the previous day's events.

"Good afternoon, class," I said. The class fell silent and I continued: "Today you're going to watch a video I recently edited where Benjamin Franklin defends the rights of the thirteen colonies and asks members of the British Parliament to repeal the Stamp Act. As you watch this video it will be very easy to imagine what it was like to actually be there. While the documentary is playing I'm going to slip out to get my horse, Liberty. As promised, Liberty is going to perform for you his stomp act about the Stamp Act. I'm going to need a couple of volunteers to help me carry in a sound system for Liberty's performance."

Several hands shot up in the air. I looked for three specific students to help me but only saw two of them. I wonder where Freedom is, I thought.

"Tommy and Cam," I said, pointing to the two boys, "please join me in the hallway. The rest of you can sit back and enjoy the show. Oh, I almost forgot." I pulled open my bottom desk drawer and pulled out a bag of bubble gum and another bag of lollipops. "You're welcome to a treat while watching the movie!"

The students eagerly passed around the bags of treats. I walked to the back of the class, dimmed the lights, and started the video projector. I slipped out the door and into the hall, where Cam was waiting for me.

"Where's Tommy?" I asked.

Before Cam could respond, Tommy slipped out of the

classroom door and joined us. He tossed a couple of pieces of bubble gum to Cam.

"Thanks," Cam said as he caught both pieces in his hands.

"Is Cam going to jump with us today?" Tommy said as he tossed an unwrapped piece of gum in his mouth.

I smiled and said, "He can if he wants to."

"Did you say jump? Aren't we just getting the sound system?" Cam asked. "I'll admit, I'm curious to see what your horse does. It looks so real when he moves his lips. It's like he's really talking. I assume the sound system is what you use for the lip sync?"

Tommy looked Cam right in the eyes and without a single sign of a smirk he said, "Cam, this is going to be tough to believe and it might blow your mind, but you've got to trust me on this. Here's the thing, a talking horse is just the tip of the iceberg. Mr. Revere has discovered how to time-travel."

We stood there in silence as Cam carefully stared at us. Finally, he said, "You guys are serious?"

Tommy nodded and looked at me.

"It's true," I said. "There's really only one way to prove it to you. Would you care to join us outside? Liberty is waiting for us there."

"Okay, sure, I'll play along," said Cam. "And I bet there's a flying pig out there, too!"

"Just don't freak out too much, okay?" said Tommy.

"Whatever," Cam said. "Let's go find your magical horse. You probably have a leprechaun in your pocket and a genie in your locker."

"Don't be ridiculous," Tommy smiled. "Leprechauns hate pockets and a genie is way too powerful to keep captive in a locker!"

Tommy thought he was being funny as he laughed at his own joke. I was amused that Tommy thought he was funny. But Cam only gave a courtesy smile as he followed us outside to join Liberty.

"So, where's your horse?" Cam asked.

"Right here!" Liberty said as he appeared directly behind Cam.

Cam jumped forward like he had just stepped on hot coals. "Whoa! Man, you have got to teach me how to do this prank!"

"His name is Liberty," I said. "Liberty, this is Cam and we've told him about your secret."

"Which secret?" Liberty asked. "Oh, you mean the time I hid inside Disneyland just before the park closed? I had always wanted to do that. Of course, it's not hard to hide when you can turn invisible but I thought it would be a lot more fun after hours when everyone was gone. Not so much. All the rides are closed and there's nothing to eat so I just wandered through Adventureland and Frontierland and Fantasyland and—"

"Liberty," I said, "I was referring to your time-travel secret."

"Ohhhhhhh," Liberty said with renewed interest. "*That* secret!"

Cam had his mouth open and was staring intently at Liberty.

"You really shouldn't stare with your mouth open," Liberty said. "No offense, but it's sort of rude."

Cam shut his mouth and then opened it and said, "He really can talk."

"Before we go anywhere, Tommy and Cam need these," I said. Opening my travel bag, I pulled out two pairs of colonial clothing.

"Okay, sure, why not." Cam laughed. "I'll play along."

The boys quickly dressed and transformed into eighteenth-century lads.

"Do I look as funny as you do?" Cam asked Tommy.

"Yep," Tommy said. "You should wear those clothes to school."

"No kidding!" Cam laughed. "These breeches and stockings are total girl magnets."

"Make sure you tuck in your shirts," I said.

"Thanks, Mom," Tommy said with a wink.

In an effort to hurry us along I said, "Tommy, why don't you climb up onto Liberty's saddle. I was going to have Freedom ride first but . . . speaking of Freedom, where is she today?"

"Oh, she had a dentist appointment," Tommy said. "But she said she was coming back for Liberty's stomp act."

"Good to know," I said. "Cam, why don't you climb up behind Tommy."

"Um, okay, sure," said Cam.

"Where are we going this time?" Tommy asked.

Cam started laughing. "Wait, wait, wait, this is all kinds of whacked-out. Are you saying that Liberty is how you time-travel?"

"Just hold on tight to the saddle," I said. "Liberty, we're ready!"

"Rush, rush, rushing to history!" Liberty said as he galloped forward.

A purple and gold whirlpool swirled in front of us as the time portal opened. I called out, "America, the colony of Virginia, 1765, Patrick Henry." As Liberty, Tommy, and Cam jumped through I followed closely behind. Just before I jumped I saw Elizabeth step out from behind the corner of the school. Only ten yards away, she started running toward the time portal, too. She wouldn't dare jump through after me, would she? In another second I was through the portal and landed in a darkened alley. Liberty, Tommy, and Cam were waiting for me. I stopped and turned back toward the portal, waiting, heart racing, eyes tracing the purple and gold to see if anyone else had time-jumped.

Chapter 5

As the boys dismounted, Liberty asked, "Why are you staring at the portal like that? You look like you've seen a ghost."

I ignored Liberty as I concentrated on the portal. After a couple of seconds the swirling vortex starting shrinking until it disappeared altogether.

"That was close," I mumbled. I was worried Elizabeth would confront me upon my return to Manchester but for now we appeared to be safe.

"Get behind the building! Quick!" whispered Tommy, who grabbed my arm and pulled me back.

Tommy, Cam, and I had our backs against a two-story colonial building with a redbrick foundation and wood-siding. I looked up and saw a solid brick chimney with smoke that drifted up into sky. I quickly surveyed my surroundings. Even though the sun had just dipped below the neighboring frontier, it was plain to see that this wasn't

England. It was a rugged landscape. No trimmed hedges or courtyards. Instead, a grove of trees thick with underbrush created an eerie scene just in front of us. A barking dog could be heard in the distance.

"I saw a bunch of guys that looked like British soldiers," said Tommy. "I don't think they saw us."

I peeked around the corner of the building and saw about six British soldiers who were leaving the establishment. Their red coats made them easy to spot.

"No wonder the thirteen colonies won the war," said Liberty, who peered over my shoulder. "Those guys stand out like a cherry on an ice-cream sundae!"

As the soldiers marched away in unison I said, "Liberty, can you verify our location?"

"Yes, Captain! Seventeen sixty-five Virginia." He turned to Tommy and Cam and said, "I pay very close attention when Rush Revere announces our future historical destination. In fact, right now my time-travel senses tell me that Patrick Henry is very close by."

"Your time-travel senses?" Tommy asked.

"Yep!" Liberty nodded. "It's hard to explain."

"Is it like a tingling feeling at the base of your skull?" Tommy said, curiously.

Liberty looked surprised and said, "Actually, yes! How did you know?"

Tommy smiled, "It's the same kind of feeling that Spider-Man gets when he senses danger. His Spider-Sense gives him a psychological awareness of his surroundings. It sounds like your Time-Travel-Sense gives you a chronological sense of history as well as a keen awareness of the historical figure we're looking for."

"You mean I have a super power?" Liberty asked, like he just found out that school had been canceled. "Wow! I never thought of it like that. Wait, let me try using my super sense!" Liberty closed his eyes as if he were concentrating.

"Your horse, he really can talk!" said Cam. "And we really did jump through some kind of worm hole to the year 1765!" He laughed and added, "That's sick!"

"You're sick?" Liberty asked. "Maybe you have time-travel motion sickness, you know, like seasickness."

"Not sick like *ill*, he means sick like *awesome*!" Tommy clarified.

"That makes no sense at all," said Liberty. "I would not be feeling awesome if I were sick." Suddenly, Liberty was distracted by the sound of someone playing the fiddle. "Where is that music coming from?" he asked, listening more intently.

"I should probably set some ground rules," I said to Tommy and Cam. "I want us to be extra cautious since we've already seen British soldiers, okay? I don't expect any problems but you never know."

"It's like we're in a virtual world, isn't it?" asked Cam.

"Yes," I nodded, "except this is not a virtual world. Those Redcoats are real and their swords and bayonets and muskets are real too. So what I'm saying is no goofing off, got it?"

"Got it," said the boys in unison.

"All right," I said, "it looks like we're ready to . . . hey, where's Liberty?"

"He was here a second ago," Cam said.

I cautiously walked around the building to where the front doors were. Across the street was a larger building with a sign that was barely visible. It said Hanover County Courthouse. A few other buildings could be seen up and down the dimly lit street.

"Hey, there's Liberty," said Cam, pointing to the building we were hiding behind. "And it sounds like there's a party going on inside."

Liberty was standing near the front door and bobbing his head to the rhythm of the fiddle. I could also hear several voices talking and laughing from inside the establishment.

"What kind of building is this?" Tommy asked.

"My guess is a tavern," I said.

"You mean, like a bar?" Tommy asked.

"Yes," I confirmed. "No worries. There aren't any biker gangs in the eighteenth century."

Liberty walked back to where we were standing and sighed, "I guess this means I have to stay out here."

"We'll be back soon," I said. "In the meantime, we need you to keep a lookout for any Redcoats," I said.

"That is sort of important," Liberty said. "I've got you covered!"

I noticed Tommy pull something from his pocket. "Have some bubble gum," he said as he unwrapped the gum and tossed it to Liberty who snatched it out of the air with his lips.

"Oh, I've always wanted to try this," Liberty said as he chewed. "How exactly do you blow a bubble?"

Tommy smiled, maneuvered his own piece of gum in his mouth, and then began to blow.

"Fascinating!" said Liberty.

I rolled my eyes and said, "Let's enter the tavern."

As we entered we saw several tables against each wall. Well-dressed men with bright-colored coats and tricorn hats like the one I wore were sitting among the tables. Other men with collarless shirts and vests were seated as well and all the men were wearing breeches, stockings, and leather shoes. Candles flickered at each table as well as in sconces fixed to the walls. Men were telling stories, drinking from mugs, or playing cards. One man sat alone at an empty table playing the fiddle.

"Let's join the man with the fiddle," I suggested. "Perhaps he can tell us which of these men is Patrick Henry."

"Wait a second," said Cam. "Do you mean *the* Patrick Henry, as in one of America's Founding Fathers?"

"The very one," I confirmed.

"No way!" Cam beamed. "You know I'm a history buff, right? Patrick Henry is a rock star! Seriously, I've read his speeches and he was amazing! He's the guy who said, 'Give me liberty or give me death!'"

"That's right," I said. "He was one of the most influential champions of the American Revolution. Benjamin Franklin highly recommended that we visit him."

"Man, this is an awesome field trip. Thanks for inviting me!" Cam said.

As we approached the man with the fiddle he stopped playing. He wore a purple vest and linen shirt. His purple coat with gold buttons was thrown over a chair. He looked to be in his late twenties, maybe thirty years old. His hair was neatly combed and pulled back into a short ponytail.

"Excuse me, sir," I said, "but can you tell me which of these men is Patrick Henry?"

"Patrick Henry!" he exclaimed in an animated whisper. "You don't want to be associated with him. Haven't you heard? He's a radical! He's an outspoken lawyer that says what he will even if he offends the King!"

I was surprised by the man's warning and said, "Yes, well, we understand he's an opponent of the King's Stamp Act."

"Shh," said the man with the fiddle. "Don't speak so loudly when you talk about the Stamp Act that way. Do you want the King's spies to hear you?" The man glanced over our shoulders at the other men in the tavern. "Come, sit with me. You tell me what you've heard and I'll tell you what I've heard about that rabble-rouser Patrick Henry."

We each grabbed a chair and sat around the table. I glanced at the other men who were talking and laughing. Any one of them could be Henry, I supposed. Unless he wasn't here, but Liberty seemed so certain about it.

"Forgive my manners," said our new host. "You must be parched. What can I get you to drink?"

"You're too kind," I said. "I'd like some tea."

"And what would your servants care to drink?" He looked toward Tommy and Cam and said, "I assume these are your servants? Or perhaps one is your son and the other a slave, a well-dressed slave I must say." He glanced at Cam's dark skin and clothes.

Cam was clearly surprised by the comment, and his face contorted into an odd look of calm and consternation that I hadn't seen in him before. I put my hand on his shoulder and was about to say something reassuring but instead Cam boldly exclaimed, "I understand this is 1765 and you aren't enlightened to the reality of freedom for all men yet, but I am free and will always be free, just like this country."

I was impressed with his strength and composure in a difficult moment.

The fiddler smiled and looked thoroughly impressed with Cam. He said, "Well, I certainly do apologize, young man. I meant no offense."

Tommy looked relieved.

Suddenly, the fiddler jumped up onto his chair and with a foot on the table and his fiddle underneath his chin he began to play a fervent tune while tapping his foot. I looked at Tommy and Cam, who were all smiles. Tommy looked back at me and mouthed the words, *I think this guy is nuts!* Cam nodded with enthusiasm and gave me the universal symbol for crazy by twirling his finger near the side of his head. And just when I thought it couldn't get any stranger, the fiddler stopped playing and sprang with both feet on top of the wooden table. That's when he started singing and acting out his song!

Our worthy forefathers—let's give them a cheer—
To climates unknown did courageously steer;
Thro' oceans to deserts, for freedom they came,
And, dying, bequeath'd us their freedom and fame!

The room burst into applause and cheers. Some of the men were louder than others but all seemed to applaud the man's song. The men soon returned to their own conversations and the room became quiet, as it had been before.

The fiddler stepped down and patted Cam on the shoulder. "We shall all drink to freedom tonight," said the fiddler. "With whom do I have the pleasure of drinking?"

I replied, "This is Tommy and Cam, my apprentices. And my name is Rush Revere. I'm a history teacher and I was—"

"Revere, you say? Hmm, are you related to Paul Revere?"

"I believe I am!" I exclaimed. "I mean I've not actually met him but I'm a great admirer and we fight for the same cause."

"I'm glad to hear that," the man said, smiling. "Now then, perhaps Tommy and Cam would enjoy a cup of chocolate?"

"That's sounds great!" Tommy said. "Thank you!"

"Yeah," Cam said with a wink, "freedom and chocolate are definitely worth fighting for!"

The man laughed and waved at the barkeep, who walked over to our table and took our orders. When he left I asked, "Where do you think we could find Patrick Henry?"

"You'd be better off without him," the man sniffed. "I heard he just gave a speech at the House of Burgesses in Virginia's capital, Williamsburg. They say he spoke like thunder as he defended the rights of the colonies. He attacked the Stamp Act and said that the British Empire had no right to tax the American colonies. He said if we don't stop King George III now he'll keep taxing the people until he has us all in chains."

"I'm curious, what did the people say when they heard his speech?" I asked.

"Ha! The governor of Virginia was furious!" said the man, who picked up his fiddle, again. "Especially when Patrick Henry said the stamp tax was a threat to our liberty! That's when some of the older men cried, 'Treason!'" The man played a fast and gloomy tune on his fiddle. He stopped playing and continued. "People say Patrick Henry is verbally attacking the King! Would you believe he actually compared King George to Julius Caesar and Charles I."

"Wow, that's harsh," Cam said. "Julius Caesar was a Roman dictator and King Charles was beheaded for crimes against England. Sounds like Patrick Henry is really going out on a dangerous limb here. He's putting himself at risk."

"Perhaps your Patrick Henry values the cause of freedom more than his life," said the fiddler.

"That's why I like him so much," said Cam as he looked around the room. "I'd really like to meet him. I was hoping he could give me a few tips on how to speak like thunder! I'm thinking about running for student body president and speaking like thunder could come in handy." Cam stood up from his chair and mimicked his presidential speech, declaring, "Students of America! You say you want freedom to speak your mind. You say you want your voice to be heard! You say you want a leader who will defend your rights and extend your lunch hour. If you vote for me I promise liberty and justice for all!"

Liberty must have thought someone called his name because his head briefly appeared in the window and I saw him rigorously chewing his bubble gum. At least he wasn't getting into trouble.

As Cam sat down the fiddler stood up and began to applaud. In a booming voice, he said, "You have my vote! You are a most excellent orator, Cam. And you are brave to be so bold. Never let fear stop you from saying what needs to be said."

The barkeep of the tavern politely interrupted and set our beverages on the table. Wisps of steam rose from the silver mugs.

Tommy leaned over his mug and smelled the wafting aroma of chocolate. "Wow, that smells delicious!"

Cam sipped from his mug and said, "It's a little different than what we have back home! This is creamier and little bit sour."

"And where is *back home* for you?" asked the fiddler.

"We just moved from Colorado. My dad is in the military so we move every year or so. I guess I really don't have a place I call home," Cam replied.

"Colorado?" the man asked. "Is this a new settlement in the West? I've not heard of it."

Just then the door burst open and a young man about seventeen or eighteen burst into the tavern. The men on either side of the room turned to see who or what the ruckus was. The boy took off his tricorn hat and wiped his brow. He scanned the room quickly and then rushed over to our table and tossed several newspapers in front of our host.

"I brought the newspapers just like you asked, Mr. Henry," the boy panted. "The other messengers arrived just like you said they would, from Maryland and Rhode Island and Massachusetts and other colonies. They've all printed your seven resolutions against the Stamp Act. It looks like the colonies have united in opposing the stamp tax!"

"Henry?" I asked the boy. "Do you mean Patrick Henry?" I asked again, this time turning to the man with the fiddle.

Patrick Henry gave a big hearty laugh to match Cam's wide smile. "I'm afraid you're sitting with a treasonous radical who defies the King of England!" thundered Patrick with a giant grin.

I could hardly believe my ears. All this time we were sitting with one of the legendary forefathers of America! I blushed and said, "Forgive me, Mr. Henry. I should've recognized you earlier!"

"Recognized me?" asked Patrick. "Have we met before?"

I realized I couldn't tell him that his picture is in every American history book.

Patrick Henry proposes the Virginia Stamp Act Resolutions to the House of Burgesses in Virginia.

"He means he should have recognized your voice of thunder," Cam joked.

Patrick laughed and said, "Cam, I enjoy your company." After a moment, he became more serious and exclaimed, "Now that you know who I am I want you to know something about me, something that has troubled me for years." He turned to look at Cam and said somberly, "The truth is I am very sorry to report that I own slaves."

"Why?" Cam asked, sincerely. "How can you say you're fighting for freedom and still own slaves? Isn't that hypocritical?"

"Slavery has become an important part of the economy here in the South," said Patrick. "But I have felt a great need to change the way things are in these southern colonies. Truly, I have felt tormented as my soul has wrestled with the owning of slaves, and I have come to realize that this wicked practice must come to an end. If we truly want to be a free people, a free land, a free America, then we must free the slaves. God cannot bless a country that allows the bondage and captivity of men, women, and children." He took a deep breath, sighed, and said, "Indeed, I believe a time will come when we shall abolish this lamentable evil called slavery."

Cam said, "That sounds like a very good start!" Then Cam raised his hand and said, "High five!" He prompted Patrick to raise his hand as well. Patrick slowly lifted his hand and Cam slapped his upraised palm.

Curious, Patrick asked, "You call that a *high five?*"

"Yeah," Cam replied. "It's a gesture of triumph or success. It also means we're friends."

"I like the high five," said Patrick.

"Wait until you learn the chest bump!" Tommy smiled.

Patrick noticed that the boy who had delivered the newspapers was watching with great curiosity about five feet away. Patrick flipped the boy a large silver coin and the boy caught it in the air.

"Thank you, Mr. Henry!" said the teenage boy, grinning from ear to ear. "If you will excuse me, sir, there is a peculiar horse out in the front of the tavern that caught my attention."

"Why did you say *peculiar* horse?" I asked nervously.

The boy replied with wonder, "In truth, this horse had a large pink bubble attached to his mouth. It was small at first but then it grew to the size of a cantaloupe until it finally popped. Then the horse used his tongue to lick up the pink sap that stuck to his nose and lips until it was all back in his mouth and he began chewing it. I'm hoping he'll do it again. I've never seen anything like it!"

"Cam and I will come with you," Tommy said. "I'm pretty sure I know what it is." The boys got up from the table, thanked Mr. Henry for the hot chocolate, and exited the tavern.

As Patrick Henry browsed the first newspaper I took out my phone, slipped it under the table, and typed a quick Facebook entry. *Virginia 1765. Sitting here drinking tea with Patrick Henry! Historians say that he was the man who sparked America's revolution. His seven resolutions to the Stamp Act articulated why America should reject and resist British taxation on the colonies. This brought on the Revolutionary War and finally separated America and England and gave independence to the colonies, which eventually became the United States of America!*

"Listen to this," said Patrick as he read from the newspaper he was holding. "This writer reports on my speeches and my opposition to the King and his Parliament. He writes, 'The tendons on Patrick Henry's neck stood out white and rigid like whipcords. His voice rose louder and louder, until the walls of the building seemed to shake. Men leaned forward in their seats, their faces pale.'" Patrick's laughter seemed to bounce off the walls. When he stopped he said, "They are scared of what the King will do when he finds out the colonies refuse to pay his stamp tax. What the King needs to understand is that before we will obey his laws we must have representation in Parliament. We want to help create the laws for the colonies. We demand the right to have our voices heard in England!"

I realized my jaw was open as I listened to Patrick Henry defend the colonies. I finally said, "I admire your fearlessness, speaking out against the King. But you realize if your words get back to England the King is bound to send his Redcoats after you for treason. This is serious. They may hang you!"

With a smile on his face and a steely gaze in his eyes he said, "If this be treason, make the most of it!"

As if on cue the door burst open again and Tommy stood in the doorway. Panicked, he said, "Mr. Revere! You better get out here. Cam's in trouble. The Redcoats are back and they've arrested him!"

Patrick and I sprang from the table and followed Tommy out of the tavern. It was nearly dark outside, and one of three British soldiers held a torch. Patrick was the first to reach the second soldier, who was nearest to Cam. His hands were cuffed and he shrugged when I looked at him. Tommy and the messenger boy were watching close by.

"What's the meaning of this?" shouted Patrick. His voice did sound like thunder and the second soldier took a step back.

Feeling threatened, the third soldier unsheathed his sword and held it in front of him. The first soldier did the same.

"It was an accident," Cam said, defending himself.

Tommy leaned close to me and whispered, "Liberty was tired of chewing his gum so Cam told him to spit it out and I sort of dared him to try and hit one of the soldiers as they walked by the tavern. The soldier was at least twenty yards away. I didn't think he'd actually do it!"

The second soldier, who must have put the cuffs on Cam, stepped forward and said, "Your slave threw a wad of pink sap and hit me in the side of the head." The soldier turned and, sure enough, a sticky mass of gum looked like it had been pulled from his hair, but it was still a gooey mess.

"He's not a slave!" shouted Tommy.

"Shut up, colonial dog!" yelled one of the soldiers. Before Tommy could react the soldier closest to him swung the butt of his gun into Tommy's head and knocked him down.

"Enough of this!" I screamed as I rushed over to make sure Tommy wasn't hurt. Tommy pulled his hand away from where the gun had hit his head and found blood on his fingers. I quickly examined the cut and said, "It's not bad. It barely broke the skin. But you're going to have a goose egg on the side of your head." I looked up and saw Patrick ready to make his move. He remained calm, but I could tell he was also worried about Tommy and nervous for his young friend, Cam.

Cam nervously laughed and said, "I didn't throw it!" His eyes darted toward Liberty, who was doing an excellent job at pretending to be just a horse. Cam firmly said, "You didn't see me throw it. You didn't see any of us throw it! I have rights! Where's a lawyer when I need one?"

"I am a lawyer!" said Patrick Henry. He walked closer to the soldier near Cam but the two soldiers with swords stood firm.

Hearing the shouts and yells, the men from the tavern came outside to see Tommy bleeding and Cam in cuffs. Their expressions turned from concern for the young boys to anger at the soldiers.

Patrick shouted, "England will always consider us inferior! I have seen the way you Lobsterbacks laugh at how we talk and the way we dress. You have forgotten that we are still British subjects. Now, you believe we are dim-witted farmers and ill-suited merchants. You would sooner keep us in a barn then invite us into your chambers as equals."

"You will never be our equals, colonial scum," said the soldier in the middle. "Now get out of our way before we lock you up with the slave. You are no better than filthy rats! We should lock up the whole lot of you and let you rot in chains."

The men from the tavern started murmuring and cursing the soldiers. These were blacksmiths and carpenters and farmers—men with burly arms and itching to fight. The Redcoats knew they were outnumbered but they stood their ground.

The soldier holding a torch in one hand and his sword in the other sneered at Patrick and said, "We are taking our prisoner and he will be judged according to his crimes. Now get out of the way!"

Cam's jaw dropped in desperation and he said, "Uh-oh. Guys? Help me. Somebody?"

Patrick Henry looked as determined as ever and bellowed, "Crimes? You dare speak of crimes? I will tell you who the criminals are. The men who sit in Parliament and a king who burdens his people with unfair taxes."

"Your words convict you of treason!" said the first soldier. "You could hang for that!"

"As I've said before, if this be treason, make the most it!" said Patrick. "I spit on your stamp tax!" Patrick spit to the right.

"You are lucky to be walking freely in these streets," said the first solider. "We have direct orders from the King to put you in jail for any disrespect to the Crown."

"The King is the one disrespecting our freedom!" said Patrick, taking a step closer. "How dare he demand that we open our homes to house Redcoats like you! You are not our guests! You don't even like the people of these colonies. You just want to keep control of us. We worked hard to build these colonies. How dare the King force us to take you into our homes! This law is absurd! I spit on what the King is calling the Quartering Act!" Patrick spit again. "You Redcoats will not step foot inside of *my* home!"

"Watch your tongue, Patriot, before we cut it out," said the third soldier, who now pointed his sword directly at Patrick Henry.

But Patrick did not back down. He turned to the men from the tavern and shouted, "If we do not oppose the Quartering Act, the Redcoats will soon be tossing your families from their bedchambers in order to move in! Your wives and your children will be out in the streets and all because the King is an oppressive, arrogant, and selfish tyrant who only cares about three things: taxes, taxes, and more taxes!"

The colonists behind us shouted and jeered at the injustice in front of them. "Let them go!" said a large colonist with the neck the size of Rhode Island.

And that's when I noticed Liberty behind the soldier with the torch. While Patrick Henry was speaking he must have slipped behind unnoticed. Before the soldiers could react, Liberty turned his hind legs toward his target and gently kicked the unsuspecting soldier in the rear end. Even a gentle kick sent the Redcoat four feet into the air. He landed with a thud in front of us, his torch and sword rolling to our feet. I took the torch and Tommy took the sword. As if to prove a point, the third soldier raised his sword and attempted to strike down Patrick. The blade was deflected as Tommy parried with his own sword. Again and again the two swords clashed and remarkably it looked like Tommy had the upper hand. As the soldier stumbled backward, Liberty conveniently tripped him and the soldier fell to the ground. The colonists cheered at the momentary victory and pressed forward against the three Redcoats, who quickly retreated, leaving Cam standing alone and handcuffed.

"It would be wise for us all to leave this place for a time," said Patrick as the men dispersed from the tavern. "We can expect more Redcoats and they will want revenge. Do you have a place to go?"

"Yes, we'll be safe," I said. "And thank you for your help today."

"No kidding," said Cam. "You basically saved my life!"

"I try to save at least one life a day." Patrick winked. "Lucky for you, I had not yet filled my quota!"

We all laughed and Patrick finally said, "Cam, you are a remarkable young man. It took me a long time to have the confidence to stand up for what I wanted to do, who I wanted to be. But I have found that I am happiest when I am defending freedom and helping others find liberty and justice."

"Me, too!" said Cam. "When I was younger I was a military

brat. My family had just moved to a new city, and it's never easy starting over at a new school. And to make it worse, I was this little runt of a kid. These bigger kids at my old school used to bully me. They did some really mean things. One time they tossed me into a trash can upside down. But one summer I had a huge growth spurt. I grew seven inches and gained almost ten pounds. That's the year I decided to act and not be acted upon. So now whenever I see someone being bullied I don't stand for it. I can't help it. I like defending the little guy. I like helping others find liberty and justice, too!"

Patrick smiled and said, "The truth is you remind me of me when I was younger. You have a gift for words, a clever mind, and a sense of humor. No wonder I feel like we are kindred spirits." He reached out to shake Cam's hand but the handcuffs made it awkward.

Cam laughed, "Oops, forgot about the cuffs."

Patrick smiled and gently placed his hand on Cam's shoulder. He looked Cam straight in the eyes and said, "And I will not forget about the evils of slavery, I promise. As God is my witness, I will give my life for the cause of freedom for all men."

"Goodbye, Mr. Henry," said Tommy.

"Goodbye, Tommy," Patrick said, beaming. "You are quite the swordsman."

"I had a good teacher," said Tommy. With all the practice he had with Myles Standish, the Pilgrims' military leader, it's no surprise that he fought like he did. Myles would be proud!

"Safe travels, Rush Revere," said Patrick. "Until we meet again!" He turned to enter the tavern for his fiddle and coat.

I turned back to Tommy, Cam, and Liberty, and said, "That was quite the adventure! But I'm ready to return to modern-day."

"Me, too!" they all said in unison.

As we walked to the back of the tavern, I took a deep breath and said, "There's a chance we'll run into Elizabeth when we return to the school."

"Why do you say that?" Tommy asked.

"Because when we time-jumped to visit Patrick Henry she was chasing after us and nearly jumped through the time portal before it closed."

"What!" Tommy exclaimed.

"Hey! Maybe we can get Elizabeth to shoot laser beams out of her eyes," said Liberty.

"How is that going to help us?" complained Tommy.

"Well, somebody's got to get those handcuffs off Cam," said Liberty.

"Now we're talking," Cam said with a chuckle. "But laser beams really aren't my first choice."

"No worries," I told him as I reached into Liberty's saddlebag in search of a solution to Cam's dilemma. "Ah, here it is!"

"That is one odd-looking key," Cam said.

"It's a skeleton key and it can pick any eighteenth-century lock." I inserted the key into the lock of Cam's handcuffs and presto!

"I can't tell you how good it feels to be free!" exclaimed Cam.

I nodded and said, "It's a great feeling, isn't it. Likewise, the laws and taxes that the King and Parliament keep mandating to the colonies are like handcuffs. They restrict and bind the colonists from living and growing and being a free America!"

"Never thought of it like that. We're going to need a much bigger key to unlock that problem," Cam said.

"No kidding," Tommy agreed. "I think it's called a revolution!"

Tommy and Cam lifted themselves up onto Liberty's saddle.

"Now, about Elizabeth. We need to return to someplace different than where we left."

"Hmm," said Liberty. "How about in the hallway in front of our classroom. We've done that before."

"Can your Time-Travel-Sense tell us if anyone is in the hallway?" Cam asked.

"It's worked before," Liberty said. "I mean, I'm still trying to figure all of this out, but I think I can do it so no one sees us."

"Okay, then let's go," I said. "Tommy, how's the cut on your head?"

"It feels like a linebacker hit me without my football helmet on," Tommy said with a smile. "Besides that, I'm good."

I sighed, relieved that we were leaving without further harm. "That was a tough one for all us," I said. "I'm just glad you're both okay. Liberty, take us home!"

"Rush, rush, rushing from history," Liberty said.

In the dark of the night, the time portal opened again and as we headed toward the swirling, circular light I readied myself for whatever was waiting for us on the other side.

Wouldn't you be scared to have soldiers force their way into your home?

Chapter 6

The fluorescent lights in the school hallway made me squint as we returned to the twenty-first century. Once again, Liberty hit the bull's-eye as we landed in front of our classroom door. I quickly surveyed the scene and noticed we were alone.

Relieved, I said, "Nice jumping, Liberty. You boys need to change your clothes and—"

Just then I heard a single pair of footsteps running down the connecting hallway. The footsteps were getting louder. I assumed we returned just seconds after we had left, just seconds after Elizabeth had seen us jump through the time portal. I was certain those were her footsteps racing back to my classroom to prove I was a neglectful and delinquent teacher. The footsteps sounded like they would turn the corner any second and Elizabeth would find us! I desperately called to Liberty, who was already disappearing, but the boys were still sitting on top of, well, nothing!

"Oops," said Tommy. "I thought we'd turn invisible with Liberty if we were sitting on top of him." Still five feet off the ground, they quickly kicked their legs over to one side and slipped off an invisible saddle.

Freedom stood there and smiled. "Real slick, guys," she said nearly laughing. "You're lucky it's just me."

"Why were you running down the hallway like that?" I asked.

"When my grandfather dropped me off in front of the school I sprinted to the classroom hoping I could still catch you before you time-jumped. But by the look of things I'm guessing you just returned."

"It was incredible!" said Cam like he had just come off a wild roller coaster. "We traveled to the year 1765 and met Patrick Henry!"

"And I learned how to blow a bubble with bubble gum!" said Liberty.

"I thought you were going to be at the dentist today?" asked Tommy, apologetically. "You told me you wouldn't be back until almost the end of class."

Freedom shrugged her shoulders and said, "No cavities."

"You're lucky," Cam said. "The worst part is when the dentist has to numb your gums. I mean, I'm glad for the anesthesia. It's the shot I don't like."

"Anesthesia, spelled A-N-E-S-T-H-E-S-I-A," said Liberty, proudly. "Now, give Tommy a word and see if he can spell it. We're having a spelling bee competition. Unless Tommy is scared," Liberty taunted. "Of course, he shouldn't feel bad losing to a horse since technically I'm no ordinary horse although I look ordinary but most people who do extraordinary things appear ordinary at first until the moment that they—"

"Thanks, Liberty," Freedom said with a smirk. "You just gave me an idea. Tommy, spell the word *logorrhea*."

"Huh?" Tommy said while raising one eyebrow.

Liberty smiled and said, "I don't know what the word means but I approve of your word choice."

Tommy took off his hat and scratched his head. "Um, can you give it to me in a sentence?"

"Sure," said Freedom. "Liberty's logorrhea can go on and on but it's one of the things I like about him."

"Oh, I think I know," Tommy said, smiling. "*Logorrhea* is spelled L-O-G-O-R-R-H-E-A."

"Correct," Freedom said.

"Wait a minute," said Liberty suspiciously. "Are you saying that I . . ."

"That you have a big mouth and talk too much? Yes!" said Elizabeth, who appeared from behind the hallway corner. She wore a long red coat with designer jeans and a matching red headband in her hair. "My, my, my, what do we have here?" Elizabeth slowly walked in between us with her hands behind her back. She stared at each of us and talked as if she knew a secret. "Do any of you have hall passes? No, I'm sure you don't because that would require one of you to have a responsible teacher." She glared at me and then looked away. "Do any of you have any fashion sense at all?" She stopped in front of Freedom with a look of disdain. "Freedom? Or should I just call you Free-*dumb*! That's spelled D-U-M-B. By the way, you looked better in that hideous Pilgrim costume that should've been burned in the seventeenth century." She released her gaze and finally approached Liberty. "Oh, and finally, do any you have a permit for this"—she scrunched up her nose in disgust—"this odoriferous horse inside Manchester Middle School?"

"Odoriferous?" said Liberty. "For the record, I'm hardly offended by your weak insults."

"Oh, that wasn't an insult," Elizabeth said. "That was simply a fact. I'm sure you know that *odoriferous* means smelly. Personally, I don't like the smell of horses. It's a foul stench that belongs in a barn, not a school." Elizabeth turned to look at all of us and said, "I'm on to your little secret. I saw you jump through that magical door thingy. It's a time portal, isn't it?" I must've looked surprised because she said, "I knew it! And don't look so surprised. It's obvious with all the colonial costumes and the movie you showed us about the Pilgrims in Holland and the talking horse who knows about American history."

"Just what is it you're going to do, Elizabeth?" I asked.

"What am I going to do?" she asked, acting surprised. "It's not about what *I'm* going to do. It's about what *you're* going to do for *me*."

"That sounds like blackmail," said Cam.

"At least one of you has some brains," Elizabeth scoffed.

"Whatever," Tommy said. "We'll all deny what you've seen and heard and you'll end up with the nurse again."

"Already thought of that," said Elizabeth. "That's why I had the custodian help me install that small camera in the corner of the ceiling." We followed her gaze and saw the lens pointing right at us. "So let's get this straight. Either you do what I say or I take the video to my daddy and it's bye-bye Mr. Revere. No more Liberty. And I'm pretty sure I can get the rest of you expelled from Manchester Middle School."

"Why are you so mean?" asked Freedom.

Elizabeth sighed and said, "Freedom, I'm not mean. I'm simply taking control of the situation. You see, when things get out of control I have to tighten the controls. Let me put it this way. Some people were meant to rule, that's me, and other people are meant to be ruled, that's you. Some people are superior, that's me. And some people are inferior, that's you."

"Mr. Revere," called Tommy, "I say we take Elizabeth with us the next time we time travel. Seriously, I know just the person she should meet. I bet she's a direct descendant."

I knew exactly whom Tommy was thinking of.

"I knew Thomas would get it," said Elizabeth.

"My name's Tommy," he said.

Elizabeth sighed, "Tommy is a child's name. Thomas is much more sophisticated. Plus, Thomas and Elizabeth sound much better together, don't you think?"

"Excuse me?" asked Tommy with a stunned look on his face.

"I've been thinking since you're the star quarterback and I'm the most popular girl in school that we'd be perfect as the homecoming king and queen. Then we can rule the school together," Elizabeth said, smiling, "just as long as you do exactly what I say."

Cam nearly laughed out loud and Freedom just rolled her eyes.

"I don't know what warped fantasy world you're living in," Tommy replied, "but keep me out of it."

Elizabeth ignored Tommy's remark and impatiently said, "The day isn't getting any younger, people. I want to time-travel now."

"Now?" Tommy asked, surprised.

Liberty looked heartbroken. "But I thought it was time for me to finally perform for the class my stomp act about the Stamp Act!" he whined.

"If she's time-traveling, then count me out," said Freedom, crossing her arms.

"Me, too," said Cam.

"Me, three," Tommy said.

Elizabeth grabbed Tommy's arm and said, "I insist that Thomas travel with me. Riding behind him will be the only thing that gets me on that horse."

"Oh brother," Tommy mumbled.

Elizabeth continued: "And another thing: I'm not wearing any colonial clothing. It makes you look like orphans. Except for you, Mr. Revere. You look like you should be in an insane asylum."

This girl was starting to get on my nerves. I took a deep breath and exhaled slowly. She would have to wear the appropriate clothing if she wanted to time-travel but I'd deal with that later. I sighed and said, "Very well, Elizabeth, if time-traveling is what you want, time-traveling is what you'll get. But for the record, you're not forcing me to do anything. I'm happy to take you and teach you what only history can share. But mark my words, history has a way of showing us the good, the bad, and the ugly. Are you prepared for that?"

Elizabeth simply shook her head and rolled her eyes. "Mr. Revere," she said, "I deal with the good, the bad, and the ugly every day at Manchester Middle School. For example, my fashion sense is the *good*. And Freedom's fashion sense is the *bad* and the *ugly*."

"I'm outta here," Freedom said, giving one last glare to Elizabeth. "Bye, guys, I'm going to class." As she walked toward the classroom door she turned back and looked at Liberty. I suspected she was sending him a telepathic message.

Liberty whinnied and smiled. He whispered, "Freedom thinks we should take Elizabeth to the past and leave her there."

"I'm outta here, too," said Cam. "I better change my clothes before all the girls see me. That's right, I've seen Elizabeth like she's all desperate to know how I make these colonial clothes look so good! We can hang later, Lizzy," Cam winked.

"My name is Elizabeth, you moron."

"Whatever," Cam said, casually. "Maybe I'll see you guys at the football game tomorrow night." Cam gave us a giant smile and strutted toward the bathroom.

I turned to Elizabeth and said, "Are you sure I can't persuade you to wear something more appropriate for our eighteenth-century visit?"

Elizabeth sighed as if she felt sorry for me. She replied, "I should be asking you the same question." And then in a very condescending tone she began pointing to what she was wearing and slowly said, "*This* is a Le Pluer jacket and *these* are Yass jeans and my Pomanelli shoes are from *It-al-y*. You, on the other hand, are wearing scraps and rags from the thrift store. I'm surprised you're not pushing a shopping cart with all your belongings inside."

My mouth dropped open slightly in disbelief. Did she just call me a hobo?

Tommy replied, "Elizabeth, you can't show up like that and not expect people to start asking questions . . ."

As he continued to try to explain the potential danger of a girl wearing jeans in the eighteenth century, I turned to Liberty and whispered an idea into his ear.

Liberty mused, "Hmm, yes, that might be the perfect solution."

"Good," I whispered, "and I still have Freedom's colonial dress;

that should fit Elizabeth." I interrupted Tommy and Elizabeth and said, "It's time we show Elizabeth what time-jumping is all about."

Tommy lifted himself up onto Liberty's saddle and I helped up Elizabeth, who sat right behind him.

"Liberty, it's time we visit Windsor Castle in England. It seems like a place that would suit Elizabeth."

"Windsor Castle is a part of American history?" Tommy asked.

"It's the residence of King George III," I said. "And he was very involved in shaping American history."

"Meeting a king sounds great but what are we waiting for?" asked Elizabeth sounding irritated. "Enough chitchat. Sitting on top of your donkey is making me gag. Seriously, the smell is like a manure pile. Let's go already!"

"Some people need a swift kick in the you-know-where," Liberty snorted.

"Let's just stick with our plan," I reassured him.

"Fine!" said Liberty. "It'll be my pleasure." He took a deep breath and firmly said, *"Rush, rush, rushing to history!"*

As the gold and purple time portal started to open, I hoped our plan would work. I ran closely behind Liberty as he galloped toward the portal. I shouted, "England, Windsor Castle, 1766, King George III."

As Liberty jumped I heard Elizabeth scream as she passed through the portal. I immediately followed and in the time it takes to hurdle a small fence I landed on the other side. The first thing I saw was Elizabeth sailing over Liberty's head and landing face-first in the middle of a small pond with several lily pads floating on the surface of the water.

Windsor Castle, Berkshire, the royal residence in England.

Tommy quickly jumped off Liberty and raced over to the edge of the shallow pond and yelled, "Elizabeth, are you okay? Let me help you out!"

Elizabeth pushed herself up, sopping wet. Her red headband was floating in the water and in its place was a limp lily pad. Her jacket and jeans were muddy and her mascara was smeared. As she slowly walked to the lawn that surrounded the pond I noticed she was missing one shoe. I could barely see it stuck in the mud about two feet under the water. Her hair was matted to her face, and although her mouth was open I wasn't sure if she was breathing.

Finally, the silence was broken when she screamed, "Ahhh! What. Just. Happened! What kind of horse stops like that! Are you kidding me?!"

Liberty confessed: "Um, well, I really didn't think you'd fall face-first into a pond. Sorry about that. The plan was to get your clothes a little muddy so you'd want to change them and wear something from the eighteenth century."

"I'm the one that makes the plans around here, remember!" Elizabeth shouted. "Ugh, just help me get out of this sewer! It smells putrid, almost as bad as Liberty."

Liberty ignored the insult, distracted by the new scenery. With wonder in his voice, he said, "Now that is a castle!"

Directly in front of us was a tall, massive, round stone tower. It was ancient-looking but matched all the smaller castle-like towers and buildings that surrounded us. The smaller towers were connected by a large stone wall that was clearly meant to keep out the unwanted. After a moment, I realized we were inside the grounds of Windsor Castle. The yard was beautifully landscaped with a variety of trees, shrubs, and flowers. The aroma from many varieties of roses was intoxicating. Birds chirped from the trees as bees buzzed around the garden. The scene was a paradise and very different from what the colonists were dealing with in a new country.

As Tommy helped Elizabeth to a small stone bench just a few yards away, I reached for my travel bag that had the colonial dress.

Suddenly, a voice from behind us yelled, "You there! What is your business?"

I turned to see three British soldiers running in our direction. Their red-coat uniforms looked brand-new. Their black boots shined and their gold buttons sparkled. Even their muskets looked polished, as if they had never been used. Life behind castle walls was certainly much different than life in the American wilderness, where British troops had to try to control headstrong colonists every day.

"How did you get into the castle?" asked the lead soldier. He sounded very annoyed.

"Would you believe we dropped out of the sky?" I said, jokingly. Apparently, my joke wasn't very funny, as the soldiers just glared at me. "As a matter of fact we have urgent news for the King," I said.

"Only those invited get to see the King," said the soldier, briskly. "Do you have an invitation?"

I paused for just a moment before Tommy butted in and lied: "We did but it's probably at the bottom of the pond. As you can see we had a little accident."

I smiled and said, "Yes, that's right. Poor girl. And now's she's

A portrait of George III, King of Great Britain and Ireland (1760–1820).

wet and freezing and I'm sure the King would not want any harm to come to one of his invited guests, especially one so young and beautiful."

Elizabeth just sat there looking cold and miserable.

The soldier looked at Elizabeth and then back to me. He paused before he finally said, "Very well. Follow me. But if the King is not expecting you—"

I interrupted and said, "I assure you the King will be glad we have arrived. Our news is of the utmost importance."

Soon we were following the lead soldier, with the other two soldiers following us. We approached a very large door big enough for Liberty to fit through. Two more Redcoats stood guard on either side of the door. We quickly entered into an immense hallway with colorful tapestries that hung from the stone walls. On one side of the hallway were full suits of armor from the Middle Ages. The armor stood like sentinels ready to come to life and protect the castle if need be. When we were halfway down the hallway we saw a tall man descend a stone stairway. The man was in his mid to late twenties. He looked young but was dressed in clothing worthy of a king. Everything he wore looked expensive and new. The rich colors of his clothes, his perfect posture, and even his powdered face intimidated me. The vision of this man was so royal, so majestic that I could barely speak.

As he reached the last step of the stairway I forced my tongue to comply with my mind and while bowing low I said, "King George, Your Excellency." Liberty bowed as well, which seemed to amuse the King. "I am Rush Revere, history teacher and historian. And these are my students, Tommy and Elizabeth. We've come to bring you news from the New World."

"Your Highness," the lead soldier said with a bow, "they insisted that their news was urgent."

The King looked me up and down as if to say *what are these peasants doing in my presence?* His eyes turned to Elizabeth and said, "Elizabeth is a fine name, a royal name. But why is she drenched from head to toe? Guard, find the maids and have them dress her in something appropriate. Take her to the Red Drawing Room when she is fit for company. And you can burn those rags she's wearing."

Elizabeth was staring at King George III as if he were a rock star. Surprisingly, she did not complain about her clothes getting burned. In fact, I wondered if she had heard him at all. Instead, she bowed low and said, "Thank you, Your Majesty. Your clothes are magnificent. You shine like gold. It's been a long journey but I am honored to be in your presence."

I was shocked by Elizabeth's sudden change in character. She was actually being nice and extremely polite! She played along perfectly and curtseyed to the King and then followed the guard while leaving a trail of water still dripping from her clothing.

"Is that the same girl we know? That's what you call sucking up!" whispered Tommy with a grin.

"Is something amusing?" King George asked, reminding us quickly of our surroundings.

"No, Your Excellency, quite the opposite," I said standing up straight. "There is a serious situation happening in the colonies."

"Let us retire to the Red Drawing Room. Guard, take Mr. Revere's horse to the livery."

It didn't take us long before we entered a magnificent room adorned with red velvet chairs with golden armrests. Huge golden-framed paintings of kings and queens lined the red fabric walls. The ceiling looked like it was painted with real gold leaf. Golden tables with intricate and expensive-looking vases and statues and golden clocks reminded me that we were indeed in a real castle with a real king and his real riches! Several of the King's guards entered the room with us.

"Tell me this important news from the colonies," said the King as he gracefully sat in a royal-looking chair and crossed his legs.

The king didn't smile but he wasn't frowning, either. Tommy and I found chairs and sat down. I said, "We are here to tell you that the people are not happy in America."

The King looked mildly interested in what I was saying but not very concerned. "What concern is that of mine?" he asked.

I was thrown off a bit by his question. I had expected him to ask me to explain further. Tommy looked at me with his eyebrows raised as if to say, what now?

I knew I couldn't change history, and I hadn't come to pick a fight. But I was determined to explain the colonial situation and, hopefully, learn some historical truth in the process. I said, "This should concern Your Majesty because the people are getting more and more angry. They left England for a reason. They were looking for freedom and the chance to really succeed with their lives."

"You came all this way to tell me that the colonists are fighting with the motherland? You think this is important information for me? You are a foolish man!" said the King in a raised voice.

I must say that his insult got under my skin. I respected that he is a king but I was born an American, and I wasn't thrilled about getting treated this way! I held my temper enough to say,

"Your Excellency, please if you would—you are mistreating the people, the taxes are too severe, and they cannot vote! This isn't the way to lead."

"Revere, I should throw you out in the moat this minute for your ridiculous statements. How dare you tell me how to be a leader! I am the head of England; I know exactly what I'm doing. The New World is our land and the people are ours. They must share their wealth with the homeland, they must pay taxes to England, and they must obey the wishes of the King!"

The guards in the room moved closer to King George as if I was some kind of threat.

Normally, I'm as cool as a cucumber, but this was getting out of control. The King was really laying into me now and I must say it was getting to me.

Tommy whispered, "No wonder Elizabeth is a fan! He's a bigger diva than she is!"

"Your Excellency, you are a smart man," I said. "Why are you pursuing this path? What benefit is there to Britain?" I was trying to remain detached as best I could, an observer of history.

"I do not need you to tell me I am smart! I do not need you to tell me anything, you buffoon!" the King said, pounding the bottom of his fist on his knee.

"With all due respect, Your Highness, I'm hardly a buffoon." I tried to maintain some sense of relaxed scholarship, but I was starting to sweat and my heart was starting to beat faster. I was either scared or angry or both! I continued: "I am just trying to figure out why you are so dedicated to limiting the rights of the Americans. Why do you treat them this way? Why are you taxing them so much?"

The King squinted at me and asked, "Do all the colonists

dress like you?" Before I could respond the King replied, "The hat you wear, it is atrocious. Your coat is that of a commoner. Your shoes look pale and unpolished. And your speech sounds ghastly. Do you have a speech impediment or was your mother simply as dumb as you are?"

Did he really just insult my mother? This king was pompous, rude, and inconsiderate. Frankly, he was a jerk!

"No matter, I will answer your insidious question," the King said. "The colonies are behaving like children. They have forgotten their mother country and for that they must be disciplined. They are not their own land or their own people! They are part of this country! They are under my rule and always will be!"

I knew I shouldn't provoke the King and was doubtful that anything I could say would get through to him. But he did insult my mother! I finally said, "Yes, children can be very rude. In fact, you, yourself, look very young. Was it you who chose to punish the colonists by creating the Stamp Act and Quartering Act?" My comment seemed to strike a nerve in the king.

"How dare you!" shouted the King.

The King's guards pressed forward and unsheathed their swords. King George raised his hand and the soldiers stopped. I imagine they thought my words had sentenced me to the dungeon. I doubt many people, if any, dared speak to the King of England like I had.

King George eased back in his chair and coldly said, "Parliament creates the rules based on what they feel is best for the colonies and best for England. The thirteen colonies need order. They need England like a baby needs its mother's milk." When he finished speaking he smirked with satisfaction.

I forced myself to remain calm and replied, "That is a good

point, Your Highness. But the colonies believe they are no longer babies. In fact, they believe they are no longer children. Their economy is thriving, their businesses are successful, and they refuse to be told what taxes they have to pay—"

The King interrupted and exclaimed, "And that is something that a child would say. I will have the colonies back under my control. These so-called Patriots will never succeed as individuals. They will bow to the King and serve the Crown. They will do what they are told. I will not tolerate anything less!"

"I'm not so sure about that," I whispered to Tommy. "The United States of America is going to be born soon."

Tommy whispered back, "This is better than Monday Night Football! Revere versus the King of England!" I was glad Tommy could have a sense of humor. The tension in the room was so thick you could slice it with a butter knife.

"You have some nerve, Revere! You took a great risk coming here and addressing me with this drivel!" The King's face was red and his eyes were fiercely focused on mine.

Whether good or bad, something inside me pushed onward. I could tell I was losing some of the history teacher and getting involved a little too much in the actual history. *Careful,* I said to myself. *Careful!*

"Your Excellency," I said, "what the people want is a vote. Why is that so hard to understand?"

"I recommended ending the stamp tax! Isn't that enough for you fools? You truly are children! I don't care what the colonists want!" the King yelled as he stood up from his chair. "I have heard from the provincial Benjamin Franklin. He is a fool to side with those who fight against the Crown. And rebels like Patrick Henry and Samuel Adams will hang from the gallows for their

treacherous words. I will have my way!" He pouted. "I will. I will! The colonists are rabble-rousers and common criminals. They are dumb, silly dressed fools who are still subject to my laws and my word. I shall not have them forget that I rule the New World. I am the King! The land and the people of the thirteen colonies are still mine. Mine, I tell you! The colonists will do anything I say and buy anything we sell them! Except for fine fashion, it appears!"

The King sneered with a wicked grin. "As a matter of fact, I am signing the Declaratory Act in the morning, which gives England and the King full authority, full power to make laws that are legally binding on the colonies."

"In other words," I said, "England's grip on America becomes even tighter."

"Like handcuffs?" asked Tommy.

"Exactly," I said. I stood and motioned for Tommy to stand as well. I tried to remain humble, realizing at any moment the King could tell the guards, Off with my head!

I took a deep breath and said, "This act, this Declaratory Act, will make my countrymen even angrier. It will feel like the freedoms their ancestors fought for are being taken away."

The King sneered and said, "You imbecile! The colonists have no idea what is best for them. They are not capable of making decisions for themselves. I am their king, and I know better than they do what is good for them! I want them totally dependent on me for everything. That is the way it always has been, that is the way it should be."

"I couldn't agree with you more Your Highness," said Elizabeth, who stood at the door of the Red Drawing Room. She was wearing the most exquisite blue gown, which seemed to sparkle.

George III, King of Great Britain and Ireland (1760–1820).

It reached all the way to the floor and looked like something from Cinderella's ball. A short white fur was draped across her shoulders and her hair was curled and beautifully arranged on top of her head. I could tell her face was powdered and she looked several years older than she really was.

"Elizabeth?" Tommy asked. "What the . . . did you bump your head when you fell into that pond?"

"The King is so wise and so amazingly handsome," Elizabeth said, ignoring Tommy. "I absolutely agree that taking control of the situation is the only thing to do. We need to do what needs to be done to help them see that the King's laws are just. We need the colonies to show more respect to England. We need to force them to obey! I declare that we put troops in every house and tax all the little fools!"

"We?" said Tommy. "And who made you queen? Maybe bringing you here wasn't such a good idea."

The King turned to Elizabeth and said, "It is reassuring to see this kind of transformation and hear this kind of loyalty from one of my colonial subjects."

"The point is a good leader is supposed to protect and preserve the rights of the people. Instead it appears as though you are trampling those rights with tyranny," I said, knowing full well I would break what little harmony there was in the room.

"I am done with you!" screamed King George. "I rule! And I grow tired of your insults." He walked toward Elizabeth, took her hand, and kissed it. "Elizabeth, I am glad for your company and wish we could have spent more time together." He then turned toward Tommy and me and shouted, "Guards! Escort my lady and the two bloody Americans to the front gate. Retrieve their horse from the livery and send them on their way."

Two guards escorted Elizabeth by the arms and another two escorted Tommy. As they left the room, King George called to me one last time. I was really not interested to hear what the King was about to say. In fact, I knew I had pushed the King too far and had overstayed my welcome.

That wicked grin returned to the King's lips and he said threateningly, "Mr. Revere, do not ever forget that I am king of the most powerful nation in the world. My word is law. Your pathetic life has been spared for one reason. I want you to sail back to your woeful America and tell those wretched rebels that I will send the entire British army to force them into submission if I have to. Do you understand? Or is that too difficult for your pea-sized brain."

"Oh, I understand," I said with a smirk. "It will be my pleasure."

Chapter 7

After leaving the castle we found a secluded area in a nearby forest to time-jump back to modern-day. Liberty suggested that I put duct tape over Elizabeth's mouth so we wouldn't have to hear her incessant complaining about getting kicked out of Windsor Castle.

"*Rush, rush, rushing from history,*" Liberty said.

Like clockwork, we arrived back at Manchester in the same hallway just seconds after we had left. In fact, Cam must have just finished changing into his modern-day clothes and was walking back to the classroom when he noticed us in the hallway.

"Haven't you guys left yet?" Cam asked. "What's taking you so . . ." That's when he noticed the dress that Elizabeth was wearing. "What happened to her?"

"Would you believe she fell into a pond?" Liberty said.

"More like thrown into a pond," Elizabeth countered.

"A pond?" asked Cam. "Was there a toad in the pond that kissed her and she turned into a princess?"

"I wouldn't let a toad kiss me! Gross! If we were in England I'd have the guards throw you into the dungeon!" Elizabeth said.

"She may look like a princess but she's acting like a toad," Cam replied.

"Let's get back into the classroom. I imagine the video of Benjamin Franklin is almost over," I said.

"Quick, someone take a picture of me wearing this dress!" said Elizabeth as she handed Tommy her phone. "It's the least you can do after ruining my visit with King George!" Tommy took a quick picture and handed the phone back to Elizabeth.

"I can't wait to post this on Facebook and Pinterest and Instagram and—"

Liberty interrupted and said, "I remember when people would simply post things to doors. For example, in 1770 I remember a posting about the Boston Massacre!"

"The mass of what?" Tommy asked.

"The Boston Massacre," Cam said.

Liberty agreed. "Yes, I saw a drawing of it that Paul Revere engraved, printed, and posted all over Boston. I suppose if Paul Revere had Facebook or Instagram he would've posted it there as well!"

"I wish I had taken a picture of King George," Elizabeth sighed as if she were daydreaming. "He looked magnificent!" Elizabeth twirled around and around as she waltzed down the hallway. "Adieu!"

I looked at Tommy and Cam, who looked as worried as I did.

"Should we try to stop her? What's going to happen when Principal Sherman sees her dress?" said Tommy.

"Yeah, she has all the evidence she needs to bust us!" Cam said.

"Let's not panic," I said. "I don't think she's in any hurry to burn the bridge that let her meet King George. I'd say she's very happy."

"I'd say she's loopy!" Cam said.

"I'd say she's nuts-o," said Tommy.

"I'd say her chimney is missing a few bricks!" said Liberty, who snorted at his own joke.

"I'd say you better get in here," said Freedom, who stuck her head out the classroom door. "The video you took of Benjamin Franklin just ended and kids are wondering where you are."

I turned to Tommy and Cam and said, "After Tommy changes his clothes I need the two of you to go to the teachers' lounge and grab the sound system and speakers. Bring them here so Liberty can perform his stomp act about the Stamp Act."

Cam started to laugh and said, "I'm sorry for laughing but it sounds really funny every time you say that."

Liberty replied, "I always laugh when I hear the question, 'How much wood could a woodchuck chuck if a woodchuck could chuck wood?' If I ever meet a woodchuck I'm going to ask him if woodchucks really do chuck wood and if so, how much wood would he really chuck if he could? I mean if he chucks too much wood could a woodchuck upchuck the chucked wood?"

The things this horse says, I thought. I smiled and pulled Liberty's halter toward the classroom door. "Let's go. It's time for Honors History," I said.

The two boys darted down the hallway and Liberty and I entered the classroom. Upon seeing us the students quickly settled down.

I walked to the front of the class and said, "We're going to have a quick test on the movie about Benjamin Franklin that you just watched. I'm going to pass out a piece of paper and I want you to answer the question, 'Why were the colonies opposed to the Stamp Act?'"

I heard a couple of moans and sighs.

I continued: "Before you answer I'll need you to give me five dollars each for the paper you're going to use to take the test."

This time I heard lots of moans, gasps, sighs, and even a "That's a rip-off!"

"Is there a problem?" I asked.

A boy in the middle of the room raised his hand and said, "It's not fair!"

And then a girl said, "Don't my parents already pay taxes for this?"

Another boy said, "Do we have to use your paper? If I use my own do I still have to pay the five dollars?"

I smiled and said, "Yes, you still have to pay the five dollars. Yes, I assume your parents are paying taxes already. And, yes, I'm requiring you to pay this paper tax because it's going to help me pay off some debts."

Now it seemed like the whole class was in an uproar.

"Mr. Revere," said Freedom from the back of the class, "this sounds a lot like the stamp tax that Parliament and the King demanded that the colonies pay. And we sound a lot like the colonists who didn't think it was fair."

"Very good, Freedom. I'm glad to know that the video you watched may have taught you something. In any case, I think Parliament and the King are right. So I need you to pay me now!"

"Seriously?" Freedom smirked, thinking I was kidding. "What if the whole class decides not to pay the tax? What if we refuse?"

"Is that how all of you feel?" I asked as I looked around the room.

"I'm with Freedom! Me, too! I'm not paying! No way! Freedom is right!" said the students until they all started chanting, "We won't pay! We won't pay! We won't pay!"

With a wide grin I finally held up my hands to quiet the student mob and said, "Congratulations, you passed the test and you all get an A!" As the class cheered, Tommy and Cam entered the room carrying the sound system and speakers. I quickly set them up and invited Liberty to come to the front of the room. With a short introduction I said, "It's my pleasure to introduce Liberty and his stomp act about the Stamp Act."

The music started, Liberty began stomping to the beat, and then he started to sing:

(Sung to the tune of "Call Me Maybe" by Carly Rae Jepsen and Tavish Crowe)
I threw a stamp on the fire
Go tell the British Empire
Your Stamp Act agents are fired
You're simply in our way

Go tell King George the III
His Stamp Act is absurd
This is our final word
You're simply in our way

This law is bogus
Taxing all our paper products
Do you really think you own us?
Listen to the Stamp Act Congress!

Hey, we just left you
And this is crazy
You never asked us
Don't tax our colonies
We've got Ben Franklin
And Patrick Henry
You never asked them
Don't tax our colonies

Because your taxes aren't fair
You make us so mad
You make us so mad
You make us so, so mad
Because your taxes aren't fair
You make us so mad
And you should know that
You make us so, so mad

As the music faded away Liberty struck a pose and the class applauded and cheered. As the bell rang, I was certain this would be a history lesson they would never forget.

The next day I had to wake up Liberty so we could have lunch before my class started. He said he was still tired and blamed it on all the time-jumping.

"Well, let's get some food in you because we'll need to time-jump today to meet Samuel Adams," I said.

Liberty yawned and replied, "Oh, I remember King George said that Samuel Adams was a rebel. Is that true?"

"Yes, Samuel Adams fanned the flames of the Revolutionary

War in Boston. He was also a cousin to the American hero John Adams. If possible I'd like to find Samuel and discover the truth. From what I've heard he was a stubborn, hotheaded, and crafty man who never doubted the cause of freedom."

"Oh, he sounds delightful," Liberty said with sarcasm.

I smiled and said, "Maybe not delightful, but he knew how to motivate people to fight for their liberties. And I want to see how he did it. I want to know what role he played in Boston and what he was truly like."

"Fine with me, but I don't think I'm adding him to my Christmas card list!"

"Well, maybe our visit will change your mind," I said.

Liberty paused before he said, "Benjamin Franklin, Patrick Henry, Samuel Adams—I'm certain I have a connection with all of these exceptional Americans but I can't seem to put my hoof on it."

"Well, you are from the revolutionary time period," I reminded him.

"Yes, I am certain of that," said Liberty. "Oh, and I'm also certain that I am famished!"

No surprise, I thought.

On our way to Manchester Middle School we stopped and ate bagels and cream cheese. Liberty ate eighteen bagels in honor of the eighteenth century.

"A full stomach always makes me sleepy," he said.

"Maybe you can take a quick nap during part of my history lesson."

As we approached the front doors of the school, Liberty turned invisible. The bell would ring at any second and students would flood the hallways as they headed toward their

A map sketched by John Adams of the taverns in Braintree and Weymouth, 1761.

…ridge

…er's

This Brook divides Weymouth from Braintree

Road to South part of Braintree, & Bridgwater

Little Pond.

Clark's.

Walis

Braintree South M: House.

Vinton's

…Meeting House in Weymouth

Nash's.

White's

The publick Houses in the southern Parts of
Braintree and Weymouth, are not too nu
merous, perhaps, if they are well provided an
well disposed, but of these Things I know noth

Samuel Adams

final class of the day. As we turned the final corner I saw Elizabeth slip into the Honors History classroom. I assume Liberty saw her, too, but just to be sure I said, "Did you see Elizabeth?"

Liberty exhaled and reappeared by my side. "Yes, and she looked a little sneaky. I'll stay invisible until we know what she's up to." He took a deep breath and disappeared again.

At the sound of the bell I saw students exit other classrooms along the hallway. We quickly slipped inside the Honors History room and I noticed Elizabeth sitting in her regular seat. She sweetly said, "Hello, Mr. Revere. I think we got off on the wrong foot. I've decided that Manchester Middle School definitely needs a horse, uh, I mean, a history teacher with your special skills. By the way, where's Liberty?"

She looked behind me as if she was waiting for Liberty to enter. I knew she was up to something. But what? I casually replied, "Thank you, Elizabeth. I'm glad to have you back in Honors History. Liberty will be here soon. What did Principal Sherman say about your new dress?"

"Oh, I told him I went shopping and just had to have it for the homecoming dance." She winked. "No worries, Mr. Revere. I've got you covered. I know how to play this game. You scratch my back and I'll scratch yours."

Tommy entered the classroom and paused when he saw Elizabeth.

"Hi, Thomas, did you miss me?" said Elizabeth, her words dripping with sweetness.

"No offense, but not really."

"No matter. I need to talk to you about the next time we

time-jump. The possibilities are so exciting! And I know just where I want to—"

Just then the door opened and several more students began walking in. I was relieved for the interruption. Something was definitely up with Elizabeth. She was acting very strange since our visit with King George. Finally, the bell rang for class to start and I noticed Cam was standing in the middle of the room unsure about where to sit.

"It looks like there's a desk in the middle of the classroom." I pointed to the empty desk next to Freedom. Once Cam was seated I took a quick roll call and welcomed everyone.

Liberty finally exhaled and appeared behind Freedom and Cam. I was always impressed at how long he could hold his breath and stay invisible.

I turned, grabbed a piece of chalk, and wrote on the chalkboard, "The Townshend Acts." I said, "The Stamp Act wasn't the only act or law that Parliament created and King George III approved to tax the thirteen colonies. The Quartering Act, the Declaratory Act, and numerous other acts continued to make the colonies boil with anger and hatred toward King George. But it was the Townshend Acts that may have finally pushed the colonies over the edge."

Elizabeth raised her hand and said, "You're making King George sound like a monster. Actually, he was a very nice guy with incredible taste in fashion, gorgeous blue eyes, and let's not forget, he was a king."

"Thank you, Elizabeth," I said. "But let's finish our discussion by saying that the Townshend Acts were a series of 1767 laws named for Charles Townshend, the British chancellor of

Boston. (Town of.)
Circular

THE Merchants and Traders in this Town in the Agreement subscribed by them the 17th of *October* last, engaged that the Orders they might send for Goods to be shipped them from *Great-Britain* should be on Condition that the Acts imposing Duties for the Purpose of raising a Revenue in *America* should be totally Repealed, at the signing of which Agreement it was expected that the Merchants in *New-York*, *Philadelphia*, and other Colonies would come into a similar Agreement; but the Merchants in the other Colonies having already ordered their Goods to be shipped in Case the Act imposing Duties on Tea, Glass, &c. is repealed, for this and other Reasons mentioned in their Letters decline concurring with us at present, but have proposed to join us in any Plan that may be thought prudent to pursue for obtaining the Repeal of the Acts of the 4th & 6th of GEORGE the Third——Therefore the Merchants here thinking it of the utmost Importance that the Traders in all the Colonies should act upon the same Plan, *have agreed to write their Correspondents that the Goods they have or may send for should be shipped on this express Condition, that the Act imposing Duties on Tea, Glass, Paper and Colours, be totally repealed, and not otherways*——And have directed their Committee to confer with the Committees of the other Colonies relative to their Proposal above-mentioned.

This Notice of the Proceedings of the Merchants, at their last Meeting, is now sent to the Gentlemen in Trade for their Government, in Case they should send any Orders for Goods.

Boston, December 6th, 1769.

Notice from Boston merchants calling for a complete repeal of the Townshend duties, 1769.

Portrait of Charles Townshend by Joshua Reynolds.

the treasury. He's the guy keeping track of all the King's money. These laws placed new taxes on glass, lead, paints, paper, and tea. How do you think the colonies felt about paying more and more taxes?"

Cam started singing the chorus from Liberty's Stamp Act song. "Because your taxes aren't fair, you make us so mad, you make us so mad, you make us so, so mad!"

The class laughed as Cam took a bow from his seat.

"Exactly," I said. "Many of the colonists protested; sometimes they showed violence against British soldiers and the British tax collectors. So King George sent more British troops to the colonies. In fact, he sent four thousand Redcoats to the city of Boston, which only had twenty thousand residents at the time."

"It sounds like Boston was swarming with Redcoats," said Tommy.

"I wish I could take all of you back to Boston on March fifth of 1770," I said. "You'll need to use your imaginations for this. If it helps to close your eyes, please do. Daydream, if you will, to March fifth, 1770. You're in Boston, Massachusetts. It is evening and the moon is full. You're on King Street in front of the Customs Office. Street lanterns dimly light the way as you walk along the cobblestone. Eighteenth-century brick buildings and—"

Suddenly, the walls of the classroom started to spin. I leaned back onto the teacher's desk for fear that I might topple over. Was I spinning or was the room spinning? I wasn't sure. The students seemed to notice it as well. A gold and purple swirling pattern raced along the walls and encircled us until the walls completely vanished and the Bostonian scene I had just described appeared all around us. Even the cobblestone street was beneath our desks and feet. I slid my foot across the ground and it was smooth like a classroom floor, not like cobblestone.

"Mr. Revere, is this supposed to be happening?" asked Tommy.

"No worries," I said, lying. "Stay in your seats. You're experiencing, uh, a new, um, technological, uh, teaching moment . . ." I honestly had no idea what was happening. It looked like we were back in time. But that was impossible! We hadn't jumped through a portal. We would need Liberty to do that. And that's when it hit me. Liberty! This had to be his doing. I looked to the back of the room and noticed him leaned up against the back wall, fast asleep. He must be dreaming this! Somehow his subconscious had the ability to simulate the historical event I was describing! Liberty was re-creating history all around us. None of it was real but the virtual experience made us feel like we were actually there. Unbelievable! I decided to make the most of the situation and continued with my storytelling.

"Suddenly, you find yourself with a mob of people who start to throw snow, ice, and rocks at the British soldiers standing in front of the Customs Office," I said.

Sure enough, as I described the scene a large mob of colonists appeared to the right of us. To the left appeared a small group of British soldiers. A colonist stood only a few yards away from me and threw a chunk of ice. It hurtled directly at me on its way toward the soldiers. Instinctively, I winced and flinched right before the ice hit me in the side of face. But, surprisingly, the ice chunk went right through my head and continued forward, hitting the chest of a British soldier. I had forgotten this was just a simulation. It was just a virtual, holographic representation that Liberty was creating while dreaming. It seemed so real! I noticed

An Account of a late Military Massacre at Boston, or the Consequences of Quartering Troops in a populous well-regulated Town, taken from the Boston-Gazette, of March 12, 1770.

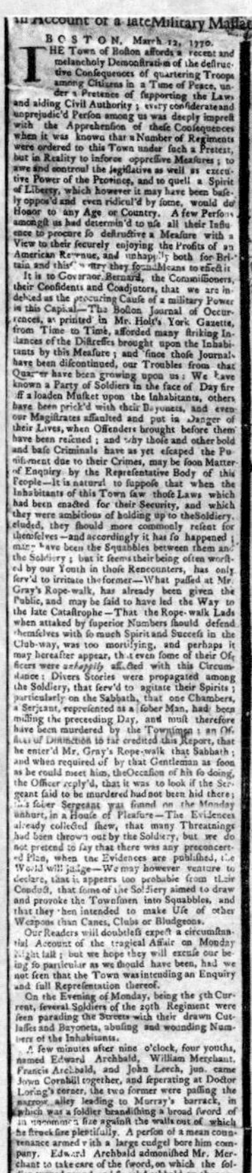

The Bloody Massacre perpetrated in King Street BOSTON on March 5th 1770 by a party of the 29th REGt

Unhappy BOSTON! see thy Sons deplore,
Thy hallow'd Walks besmear'd with guiltless Gore:
While faithless P—n and his savage Bands,
With murd'rous Rancour stretch their bloody Hands;
Like fierce Barbarians grinning o'er their Prey,
Approve the Carnage and enjoy the Day.

If scalding drops from Rage from Anguish Wrung
If speechless Sorrows lab'ring for a Tongue,
Or if a weeping World can ought appease
The plaintive Ghosts of Victims such as these;
The Patriot's copious Tears for each are shed,
A glorious Tribute which embalms the Dead.

But know, Fate summons to that awful Goal,
Where JUSTICE strips the Murd'rer of his Soul:
Should venal C—ts the scandal of the Land,
Snatch the relentless Villain from her Hand,
Keen Execrations on this Plate inscrib'd,
Shall reach a JUDGE who never can be brib'd.

The unhappy Sufferers were Messrs. SAML. GRAY, SAML. MAVERICK, JAMS. CALDWELL, CRISPUS ATTUCKS & PATK. CARR Killed. Six wounded; two of them (CHRISTR. MONK & JOHN CLARK) Mortally

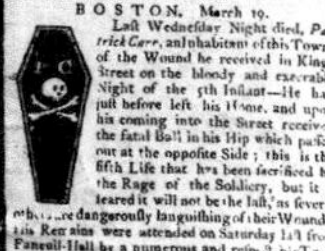

A broadside (poster) describing the Boston Massacre, March 5, 1770.

other students dodging snow, ice, and rocks as the projectiles flew through the air.

I continued with my narration and shouted, "The Redcoats tried to keep order and stop the colonists from demonstrating against the Townshend Acts. However, the soldiers were forbidden to shoot anyone unless they had an order from a civil magistrate who was like a judge. The Americans and Patriots knew this so they kept trash-talking and taunting the British troops. Confusion and chaos only increased when the bells began to ring from the nearby Old Brick Church."

Again, the literal sound of church bells rang through my ears as the chaos continued all around us. I knew the bell was normally used as a fire alarm in eighteenth-century Boston so it wasn't surprising when people started shouting, "Where's the fire?"

I continued: "The large, angry crowd pressed in on the nine British soldiers, who were desperately outnumbered. Suddenly, one of the British soldiers is knocked down by something hitting his head and someone yells, 'Fire!'"

The sound of gunshots ripped through the air and suddenly, the classroom walls returned as the sights and sounds of 1770 Boston vanished like a magical act.

"Oh, sorry, I must have dozed off for a minute," said Liberty, a bit startled. "Did I miss anything? The last thing I remember, you were talking about Boston and then I had the strangest dream. More like a nightmare."

"That was awesome!" said a boy in the front row.

"This class rocks!" said another boy.

"You're the best teacher ever!" said a girl sitting by the window. "How did you do that?"

Gratefully, the students seemed clueless that Liberty was the source of the simulation.

"Oh, it's, um, all high-tech cinematronics," I said, hoping it was enough.

"Seriously," said Liberty, "I feel like I missed something."

Just when I tried to get the class back on track, the school fire alarm sounded.

Principal Sherman's voice was heard on the school intercom system. He said, "Dear students, this is our annual school fire drill. Please calmly leave your classrooms and head outside to the blacktop. Thank you."

I followed the students out of the room but just before I passed through the doorway I noticed Freedom and Cam huddled with Liberty. I walked to the back of the room and asked, "I take it the three of you have something on your mind?"

"Mr. Revere," said Cam. "Since Freedom and I didn't time-travel with you last time, do you think we could go now? I'd love to go to Boston in 1770. We could learn more about the Boston Massacre!"

"I'm in!" said Freedom, enthusiastically. "We could be back before anyone realizes we're missing!"

Liberty nodded rapidly and nearly danced in place.

"All right," I said.

The three of them cheered in unison.

"You'll have to change your clothes in the past. If you run to the restroom now you may get caught by another teacher. Help me move these desks to either side of the room so we have a running path for Liberty."

In a matter of seconds we were ready to go. Freedom and Cam rode on Liberty and I followed close behind.

"Rush, rush, rushing to history!" said Liberty.

We were headed to Boston and I was excited to find Samuel Adams. I was nervous at the same time. I had just witnessed what happened in Boston on March 5, 1770. It was a dreadful day in American history, and when five Americans died and more were wounded, I knew this was the beginning of a revolutionary war.

Chapter 8

On a crisp winter morning we landed alongside a large, redbrick building. The bottom level looked like a marketplace where several merchants, fishermen, meat and produce sellers, and peddlers of every kind were selling their goods. The second level had several windows; some were opened and many voices could be heard inside.

"You realize we landed a day after the Boston Massacre, right?" Liberty said.

"Is this March sixth, 1770?" I asked.

"Yes, but you said the massacre happened on March fifth," Liberty reminded me.

"Yes, I'm aware of that," I whispered. "But I didn't want my students to witness the Boston civilians who died."

"Why is it that the past always seems colder than the future?" said Freedom. "It's freezing out here!"

I reached for my travel bag and handed Freedom and

Cam their colonial clothes. "Put these clothes over your modern-day clothes. You should be warmer with a double layer."

Freedom and Cam eagerly put on the clothes like they were racing each other.

"I want the two of you to stay close to me," I said. "Let's walk to the front of the building and see where we are."

"Why don't we just ask Liberty?" said Cam. "Isn't he supposed to have special powers that let him know when and where we are?"

Liberty closed his eyes and concentrated before saying, "We're definitely in Boston and this building is . . . I can see the name but I'm not sure I can pronounce it."

"Faneuil Hall," said Freedom. "It must be a French name."

"How did you know that?" asked Cam.

"I read Liberty's mind," Freedom said, smiling.

"You can read minds?" asked Cam with a worried expression on his face.

"Don't worry, I can only communicate with animals. But I do have X-ray vision!"

"What?!" Cam blurted out as he walked behind Liberty.

"I'm just kidding." Freedom laughed.

"But wouldn't that be cool?" Liberty said. "I wish I had X-ray vision."

"You don't need it," I said. "You have your Time-Travel Sense. Can you sense Samuel Adams in this building?"

Liberty paused and then said, "Yep, he's definitely in there."

"And Faneuil Hall is a special building," I said. "It served as the Patriot headquarters or meeting place to discuss the Stamp Act, the Boston Massacre, the tea crisis, and other British laws that burdened the colonists."

"Where's Liberty?" Freedom asked.

We turned and spotted Liberty near the front of Faneuil Hall. He was staring at what looked like a sign. We followed Liberty and as we got closer I read the sign that had caught his complete attention. It read, *Faneuil Hall Boston, the Cradle of Liberty. Dedicated in 1763 in the cause of liberty!*

"Have you ever seen anything so beautiful?" asked Liberty, who was nearly crying. "Although I don't remember sleeping in a cradle. In fact, I don't think I'd fit inside a cradle unless it was a giant one. Oh well. Hey, you should take a picture of me beside this sign!"

After a quick photo I said, "Let's look inside the building."

"What are we looking for?" asked Freedom.

"I want to meet Samuel Adams," I said. "Today, he's giving an impassioned speech about last night's horrific events."

Liberty replied, "I'm going to sit this one out. I mean I'm glad this Adams guy is on our side but I don't want to risk getting yelled at."

"Why do you say that?" Freedom asked, a little worried.

I interjected: "From what I've learned Samuel Adams is not a patient person but I'm sure he's—"

"You said he was pigheaded and needs anger-management classes," Liberty said.

"Well, I, uh, I've never actually met the man. It's just what I've read in history books," I said defensively.

"So why are we meeting him?" Cam asked.

I sighed and explained: "Samuel Adams may not have the genius and social skills of Benjamin Franklin and he may not be as brilliant and lighthearted as Patrick Henry but he definitely played an important role in America's independence. Let me tell the three of you something that I hope you never forget. You will meet people in your life that get on your nerves. Maybe they challenge your ideas or they're not willing to completely agree with you. That doesn't mean they're bad people. Yes, Samuel Adams was said to be a stubborn and quick-tempered man. But I think we'll see that he was an incredible motivator. The point is I believe that God knew He would need different people with a variety of personalities to create a free America. He needed men and women who weren't afraid to speak their minds. He needed people who would not back down. And, frankly, this country needs more of that today. Our country needs kids like you to speak up when our liberties are being threatened. Our forefathers said and did hard things even when they knew it might not be the popular thing. Samuel Adams is one of those people. He wasn't trying to win a popularity contest. He was trying to motivate people to take a stand and fight for their liberties!"

"Thanks, Mr. Revere," said Cam. "I know peer pressure makes a lot of kids go along with the crowd even when they know it's not the right thing."

"Yeah, thanks, Mr. Revere," echoed Freedom. "My mom named me Freedom because she hoped that it would give me the courage to stand up to others who might take advantage of me. I don't do a very good job at that. But now I'm anxious to meet Samuel Adams. Maybe I can pick up a few tips from him."

"No kidding," agreed Cam. "Let's go meet the Samuelator!"

"The what?" Liberty said.

"You know, like the Terminator! The Samuelator!"

"Oh, well, good luck with that. I'll meet you outside when you're finished," said Liberty.

As we entered the front doors I noticed the hall inside was

packed with people, from the entrance all the way to the platform on the other side. The man standing near the podium was dressed in simple colonial fashion. He looked like he was in his late forties. I immediately felt his penetrating stare, which seemed to reach all the way across the room and into my soul. When he started to speak I knew instantly that this was the exceptional American Samuel Adams. "There he is," I said.

"That's the Samuelator?" asked Cam.

"Show some respect," said Freedom. "It's Samuel Adams."

"Yes, that's him!" I said, mesmerized by what he was saying.

Samuel looked over the crowd and boldly said, "The governor of Massachusetts says that I'm the great incendiary. He says I spread lies about the British Empire and spread stories about the injustice of the King. But I will tell you that my purpose and my passion is to warn against the hostile designs of Great Britain!"

The crowded room erupted with shouts and cheers.

Samuel Adams continued: "Furthermore, I accept your nomination to chair a committee that will petition Governor Hutchinson for the immediate removal of British troops from the city of Boston!"

"Hear, hear!" shouted members of the crowd.

"America should never forget the horrid massacre in Boston," said Samuel, "when five innocent Patriots were shot by British muskets. We will honor men like Crispus Attucks, who was the first to fall, struck twice in the chest by bullets."

Again, the crowd erupted with anger. It was beginning to look and sound like a mob.

"That's harsh!" said Cam. "I remember hearing the gunshots in the classroom. I bet that's when the Patriots got shot."

"Yeah," said Freedom. "But I don't like that innocent people are getting killed."

"No kidding," said Cam, somberly. "And too bad about Crispus Attucks. I've never heard of him before."

I whispered, "History tells us that Attucks was of African and Native American descent and had fled to Boston after escaping his enslavers. In fact, he has a monument in Boston that hails him as a hero of the American Revolution, the first Patriot to give his life for the cause."

"I wonder if he would've still gone to King Street and protested like that if he knew he might die," said Freedom thoughtfully.

"That's a good question, Freedom," I said. "But I think a hero does what needs to be done and says what needs to be said despite the consequence, even if it means giving your life. That's why I consider Samuel Adams an American hero. He could have hanged for the things he said, but it didn't stop him."

As the public meeting ended we weaved our way through the crowded hall and headed toward the podium.

"We'll try to introduce ourselves to Samuel Adams. It would be great to meet him and ask a few questions," I said. "But I'm not sure I see him anymore."

"It feels like everyone's really fired up!" Freedom said.

"No kidding," Cam said. "It feels like we're at a tailgate party before a football game. It's too bad Samuel Adams can't come to a game. I bet he'd be an awesome cheerleader!"

"Oh, sure, let's invite Samuel Adams to a football game. I'm sure he doesn't have anything better to do," Freedom said, a voice of reason.

Crispus Attucks, one of the men killed in the Boston Massacre.

"And just what am I being invited to?" asked Samuel from behind us.

I could hardly believe I was standing face-to-face with the legendary Samuel Adams. I said, "Sir, Mr. Adams, Samuel or do you go by Sam, I mean, it's a pleasure to meet you. We're huge admirers of yours and fellow Patriots!"

"I'm not looking for admirers," stated Samuel. "But I am looking to grow the cause of freedom. Now, tell me about this *football* game. Is this a game for Patriots?"

"Actually, yes," laughed Cam. "The New England Patriots are a football team in Massachusetts! Personally, I like the Broncos but—"

Freedom elbowed Cam in the ribs.

I quickly tried to change the subject and said, "These are two of my students, Cam and Freedom. And I'm Rush Revere, history teacher and historian. I brought them to hear your speech and, hopefully, help them understand the importance of fighting for freedom. We were very inspired and motivated by your speech. In fact, we'd love to help support the cause any way we can."

"Your name is Freedom, you say?" asked Samuel, who turned to look at Freedom. "That is a name worth having and a cause worth fighting for."

"Well, I'm not really a fighter," said Freedom.

"Nonsense!" shouted Samuel.

His word made Freedom practically jump.

Samuel firmly said, "We were born to fight. A baby fights for his first breath! Our hearts fight to beat every second of every day. If you stood between a hungry wolf who was after a younger sister or brother and you had a club in your hand, what would you do?"

Freedom looked nervous about answering but finally said, "I would fight it off."

"What? I didn't hear you. Say it louder!" Samuel prodded.

Freedom tried again, this time a little louder: "I said, I would fight off the wolf."

"Of course you would!" Samuel said, sounding almost angry. "And King George is simply a wolf that wears a crown! Do you understand?"

"Yes," said Freedom timidly.

"Don't ever forget that you are a fighter, Freedom. You are worth fighting for."

Freedom nodded and gave a weak but sincere smile.

Samuel turned toward me and asked, "Did you say your name is Rush Revere?"

"Yes, that's right," I said and smiled.

"I am a good friend with Paul Revere, a fellow Patriot here in Boston," said Samuel. "In fact, I'm on my way to visit with him now. He is a master silversmith and I am in need of his services. Would you care to join me?"

"Really?!" I asked with wonder. "It would be a great honor to meet him as well. I'm sure we're related."

"Come, then," said Samuel, "we will travel together. His shop isn't far from here."

"Thank you! That is very generous of you," I stammered. I was practically shaking from the anticipation and excitement of meeting my favorite exceptional American, Paul Revere.

As we followed Samuel out the doors and down the stairs of

Faneuil Hall, a man who I assumed was a fellow Patriot called to speak with Samuel. Samuel stepped away briefly and as I waited I overheard bits and pieces of their conversation. Something about a secret meeting and the Sons of Liberty. Interesting.

Cam interrupted and said, "Mr. Revere, we found Liberty. He's down by those food vendors. Apparently, someone spilled a whole pot of baked beans and Liberty decided he'd help clean things up."

"Yes, cleaning up food is his specialty!" I laughed. "Tell him to hurry because we're following Samuel Adams to Paul Revere's silversmith shop.

Samuel finished his conversation about the "secret meeting" and said, "I apologize for keeping you waiting."

"Not a problem," I said. "Lead the way, Mr. Adams."

Cam and Freedom followed close behind and Freedom led Liberty by the halter. The streets of Boston were buzzing with colonists. Their mood seemed somber as they went about their errands. I noticed many dirt streets that branched off from the main cobblestone street that we traveled on. Samuel pointed out several of his favorite shops along Main Street. A tavern, a fruit vendor, a bakery, and a barbershop. A hat store, a fish market, a pipe maker, and a flower shop. Merchants lined the streets and a variety of signs hung over their doors and windows. "The Hoop Petticoat," "The Four Sugar Loaves," "The Chest of Drawers," and "The Spring Clock & Watches" were just a few of the signs that caught my eye.

"For the most part we have all the luxuries we need. England does ship goods for us to purchase but I prefer to purchase items made in America," Samuel said.

Faneuil Hall as it looked in Boston around this period.

In addition, Redcoats could be seen policing the streets. They traveled together in groups of five or six. We crossed the street whenever Redcoats were approaching. In fact, I noticed most of the colonists tried to avoid the British soldiers.

As we walked, Samuel said, "Paul Revere is a master silversmith. After he fought in the French and Indian War he took over his father's shop."

Curious, I asked, "Exactly what kinds of things does he make?"

"I don't think there's anything he couldn't make. He is a true artisan of silver."

"And is this why you are visiting Paul Revere, today? You want to purchase one of his silver pieces?" I inquired.

"No, I'm going to ask Paul to use his skills to engrave a piece of copper. You see, Paul Revere has a small printing press in his shop. Whatever he engraves on a thin piece of copper can be used as a template for his printing press. The piece of copper can be printed over and over again," said Samuel.

"And what exactly do you plan to engrave on the piece of copper?"

"You get right to the point, Rush Revere! I like that," said Samuel. "The British army has given us a golden opportunity. I have called it the Boston Massacre. In fact, we approach King Street now. This is where the tragedy occurred last night."

Overhearing our conversation, Cam said, "I recognize the Customs Office and the Old Brick Church."

Indeed, back in the classroom Liberty had dreamed a remarkable simulation of the crime scene. As we walked to the place where the crowd of colonists stood shouting at the British soldiers, I saw thin patches of snow in the shadows of the buildings. A large icicle fell from a two-story building and shattered into dozens of large chunks. A thick, jagged piece tumbled across the street until it hit my leather shoe. I looked down at the piece of broken ice and saw a large dark stain on the cobblestone. A cold wind blew across my face and gave me goose bumps. I knelt to get a better look and shivered at the thought of what had happened at this very spot last night.

Behind me, Samuel said, "I have talked to many witnesses about the event last night and it appears that the British soldiers indeed fired upon several Americans. However, I've also discovered that the Americans who gathered were not all peaceful bystanders. Most likely, some provoked and taunted the soldiers. Sticks and stones and ice were thrown at the Redcoats. The angry crowd started pressing in on the nine soldiers."

"And that's when someone shouted, 'Fire!'" I softly said, remembering the event from the classroom.

"Correct," said Samuel. "My investigation tells me that Captain Thomas Preston ordered his soldiers not to fire. However, by then it was too late. One of his men fired his musket and soon after, several more shots were fired, killing five unarmed men. It was bound to happen with the Quartering Act, quartering troops so close to the civilian population. It is like putting a fuse so close to flame."

"Perhaps both sides are guilty," I said, finally standing and looking at Samuel.

"Perhaps," said Samuel. "My cousin John Adams has been asked to defend the British soldiers who were at the massacre. Only a handful of witnesses will ever know what truly happened.

However, I'm a big believer that people will believe what we tell them, and I intend to spread the word to help spread the cause of the Patriots. We can use this to our advantage."

"And this plan involves Paul Revere," I said matter-of-factly.

"It does," Samuel said. "Paul Revere's silversmith shop is not far from here."

I looked for Cam and Freedom and saw them near Liberty. Freedom was huddled up close against Liberty's neck. I walked over and asked, "Are you cold?"

"I'm fine," said Freedom, quietly.

Cam replied, "I guess this is the ugly part of history, eh?"

"Yes," I said. "I am sorry if this was a hard thing to experience. I hadn't planned to—"

"It's okay, I'm glad we came," said Freedom. "But it's a weird feeling to think about what happened here last night."

Cam agreed. "Yeah, I know it's just a street but it feels like a cemetery."

Samuel called from across the street and said, "We must be on our way!"

A cold wind blew again across our faces. It chilled me to the bone as the image of those who lost their lives seemed to lie very near the stain-filled streets.

We continued following Samuel in silence and soon heard the sound of someone pounding metal.

"Ah, here we are. Paul Revere's silversmith shop," said Samuel.

I was glad we'd arrived. My somber mood changed to wonder as I thought about meeting the one and only Paul Revere. I straightened my coat and I felt like I was a little boy again ready to meet Santa Claus.

I peered through the shop window and noticed the most

The Boston Tea Party was planned here at the Green Dragon tavern.

beautiful, handcrafted pieces of silver I had ever seen. Spoons, cups, trays, bowls, and teapots adorned the window display.

"I like that bowl with the horse engraved on the side of it," said Freedom.

"I like it, too," whispered Liberty into Freedom's ear.

"His craftsmanship is impressive," Samuel said. "Believe it or not, he even crafted a small, silver chain for a pet squirrel."

I laughed at the thought of it.

"Seriously?" laughed Cam. "I wish I could get a picture of that!"

"Such a picture would be senseless," said Samuel, clearly not seeing the humor of it.

As Samuel opened the door I saw a man sitting behind an anvil. Hot sparks burst between the anvil and the heavy hammer each time it connected with the silver that he worked with. I could practically feel the hot furnace from the doorway and certainly smelled the melting metal. As we walked through the doorway I left the door ajar just a bit so Liberty could hear our conversation. My heart was beating fast and my palms felt cold and sweaty. I didn't realize how nervous I would feel upon meeting my boyhood hero. I had met dozens of exceptional Americans, but this one was extra special for me.

"Paul, my good friend," said Samuel, "may I introduce you to my new friends, Rush Revere and his students Cam and Freedom?"

Paul set down his hammer and wiped his brow. He looked like a strong man with broad shoulders and mighty forearms. He wore a leather apron over his linen shirt, which was rolled up at the sleeves. His hair was pulled back into a ponytail and he immediately smiled at me like we were long-lost brothers.

"With a last name like that, I'm sure you must be a brilliant man!" said Paul, laughing. "It's a pleasure to meet you." He reached out his hand and I did the same. His handshake was firm and he looked me straight in the eyes. "To what do I owe this visit?"

I said, "I am a history teacher and historian, and I have been a great admirer of all you've done for America's independence."

Paul laughed heartily and said, "I like this Revere. He speaks of our independence as if it has already happened!"

"Yes, it seems all the Reveres are true Patriots!" said Samuel. "I will tell you why I have come. But first, I must show you this drawing." Samuel unrolled a piece of parchment that he was carrying. "I asked a man by the name of Henry Pelham to draw this illustration of the massacre on King Street last night." He showed it to Paul Revere.

"Massacre?" Paul said with a surprised grin.

I found myself smiling with him and not knowing why. It's as if his smile was contagious.

Paul said, "Ha! I should not be surprised that you chose a word with such drama!" Paul laughed again. I could see that this was a man who loved life. He made me feel right at home in a way that Samuel Adams definitely didn't. He was good at his craft and his customers probably enjoyed him as much as his handiwork. Paul turned in my direction and said, "Be careful of what Samuel tells you. He is very good at spinning a story to his own benefit. Bending the truth is his specialty!" Paul slapped Samuel on the back and laughed again while Samuel grimaced. Paul continued, "The word *massacre* makes it sound like the Redcoats were premeditated and cold-blooded."

"Some of us fight with swords and some of us fight with words," said Samuel with a glint in his eye. "I call it the Boston

Massacre because I want Americans to always remember the horrific event of March fifth, 1770."

I peered at the drawing and noticed that it showed British soldiers firing at peaceful Boston citizens.

With a bit of anger Samuel said to Paul, "And why do you criticize me for lighting a fire under our fight for freedom?! My intent is to remind all Americans how unjust and unfair King George has been to the colonies. He is trying to cripple our economy by taxing everything. He wants to crush our hopes of independence. He will stop at nothing until he kills our chance for freedom."

"I agree," said Paul, smiling. "No need to bark up my tree. Boston is clearly being targeted by the British Empire. King George sends more and more troops to Boston. We must do something! I assume you have a plan? You always do," Paul said, laughing.

Samuel nodded and said, "Yes, I do. I need the help of a master silversmith to engrave this picture on a copperplate so we can print and distribute it to as many Americans as possible."

"I can do it," said Paul. "It will take some time, but I can do it."

"Well, if you cannot do it, perhaps the printer and Patriot Benjamin Franklin can?" teased Samuel with a serious look on his face.

Paul's laughter bounced off the walls of the small silversmith shop. He said, "You really know how to motivate a person!"

Surely I was biased, but I loved Paul Revere's attitude. He never seemed to doubt his own ability and he was always optimistic about getting the job done. I wished I could stay with him all day and listen to his adventures and stories.

Just then the door creaked open and Liberty stumbled inside.

Paul Revere, American Patriot (1735–1818).

Freedom whispered, "He was listening too closely and accidentally fell into the door."

"Is this your horse," Paul asked, walking to the door.

"Oh, uh, yes, I apologize. He is a curious animal, and I'm sure he was just looking for us," I said.

"I am looking for a new horse," said Paul. "Would you consider selling him?"

"No, I couldn't," I said. "We've been through a lot together."

"Before you go, I have a gift for Cam and Freedom," said Paul. He walked to the back of his shop and then returned with two silver objects. "These are whistles," said Paul, proudly. "They make a very loud, high-pitched sound. I recommend you use this in case of an emergency only." He laughed again and we all laughed with him.

I turned to Samuel Adams and Paul Revere and said, "I will forever remember this day, gentlemen. Thank you for your dedication and your bravery. As a teacher of history I will make sure your names are remembered as exceptional Americans!"

"We are far from exceptional," said Samuel seriously.

"True, but I'm a little closer than Samuel," Paul said jokingly.

As Cam and Freedom left the shop, Samuel lowered his voice and said, "I invite you to join our secret society of Patriots, called the Sons of Liberty. Paul is also a Son of Liberty. I feel I can trust you and we need good men who have the courage to fight for freedom no matter the cost."

"I'm honored," I said without hesitation. "I will find you the next time I am in town."

As we parted ways I thought about the commitment I had just made, the commitment that all the Sons of Liberty had

made. Their imprint in American history would forever be remembered during the famous Boston Tea Party.

As I left the shop I saw Cam and Freedom sitting on Liberty's saddle. Both were plugging their noses. As I got closer to Liberty I realized why.

"What's that smell?" I asked, grimacing.

Just then Liberty tooted and said, "Excuse me. I, um, may have sampled some beans earlier and, well, let's just say I'll have plenty of gas to get us through the time portal."

I simply shook my head and smiled. It was definitely time to jump back to Manchester Middle School.

The Old State House as it looks today in Boston, Massachusetts.

Chapter 9

While we waited for the bell that signaled the end of the fire drill, Liberty quickly exited the classroom.

"Did you see the look on Liberty's face?" Cam asked as he started laughing. "So funny! He kept passing gas every time he took a step!"

"I know, right?" said Freedom with a big grin. "Even after he turned invisible we could still hear him tooting all the way down the hallway!"

Their laughter was contagious.

Tommy walked over and whispered, "I still can't believe you time-jumped without me!"

Freedom replied, "Oh, I almost forgot. This is for you." Freedom handed Tommy her silver whistle. "I'm not much of a whistle blower. And since you couldn't come, I want you to have it. Paul Revere made it."

"Wow, thanks, Freedom!" Tommy said and gave Freedom a giant grin.

When the bell rang, Freedom said, "Gotta catch my ride. Bye! And thanks again for the field trip!"

"But I'm still jealous that I didn't get to go with you guys," said Tommy to Cam.

"It just sort of happened," Cam said. "Plus, you and Elizabeth got to time-jump when you visited King George."

"Speaking of Elizabeth, I didn't see her when the class returned," I said.

"Oh, yeah," Tommy said softly. "I almost forgot. I spoke with her outside while we waited for the fire alarm to stop. She kept talking about King George III and how excited she was to see him again. I told her I didn't think we were going back there, and she said, 'Yes, we are, Thomas.' Ugh, I hate when she calls me that."

"What else did she say?" I asked.

Tommy looked around the room to make sure we were alone and said, "Ever since she came back from Windsor Castle she's been acting really strange." He did his best Elizabeth impersonation: "Oh, Thomas, it's my destiny to return to England. I have plans and they involve King George."

"Hey, you sound just like her," Cam said and laughed.

The two boys high-fived each other and Tommy said, "So, anyway, I asked her what her *plans* were. I told her maybe I could help. I was curious to know what she's up to."

"What did she say?" Cam asked.

Again, pretending to be Elizabeth, Tommy said, "Oh, Thomas, wouldn't you like to know!"

Cam raised one eyebrow and said, "On second thought, you probably shouldn't talk like that. It's sort of creepin' me out!"

Tommy chuckled. "Anyway, while we were waiting for the fire drill to end a couple of kids were throwing a football back and forth but one of their passes went wide. It soared like a heat-seeking missile headed right for Elizabeth."

"Let me guess—KABLAM!" Cam said.

"Yep, it was a direct hit! Her books and folders and papers went everywhere. As soon as those kids saw what happened they ran away like a quarterback running from a linebacker."

"I don't blame them," I said, smiling. "Elizabeth is a pretty mean linebacker!"

"Anyway, I'm not sure what came over me," said Tommy, "but I decided to help her gather her things and that's when I came across this." He pulled out a folded piece of paper that was stuffed into his pocket. "I saw the words 'Top Secret' written on it so I snatched it when she wasn't looking." He handed the paper to me.

I unfolded the note and then smoothed out the paper. The note had a few words written on three lines. The first line said, *Jump to Great Britain*. The second line said, *Impress the King*. The third line said, *Tell secret about BTP*. And underneath that were several signatures. One said, *Queen Elizabeth*. Another said, *President Elizabeth*. And a third said, *Elizabeth the Great*.

"She definitely bumped her head back in the eighteenth century. She's nuts!" Cam said.

"What does BTP stand for?" asked Tommy. "British Toilet Paper?"

Cam laughed and said, "Or maybe it stands for Boston Triple-Cream Pie? I love a good pie!"

"That's something Liberty would say," I said. "Wait a second, I think you're on to something, Cam."

"I am?" Cam replied, confused. "You think Elizabeth's secret is about a pie recipe?"

"No," I corrected. "I think her secret is about Boston. In

particular, a secret event that will happen in Boston, a big secret that involves a lot of tea!"

"Ohhhhhh," Cam said, snapping his fingers. "BTP. Boston Tea Party! Of course!"

"Exactly," I exclaimed. "If the King knew about the Boston Tea Party before it happened, well, he could probably stop it and it could be the beginning of the end of the American Revolution."

Tommy raised his hand like he was in class. "What exactly is the Boston Tea Party? And why would Elizabeth plan something like that?"

"Elizabeth isn't planning it," I said. "The Boston Tea Party is a secret mission planned by the Sons of Liberty."

"Liberty has sons?" asked Tommy, surprised.

"No, I'm referring to a secret organization called the Sons of Liberty. It was a well-organized group of Patriots who banded together to resist the British and unfair laws like the Stamp Act. The Sons of Liberty were sort of like Robin Hood and Batman mixed into one. When the colonists were burdened and suffering because of King George and his minions, the Sons of Liberty would come to the rescue! Their most famous operation was the Boston Tea Party!"

"Cool!" Tommy was smiling. "I wish I could be a Son of Liberty. What else did they do, Mr. Revere?"

"They once tried to persuade Governor Thomas Hutchinson of Massachusetts to reject the Stamp Act in his official letters to London. The governor was a loyalist so, of course, he refused. In fact, Governor Hutchinson sent and received many letters to and from England. These letters made it very clear that the British were superior. King George and his Parliament thought the colonists were sloppy and stupid so they granted fewer rights to people living in America. Simply, the letters said that Britain was better and America was blech! Governor Hutchinson agreed and that made the Sons of Liberty really mad so they attacked the governor's mansion. They axed his door, uprooted his garden, and destroyed much of his home. Of course, they didn't harm the governor, but they told him that he didn't belong in America. Eventually, he left Massachusetts and returned to England."

"Okay, wait, back up," said Tommy. "You said the Sons of Liberty were the ones who planned the Boston Tea Party. A tea party? I don't get it. I mean, my little sister likes to have tea parties with all her friends. I just don't see the Sons of Liberty doing that."

Cam laughed. "Not that kind of tea party!" he said.

I laughed as well and said, "The best way for me to explain it is to simply show you!"

"Awesome!" Tommy said. "Road trip!"

"Let's go find Liberty," I said.

"Yeah, it shouldn't be too hard to find him." Cam smiled. "All we have to do is to listen for someone cutting the cheese!"

Tommy chuckled and asked, "Seriously?"

"Oh yeah," said Cam. "He ate a boatload of beans in Boston."

After fifteen minutes, we found Liberty. He was waiting for us by the big oak tree near the back door of the school.

"Is everything okay?" I asked.

"Let's just say I've *bean* better," Liberty said with a half smile.

"Are you up to jumping again?" I asked Liberty.

"Did the *Mayflower* make it to the New World? Did Benjamin Franklin invent the lightning rod? Was Paul Revere a master blacksmith?" asked Liberty.

"I think he means *yes,*" said Cam.

All the students and buses had left by now, and the schoolyard

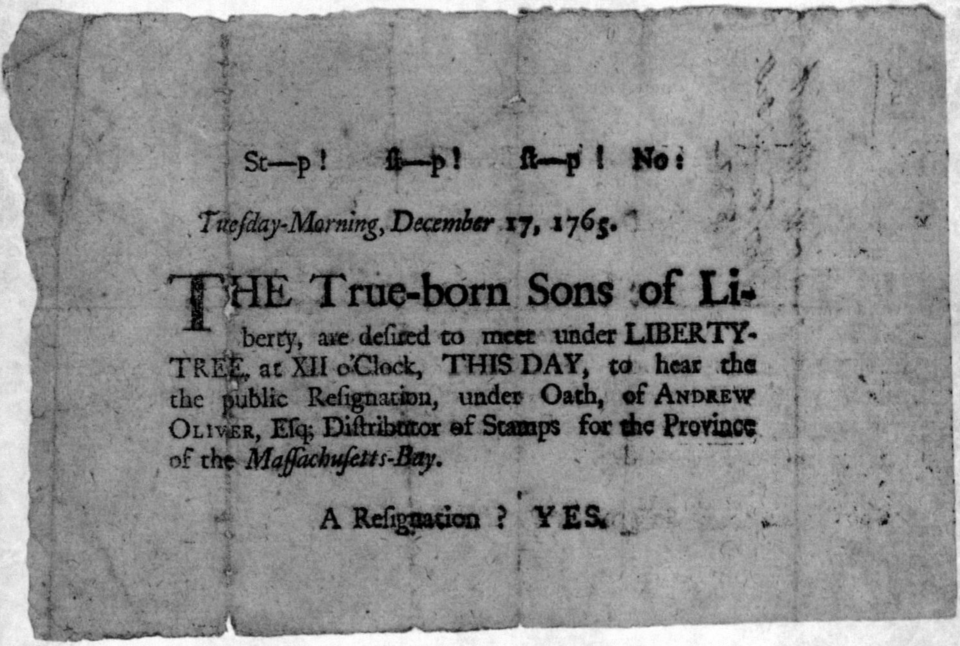

St—p! st—p! st—p! No:

Tuesday-Morning, December 17, 1765.

THE True-born Sons of Liberty, are desired to meet under LIBERTY-TREE, at XII o'Clock, THIS DAY, to hear the the public Resignation, under Oath, of ANDREW OLIVER, Esq; Distributor of Stamps for the Province of the *Massachusetts-Bay*.

A Resignation? YES.

A broadside (poster) calling the Sons of Liberty to a meeting at twelve o'clock on December 17, 1765.

looked deserted. After Tommy and Cam climbed up onto Liberty's saddle, Liberty said, *"Rush, rush, rushing to history!"*

Swirling colors of purple and gold grew to the size of a Hobbit hole. As we rushed to the time portal I said, "December sixteenth, 1773, Boston, Massachusetts, the Old South Meeting House!" We jumped and the next thing I felt was the chilled air. Were we in a field or a park? It was hard to tell since the only light came from the moon and the flickering lanterns and candles in a building straight ahead of us. It looked like an old church with a large steeple that stood like a single sentinel keeping watch over the large crowd of colonists below. The boys quickly jumped off Liberty and put on their colonial clothes over their modern-day clothes.

"There must be five thousand people over there," said Tommy.

I nodded. "We're about to witness another key event that brings the thirteen colonies that much closer to their revolution against Great Britain."

"Can we get a closer look?" asked Cam. "I want to hear what they say."

As we approached the front doors to the meetinghouse a man rushed outside and pushed his way through the crowd. He wore cream-colored breeches and white stockings as well as a cream-colored vest buttoned nearly to the neck. His royal blue coat with golden buttons and gold trim hung low to his knees and reminded me of something a ship's captain would wear. The man was searching for something. When he saw us he hurried over and said, "I'm in need of a swift horse. I'm Mr. Francis Rotch, owner of the *Dartmouth* out of England. I've been asked to seek a pass from Governor Hutchinson so my ship might return to England with its crates of tea. May I borrow your horse? I expect to return shortly with the governor's answer."

Before I could respond, Liberty was enthusiastically nodding his head. He looked excited for this unexpected adventure. I knew Liberty was a fast horse and would enjoy the task of an important mission. I finally said, "Oh, why not?"

"Thank you, my good sir. I shall return shortly," said Francis. Within seconds he was sitting in Liberty's saddle and dashing off into the night.

I turned to the boys and said, "Let's squeeze our way into the meetinghouse."

"I think the *Dartmouth* is the name of a ship," said Cam.

"Yes, that's right," I confirmed. "The *Dartmouth* is one of three ships that are sitting in Boston Harbor right now with hundreds of crates of tea from England. King George and Parliament are trying to force the colonists to purchase only British tea. In fact, the King has made his tea cheaper than anything else the colonists could buy."

"Yeah, but he's also making the colonists pay a tax on the tea!" said Cam.

"More taxes?" asked Tommy. "King George doesn't give up! I mean, it's pretty obvious the colonies don't want to be taxed by England anymore. You'd think the King would've learned that lesson with the Stamp Act!"

"History shows that King George III was not a very smart man," I said.

"Okay, but wait a second," said Tommy. "The guy who rode off on Liberty said that his ship can't leave the harbor without a pass from the governor?"

"That's right," I said. "You see, the *Dartmouth* arrived in Boston a few weeks ago. A tax has to be paid the moment the cargo of tea is removed from the ship. However, the colonists refuse to pay the tax and, therefore, don't want the tea to leave the ship.

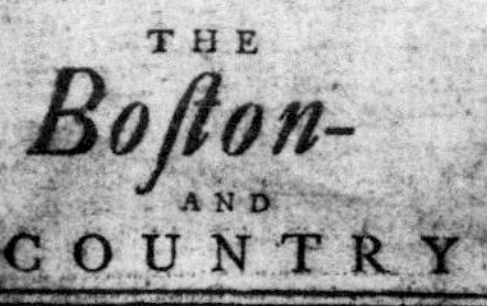

No. 769.

THE *Boſton-* Gazette, AND COUNTRY JOURNAL.

Containing the freſheſt Advices, Foreign and Domeſtic.

MONDAY, January 1, 1770.

A LIST of the Names of *thoſe* who AUDACIOUSLY continue to counteract the UNITED SENTIMENTS of the BODY of Merchants thro'out NORTH-AMERICA; by importing British Goods contrary to the Agreement.

John Bernard,
(In King-Street, almoſt oppoſite Vernon's Head.

James McMaſters,
(On Treat's Wharf.

Patrick McMaſters,
(Oppoſite the Sign of the Lamb.

John Mein,
(Oppoſite the White-Horſe, and in King-Street.

Ame & Elizabeth Cummings,
(Oppoſite the Old Brick Meeting Houſe, all of Boſton.

And, *Henry Barnes,*
(Trader in the Town of Marlboro'.

HAVE, and do ſtill continue to import Goods from London, contrary to the Agreement of the Merchants.—They have been requeſted to Store their Goods upon the ſame Terms as the reſt of the Importers have done, but abſolutely refuſe, by conducting in this Manner.

IT muſt evidently appear that they have prefered their own little private Advantage to the Welfare of America: It is therefore highly proper that the Public ſhould know who they are, that have at this critical Time, ſordidly detached themſelves from the public Intereſt; and as they will be deemed Enemies to their Country, by all who are well-wiſhers to it; ſo thoſe who afford them their Countenance or give them their Cuſtom, muſt expect to be conſidered in the ſame diſagreeable Light.

On WEDNESDAY Next the 3d Inſt.
At TEN o'Clock in the Morning,
Will be Sold by PUBLIC VENDUE, at the Store of the late Mr. JOHN SPOONER, next Door Eaſtward of the Heart and Crown.

All his Warehouſe Goods,

Conſiſting of a large Quantity of

KNIVES and Forks, Cuttoes, Shoe Knives, Butchers Knives, all kinds of Penknives, all kinds of Shears and Sciſſars, Borax, Fountain Pens, Pins, Needles, Razors, Temple and Bow Spectacles, Hand Saws, all ſorts Carpenters Irons and Chizzels, Braſs Ladles, Skimmers, Braſs Candleſticks, Steel Spring Tobacco Boxes, Handles and Eſcutcheons, FlatIrons, FryingPans, RubStones, Pewter Tankards, Quart and Pint Pots, Porringers and Tea Pots, all kind of Locks, HL and other Hinges, Compaſſes, Squares and Rules, Bell-metal and Braſs Skillets, Braſs Kettles made and un-made, Shoe and Carpenters Hammers, Fire Arms, Piſtols, Stone Sleeve Buttons ſet in Silver, large and ſmall Fiſh Hooks, Gimblets, Tobacco-Tongs, Pincers, Awl & Awl Blades, Braſs head & other Andirons, Steel and Braſs Thimbles, Knitting Needles, Horn and Ivory Combs, Matthewman's Buttons, Beams, Scales and Weights, &c. &c. *A four Wheel Carriage.*

The Sale to continue from Day to Day 'till the whole is Sold.
J. RUSSELL, Auctioneer.

BOSTON, 28th of December, 1769.

RUN-away from the Snow Union, John Copithorn, Maſter, from Briſtol, James Clifford and Nicholas Giles, two Seamen.——This is to deſire they will return to their Duty, and they ſhall be well received.—If they do not, to forewarn all Perſons from entertaining them, as they may expect being proſecuted according to Law.

CHARLESTOWN, (*South-Carolina,*) *Nov.* 27.

Mr. Goodacre of the 9th regiment, was not killed in a duel with a gentleman from Penſacola, as formerly mentioned, but with Mr. G——— of the ſame regiment, who remains there to take his trial. The deceaſed declared himſelf the aggreſſor, and that his antagoniſt was not in the leaſt blameable.

Nov. 9. At a meeting of the general committee on Tueſday laſt, and an adjournment thereof to Yeſterday ſeveral matters of importance reſpecting the general agreement entered into by the inhabitants of this province on the 22d day of July laſt, were taken into conſideration; and a committee of inſpection appointed, whoſe particular buſineſs it will be, to ſee ſuch Goods ſtored or re-ſhipped, (at the Option of the importers) as may be brought here contrary to the true intent and meaning of the ſaid agreement. It was at the ſame time agreed, that the general committee do meet on Tueſday in every week.

We have the pleaſure to inform our readers, that Mr. Thomas Eveleigh, who arrived here laſt Sunday, has readily agreed, that the goods which he imported in the Flora, Captain Carter, from Briſtol, ſhall be re-ſhipped or ſtored: and that Mr. Andrew Marr, has done the ſame, in regard to a conſignment of goods by the Brigantine Matty, arrived from Glaſgow.

The ſubſcribers to the reſolutions are ſo conſcious of the juſtneſs of their proceedings, that they appear determined to adhere to them; and have not only refuſed to purchaſe ſome ſlaves lately arrived from Penſacola, but alſo rejected a parcel of rice, belonging to a gentleman on John's iſland, who is a non-ſubſcriber.

'The few intereſted individuals in the colonies of Rhode-iſland and Georgia, who have hitherto miſled thoſe unhappy colonies by ſkim'd milk reaſonings, which has been attempted even in our province, we hear, have begun to loſe ſo much of their influence.

On Monday, January 1, 1770, the *Boston Gazette* published a list of merchants who imported British goods into Boston despite the boycott.

And to make matters worse, two more ships have arrived with more tea! So the Patriots, the colonists who are fighting for a free America, have posted guards around all the ships so that not a single crate is removed. They want the ships to return to England. But only the governor can approve such a thing."

"I get it. They want the governor to tell the King to go jump in a lake because they're not paying the stinkin' royal tea tax!" said Cam.

"In manner of speaking, yes. But the governor is not a Patriot. He's a loyalist, remember? He supports the King. So, I'm afraid Liberty will return with bad news for the Patriots."

As we entered the front door Cam said, "There's a great spot for us to the right in the corner." There was standing room only so we shuffled across the wooden floor and squeezed our way over and against the back wall near the corner of the room. I immediately recognized Samuel Adams at the front of the large gathering. Just seeing him reminded me of his clever plan to use the Boston Massacre as a way to incite the colonists to hate Great Britain. He was always ready to get the Patriots fired up to fight against the British Empire. Tonight was no different. He was standing behind a podium with a firm scowl. He raked his fingers through his wild hair and then tried to get the attention of the raucous crowd, but the men in the room were arguing and yelling with each other. The sound was deafening and the smell reminded me that underarm deodorant hadn't been invented yet. It might have been chilly outside but it was warm and stuffy inside.

"Gentlemen, order! We will have order!" Samuel demanded. Finally, the crowd calmed down, and Samuel pointed to a man who was sitting in the balcony.

"Three pence a pound is a small sum to pay for tea!" said the man, who was surely a loyalist.

"It's not the cost that angers me. It is the tax that comes with the tea!" yelled a Patriot. "I will not pay it. The tea tax is an insult to the citizens of Boston! The British Empire does not treat us as equals! We have no representation in Parliament! They think we are fools, children, and worse—slaves!"

Cam rolled his eyes and said, "Ironic, isn't it?"

"Indeed," I said.

"But we must pay for the French and Indian War debt!" yelled a loyalist. "If not for the King we might all be speaking French!"

Tommy whispered, "What does he mean by that?"

I whispered back, "King George sent thousands of British troops to help the colonists fight the French and Indians. Without the King's help the colonies would not have been able to defend their lands and defeat the French. The King wants the colonies to help pay for the war. That's partly why he's taxing them. The colonies believe they did pay for the war; many gave their lives for it. But the King and Parliament feel like the colonies still owe England."

"And that's why the King is taxing them," said Tommy.

"Correct," I said. "But as you can see and hear, the colonists can't agree on what's best for America."

"Sort of like the Senate and the House of Representatives in Congress today," said Cam with a smirk. "When our leaders can't agree, well, it can lead to a government shutdown!"

I nodded sadly. "Yes, you're getting a taste of our future government in this very room."

Although it was cold outside, the meetinghouse was getting very warm, the crowd was getting louder, and some men started shoving and pushing to get their point across.

"Mr. Revere!" Tommy shouted. "Maybe we should leave."

The idea was a good one, I thought. Unfortunately, we were

boxed into a corner with Patriots and loyalists on either side of us who looked like they were ready to come to blows.

Samuel Adams tried to retain order but he looked just as angry as the rest of them. It was apparent that neither side was willing to back down.

"We should have the right to tax ourselves and keep it in the colonies! Not send it to the King!" said a Patriot.

"And we must not let the tea leave the ships!" said another Patriot. "Our colonies in Charleston, New York, and Philadelphia all refused to accept the tea shipments. Boston must do the same!"

Suddenly, the owner of the *Dartmouth* rushed back into the assembly and yelled, "I have news from the governor!" He panted and said, "He is not willing to send the tea back to England. He said it must be landed and the tea tax must be paid!"

Patriots shouted with anger and loyalists yelled in support of what the governor had decided. It was so loud I could barely hear my own voice. I yelled to Tommy and Cam again, "Stay close by me. This could get ugly!"

"This is like a Boston Bruins ice hockey brawl!" said Tommy.

Samuel Adams raised his hands to quiet the crowd but without success. He looked like he was ready to explode.

"Hey, I have an idea!" said Cam. He pulled out the silver whistle that Paul Revere gave him.

"Good idea," said Tommy, who pulled out the whistle that Freedom gave him.

"On the count of three," Cam said.

They each put the tip of their whistle in their mouths. Cam counted to three with his fingers. One, two, three! After a deep breath the boys blew as long and as loud as they could. A high-pitched sound sliced through the room like a hot knife through

butter. The sirenlike sound seemed to bounce off the Old South Meeting House walls until all eyes turned toward Cam.

Cam smiled and said, "I think Mr. Samuel Adams has something to say."

With gratitude, Samuel nodded at Cam but he was in no mood to smile. With a stern expression on his face he looked out across the crowd of Patriots and loyalists and said, "It is clear that we are divided among ourselves. I will say only this, gentlemen. This meeting can do nothing more to save the country!" With that, Samuel Adams left the platform of the meetinghouse and slipped out the back door.

I felt someone tap me on the shoulder. As I turned I saw that it was my hero Paul Revere. "Come," he said. "Samuel said the secret words '*This meeting can do nothing more to save the country!*' We agreed that if and when he said these words the Sons of Liberty would meet behind the Old South Meeting House."

Tommy smiled and said, "Is it time for the Boston Tea Party?"

Paul looked at Tommy and while raising his eyebrows said, "Yes, that is correct." He turned his gaze toward me and said, "Rush Revere, you agreed to be a Son of Liberty, did you not?"

"Uh, yes, I did," I said.

Paul smiled and slapped me on the back. "Good, the Sons of Liberty need good men like you. And your students are welcome to join us."

"Awesome!" said Tommy. He turned to Cam and said, "You can be Robin Hood and I'll be Batman."

"No way," argued Cam. "You're Robin Hood and I'm Batman."

Paul Revere interrupted, "Robin Hood is a legendary hero who fights to destroy tyranny. A bat is a creature that cowers in caves and spreads filth and disease."

In unison, Tommy and Cam said, "I'm Robin Hood!"

"I approve. The Sons of Liberty are very much like Robin Hood of Sherwood Forest. Come, follow me," Paul said.

We scurried along the wall and then through and around several men who were still arguing about what should be done with the tea. In less than a minute we had reached the back door. We exited and found ourselves in the middle of forty or fifty Indians. No, they weren't real Native Americans, but their faces were covered with red and black war paint. They had feathers in their hair and many carried hatchets. Some were still in the process of changing from colonist to Indian, including Samuel Adams.

"We need to change our appearance," said Paul, smiling. "Come, we have enough clothes for the three of you."

I was thrilled to join the Sons of Liberty, disguised as Mohawk Indians in a unified act against the British Empire.

Cam turned to Tommy and whispered, "Dude, do you realize what we're about to do? We're going undercover! We're like eighteenth-century special ops or Navy SEALs!"

"Except we don't have night vision goggles," said Tommy. "But this is way better than playing a video game! I mean we're actually here in 1773 Boston! And we're about to be a part of history!"

"Yeah," said Cam. "Operation BTP, here we come!"

"This is going to be so awesome!" squealed Tommy.

In a few minutes we were all dressed like Indians. Well, sort of. It was a good thing it was dark, because in the daylight I bet we looked more like Peter Pan's lost boys. In any case, we used coal dust to darken our faces and arms.

"I'm just glad it's not too cold tonight or I'd be freezing," Cam said.

"I think I'll grab a couple of feathers for Liberty," I said. "I'm sure he's close and I bet he'll want to join us if he can."

Samuel Adams joined us as others formed a circle around him. Firmly, he said, "Tonight we send a message to the King. If his ships will not leave Boston so be it. But we will toss his tea overboard and let it float back to England!" Then Samuel let out a loud war whoop.

Many other war whoops echoed in response as we began marching down to Griffin's Wharf, where the three ships, the *Dartmouth,* the *Eleanor,* and the *Beaver,* were moored. Men shouted and cheered us on as we hurried down Milk Street. "Boston Harbor will be a tea pot tonight!" yelled a Patriot who slapped me on the shoulder as I passed by.

The moon overhead was bright and I was amazed at how well I could see. Was this a bit of divine intervention? Perhaps God provided the perfect weather and the perfect moon for what I hoped was a perfect tea party. Soon we were at the wharf and I felt a cold breeze come off the water and into my face. It was dark and hard to see who might be looking at us. I could barely see the faces of the other Sons of Liberty dressed as Mohawk Indians. It was a little spooky, especially hearing the creaking and squeaking of the boats as the sea pushed their hulls back and forth against the docks. It was like the three ships were trying to warn the British army. *Danger!* squeaked the *Dartmouth. Look! Thieves!* creaked the *Beaver. Don't let them take our precious chests of tea!* groaned the *Eleanor.*

Within minutes we were divided up into three different groups and ready to board the three different ships.

Suddenly, Liberty appeared out of nowhere and said, "Let's get the party started!"

"Liberty!" we all shouted, excited that he had joined us.

"It just wouldn't be the same without you," Tommy said.

"Here, let me attach these feathers to your mane. Now you're an Indian horse," I said.

"I would've joined you earlier but I was speaking with Freedom. You know, with my mind."

"Wow, that's amazing," said Tommy. "I didn't think that would be possible once we passed through the time portal."

"Neither did I," said Liberty. "But our connection has been getting stronger and stronger."

"And what did Freedom have to say?" I asked.

"Oh, she just asked how I was feeling after eating all those beans. She was genuinely concerned about my well-being. That's what I like most about Freedom. Well, that and also her name. Hey, maybe that's why we have such a strong connection! Freedom and Liberty sort of go together, if you know what I mean!"

"Here come Samuel Adams and Paul Revere," I interrupted. "It looks like they'll be joining us on the *Dartmouth*."

Liberty sighed, "I'm just relieved we're not boarding the *Eleanor*. Seriously, I once had a great-aunt Eleanor who loved to suck on garlic."

"Did you say *suck* on garlic?" Tommy asked.

"Oh yeah," Liberty said. "She said it kept away the vampires!"

"Vampires?" Tommy said, doubtfully.

"Well, vampire bats. Yeah, she was a strange old mare who would stay up all night watching for bats. I guess you could call her a night-mare!" Liberty started laughing and stomping his hoof. "Get it? Nightmare! Oh, I am so funny!" he whispered as Samuel Adams and Paul Revere drew near.

"It is midnight," said Samuel. He looked up at the starlit sky and said, "It appears that heaven smiles down upon us. Yet there is still great danger. The British are all around us. Have a prayer in your heart that we shall be undetected. We must work quickly and finish before dawn."

Tommy raised his hand and asked, "What if one of those warships sees us? What if a troop of Redcoats catches us throwing the King's tea overboard?"

"I know," said Cam. "I still remember what happened to me back in Virginia. They'll cuff us until they can hang us!"

Samuel stared at Tommy and Cam for a moment as all the men around us were listening. He finally said, "I believe God wants men to be free. I choose to believe that there is a force greater than our own here tonight. I can feel it in the air and see it in the stars. God willing, we will accomplish this mission. It is only the beginning of what we will need to do. Fear will try to stop us, but we will not let it. People who live with fear will never be free. Remember this, Tommy and Cam: We are the fear chasers. We are the hope givers. We are the freedom builders. We are the Sons of Liberty!"

I felt invigorated by Samuel's words! I felt unstoppable, like I could accomplish anything. I could see that the men with me felt the same way. Even Tommy and Cam looked ready to take on the world.

Cam fumed and punched his fist into his palm. "Seriously, after what those Redcoats did to me back in Virginia with Patrick Henry, I can't wait to get my hands on that tea!"

"It's tea time!" whispered Liberty.

We walked across the gangplank of the ship and joined the other "Indians." Some were breaking open chests with hatchets to get to the tea. Since we didn't have any hatchets, Liberty kicked open a chest with his back legs and the three of us jettisoned the tea into the water below. It was too dark to see much but up close I saw thousands of little green tea leaves flitting down to the water and creating a sea of tea in the harbor below. Tea party, indeed! A really big one! Maybe some of the fish thought the tea leaves were fish flakes and decided to make a meal of it.

As Liberty stomped and kicked he softly sang his Stamp Act song, "Because your taxes aren't fair, you make us so mad, and you should know that, you make us so, so mad!"

I kept looking over my shoulder at the docks to see if any Redcoats had spotted us. The noise we were making as we busted up the wooden crates seemed loud, but it was hard to know how far-reaching it was.

After nearly four hours, we had finished. I remembered from history that there were 342 chests or crates of tea. King George would be furious when word got back to him. And you know what? I was okay with that. After all, he did insult my mother.

"I think that's the last of it," said Cam.

"Now I know what you mean by the Boston Tea Party!" said Tommy.

Cam nodded and said, "Did you see Paul Revere? That dude is strong! It must be from being a blacksmith because he was smashing through those chests like they were made of graham crackers!"

"Does someone have graham crackers?" Liberty asked. "I love graham crackers!"

"Shh," I said, patting Liberty's neck. "Here comes Paul Revere."

"Well done!" Paul said with a huge grin on his face. "The *Beaver* has also finished dumping its tea and I expect to hear word about the *Eleanor* soon."

In the light of the moon we silently rejoiced in our success, and I silently thanked God.

"So what's next?" asked Tommy.

"The King will not let this act go unpunished," said Paul. "Certainly, he will try to make an example out of Boston's rebellion. We need to do what we can to store food and supplies for our families. I would not be surprised if the King chose to close our ports. We must ready ourselves for England's retribution."

I was still in awe by the fact that I was standing just inches away from the legendary Paul Revere. I mustered up my courage and said, "Thank you, Paul Revere, for what you've done and what you'll do for this country. I don't know how you find the time to do all that you do to support the cause of freedom."

Paul beamed at my compliment. He said, "Rush Revere, you are a good man and I am honored we share the same name. Freedom is in your blood. It is in the blood of every true American. It is part of who we are. And freedom needs our effort. It needs our attention. If we are not watchful, freedom can and will be taken from us." Paul breathed deeply and exhaled. He looked deep in thought and said, "Only when we are free can we be all that God wants us to be. Only when we are free can we do all that God wants us to do. Remember this, my friend, freedom is from God. And when we fight for freedom we always fight on the side of God."

"Thank you, Paul," I said, humbly. "I will always remember that. Godspeed."

We parted ways and after leaving our boat we found an empty street and time-jumped back to Manchester Middle School. The boys changed their clothes, cleaned their faces, and walked home together. I, too, changed from my Indian attire and was glad to be back in my colonial clothing. However, Liberty left the feathers in his hair. He said he was excited to show Freedom.

I thought about tomorrow and remembered that it would be

my last day before Mrs. Borrington returned. I knew there was still one more important history lesson I wanted to teach before leaving. The fact is, England was not going to give up. And the thirteen colonies would not be able to withstand the power and might of Great Britain unless they united together. Let's face it, Boston, Massachusetts, was getting beat up pretty badly. Other colonies would experience the same punishment from the bully of Britain, King George III. I wanted Tommy, Cam, Freedom, and, yes, even Elizabeth to understand that America's freedoms were hanging by a thread. And King George was ready to take his sword and cut us off from freedom forever. Our only chance, our only hope was to unite with the other colonies and fight back. I wanted them to see and experience what really happened! For that to happen I would need to get them to the First Continental Congress.

We were just about to leave the classroom when a note was slid under the door. I walked over and picked it up. The writing on the front said, "To: Mr. Revere. From: Elizabeth." I'd forgotten about Elizabeth's secret plan to leak information about the Boston Tea Party. All she needed was someone who could open the time portal. If she could go back in time she could rewrite the history we had just experienced. And a personal visit with King George before the BTP happened could certainly do that. Well, I wouldn't let that happen. I knew I had the upper hand because I knew what she was plotting. Then again, Elizabeth was both clever and crafty. Maybe this was all a setup. Maybe she had something else up her sleeve.

Chapter 10

The next morning I did just what Elizabeth's note asked me to do. Liberty and I arrived at Manchester Middle School thirty minutes before school started. In addition, I texted Tommy, and only Tommy, to meet us near the big oak tree at the back of the school.

The back door of the school opened and Elizabeth walked out. She was dressed in the blue gown that she'd received from King George III. Her hair was expertly curled and pinned to the top of her head. She looked like a fairy princess; all she was missing was a magical wand.

"Where's Thomas?" said Elizabeth, sounding annoyed.

"Good morning, Elizabeth," I said. "You look especially pretty today. Is there a special occasion?" Of course, I knew she intended to time-jump to eighteenth-century England and visit with King George III.

"As a matter of fact, yes, there is a special occasion," she said. "And you're my ride."

"Sorry I'm late," said Tommy, who sounded a little winded. "I practically ran the whole way here."

Elizabeth sighed, "Ugh, I hope you're not sweaty."

Tommy lifted one of his arms and smelled under his armpit. "Nope," he said, "I still smell like an ocean breeze. At least that's what my deodorant said."

Liberty turned to smell Tommy's armpit as well.

"That's disgusting!" Elizabeth said.

Liberty replied, "I think you smell way better than an ocean breeze. Seriously, sometimes the breeze from the ocean smells like dead fish. I'm just saying that I don't think the person who picked the name of that deodorant has ever been to the ocean."

Elizabeth sighed and said, "Thomas, help me get in the saddle. And make sure my dress doesn't get snagged!"

"Pardon me, Elizabeth," I said, "but I don't remember us discussing any sort of field trip."

"Mr. Revere," said Elizabeth, sounding bothered by my question, "I thought we'd been over this once. I'm in charge, remember? I have the video of all of you time-jumping, so if you want to keep teaching the Honors History class you'll do what I say, and don't ask questions."

"Somebody woke up on the wrong side of the barn," Liberty mumbled.

I pondered the situation and an idea popped into my head. I called for Tommy. "You better get dressed in your colonial clothes," I told him.

As Tommy walked over to get his clothes I whispered in his ear, "When I give you the signal tell Liberty to ignore whatever Elizabeth says and concentrate on time-jumping to Philadelphia, October 1774, Carpenters' Hall."

"What's taking you guys so long?" Elizabeth huffed.

"Got it," Tommy whispered back as he finished buttoning up his vest.

Tommy quickly climbed up onto Liberty's saddle and we both helped Elizabeth to sit behind him.

"Let's go, Liberty! Open the time portal," Elizabeth said impatiently.

"Aren't you going to tell us where we're going?" Liberty questioned.

"I'll give you the destination when you're ready to jump," Elizabeth said slyly.

She was a sneaky girl. But I was not going to allow her to time-jump to England and divulge future secrets to King George. I knew her plan was to change history and I couldn't let that happen. I said, "This meeting can do nothing more to save the country!" I hoped Tommy remembered that this was the secret signal.

"Huh?" Liberty said, confused.

"Hey, that's what Samuel Adams said as . . . oh, I get it!" Tommy said. He leaned over and whispered into Liberty's ear.

"My destiny awaits!" said Elizabeth. "Giddy-up. Charge! Let's go already."

Liberty started to gallop and said, *"Rush, rush, rushing to history!"*

As we approached the time portal Elizabeth yelled, "England, November 1773, Windsor Castle."

The next second we jumped through a cosmic curtain of purple and gold and landed near a two-story colonial brick building. Other colonial buildings could be seen nearby and it was obvious that we were not at Windsor Castle, or in England for that matter. The primitive plaza was nothing like the grandiose gardens of England. And the few people we saw wore simple coats or dresses, not the fancy fashions of eighteenth-century England. The cold breeze whipped through the plaza and up through the nearby trees. Mother Nature had been busy painting the leaves a bright orange, a brilliant yellow, and a vibrant red. The leaves clung to nearby branches as they spastically fluttered in the wind.

"Where's the castle? This isn't England. You imbecile! Ugh! Where are we and what year is this?!" Elizabeth demanded.

"As your time-travel tour guide I'm obligated to tell you that we're in Philadelphia, Pennsylvania, and it's October twenty-sixth, 1774," said Liberty.

"What!" Elizabeth yelled. "Are you deaf? I specifically said Windsor Castle. It's supposed to be November 1773!" She took a deep breath and tried to calm herself. With a venomous tone she said, "I'm going to give you one more chance to get this right. Liberty! Open the time portal!"

"I'm afraid he won't do that," I said. "You see, Elizabeth, we know your plan to meet with King George and leak information about the Boston Tea Party."

Elizabeth scowled and said, "Get me off this thing!"

I quickly helped Elizabeth down from the saddle. She folded her arms and said, "You found my note, didn't you?" She looked back and forth between Tommy and me. Finally, she said, "I confess. You caught me. But it doesn't change anything."

"Yes, it does," blurted Tommy.

"Oh, my dear Thomas," said Elizabeth like she was speaking to five-year-old. "You can't stop a falling star from streaking across the sky. You can't stop an avalanche once it's racing down

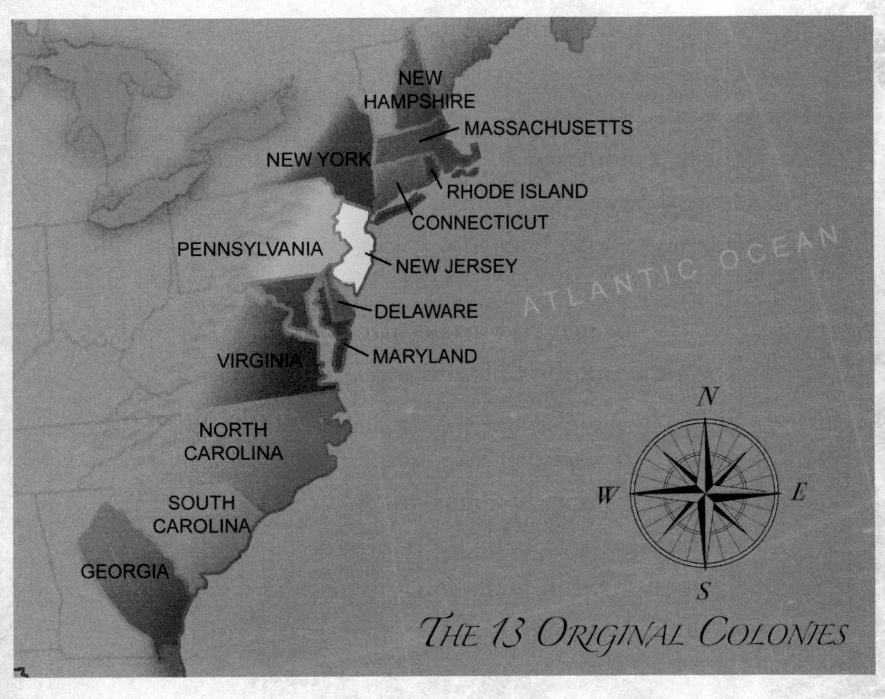
NEW HAMPSHIRE
MASSACHUSETTS
NEW YORK
RHODE ISLAND
CONNECTICUT
PENNSYLVANIA
NEW JERSEY
ATLANTIC OCEAN
DELAWARE
MARYLAND
VIRGINIA
N
W
E
S
NORTH CAROLINA
SOUTH CAROLINA
GEORGIA
THE 13 ORIGINAL COLONIES

a mountain. And you can't stop me from reaching the greatness I was born to reach. I really should be thanking you because with Liberty I can reach that greatness a lot faster."

"You were really going to tell the King about the Boston Tea Party?" Tommy asked.

"Duh!" said Elizabeth. "It wasn't going to hurt anyone. And I would look like a hero to King George! I bet he would've given me a crown or at least a title and I could have a hundred dresses just like this one!" She twirled around and watched her dress fluff out as she spun.

"It's all about you, isn't it?" said Tommy.

"Double-duh!" said Elizabeth. "But it could be about us! Help me reach King George and I'll tell him to reward you, too!"

"I'm sorry, Elizabeth, but I would never sacrifice the future of America for my own gain or needs," I said.

"I'm with Mr. Revere," said Tommy, firmly.

"Ugh, you're such losers!" Elizabeth whined.

"Well, you were trying to ruin the Boston Tea Party and stop it from happening so technically you're captain of the losers," said Liberty as he stuck his tongue out at her.

"That's enough, you two," I said. "We've arrived at a very important time in America. History tells us that the King and Parliament were furious about the Boston Tea Party. In fact, the King was so mad he punished the colonists by closing Boston Harbor so ships weren't allowed to leave or enter."

"How did families get food?" Tommy asked, concerned.

"Sister colonies were able to send some food and supplies," I said. "But many families suffered with many men out of work. And the Redcoats swarmed Boston like red army ants."

"Good! I hope the King locks up the whole city!" said

Elizabeth. "He should ground everyone, feed them cooked spinach, and put coal in their Christmas stockings!"

"That's a bit cruel," Liberty said, "especially the cooked spinach part! Seriously, why do people ruin perfectly good spinach by cooking it?"

"Liberty," I interrupted, "we're in the middle of an important conversation."

"Oh, sorry. I'll let you and the Grinch finish," Liberty said.

"As I was saying—" I turned to Elizabeth. "The Grinch, err, I mean, the King definitely punished the Bostonians. When the other colonies heard what the King was doing they were really mad."

"No kidding!" said Tommy. "I mean King George really is the Grinch and he ticks me off big-time! I'm surprised the colonists didn't freak out earlier. Seriously, I'm not a colonist but I don't have to be to know why they're so angry! The King doesn't let them vote! He taxes everything! He sends troops into their homes and harasses them on the streets! His laws are stealing the people's hard-earned money and causing families to go hungry! And he doesn't care who he's hurting! He's not a king. He's a tyrant, thief, whiner, jerk, and a bully. Sorry, Elizabeth, but King George is the biggest loser! He's out of control and he's got to be stopped!"

Elizabeth just looked away, nearly expressionless, with her arms folded.

"Tommy," I said, "I'm very glad you understand the real issue here. In fact, the colonies have banded together in Philadelphia to fight back. Representatives, called delegates, from each of the colonies except for Georgia have come together here to decide what the colonies should do."

"Sweet!" said Tommy with wide eyes. "Is that why we're here? Is it a secret meeting? Do I know anybody that's coming? Is there a secret handshake? I wish Cam was here!"

I chuckled at Tommy's wild enthusiasm. I nodded. "Tommy, you are about to meet some of the most educated, intelligent, skillful, and courageous men in America. In fact, they are gathered in that redbrick building in front of us." I pointed to Carpenters' Hall. "They are attending the First Continental Congress."

"Awesome!" said Tommy.

"Exciting!" said Liberty.

"Boring!" complained Elizabeth. "I'm tired of you babbling on about the colonists fighting back. I insist that we visit King George this instant! Or else!"

"What are you going to do?" Tommy asked, smiling. "You don't have much leverage without your blackmail video."

Elizabeth huffed and puffed with exasperation. She finally said, "Just wait until we get back to Manchester Middle School!"

"Who says we're bringing you back?" said Liberty. "Seriously, I think she'd be fine as a colonist. I survived moving from one century to another and I think I'm a better horse because of it."

Elizabeth gasped, "You wouldn't dare!" She looked desperately at Tommy. "Thomas, you can't let them leave me here!"

Tommy looked at me and then back at Elizabeth. He finally said, "Elizabeth, you have a lot of things going for you, but nobody likes the way you treat them. You act like you're better than everyone else. You make Freedom feel like she's a fashion moron. You tell Liberty that he stinks. And you threaten to send Mr. Revere to a different school. And you want us to bring you back to Manchester Middle School so you can keep treating people like a piece of chewed gum stuck to the bottom of your shoe? No, thank you. If we bring you back, you're going to have to start treating people differently."

"Hey, I bring the teachers cupcakes!" Elizabeth said in defense.

"Only when you're trying to bribe them to give you a good grade," said Tommy. "Being truly nice to someone means being kind and thoughtful and considerate of others. It means complimenting Freedom about her hair or her smile or how smart she is."

"Okay, let's not go overboard," Elizabeth said.

"Being nice means not saying stuff that would make someone feel bad. For example, Liberty smells like a horse. He can't help it. It's just the way he is."

Elizabeth rolled her eyes. It was hard to know what she was thinking or feeling. She said, "Okay, I'm sorry, Liberty, for calling you odoriferous. But a body spray wouldn't hurt. Is that considered offensive?"

"Here's the thing, you'll know when you're really being nice when you do something for someone else without expecting anything in return."

"People actually do that?" Elizabeth gawked.

Suddenly, we heard the sound of a bell from a distant bell tower.

"You don't need to tell me what time it is!" Liberty grinned. "It starts with an *L* and ends with an *E*."

"Latrine?" asked Tommy. "Most people just say 'I have to go to the bathroom.'"

"Oh, brother," Liberty sighed. "It's lunchtime!"

The doors of Carpenters' Hall opened and several

George Washington, Patrick Henry, and Edmund Pendleton travel to the First Continental Congress at Carpenters' Hall, Philadelphia, September 1774.

distinguished-looking men dressed in colonial clothing exited the building. I didn't recognize most of them but some of them I did.

"Look, there's Patrick Henry!" Tommy said. "Can I go say hi?"

"Absolutely," I said.

"Come on, Elizabeth," Tommy said, "I'll introduce you. Cam is going to die when I tell him we bumped into Patrick Henry. He and Cam totally hit it off back in 1765."

Suddenly, I noticed Samuel Adams coming out of the building with two other men standing on either side of him. I didn't recognize the one on the left but the tall gentleman on the right was a dead ringer for George Washington!

"Liberty! Do you see who that is?" I pointed.

"Which one? Oh! I see. Wow! That's George Washington," Liberty whispered. "He's as regal as ever. I've always loved the way he commands respect. They should teach that in school."

"And exactly what would the class be called?" I asked, amused.

"Hmm," Liberty pondered, "how about *Awesomeness 101*. Seriously, George Washington is the man. People can't help but stare at him because he's just so awesome."

Within seconds, Samuel Adams, whom I had met in Boston, recognized me and said, "Rush Revere. Welcome! When did you arrive in Philadelphia?"

"Just today in fact," I said.

"Let me introduce you to my cousin John Adams, who is a fellow delegate from Massachusetts," said Samuel.

"A pleasure to meet you, sir," said John.

"You have no idea how excited I am to be here and meet all of you," I said, trembling with excitement. "I'm a history teacher and I've brought a couple of students with me."

A portrait of George Washington.

Portrait of John Adams by Gilbert Stuart.

"And what will you teach them about?" asked John Adams.

"Well, funny you should ask," I chuckled. "We are studying the events that led to the colonizing of America and the events leading up to the American Revolution."

"Yes, indeed, an American revolution. I like the sound of that," said the tall and regal-looking man who just had to be George Washington. "However, we must be united before we ever dare revolt. There is still much discord among the thirteen colonies."

Samuel Adams stepped forward and said, "Rush Revere, let me introduce you to one of our delegates from Virginia, the illustrious George Washington," said Samuel.

"I'm truly honored and overwhelmed," I said. "I barely know what to say. You are as presidential as I imagined."

"Are you running for political office, Mr. Washington?" asked John Adams.

"I doubt Mr. Washington is looking for this kind of office," I said knowingly.

"That is absolutely correct," said George Washington. "But I am looking for some food before we return to the Congress."

"Is George hungry again?" said a jovial voice from behind me. I turned to see Patrick Henry with Tommy and Elizabeth. Patrick laughed and slapped George Washington on the back. The future first president scowled and stood erect, ready to confront the man who dared invade his personal space. When he saw it was his fellow delegate Patrick Henry he only sighed, shook his head, and returned to his military posture.

Patrick laughed again and said, "I try to make sure that my fellow delegate from Virginia gets fed at least every other day but he seems to think he needs food every day!" This time everyone laughed, and even George Washington gave a half smile, but Patrick Henry laughed the loudest. "And where is my eloquent young friend, Cameron?" asked Patrick.

"I'm afraid he was unable to make this trip," I said. "But he is doing well and I know he will be sorry he missed you."

"It is good to be missed," said Patrick. "Better than being shot!" He laughed again and was joined by the others. "You must take this back to Cameron." Patrick raised his hand in the air and prompted me to do the same. When I did he slapped my upraised palm and said, "High five!" He laughed and exclaimed, "Cameron will know what that means."

I grinned and said, "Thank you, I'm sure he will enjoy it."

"And I am sure that my hunger grows more persistent," George Washington said. "Come, I know where we can get some hearty meat pies."

The others followed him as he led the way down a cobblestone street. His long stride and tall stature made him look the part of a natural leader.

"A good choice," said John Adams. "Meat pies are both delicious and filling. Even my cranky cousin would agree with me. Isn't that right, Samuel?"

"*Filling* is not the word I would choose," Samuel argued. "I prefer *satisfying*."

John rolled his eyes as the eight of us followed with growing appetites.

I marveled to think of who I was walking with. These were four of the Founding Fathers of America. And two of them, George Washington and John Adams, would be future presidents of the United States of America.

"Mr. Revere," Tommy said, "is Benjamin Franklin here?"

"No, he is not a delegate at this First Continental Congress," I said.

"I'm afraid he's licking his wounds after getting lambasted by Parliament for the Hutchinson letters," said John.

"The what letters?" asked Tommy.

John Adams continued: "The royal governor of Boston, Thomas Hutchinson, wrote letters to England asking for more British troops to fight against the American rebels as well as advice on how to subdue America by restricting its liberties. Somehow the letters were taken and printed in the Boston newspapers. As you can imagine, the citizens of Boston were furious and wanted Hutchinson's head. He had to flee to England and the British government demanded to know who leaked the letters."

"But what does that have to do with Benjamin Franklin?" asked Tommy.

John clarified, "At one point, Franklin had the letters in his possession. He was not responsible for the letters getting printed, but he took the blame so others who were innocent and wrongly accused would not get punished."

"He was verbally abused again and again. The brutal criticism must have been tormenting for him. It is said that he stood there silent yet standing firm. They wanted to show he was inferior and tried to make him feel worthless," said Samuel.

"The King and his Parliament think all the colonists in America are inferior. It is clear that they no longer consider us British citizens!" exclaimed Patrick Henry.

"I wish that were all that Franklin was dealing with," said George Washington. "It is well-known that Franklin's son,

Benjamin Franklin, assisted by his son William, proving the identity of electricity in lightning with his famous kite and key experiment of June, 1752.

Chaplain Jacob Duché leading the first prayer in the First Continental Congress at Carpenters' Hall, Philadelphia, September 1774.

William, is a fierce loyalist who refuses to listen to his father's pleas to join the Patriots. They have exchanged bitter words and I am sure it must feel as if he has lost his son to the darkness that blinds men of the truth."

"Indeed, it is a sad and difficult time for all who live in America," I said.

Tommy pulled me back with Liberty and Elizabeth and whispered, "I remember when we visited with Benjamin Franklin outside the Palace of Westminster. He was so kind and gave me some great fatherly advice."

Liberty butted in and whispered, "He called you the Future of America, remember?"

"Yeah." Tommy nodded. "How can his son not see and appreciate a father with so much wisdom and goodness? But I suppose we don't really know what happens inside of families."

Liberty nodded and whispered, "Remember when Benjamin called me a *natural phenomenon*? And he said I was exactly who I was meant to be. He basically said I was awesome and the most amazing creature on the planet."

"Are you sure he didn't say you're naturally delusional and the most annoying creature on the planet?" asked Elizabeth with an attitude.

"Ahh, there's the Elizabeth we all know and love." I smiled. "It's good to have you join in the conversation."

Elizabeth just rolled her eyes and turned the other way.

"Here! We have arrived at our destination," said George Washington.

Before too long I was eating a slice of warm meat pie made with ground pork, potatoes, onions, and spices. It was absolutely delicious.

"I'm going to that vegetable cart," whispered Elizabeth. "I'm not a big fan of meat pies."

"I'm coming with you," whispered Liberty. "I'm not a carnivore."

I called to Tommy and said, "Why don't you go with Elizabeth and Liberty."

Elizabeth gave me a suspicious look and said, "What? You think I'm going to escape with Liberty when you're not looking?"

"It's not that I don't trust you, Elizabeth," I said. "Oh, wait, on second thought, I don't trust you." I smiled.

"Whatever," she said as she headed toward the vegetable cart.

I turned to these legendary Founding Fathers and asked, "I know you are about to make a decision that could separate America from Great Britain. Are you truly ready to face the consequences of this decision? I'm sure you know that King George will not give up without a fight."

Patrick Henry squared his shoulders to mine and boldly said, "As God is my witness I say give me liberty or give me death. I will give my life for the cause of freedom. I will not support a crown that restricts our liberties. I will not pay the King's debt or feed his soldiers or obey without question. He will take everything from us if we let him. Parliament laughs at the thought of us governing ourselves. It is time we make America free!"

"But we are a free people," said John Adams. "Always were and always will be. As the first colonists arrived on the *Mayflower* and fought the elements, we will fight against tyranny always!"

"We may be hanged, but we will die for our beloved freedom!" Samuel Adams joined in.

I nodded as George Washington stepped forward. As he spoke it was as if the clouds parted and the sun rested upon

his back and shoulders. He smiled as he looked down at each of us before saying, "America was founded on freedom. Heaven opened a way for the Puritans to come and thrive in a hard and hostile land. Were they smart men? Of course they were. But I have read that men like William Bradford were more than just smart. They were people of faith and courage and integrity. I believe the only way America can prosper is to remember the religious freedoms that our forefathers fought for. Only then can the smiles of heaven bless this sacred land."

We all nodded at the wisdom from the man who would be the first president of the greatest nation on earth. And for a quick moment I thought of my Pilgrim hero William Bradford and how sad he would be to hear that all the freedoms that they fled England for were in jeopardy. But how happy he would be to know that many brave men in this century were fighting to keep their dreams alive!

"This Congress," I said. "Do you think it has been successful?"

"This First Continental Congress represents the willingness of the thirteen separate colonies to join together as one united government," said Patrick.

"Sort of like a united states of America?" I hinted.

"Yes, you could say that," said John Adams. "In fact, I quite like the thought of it."

"And now we must return to vote as a united America," John said.

"We must all pray more fervently that God will help us in this most important decision," said Patrick Henry.

Tommy, Elizabeth, Liberty, and I were outside Carpenters' Hall when the final session of the First Continental Congress ended. I'll admit I was extremely anxious to know if the colonies decided to separate from England or not. As the doors opened and the delegates began exiting the building I saw Samuel Adams first.

"I'll be right back," I said as I ran to learn the real history of what had happened.

Samuel looked satisfied as he said, "A vote was taken and the delegates of the First Continental Congress decided to cut off colonial trade with Great Britain unless Parliament abolishes the Intolerable Acts."

"If I'm not mistaken," I mused, "the Intolerable Acts caused the port of Boston to be closed, forced the people of Boston to open their homes so the King's soldiers would have a place to live, and denied any Bostonian to govern their own city."

"That is correct," said Samuel. "The King must reopen Boston Harbor, remove the Redcoats from living in our homes, allow Boston to govern itself, and remove other punitive laws."

"And you are happy with this?" I asked.

"Yes, of course," Samuel said. "But the delegates were asked to return to their colonies and begin training their citizens for potential war against Britain."

A sense of worry and dread touched my heart and mind. My own feelings surprised me. I knew the history. I knew the outcome. So why did I feel so much angst about the news from Samuel? As I pondered I realized what it was. Simply, war means death. The men, women, and children that I had seen in Massachusetts and Virginia, the families in all the colonies, would sacrifice so much for something many Americans today take for granted. Freedom. Is freedom something worth dying for? I believe it is. But not all the delegates were happy about this. However, in the end the votes were cast and the decision was made to officially make a stand against the King of England.

And I knew that in less than six months the war for America's independence would officially begin at the Battle of Lexington.

"Godspeed, Rush Revere," said Samuel.

"Godspeed, Samuel Adams," I said in return.

As I walked back toward my little band of time travelers I noticed that Tommy, Elizabeth, and Liberty had walked over to a group of boys about thirty yards away. It looked like they were taunting and teasing Elizabeth and, no surprise, Elizabeth wasn't standing for it.

As I got closer I began to hear their conversation.

"You don't belong in America!" said a large colonial boy.

"I was born in America, you idiots!" shouted Elizabeth. "You all stink like pigs. It's like you haven't bathed in days!"

The boys thought that was the funniest thing ever. "We do not bathe," they all said.

"But we think you should jump in the sea and swim back to your precious England," said a boy with red hair.

"Hey, maybe we should send her back with a little gift for the King," laughed a scrawny kid who was missing a front tooth and carrying a wooden bucket.

The other boys cheered him on and before I could interfere, the scrawny kid ran up to Elizabeth with the wooden bucket. My fears were realized when I saw a mess of soupy mud launch from the bucket with deadly aim toward Elizabeth's face and dress. Suddenly, everything stopped and everything was silent. The mud hung in the air like an ugly piece of modern art. The boys pointed and laughed like they were colonial statues. I looked for Liberty, certain he was behind this. Unblinking, Liberty's eyes were focused like lasers on Elizabeth. Although everything in the past had ceased moving, those of us from the future were still free to act. In a flash, Tommy quickly moved Elizabeth several feet to the left and that's when Liberty finally blinked and everything went back to normal.

The mud splashed to the ground and the boy with the bucket looked shocked that he had missed his target by that much. His friends laughed at the scrawny kid like he was the one that got covered in mud.

Elizabeth was stunned and confused at the same time. "What just . . . how did . . ."

"It was Liberty," said Tommy. "He can do more than just open a portal to the past."

As we walked away from the boys, Liberty stood between Elizabeth and the menacing boys like he was protecting her.

"Why did you do that?" Elizabeth asked Liberty. "Why did you help me when I've been so mean to you?"

"Maybe we aren't friends yet," Liberty said. "But we could be. And I wanted to show you that I don't hold any grudges. America is a land of the free where people, like the Pilgrims and the colonists, were able to start over in a new place with a new life."

"True, but it's not free of bullies," said Tommy.

"No," said Liberty, "unfortunately, there will always be bullies. But that's why friends are so important."

"That's right," I said. "When the colonists in Boston were bullied by King George and his Intolerable Acts, twelve other colonies were willing to help and support their sister colony."

"We're sort of like secret sisters now," Liberty chuckled. "Well, except I'm a male and we don't have the same mother and if we did that would be really weird."

"This whole thing is weird!" said Elizabeth firmly. "I-I think I just want to go back to the school now."

"I think that's a good idea," I said.

Within minutes we found a secluded place to time-jump. Within seconds we were back at Manchester Middle School. Elizabeth quickly dismounted and ran off like Cinderella at midnight.

"That was weird," said Tommy.

"Maybe she had to go to the bathroom," Liberty said.

"I think Elizabeth is at a crossroads right now," I said. "I believe her greed for power and her need for friendship are battling inside of her."

"Well, I hope the good Elizabeth wins," said Liberty. "The evil one scares me."

"Thanks, again, Mr. Revere," said Tommy. "And thanks, Liberty. It's been another amazing adventure through time."

"I'm glad you enjoyed it," I said. "And I almost forgot, you better take these with you." I pulled out the three musket balls from my coat pocket. As I did, I purposefully let a small seed packet slip from my pocket and land in front of Tommy's feet.

"You dropped something," Tommy said.

"Oh, clumsy me," I said. "I'd only meant to give you these musket balls for good luck. They seemed to help you with your last game so I thought you might enjoy having these before your next one."

"Oh, yeah, I forgot about those. Thanks!" said Tommy. He eyed the small packet I had in my other hand and asked, "So what's with the little packet? Hey, does that say 'From B. Franklin' on it?"

"Oh, this?" I said, innocently. "Yes, well, these are from Benjamin Franklin. I'd forgotten he gave these to me the last time we visited. It's an experiment he's been working on and he said he finally succeeded in creating the first spaghetti seeds."

"Spaghetti seeds?" Tommy asked.

"Yes," I replied, "apparently these seeds can grow spaghetti noodles in your garden."

"That's amazing!" Tommy said. "That guy can do anything! Any chance I could try them in my mom's garden?"

"I don't see why not. Just take these and bring me back what you don't use," I said, handing Tommy the packet.

"Awesome, thanks! See ya!" he said as he jogged up the stairs and into the school.

As I watched Tommy leave, Liberty said, "When do you think he'll discover that those spaghetti seeds are fake? Personally, I'm surprised he fell for it."

"Me, too," I chuckled. "Let's go and get some breakfast. How about bagels and cream cheese?"

"Sounds good to me!"

As we started to leave the school, I was surprised to see Elizabeth again. She had already changed into her modern-day clothes and was waiting for us by the big oak tree. As we got closer she quickly handed me a small disk.

"What's this?" I asked.

"Just take it before I change my mind," Elizabeth abruptly replied.

I reached out and took the disk.

"It's the memory card from my video camera," Elizabeth said.

"The blackmail video?" Liberty asked.

Elizabeth sighed. "It sounds so mean when you say it like that. But, yes, it's the video of you and Mr. Revere jumping through the time portal."

"Thank you, Elizabeth," I said, sincerely.

"Yes, thank you," said Liberty. "What happened? I mean I don't know if you realize this or not but what you're doing right now could be considered, um, well, it could be considered a *nice gesture*."

"Whatever," Elizabeth said as she looked around to see if anyone was watching.

"Seriously," Liberty continued. "If word got out that you were doing nice things for other people, well, your reputation could be ruined."

Elizabeth kept her head down and her arms folded. I could tell she was trying to decide what to say next. Finally, she lifted her head and looked at Liberty. Her voice cracked just a little when she said, "You protected me. You know, back in Philadelphia. So I . . . I wanted to thank you. You helped me and now I'm helping you. Now we're even." As she turned to leave she looked one last time at me and said, "Mr. Revere, just to be clear, you and I are *not* even. I believe it was your plan to throw me into that pond at Windsor castle. Anyway, you haven't seen the last of me. And I can't wait until our next adventure," she said with a smirk. With a flip of her long blond hair she turned and walked away.

"Don't you just love happy endings," said Liberty, smiling.

Happy endings? "Maybe for you," I mumbled and decided that maybe I should start sleeping with one eye open.

As we walked away from Manchester Middle School, Liberty asked, "Who did you enjoy visiting the most? Benjamin Franklin? Patrick Henry? Samuel Adams? Paul Revere . . ."

I laughed and said, "Well, they were all very different. Benjamin Franklin's creative energy, his calm wisdom, and his brilliant mind were certainly gifts to America. His speech in Parliament may have been the reason that the King finally repealed the

Stamp Act. And I know he plays a bigger role in the Second Continental Congress and the Declaration of Independence."

"And . . ." Liberty prodded.

"And Patrick Henry's bold and courageous speeches against the King's injustice created a spark for the American Revolution. I loved his enthusiasm for life and his courage to defend freedom. Oh, and I must remember to give Cam his high five from Patrick Henry."

"And did you ever warm up to the Samuelator?" Liberty joked.

"Are you kidding? I loved Samuel Adams! I mean he wasn't really looking for friends, he was looking for freedom and he never doubted the cause."

"Well, he always seemed a little angry to me," Liberty said.

"Some people call it anger. I call it one hundred percent colonial stubbornness! It was a determination mixed with a whole lot of passion. He was always ready to tell people what to believe. He was a fire starter and really good at fanning the flames of the Revolution!"

"And, of course, your boyhood hero, Paul Revere!" Liberty said with a big smile.

"Wow, he was involved in everything," I said. "He was ready to serve wherever he was needed. He was strong, talented, happy, I mean, what's not to like! He's the kind of guy I want as my next-door neighbor. Dependable, always there when you need him. And his courage as a Patriot with the Sons of Liberty is exactly what America needed. Although, I plan to see more of him. I mean we definitely need to time-jump to witness his famous midnight ride!"

"Oooh, I'm all for that!" Liberty nodded.

"What about you?" I asked. "Who impressed you the most?"

"Not who, but what!" Liberty said. "For me it was all about freedom."

"What's all about me?" asked Freedom, who surprised me from behind.

"You startled me," I said.

"I knew you were there," said Liberty. "I could sense you a mile away!"

"I'm glad you're back," said Freedom. "So, what about me?" she asked again as she slung her backpack to her other shoulder. "Liberty said something like it was all about Freedom."

"Not you," Liberty corrected. "It's all about fighting for freedom. That's what I've learned the most the last few days."

"Me, too," Freedom said. "I mean I haven't always believed that. But I think Samuel Adams is right when he said my freedom is worth fighting for. Sometimes we really do have to fight to live free. So starting today I'm going to start living my name! You're looking at the new Freedom!"

"Good for you!" I said.

"Yeah," Liberty agreed. "You look different already!"

"Speaking of looking different," said Freedom suspiciously as she reached out for the Indian feathers still in Liberty's mane. "What are these? Oh, that's right. You guys visited the Boston Tea Party! That was so weird that we could talk to each other through time."

"I know, right?" said Liberty.

"Well, I better get to my first class," said Freedom, laughing, as she skipped toward the school. "But tell me all about your trip on my way to school. You know, telepathically! Oh, and bye,

Mr. Revere! Great seeing you! Did I mention that having freedom is a great feeling!" she yelled, skipping backward. "And it's worth fighting for!"

"Well, that was fun!" said Liberty. "For the record, I think your students really like you as their substitute history teacher, especially Freedom, Tommy, and Cam. Oh, and we never got to tell Cam about our adventure at the First Continental Congress! Maybe I'll meet him for lunch and give him all the details. Hmm, I know it's still early, but lunch sounds really good about now." Instantly, Liberty looked panicked and said, "Wait a minute, have we eaten breakfast? With all the excitement I almost skipped a meal!"

The excitement has just begun, I thought as I patted Liberty. America was definitely feeling growing pains. It was plagued with evils like slavery and burdened by a tyrant king. It was clear our country was not perfect and neither were our Founding Fathers. But our visit with these exceptional Americans had reminded me what it means to fight for freedom and endure hard things. More than ever I was ready for our next adventure and the truths we would learn about the American Revolution!

Be sure to explore the *Adventures of Rush Revere* at www.twoifbytea.com!

David and Rush

Acknowledgments

There isn't a single day when I don't sincerely appreciate my loyal, unwavering audience, great people who make me eager to wake up each day and join them on the radio. The bond of loyalty that has developed over the past twenty-five years still has me in awe and I am more motivated than ever each day to meet and surpass their expectations. You really have no idea how much I appreciate and love you all. My heartfelt appreciation further extends to all of the children, parents, grandparents, aunts, and uncles across America who love this phenomenal country like I do. Their support over the years has allowed me to want to take on new projects like this one because I know we are unified in our mission to teach the younger generations why the United States is a place to be cherished.

Once again I give thanks and have tremendous gratitude to my wife, Kathryn, for developing and shepherding this series. She manages and coordinates all aspects of the assembly of the many parts that make up each book. She is tireless and devoted beyond a level I deserve. Her intelligent creativity and insight are unparalleled. I am indeed a lucky man.

Writing a book for children is brand-new for me and I could not do it without our incredible small team pouring their very hearts into every aspect of the undertaking. It requires countless hours going over every detail. Nothing is farmed out, nothing is phoned in. There are no half measures taken. Their commitment and passion make this something special to be part of. Thank you to Christopher Schoebinger for your creativity, adaptability, and devotion from day one. You are the Best. Thank you to Chris Hiers for the unbelievable attention to detail and perfection in every illustration. Spero Mehallis defines loyal and hardworking.

Jonathan Adams Rogers has been indispensable. There aren't many about whom that can be said. I sincerely appreciate his dedication and help, which was limitless while also being great.

My brother, David Limbaugh, grants us all peace of mind. His unwavering support of every endeavor and positive attitude is a constant inspiration.

After hearing about the idea to create a children's series, my good friend, the late Vince Flynn, put me in touch with Louise Burke at Simon & Schuster. Thank you to Vince, Louise, and everyone at Simon & Schuster, especially Mitchell Ivers, who helped bring this vision to life.

Photo Credits

PAGE

iv Chris Hiers
viii Chris Hiers
9 Chris Hiers
19 Chris Hiers
24 UIG via Getty Images
33 Chris Hiers
37 Photo Researchers, Getty Images
39 Print Collection, Miriam and Ira D. Wallach Division of Art, Prints and Photographs, The New York Public Library, Astor, Lenox and Tilden Foundations
40 Wikimedia Commons
41 mbbirdy, Getty Images
45 The Granger Collection, NYC
47 Library of Congress via Wikimedia Commons
53 Chris Hiers
55 The Granger Collection, NYC
57 The Granger Collection, NYC
58 Wikimedia Commons
63 © Stapleton Collection/Corbis
65 Chris Hiers

70 Peter Tillemans, Getty Images
73 Chris Hiers
78 Image Asset Management Ltd./SuperStock
85 Chris Hiers
95 Chris Hiers
97 SuperStock
105 Chris Hiers
109 Chris Hiers
116 Chris Hiers
119 © The Print Collector/Corbis
122 National Portrait Gallery/SuperStock
129 Chris Hiers
131 Prism/Superstock
136 Chris Hiers
142 The Granger Collection, NYC
144 The Granger Collection, NYC
147 Library of Congress
148 Wikimedia Commons
151 Getty Images
161 Getty Images
165 The Granger Collection, NYC
169 Everett Collection/SuperStock
173 The Granger Collection, NYC
175 Chris Hiers
177 Images Etc Ltd., Getty Images
183 Wikimedia Commons
186 Getty Images
190 Chris Hiers
203 Chris Hiers
208 The Granger Collection, NYC
210 Superstock
211 National Gallery of Art
215 SuperStock
216 The Granger Collection, NYC
219 Chris Hiers
224 Chris Hiers

231 Chris Hiers
232 Author's Collection
241 Getty Images
242 Chris Hiers

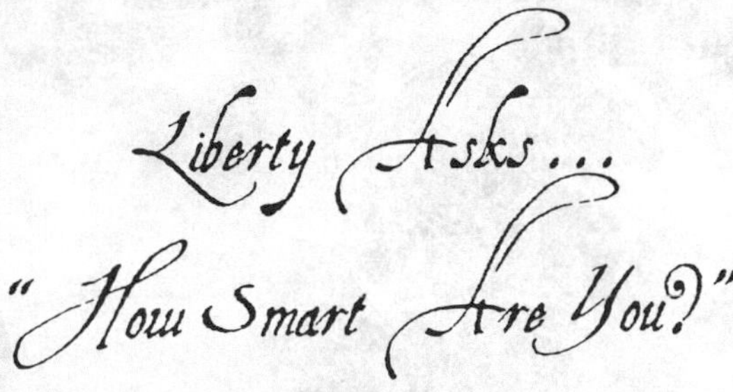
Liberty Asks . . .
"How Smart Are You?"

(Beware—He Thinks He Can Stump You!)

1. What kind of animal is the Manchester Middle School mascot?
2. How many colonies were there in 1774?
3. What is the prank that Tommy and Cam played in front of the class?
4. Who invented swim fins?
5. What is Liberty's favorite type of food in Boston?
6. In what city can the Palace of Westminster be found?
7. What were the British soldiers called?
8. Who played the fiddle in the tavern?
9. True or false, the Stamp Act meant that no one could use postage stamps on their envelopes?
10. In what country can Windsor Castle be found?
11. In what city did the famous massacre take place described in this book?
12. Which patriot is Rush Revere's idol?

13. Who identified that there is electricity in lightning?
14. Who lived at Windsor Castle?
15. True or false: the Quartering Act of 1765 required the colonists to house British soldiers?
16. What did members of the crowd shout at Patrick Henry when he spoke in the Virginia House of Burgesses?
17. What was Paul Revere's profession?
18. What did they throw off the boats in Boston Harbor?
19. What famous American spoke in front of British Parliament about the Stamp Act?
20. What is the meeting that Rush Revere, Ben Franklin, George Washington, and others attended at the end of the book called?

Looking for answers?

Visit the *Adventures of Rush Revere* at www.twoifbytea.com!

Do you know what this is?

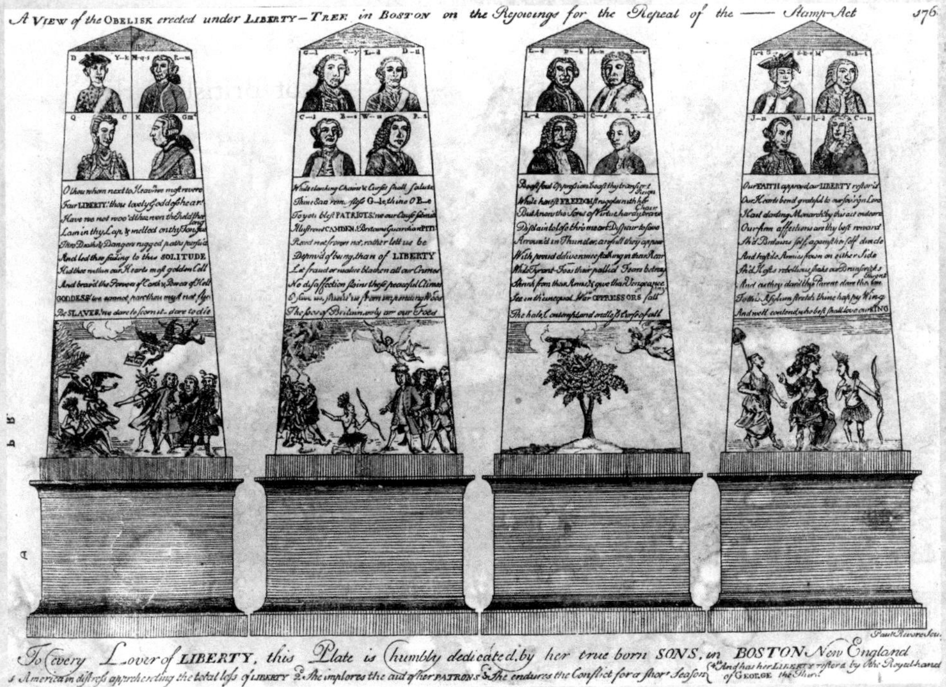

An obelisk engraved by Paul Revere and erected under Liberty Tree in Boston to celebrate the repeal of the Stamp Act, 1766.

What's your
favorite snack?